OHIO

Archæological and Historical

PUBLICATIONS.

Volume XIV.

WILDSIDE PRESS

CONTENTS.

(iii)

ILLUSTRATIONS.

OHIO
Archaeological and Historical
PUBLICATIONS.

THE SHANDON CENTENNIAL.

ALBERT SHAW, NEW YORK.

[On August 26 and 27, 1903, there was held at Shandon, Butler County, Ohio, a centennial celebration of the Congregational Church and community of that place. The order of exercises embraced addresses by the Reverend M. P. Jones, Pastor of the Church, Mrs. M. P. Jones, Mr. Stephen R. Williams, Mr. Minter C. Morris, Mr. Stanley M. Roland, Mr. Michael Jones, Miss Edna Manuel, Dr. W. O. Thompson, Mr. Murat Halstead and Dr. Albert Shaw. The proceedings of that centennial have not been published and it is through the courtesy of Mr. Albert Shaw, the editor of the Review of Reviews, that we are herewith permitted to put in public print for the first time his admirable address delivered upon that occasion. Dr. Albert Shaw was born in Shandon, Butler County, Ohio, July 23, 1857. — EDITOR.]

As this centennial occasion has from time to time been in my thoughts, I have found one idea presenting itself in a more fixed and definite way than any other. That idea is the sense of gratitude and pride we ought to feel in being the sons and daughters of a race of sterling pioneers. It is a great thing to found a nation or a state or a worthy community. In all history we can discover the records of no better or braver people than the men and women who subdued the American wilderness; prepared it to be the home of millions of people speaking the same language and possessing the same kind of civilization, and left to us the heritage of their hope, their courage and their faith.

Our ancestors in England or Wales, or Scotland or Ireland, or Germany — or whatever other ancient land — may have been very humble, or they may have been of educated or even of aristocratic lineage. We are willing, indeed, to know anything about them that we can find out. But, after all, for most Americans it will always suffice to trace their ancestry back to the first of their forefathers who crossed the seas and cast in his lot with the makers of this new world.

Very many, perhaps the majority, of the English nobility do not run their pedigree back more than two or three hundred years. We have, on the other hand, a great many families in this country who clearly trace their descent from ancestors who helped create our original Eastern colonies more than two hundred and fifty years ago. In April last, I was on the James River, in Virginia, conferring with the men who are preparing four years hence to celebrate the three hundredth anniversary of the first permanent white settlement north of the Spanish post at St. Augustine. New York City has just celebrated the two hundred and fiftieth anniversary of the town's original charter. Our oldest Eastern universities have been observing the anniversaries that remind us of the devotion to educa-

ALBERT SHAW, EDITOR OF REVIEW OF REVIEWS.

tion of the early pioneers. My own home is now on the Hudson River, and the highway that passes my house was opened almost two hundred and sixty years ago. When Washington was in camp there, during the Revolution, the village was already much more than a hundred years old.

And yet, it was only the merest fringes of our great country that were occupied before the Revolutionary period. It was not until after the Revolution that the great movement of expansion set in, and the United States began to develop in earnest. To some of us who have been in the habit of thinking that New York and New England are comparatively old regions, it might be interesting to call to mind the fact that in the East, as well as in the West, the country's development has been principally in the past one hundred years.

Thus, to be personal, I might illustrate by saying that while two of my four great-grandfathers were pioneering in the Ohio River country, the other two had gone out from Massachusetts and Connecticut respectively as pioneers to help open the then unbroken wilderness of Vermont. Northern New England and Northern and Western New York are of just as recent development as Ohio. The same thing is true of almost the entire area of the Southern States. There were settlements along the tidal streams of Maryland and Virginia, and along the coasts and the navigable rivers of the Carolinas and Georgia; but there was little or no development of the great interior areas and valleys of those States until well after the Revolutionary War.

Our own ancestors, who came to this particular neighborhood, belonged, therefore, to the true pioneering generation. The process of pioneering went on subsequently in successive waves until it reached the great Mississippi prairies, the plain beyond the Missouri; the Rocky Mountain regions, and the Pacific coast. It has been a part of my experience to have seen something of the methods of pioneering in Iowa, the Dakotas, Montana, and other parts of the West. But the great generation of American pioneers was that which lived and worked in the thirty or forty years following the Revolutionary War — the period before railroads were built, and before river and lake steamboats had come into much use.

This was the generation that floated down the rivers on flatboats, and that crossed the mountain passes with ox-teams and antique wagons. Washington's interest in Ohio had done much to give the region fame, and the circumstances under which the colonies had ceded their northwestern territories to the Union had left several of them with lands to dispose of, either as free grants to Revolutionary soldiers or else as bargains to homeseekers. The northwestern ordinance, forever excluding slavery from the country north of the Ohio River, had its influence also

in helping to fix the character of the people who chose to participate in the arduous work of redeeming this region from its
wilderness condition and making here a home for themselves
and their posterity.

Ohio has recently had a great centennial Statehood anniversary, and there have already been numerous local celebrations.
Much has been written and much has been said by way of a
review of the origins of this great commonwealth. I shall not
attempt to add anything on that score of an historical character.
Surely nature was lavish in her gifts to this beautiful and productive region that lies west of the Alleghanies and south of the
Great Lakes, and that embraces the better-favored side of the
Ohio River valley, with its marvelously rich tributary valleys.
But, there are other fair and rich countries — some of them fairer
and richer even than this — that lie desolate to-day because they
have lacked the right kind of men. They have needed but have
not found men with brawn and brain and heart to wrest wealth
from the soil; to utilize the forces and bounties of nature; and to
plant those seeds of social life and of religious and political institutions, that count for more, after all, than fields of waving
corn or golden grain.

Last week I was wandering over the rock-ribbed pasture
lands of old Connecticut. At best the thin covering of soil
seemed only a few inches deep. In lieu of fences, the tiny fields
were separated by massive granite stone walls, blasted and hewn
out of the solid rock, or else heaped up with giant boulders by
those Yankees of prodigious industry a hundred years or more
ago. They raised poor crops, those hardy farmers, but they
planted churches and schools, and they produced men and women.
These are the real tests of the greatness of a community or a
State. If rural life has since decayed a good deal in those New
England regions, it lives and flourishes yet, where New England
has been transplanted, in the Western Reserve of Ohio, in Illinois, Iowa, Michigan, Wisconsin, Minnesota, Kansas and Nebraska, Colorado and California.

If in the same spirit of devotion and courage those New England pioneers had perchance made their farms on richer soil, they
would have been none the worse for it, and the results in a local

sense would have been more enduring. They built up men and women for the glory of the nation and the peopling of prairie States yet unborn. But in thousands of instances their farms, so painfully redeemed from forest and from rock, have now relapsed to a state of wilderness, where some gnarled old apple tree, in the very thick of a dense young growth of scrub oak, birch, spruce and pine, reminds us that here were once cleared fields and orchards, thrifty homesteads, men who plowed and women who spun, all for the glory of God and the greatness of the American name.

Only a hundred years ago — or even seventy-five years or fifty years ago — these were tidy, decent farms. To-day they are lost in mile after mile of tangled young forest, where the fox dwells, where the wild deer has come back, and where even the wolves and panthers are likely soon to reappear. Of course, within a few miles there are thriving manufacturing towns, and there is progress along other lines. But these manufacturing towns are made up of a new and strange population of polyglot origin; and in the lesser of the farming hamlets, there remain few, if any, who would care to celebrate the one-hundredth or the two-hundredth anniversary of the neighborhood, or who possess either the knowledge, the reverence, or the personal interest to save the tombs of the stalwart forefathers from neglect and decay.

From the spectacle of these deserted New England farms, and these ruined New England villages, I come with congratulation and thanksgiving to greet you, my friends and old neighbors, and to rejoice with you in the preservation intact of our own beautiful Ohio community. It has not, like some of those Eastern places, forgotten itself. Its farms are better tilled than ever. Our forefathers, with faith and devotion akin to that which set a beacon light for the world on the hills of New England, had the further wisdom and good fortune to pitch their tents and make their abiding place where the soil was rich, the rainfall was equable, the climate was wholesome, and the geographical situation was bound to give permanence and continuity to the work of their hands.

When they cleared the land in this valley, they knew that the conditions were such as to give long and abiding prosperity to the neighborhood, and to justify at least a part of their descendents in remaining here to maintain the high character of the neighborhood's life, and to keep the memories and traditions of the men and women of the first half of the nineteenth century from lapsing into oblivion.

They were large-minded people, who from the very first were determined to possess good church advantages, good school advantages, and a home life made the more dignified and refined by good houses and substantial improvements. They were people of high ideals and unbounded self-respect.

The life of a little country community, when it is stagnant and listless and without the touch of idealism and other worldliness, is about the pettiest and worst of all possible kinds of life. The city, even with its darker aspects of misery and vice, stimulates the mind by its rush and roar — its external activities — its ever-changing sensations and novelties. But the dull, dead, rustic hamlet, where nobody cares for anything or believes in anything beyond the gratification of a few sordid material wants, is in danger of sinking to a lower moral level than the slums of the great towns. We all know that there are such depraved neighborhoods, where fair skies shine on scenes of natural loveliness without seeming in the very least to lift up the minds and souls of men to noble thoughts and aspirations.

It is not in a spirit of pride or boastfulness that we proclaim the fact that ours has always been a good neighborhood to live in. Its superiority has been due, as we all know, primarily to the religious and intellectual qualities of the early settlers, and secondarily to those distinctive facts that made the community so largely homogeneous. Narrow sectarianism has been a blighting curse to many a small community. It has destroyed all unity of feeling. It has kept the people from forming the habit of co-operation, and from developing the neighborly spirit which is so essential for the best purposes of local life.

The greatest boon we owe to our noble Welsh pioneers of this valley is the strong undenominational church they formed. It was more than a church — it was a veritable center of light and leading; a focus of intelligence; a nursery of patriotism; a mother of schools; a patron of music; a rallying place for innocent social life; a teacher of the art of public speaking; a rewarder and promoter of eloquence — a place ever hospitable to those having a message to the heart or to the head, from the great outside world.

This undenominational church — which called itself Congregational in order to have some sisterly relations with other independent churches — readily assimilated Presbyterians, Methodists, Baptists, Episcopalians or Lutherans. Its influence was benignant and its spirit was tolerant through a period of such sectarian throat-cutting in many another place as our younger friends here to-day cannot understand, or even imagine. Such a church attracted and held good preachers. It was known and respected in Cincinnati, Oxford, Columbus, Oberlin and Cleveland — and it was highly appreciated in the New York and Boston headquarters of benevolent and missionary societies. It was also well known in Wales, and in the other Welsh settlements of this country.

What more can be said for the church and community in those early days than that it had such a man as Dr. Chidlaw for its spiritual and intellectual leader, and that it so held itself as to be worthy of such leadership? Wales, as you all know, was a famous center of Bible study and pulpit eloquence in the period which furnished the chief Welsh emigration to this country. It was in that regard superior even to Scotland. A finer race never came to America than these devout, keen-witted Welsh folk. I am not able to claim any blood kinship with them; but at least I may hope to have derived benefit from close association with them in home and school and church, and to have inherited something of what my father gained as a pupil of Dr. Chidlaw and of other distinguished Welshmen who were school-masters here in the old days.

Thankful, then, we all should be for the circumstances that brought here in the early period men of such force of mind and character as to leave their impress through a rounded century. These men believed in learning, as only next in importance to religion. There never has been a time when this community was not prepared to transmit a considerable degree of scholarship and knowledge of books to the rising generation. The old-fashioned school-master, such as our fathers knew, was an educator of no mean ability. I am not on this programme as local historian, and

I am not thoroughly versed in the earliest annals of the neighbor-hood; but I have heard of a number of men of masterly minds who taught school here in the days when my own father, for instance, was a pupil.

They were not all Welshmen. A young man named Dennison, who afterward became Governor of the State, was one of them, and I believe Congressman Shields, before he went to Washington, had some teaching experience. I know that later on, in the fifties and early sixties, there were teachers of marked culture and enthusiasm. Among these were Scott and McClung, and various others.

My own first teacher was the Rev. Mark Williams. While he was fitting older boys for college, he was looking after a few children who were too small to go to the district school.

It was his brother-in-law, the lamented James A. Clark, who afterwards prepared me to enter college — as he prepared others of you — and to whose patience and thoroughness I have always felt myself greatly indebted. In the old days, our schools attracted here a great many good pupils from other communities round about, and gave their educational beginnings to a large number of able, well-instructed men.

Just now the educators of the whole country are giving their attention to what for many of them is the new idea of uniting districts and consolidating country schools, in order to supply a central school with better equipment and teaching, and with a graded system such as one finds in larger towns and cities. This very thing is what you were able to accomplish fully thirty years ago, when the old district schools were abandoned, the private high school superseded, and the present free, graded school established. This helped to sustain and continue the idea of a well-ordered, unified neighborhood that had been fostered from the beginning by the Church. For that achievement we were indebted to such energetic and able citizens as Abner Francis, Griffith Morris, Evan Evans and others.

The tradition of scholarship is a persistent one in families and communities. There are good things, fortunately, as well as bad ones, that are catching. Ambition to study and to learn is one of these good things that may become endemic, so to speak, in a neighborhood; and it has flourished here persistently to the fourth and — in some families, perhaps — to the fifth generation of those who came here in the beginning.

Our friends of Virginia and the South love to throw all possible glamour about the conditions of life in the earlier days of their States. They glorify their ancestors almost as if those tobacco planters were some fabled race of demigods. They were, indeed, a stanch, noble people; and the Southerners of to-day honor themselves in thus clinging to the memories of their forefathers. Few, if any, of our Ohio pioneers, could or did live in the manner of the cultivated and aristocratic families who built stately homes on the navigable rivers of tide-water Virginia, raised tobacco by slave labor, and sent their own ships to English markets. Our farmers raised wheat and corn, worked in the fields with their own hands, and helped enlarge the area of cultivation by clearing away the heaviest of forests.

But it is all the more to their credit that many of them successfully kept — through the roughest and hardest log-cabin period of their pioneer efforts — a gentle and refined side to their lives. And it was their good fortune to prosper so rapidly and substantially that in due time many of their farm-houses were as large and substantial as all but the very best of the Southern plantation mansions. For tobacco and cotton were not the only profitable cash crops of the first half of the nineteenth century. Cincinnati in those days was dubbed Porkopolis. It was the greatest meat packing and shipping center in the world. The flush days of the cotton and sugar planters of Mississippi, Alabama and Louisiana had arrived; and the plantations lived and thrived on our Ohio flour and cured meats.

In the winter and spring our turnpikes were almost impassable for the long droves of fat hogs waddling marketwards reluctantly. Thus many of our farmers became comparatively rich men, and thus they built durable and even stately brick houses, and constructed solid, stone-ballasted roads, along which — like golden argosies of old — their massive corn-fed treasures moved safely, without danger of being stuck in the mire. Less picturesque, doubtless, than the white-winged fleets that served the tobacco planters of the Virginia shores, or the smart, square-

rigged ships that brought riches to the pious New England forefathers who trafficked in rum and slaves; not majestic, like parad-
ing elephants in gilded trappings on occasion of some pompous
ceremonial in India; not so dignified, nor so suggestive of poetry
as the long caravans of camels that bear precious fabrics across
Arabian deserts; yet worthy of all honor, and to be named with
respect on this occasion, I repeat, is the hog — the prime factor in
our community's prosperity for half or three-quarters of a century. Not the varieties known as the Virginia razor-back or the
Kentucky shoat, but the large-framed, broad-beamed, well-
rounded Ohio hog that weighed half a ton, and that gave ample
bacon, pork and lard to the field-hands of the down-river plantations, while providing in return the cash that bought the black
silk dresses our mothers wore, the top-buggies our older brothers
drove, and the pianos and organs that our sisters rejoiced in.

Through the more recent period of feverish rush to the
cities that has in many regions brought country life to a condition of sad decline and stagnation, you have safely passed. You
have contributed your full quota of young men and women to
the making of the farther West, and to the throbbing activities
of the business and professional life of our towns and cities.
But you have meanwhile kept the old neighborhood running —
all decently and in good order.

When, after years of absence, we of my family came back
here to bury our beloved mother, we were comforted by the sympathy of a host of friends who also loved her and had not forgotten us. When later I came here for a day or two, with my
wife, there was all the welcome of a real home-coming for her,
though a stranger. It has always been so. My father, also
born and bred here, had, as a very young man, gone to practice
medicine in newer but larger communities further west. He
came back some fifty years ago with his family, in order to find
healthful surroundings for them. Only a few days ago, letters
were placed in my hands written at that time by my mother;
and they show how hospitable and kindly was the welcome given
here to this New England girl. I have no hesitation in making
these personal allusions, because this is an intimate occasion,
where friends are conferring with one another and where the

outside world has no interest or curiosity. I am trying merely to illustrate the fact that the neighborhood life has been absolutely unbroken in its continuity. Many a family, readily for itself, bounds the local life of the century now past. My grandfather, whom I well remember, and who was married here in his early manhood to Rebecca Halstead, was born in 1783, and would have been 120 years old if he had lived to attend this celebration.

The future of our country communities has very good promise. Communication grows easier, through the multiplication of railways and telegraph and telephone lines. Books, periodicals and newspapers are entirely accessible, and somehow they are much more thoroughly read in the country than in the city. The tide has turned, it would seem, and there is less rush for the towns, and better appreciation of the advantages of country life. I beg you, therefore, who still call this place home, to believe in it as a good place to live in and to determine to make it ever better. Let it continue to stand pre-eminent before its neighboring communities for the intelligence and character of its people. Let its life continue to center around the church, and the school, and let it make another century record worthy of the one now complete and secure.

HORACE MANN AND ANTIOCH COLLEGE.

GEORGE ALLEN HUBBELL, PH. D.,

[Mr. Hubbell is a member of the Faculty of Berea College, Kentucky, and was formerly a professor at Antioch College of which Mr. Horace Mann was president. — EDITOR.]

Ohio is the favorite daughter of the Eastern States. The cannon of the Revolution had scarcely cooled when the Ordinance of 1787 was adopted, and sturdy men began to look over the borders of Virginia, Pennsylvania, New York, Connecticut and Massachusetts to the rich land of the great West.

HORACE MANN — FIRST PRESIDENT
OF ANTIOCH COLLEGE.

Many of Virginia's sons went by way of Kentucky; the sons of the Keystone State crossed over the mountains, and dropped down the Ohio River on flatboats; while the sons of far Connecticut and Massachusetts came through New York and down by Lake Erie to establish themselves in the Western Reserve.

Thus, things went on for half a century, with new settlers ever pouring out from the old home into this new State, so rich in natural resources, so rapidly developing, so strong in the enterprise and the daring spirit of its people, that in 1824 Lafayette called it "the eighth wonder of the world." In 1850 the population had reached nearly two millions. Cincinnati

(12)

was a city of 116,000. Cleveland and Sandusky were important lake ports. The little Miami Railroad, from Cincinnati to Columbus, was opened in this year, and Columbus felt a new spirit of enterprise.

Education had kept pace. In 1802, even before Ohio was definitely set off as a state, a bill was passed establishing Ohio University, at Athens. This was opened in 1804. Next, Miami University was established in the township of Oxford. But colleges increased most rapidly from 1835 to 1845, reaching by 1845 more than twenty denominational institutions. Within the next ten years eight institutions were added; one of these was Antioch College. Its source was religious.

Late in the seventeen hundreds, a great religious revival swept over the United States. Its effect was to send men with tender hearts and open minds to their Bibles to learn the truth. From this condition arose many denominations, and, about the time Washington was entering upon his second term, there sprang up in North Carolina, Kentucky, New York and Vermont, congregations of believers holding the Bible as their "only rule of faith and practice," and answering to no other name than Christians. At first these people had not looked with favor upon an educated ministry, but fifty years' experience had taught them many things and a great wave of educational enthusiasm swept over the country, leaving deep in their hearts the determination to found a college.

It was supposed that the institution would be located in some pleasant town between Buffalo and Albany, on the highway of travel made famous by the Erie Canal; but Yellow Springs, Ohio, offered special advantages in central location, in climate, in money, in citizens, and, most of all, in its leading citizen, Judge Mills, who gave a tract of twenty acres of land for the college campus, and contributed liberally of his money for the founding of the institution. He laid out a large part of his farm in town lots, and in every way sought to promote the interests of the town and of the college. He was a broad-minded, far-sighted man, devoted to the welfare of the community and to the cause of education in the West. Friends, under the leadership of Elder John

Phillips, agent for the college, raised within the borders of the State nearly $100,000.

The wheat field which Judge Mills had given as a college campus was measured off, the best point selected, and the foundations of the college buildings were laid. But other things besides the buildings were in the making; the process of construction was slow, being hindered by many uncertainties and insecure arrangements, particularly on the financial side. The master-builder had been called from Massachusetts, but many of his workmen were of slight experience and the undertaking, for that time and place, was a great one. The leaders had planned largely, and they were building largely. Their ambitions were high, and with the spirit of true liberality they looked the country over to find a man worthy to be the first president of the new college.

Head and shoulders above all other educators in the land, stood Horace Mann, of Massachusetts. He had developed and established there the common school system. He had traveled in Europe, and brought home ideas, ideals and methods. He had enlisted in the work of education the foremost men of the nation. At his call Daniel Webster, Henry Ward Beecher, Gov. Andrews, John Quincy Adams, Dr. Channing, Ralph Waldo Emerson, Dr. S. G. Howe, Rev. Cyrus Pierce, Hon. Henry Wilson and R. G. Wintrop, leading men of the state and nation, had campaigned Massachusetts for education from one boundary to the other.

Ohio was eager for the best things. Its eyes were continually turned to New England, and when Horace Mann was finishing his second term in Congress, the leaders of the college, movement in Ohio met in the little town of Enon, near the present line of the Big Four Railroad, between Springfield and Dayton, and named Horace Mann as their first president. This had not been done without many an anxious thought and much correspondence among friends. When the matter was first mentioned to Mr. Mann, he gave it slight consideration, but with the turn in political affairs and with the renewed ascendency of his interest in the cause of education, he paused and pondered, and, at the age of fifty-eight, again entered on the work of a pioneer in education.

The founders of the college had already determined that the institution should be co-educational and non-sectarian in character. It remained for Mr. Mann to interpret and apply these two great principles. He really undertook to apply to college work his ideals of public school education. To this he added a new interpretation of the code of honor; the practice of using time more wisely than in many other colleges; and the golden rule of practical joking, "Indulge only in those jokes that are amusing to both parties." With a wisdom beyond his age he sought to

BIRTHPLACE OF HORACE MANN.

give the students definite instruction and discipline in observing the laws of health, hoping that the years in college would establish habits which would conserve the vitality of youth.

The first concern of the institution was to deal with spiritual value as the basis of all values, and to this was added the care of health, the economy of time, and the whole round of gifts and graces, including dress and manners. He taught science, to give a mastery of natural forces; but he dwelt much upon the duties that were owing to the ideal state, insisting that it should provide for the largest individual liberty consistent with the general good. Every student was his brother's keeper and was to render him all services within his power, but he was also the keeper of the honor of the State and his was the duty of keeping its banner unstained by falsity, dishonor or political corruption. Mr. Mann's new interpretation of the code of honor among college students held that the reputation of each was the concern of all, and that whoever knew of a serious fault in his fellow was bound to acquaint those in authority with it, in order that the student might be reclaimed from the error of his way. He held that the doctrine of emulation might develop keenness, but that it would produce tricky merchants and dishonorable politicians. The ideal was sublime, the effort to accomplish it heroic. .

He had put his hand to the plow and would not turn back, but when a man of fifty-eight undertakes to plant himself in wholly new surroundings and to establish not only himself and family, but wholly new ideals and a new institution in a young and growing community, he is attempting a work for which even the vigor and enthusiasm of youth are not more than adequate. The journey from Massachusetts was long and difficult. At Antioch nothing was in readiness. "Though the trustees had resolved that the college should be opened early in October, yet, said Mr. Mann, 'nothing was ready but our own hearts,' adding, 'if Adam and Eve had been introduced into Paradise, as early in the progress of creation, in proportion, as the faculty were introduced at Antioch, they would have been created about Wednesday night.'"

The days of summer slipped away; it was now October. Though the main college building was still unplastered and unheated, the leaders, with undaunted courage, determined to launch the great enterprise. The dedication was but little advertised, lest the village could but half accommodate the people who would come. October 5th arrived, and more than three thousand people in wagons, in carts, on horseback and afoot, came from far and near to the dedication of this joy and hope of the Christians. It was an imposing sight. On the great white steps at the east front stood Horace Mann, tall, erect, refined, intelligent, with keen eyes, and face luminous and sensitive. About him stood the leaders of the Christian connection and of that part of Ohio — judges, lawyers, and officers of State were in that little group; and in the audience were sturdy farmers, dressed in their Sunday best, young men and maidens, mothers with children in arms — a miscellaneous collection from far and near, all waiting to see what would happen next. But for the great leaders there was no hesitation. After a hymn and prayer, Rev. John Phillips, a man of God, came forward with three Bibles, and delivered them to Mr. Mann with these words: "In the name of the Great God, I present these to you as the Constitution of the world. I pray that you, and those under your care, may be guided by their heavenly teachings, and made better by their counsels." Horace Mann answered thus, in manly words of high purpose and unfailing faith: "Did time and occasion permit, I might give myself free scope to enumerate and enlarge upon the grand characteristics and prerogatives of this volume of the sacred Scriptures; I might speak of the venerableness of its antiquity; of the sublimity of its eloquence; of the splendor of its poetry, whose words shine out as though precious stones had been scattered over the page; of its touching pathos; of its precepts and examples of wisdom and truth, and its inspirations of devotion and love; but in this pressure and urgency of the hour it seems more fitting that I should, so far as I am able, accumulate all excellences in one phrase, concentrate all eulogiums into a single expression; ay, sweep the horizon of time, and of eternity, too, gathering their glories into one refulgent blaze, and say that it is a book which contains the truths that are able to make men wise unto salvation."

"Now, sir, no one knows better than yourself that a single institution cannot compass all purposes. As our college is not to be a theological or divinity school, we do not propose to inculcate creeds, articles or confessions of faith; but we do intend, and, with the blessing of God, we do hope, to train our pupils to a practical Christian life, and to make divine thoughts and contemplations become to them, as it were, their daily bread." These exercises occurred at ten o'clock.

At twelve o'clock a procession was formed, which moved
into the college chapel, a spacious apartment seating fifteen hundred people. After a hymn by the choir, Rev. Isaac Walter
delivered to the President the charter and keys of the institution.
A man of large mold, he voiced in noble words the hope of the
Christians for this great institution, and their ambition "that its
light might continue to attract the seekers after truth and the
lovers of duty until it should shed its radiance on the evening
of the world."

It was a great occasion, but Horace Mann was worthy of
it all. He saw a beginning, which, stretching out into the centuries, would grow to the largest plans and hopes. In thrilling
word he dedicated the building to the glory of God and the service of man. I have heard a few inaugural addresses and I have
read many more, but not one that equals the inaugural address
of Horace Mann. Throughout its thrilling words were tuned
to the grand key, "God, Duty, Humanity." He saw, as with a
prophet's vision, the great opportunity, and voiced it in noble
words to men who were to help him build it into the life of the
great new West!

"And a youthful community or State is like a child. Its
bones are in the gristle, and can be shaped into symmetry of
form and nobleness of stature. Its heart overflows with generosity and hope, and its habits of thought have not yet been
hardened into insoluble dogmatism. This youthful Western
world is gigantic youth, and therefore its education must be such
as befits a giant. It is born to such power as no heir to an earthly
throne ever inherited, and it must be trained to make that power
a blessing and not a curse to mankind. With its mighty frame
stretching from the Alleghanies to the Rocky Mountains, and
with great rivers for arteries to circulate its blood, it must have
a sensorium in which all mighty interests of mankind can be
mapped out; and, in its colossal and Briarean form, there must
be a heart large enough for worlds to swim in. Wherever the
capital of the United States may be, this valley will be its seat
of empire. No other valley — the Danube, the Ganges, the Nile
or the Amazon — is ever to exert so formative an influence as
this upon the destinies of men; and, therefore, in civil polity, in

ethics, in studying and obeying the laws of God, it must ascend to a contemplation of a future and enduring reign of beneficence and peace."

But no teacher's life can be always on the mountain top. The tables in the dining hall were cleared, and here examinations for entrance to college began. Out of the uneven company of one hundred and fifty who presented themselves, eight persons were ranked as freshmen, while all the others entered lower classes.

And so Horace Mann's great work for Ohio began. The professors who came to the West to do college work found them-

PRESIDENT'S RESIDENCE AT ANTIOCH.

selves busy in sorting and arranging this company, nearly all of whom were busy with preparatory subjects. But they went to the work with high enthusiasm. And well they might! Here were ministers who had given up their parishes to gain an education. Men who had thought their life course already determined, and who had settled down and begun to rear families, gathered their belongings together and moved to Yellow Springs,

to garner the fruits of knowledge under the guidance of this
great apostle of education. It was a slow process, but with a
heart of love, with unfailing patience, and with all the richness
of personal magnetism and wide experience, Horace Mann and
his devoted colleagues gave themselves to the work of enduing
this company with life and power.

Although the Christians had already announced as the leading principle of the institution the non-sectarian and co-educational ideals, yet, for most of them, the non-sectarian ideal was
only that all might become Christians. As for the co-educational
ideal, it was still in the experimental stage.

To Mr. Mann's surprise and disappointment, he found himself restricted in all quarters save with the students. Many of
the ministers who came there to co-operate in the work of the
institution were unable to realize the plan which he had been
asked to finish and make effective. He was an educated man,
a person of rapid action, impatient of delay, and of great
resources in bringing things to pass. They were not accustomed to the surroundings and the spirit of labor, nor to the rapid
method by which he had wrought all the large things which he
had already accomplished. Soon distrust began to be felt in the
hearts of the ministers in the smaller churches. It spread far
and wide, and he found himself growingly restricted. But there
were two obstacles that were sufficient to discourage the stoutest
heart — lack of money and conflict of authority. Bills began to
come in much more rapidly than the money with which to pay
them. A committee was called to examine the accounts of the
institution, and, after sitting almost steadily for forty hours, they
thoroughly satisfied themselves that there were no satisfactory
records of the debts of the institution. Representatives of the
college were sent to the various banking institutions at Springfield, Xenia and other cities near at hand, to inquire what paper
was held against the college. After a time, a somewhat unsatisfactory list of claims was made out, but this working in the dark
with reference to debts against the college continued until the
institution was sold by the sheriff.

The conflict of authority grew out of the peculiar form of
the organization, which left in the hand of the Superintendent

the many questions of policy and administrative detail which in this day would without question pass into the hands of the President. This conflict of authority produced continual irritation and misunderstanding. Mr. Mann was not really able to build in the small way which these men demanded of him, and he lacked the patience and insight to deal with them according to their limitations.

The story of Mr. Mann's work is one of sunshine and shadow. The high hope and inspiration and courage and patience of this man were marvelous. The young people were open-minded and teachable. Many were crude and in some respects uncouth, but their hearts were rich and their aspirations were high. They may have lacked the best ideals, but it was these they were seeking, and within the year the company that Horace Mann and his fellow-laborers had met, were transformed. Love, kindness and gentlemanly behavior had been instilled, and the aspirations of the college group had been turned into new channels. But it had cost hardships not a few. There was a kind of raw democracy, which tended to a constant leveling down. All the little arts and refinements of cultivated life were looked upon as so many earmarks of a supercilious aristocracy. Stools were used for seats, and when some of the ladies of the President's household brought chairs, their action was regarded as extreme and unreasonable. Napkins found no place, and the effort to secure clean plates for the pie was made a matter of dispute and contest.

To aid in instruction, Horace Mann had brought his nephew, C. F. Pennell, and his niece, Rebecca Pennell, two well educated, finely trained, Massachusetts teachers. All the other officers and teachers of the institution were selected by the Superintendent and the local trustees, upon little or no consultation with Mr. Mann. Bookkeeping had been advertised as one of the branches, and the man selected to teach it had never studied it a day in his life, but the Board had felt that he would be a good man because he represented certain religious ideals for which they were jealous. Like incidents were of frequent occurrence.

The deepest and darkest of all the trials which fell on Horace Mann was the great spirit of doubt and distrust growing out of the sectarianism which was called non-sectarian, but which had its set of definite beliefs and requirements that were as inexorable as any Thirty-nine Articles that were ever penned. Mr. Mann's motives were impugned, and the ignorance and intolerance which failed to understand him embarrassed his work on every hand.

But there is another side to the picture. Though the contest had cost him many a heart throb and many a waking hour, the men who wronged him so sadly believed in their own hearts that he had as sadly wronged them. They charged him with having sold out the Christian interests to Unitarian friends in the East. They believed that his interpretation of non-sectarianism was permeated with rank infidelity. They thought that his demand for higher educational standards for students and teachers was only that he might bring Eastern friends of Unitarian faith to displace the sons and daughters of their neighbors and friends. However deep may have been his trials, theirs were no less deep. At many a family altar, and in many a pastor's prayer, a cry went up to God that He might save the faith of the Christians and bring to naught the counsels and plans of this strong man, who had proved untrue to the trust they had placed in him. But the struggle grew more bitter. Mr. Mann took a stand against them. He was strong, resourceful and aggressive; they were less so. The friends of his early manhood were loyal, every one feeling that his was a mission from God, who wrought mightily to accomplish His purpose through Horace Mann.

The institution was practically bankrupt when Mr. Mann entered upon his work as President. Though by the plan of organization, he was in no way responsible for the financial management, yet it is evident that until the matter was pressed upon him, he had given so little attention to the financial standing of the institution as not to show ordinary business prudence. Those who had the construction in charge had given notes in many quarters, and kept no record of them. Agents had been sent to solicit funds throughout the Christian Connection, but with the customary negligence of the time no records were kept, and contributions were not sent promptly to the college. As the financial stress became greater, more agents were employed, and some of these received large commissions, which, with their traveling expenses, materially reduced the funds collected. Worse still, the institution was founded on a scholarship plan, which, in the very nature of things, was fatal. The holder of a $100 scholarship was promised that he might keep one student in the college free of tuition perpetually. Many of these scholarships were represented only by notes, and it came to be understood that the giver would never be required to pay the principal so long as the interest was promptly paid. In some cases there was not even a note, but simply the promise of some well-to-do man to help the college. There is little wonder that such a financial plan proved disastrous.

The institution was steadily running behind; salaries were unpaid, and bills were accumulating far more rapidly than donations. From time to time new claims would appear. There seemed to be no hope of adjustment except assignment; accordingly, steps were taken to that end, and on the twentieth day of April, 1859, the institution was sold in Cincinnati, O., by Hon. John Kebler, Master Commissioner, for the sum of $40,200. It was "knocked off" to the only bidder, Moses Cummings, for Frank A. Palmer, of the Broadway Bank, New York City, a member of the Christian denomination. Later, Mr. Palmer agreed to turn it over to a close board, consisting of Josiah Quincy, Charles E. Bidler, Eli Fay, Artemus Carter and Thomas McWhinney. At the same time he surrendered his claim of $18,000, which thus became his gift to the new college. These men prepared articles of incorporation, and in that form duly carried on the institution until the succeeding June, when a full Board of Trustees was appointed under the new charter. The tuition was raised and the general management of the institution was very much the same as before, except that closer attention was given to finances.

The new Antioch, free from its old promises to pay when there was nothing to pay with, and its old false hopes, built on a speculation, in its way, as wild as that of the South Sea Bubble, was formally opened, and Horace Mann looked forward to a few years of joy, comfort and triumph in this educational child of his old age, developing in the new West, with new opportunities and new hopes, surrounded by a fresh, strong civilization, somewhat crude it is true, but virile and promising. For him this was not to be!

For months preceding the Commencement of 1859, Mr. Mann had been giving himself with the strength of his whole nature to the effort of adjusting the financial affairs of the institution. It was seen at last that assignment was the only course, and with tireless energy he labored to organize a new company of friends to take hold of the institution and carry it on after assignment. The earlier weeks of summer were spent in this way, and soon after Commencement he found himself prostrated with fever. It did not seem serious, but his health was failing. On the morning of the second of August, the physicians announced that he had but a few hours to live. With steady courage he called about him his students and friends, some forty in number, and gave to each one the caution or encouragement which he felt to be the special need of the hour. It was near sunset, and he was heard to say, faintly, "Now I bid you all good-night!" . . . The great heart ceased to beat — Horace Mann was dead.

The whole community was stricken. One hundred of the students came from their summer homes to take a last look at the face of him whom they loved and honored. On the day of burial a great concourse of men and women came to pay the last sad tributes of respect and affection. A hymn was sung by the choir of the village church where he used to worship. Prayer was offered by Rev. H. I. Nye, and the Rev. Eli Fay spoke earnest and stirring words in testimony of Mr. Mann's great worth and the mighty work he had undertaken and carried forward in Ohio.

A year later his body was disinterred and removed to the Old North Burial ground, at Providence, R. I., and laid in eternal rest beside his first wife, the daughter of Dr. Messer, once President of Brown University.

But what are the tangible results of Horace Mann's work in Ohio? Like the influence of the sunlight as it plays on a thousand hills, or the dew as it blesses the varied landscape, these influences are hard to gather and to name. Horace Mann worked

out for Ohio, and for our great Middle West, some of the marvelous problems which have helped to make the Ordinance of
1787 more than a high-sounding phrase of campaign orators.
He taught such an interpretation of non-sectarianism as has been
a blessing to the great people of our State and far away to the
westward. He did much to fix the rank and standing of women

MONUMENT OF HORACE MANN ON ANTIOCH CAMPUS.

in co-educational institutions. But, most of all, he and his colleagues gave to Antioch, and to the wide territory since influ-
enced by her, those ideals of scholarship, devotion to duty and
interest in the public welfare, which, through his students and
by his writings, have been wrought into schools from Ohio to
California.

Altogether apart from Mr. Mann's visible work in the institution, may be found agencies which he set in operation, whose influence only eternity can measure. It was a great thing for the new West that a high standard of scholarship should be placed before her sons and daughters, and that a few of them, trained by "teachers with the discipline of West Point and the conscience of the Massachusetts Normal School," should be sent out into every corner of the State and ultimately to the farthest boundaries of the nation, with the sound scholarship and the love of truth that never failed.

Mr. Mann's reputation as a great apostle of education gave his opinions greater weight than those of almost any other man in the country. As a result, the most radical educational ideas were received from him with respect, and he carried forward the practical embodiment of co-education and non-sectarianism as few other educators could have done. He went into every corner of the State and into the great West, and by public addresses and personal contact kindled in the minds of thousands of the young people a devotion to truth and duty which, in their old age, still holds its inspiration.

But, with due allowance for all other things, Mr. Mann's greatest work in the West was done in Antioch and through Antioch. Many of his students have followed his ideals with a high devotion, and have made them living forces in education, particularly in Ohio, Indiana, Illinois, Missouri and California. In the great work that Dr. Harris did in St. Louis none supported him more loyally and none contributed more largely in patience and faith, in enthusiasm and the vision of truth, than the Antioch trained men and women.

Horace Mann's life at Antioch was full of petty annoyances, grievous disappointment and heart sacrifices, but at the same time it was rich in victory for the cause in which he labored. In those years he wrought mightily for the higher education and elevation of woman. He demonstrated that men and women can be educated together with profit to intellect and to morals. He gave an interpretation of non-sectarianism which was wholly new to the thought of his time. He showed that conduct and character are the central elements in the intellectual and moral life. Greater than all, in those six years he stamped upon hundreds of young people such high ideals and touched them with such glowing inspiration that their influence was always to count mightily for the highest and best. Far and near he stimulated thousands of people to nobler thinking and higher living.

After his death friends carried on as best they might the work which he had undertaken. Willing hands were found and tender hearts and true, but the great master spirit was gone. The college has undergone many hardships, and its work at times has suffered sorely, but still there are found signs of the old ideals and there breathes yet about its spacious halls something of the large devotion to truth, of the steady following of science, of the earnest love of learning, and, most of all, of that large-minded devotion to truth which has gone so far to make ours the land of free thought and of free speech. The spirit of the real Antioch could never be kept within bounds. It must have a field proportionate to the high ideals and the broad range of its interests.

"The real Antioch promptly slipped the fetters of the little Ohio town. It took possession of great hearts in great communities, backed by great commonwealths. A non-sectarian, co-educational, co-racial war-cry became the bugle notes that gave success to Ann Arbor, Cornell and the long line of State Universities that have come to be in the Western States since Antioch was born. . . . Whatever becomes of the Yellow Springs Antioch, the Antioch of Horace Mann is one of the greatest educational successes of the century."*

---

* Rev. Jenkin Lloyd Jones, in New Unity.

HOMES OF THE MOUND BUILDERS.

WILLIAM JACKSON ARMSTRONG.

[Col. W. J. Armstrong was inspector of the United States consulates under the administrations of President Grant. He is the author of "Siberia and the Nihilists," "The Heroes of Defeat," etc. — EDITOR.]

The Mound Builder is still a mystery. His story has not been told. He is not yet intelligibly tangent to any known race. He is not only prehistoric, but unconnected. His clues are shy and evasive, lacking the thread of either written speech or hieroglyphic memorials. His silence is impressive. He is the Pelasgian of the Western World, without articulate voice to reach his successors. On the Latin theory, *omne ignotum pro magnifico,* he tends in popular fancy to enlargement and idealization. Something, however, is being concretely, if slowly, learned of him. For a century or more he has been studied empirically and superficially in these western valleys along the great Mississippi basin. Generations of the early modern settlers here, the pioneers of the woods, and their successors, the cultivators of the soil, looked with inquiring wonder on his huge traces, his burial tumuli, his gigantic earth-works, his implements of flint and diorite. Then they gave him up as an unresolved and impossible problem. They had dimly heard, however, that he was an "Aztec," or "Toltec," or possibly a Tartar. And learned investigation has not proceeded much further. The scholar is still a fumbling sciolist, dealing with the now mute inhabitant, who, in the twilight centuries, settled down here amid the mysterious forests. Or, who knows, he may have been, like the forest themselves, autochthonous — the Adam and Eve of the occident?

But, as has been intimated, some progress has been made in the knowledge of this misty and elusive denizen of the early wilds. The unearthing and inspection of his remains in recent years having thrown new light upon his habits and customs, possibly, his grade in civilization. As is fitting, in the region where

(28)

the evidences most abound, Ohio has taken the lead in this more minute and scientific search; the work being undertaken here, as in other sections of the country, under the direction of the Ohio State Archæological and Historical Society, whose field examinations have been latterly conducted by Professor W. C. Mills, curator of the Society and to the Museum of the State University.

I accepted, in a recent year, the invitation of the Ohio Archæological and Historical Society to accompany its annual field party in search of the relics of the mysterious race. The site of explorations was fixed near the village of Bourneville, in Ross County, central in the tier of counties crossing the southern regions of the State, this site having already yielded in one or two previous years valuable osteological results to the pick and shovel.

For, to-day, the inquisition for these early settlers, the "first families" of Ohio, so to speak, is largely a matter of bones. Though his origin and scheme of empire be elusive, the primitive citizen did not fail to manufacture abundant testimony of his occupation here. The colossal mounds still rear their heads along the lowlands of the river courses, and their builders, whithersoever their race may have finally departed, have left their skeletons in and around these monumental earth-heaps, where they remain to-day as startlingly distinct effigies of humanity as at the hour of their deposit. *The Mound Builder lies by the side of his mound.* He is neither speculative nor a myth. Whatever may have been his aspirations in the flesh, or whether his intentions may have been more or less honorable in his furtive residence here, he is as obvious and clear in his osteology as the Anglo-Saxon who has succeeded him. His physical proportions and cranial architecture are in substantial evidence.

The scene selected for his exhumation under review was a magnificent valley two miles in breadth, winding along Paint Creek, or river, a stream of irregular turbulence, watering the fertile Ohio lowlands and emptying into the Scioto. Along its sides stretches to-day, for twenty miles, an expanse of rank, opulent grain fields, the soil now tame under four generations of the civilized plough and harrow. The county of Ross prides itself on its fecund fields and its antiquity among Ohio communities.

Chillicothe, its county seat, from the tower of whose ancient Court House Daniel Webster, on a passage through the State, three quarters of a century ago, praised the unrivaled prospect of springing crops, was the early capital of the commonwealth. The opening years of the late century mark, on the headstones in the local graveyards, the dates of demise of the early pioneers from the trans-Alleghany settlements. But over the smooth, culti-vated fields, along the water of Paint River, the landmarks of nature are still unchanged, wild and rugged, as in the days when the Mound Builders, with an unerring eye to succulence, pitched on the valley for an enduring habitat. The straight line of hills lifted almost to grandeur on one side of the stream, and clad as then with primeval forests, is the same in aspect as when it looked down on his encampment on the opposite shore of the river; while rearward of his ancient abode, the heights, similarly clad in their aboriginal green, swing into superb amphitheater, rising in suc-cessive terraces to miniature mountain cones against the sky line. For imposingly picturesque effect the hills of the Rhine and lower Hudson are hardly their superior. The crescent arena under-neath, two miles in breadth, forming the hoar camp of the departed race, on which we pitched our modern tents, looked on every side toward this frowning circlet of heights. The prospect was magnificent, with a touch of gloom; the shadow of this lofty environment, even through the sunny days, falling upon us in the level of the sombre cornfields with suggestions of the gray primeval time. Without much effort of the imagination, the olden scene could be nearly perfectly recalled — the pre-historic squatters from their valley settlement looking to these green-robed hills. It was to become yet more real through our subse-quent diggings here. But the antique settler on this site, as else-where in his selection of locality, gave evidence of an eye for natural beauty as well as of a solicitude for venison and corn. For the Mound Builder, though singularly carnivorous, was a cultivator of the maize.

The immediate spot chosen for our summer exploitation was in an open field of newly-mown wheat stubble, over an ancient village site extending from the base of a lofty mound — one of several tumuli dotted along the twenty miles of this fertile valley plain. From the center and slope of the mound itself had been taken, in a previous year, bones and relics of the mysterious architects, not less than seventy of their skeletons having been unearthed from the level of the cornfield neighboring its base. Over this whole lowland, or river-bottom plain, indeed, to the distance of a quarter of a mile in superficial extent, and possibly in yet uninspected territory far beyond, are the profuse relics of the ancient occupation; arrow point, wrought spear-heads in flint, and obsidian, fragments of pottery, carved shells and implements of diorite, lying so thickly strewn over the alluvial soil that the plowboy, for a century back, has only needed to stoop and select at pleasure from these mementoes of the forgotten epoch; though, in fact, they are so thickly and visibly cast that they have gone for generations virtually unheeded by the residents here. The listless curiosity, however, even of these practical sons of agriculture would have been stirred had they realized over what they stepped. It was a city of the dead that, within a few inches of the disturbing plowshare, lay with its grinning skeletons upturned to their feet!

It is to these previously unnoted village sites, rather than to the imposing and more sensational tumuli, that the recent quest for the secret of the Mound Builder has been chiefly attracted. His true vestiges and inwardness are to be uncovered here — his home, his habits, his tastes, his relations to his dead.

In this new and curious archæologic quest, the Ohio Society, so liberally sustained by the State representative assembly, is taking, as has been said, a marked prominence; the fact being due to its enlightened board of officers, aided by the vigorous and intelligent labors of its distinguished secretary.

To me, a neophyte in necrologic search, the accounts of these mysterious village habitations, with their domestic graveyards and refuse-heaped ash pits yielding testimony of the daily life of the outworn folk, sounded strange and unreal. The Mound Builder found in his alleged identical skeleton was a probable myth, or, at best, a galvanized Indian of the later and tangible epoch — whose tribe could have deposited him at will, by way of conspicuous sepulture, in or near the barrows of the more ancient people. But on the first day of our operations on this

Bourneville site, under the first thrust of the spade, there, yellow and shining in the July sun, lay the clean, indubitable skull of the pre-historic man! At its side was a pot of coarse, heavy earthenware, with crudely ornamented rim. The spot was only a few hundred feet distant from the central mound, around whose base nearly a hundred other skeletons had been previously unearthed. The Indian tribes of the Ohio Valley did not build mounds nor fashion clay pots. To them, as to their pale modern successors, these monumental earth-heaps were a mystery beyond the call of tradition.

The skull at our feet, then, was not the cranial relic of an Indian, but that of an architect of the giant barrow under whose shadow it reposed. Here was reality and history! The burial plat was the rounding bank of the ancient river bed, the soil worn thin and close to the features of the olden dead by the modern plow.

As from the initial spade stroke we proceeded into this shallow shore, the skeletons came everywhere thickly into sight; the burials in places seemingly having been imposed upon one another, as if occurring at widely separated intervals. The work grew interesting almost to excitement. We were face to face with the representatives of the vanished race! Under the heads of a few were polished stones for head-rests, while, near others, were broken or entire pots of varying size, containing flint arrowheads, ornamental trinkets in bone, minute fragments of copper and deposits of food for the dead; this latter persisting in the form of kernels of Indian corn and the shriveled seeds of fruits, distinct in their identity as on the day of interment.

How long had these human remnants laid here thus, integral and intact? One hundred, two hundred, four hundred years? Longer than that. The Indian tribes that met our fathers on this soil knew nothing of these burials. Probably six hundred, ten hundred, two thousand years, then — from the days when the Montagus warred with the Capulets or the skin-clad ancestors of the civilized Saxon, now exhuming them, fell under the sword of the Celtic Dagobert in the forests by the Rhine — or from still beyond in the pagan mists. How long will the frame of man last, anyhow? That depends: three thousand years, as exampled in the cairns of western France, or by the experience of Schliemann with his Mycenæan kings — five thousand, ten thousand, as instanced by the remains of upper Egypt. Here, at least, grinning and pertinent before us, lay the bony relics of departed tribes of men, infract and substantial as in their days under the sunlight, shocking the senses almost with their mockery of contrast with man's brief day in the flesh. The soil in this Bourneville burial camp is alluvial over a porous clay, itself imposed on a drainage stratum of loose river gravel — offering the Mound Builder unusual conditions for posthumous endurance. He thus remains to-day in conspicuous evidence.

Before the end of a week, we had exposed not less than twenty of these amazingly distinct human forms, lying in the veritable attitudes in which they had been laid away in the long-ago epochs. Method of direction as to the points of the compass had been ignored in these burials, as there was also lacking evidence of religious or superstitious rites of interment. Scrupulous care, however, had in many instances been taken as to the decorous composure of the bodies and limbs of the dead.

The process of uncovering these remains was exceedingly careful; for, although perfectly natural in appearance, the bones of these age-worn deposits were, for the most part, soft and brittle. After throwing off, therefore, by the aid of mattock and shovel, the superficial layers of soil, it was necessary to complete the exposure with minute trowels or even with the blades of penknives; the delicate, painstaking care of the proceeding being equal to that of the anatomical expert with his specimens for a museum.

Sometimes a group of not less than seven or eight skeletons would be thus prepared for the photographer's camera; the human shapes, with their deliberate meaning attitudes and grinning skulls, so outlined in relief against the earth, having, at times, a sinister and even menacing distinctness, as if in sardonic rebuke of our intrusion on their ancient rest. Faced to the living, the mysterious dead — our unmistakable kindred — seemed to speak in irony out of the ages. There was no answering back; though, at times, the prolonged, almost intelligent stare of these reproachful relics produced an effect so nearly appalling that the tension of nerves found its natural physiological relief in bursts of hilarious counter-mockery. We addressed the outraged victims of our spades as "John," "Jonathan," the "first citizens," the "late lamented," etc. But the limit of gruesome humor was reached when our artist, taking conventional stand, admonished his helpless subject, with professional courtesy, to "lie still" and "look pleasant!"

In our preliminary diggings during the first ten days, more than thirty skeletons, lying over an area of scarcely more than as many square feet, were thus uncovered and photographed; the place seeming in sections, a veritable teeming charnel pit of the mound-building tribe. The forms ranged from untoothed infancy, to toothless old age, more than one-half of the burials, however, being those of infants and children from a few weeks to a few months or years of age. The early inhabitants here were clearly not economical of babies. Scarlet rash, teething and a diet of imperfectly boiled green corn had inferentially done their perfect work.

At the head or by the side of an occasional adult lay the carved pipe of stone, the model, in size and form, of the conventional pipe, savage or civilized, in all the centuries since. A thousand years, mayhap, earlier than Raleigh and his pampered North Carolina aristocrats knew the luxury of the weed, the primeval American in the enjoyment of its curling fragrance sat here before his hut door, on the river bank, watching the failing sun over the wooded magnificence of these hills. From all evidences the Mound Builder was an ardent lover of tobacco.

Here and there, also, near the skeletons, lay the spearhead, the stone hatchet or other implements, in bone or flint, of the primitive warrior or hunter — notably among these being the shapely, carved bone awl, for the piercing of skins, or similar domestic use.

The physical proportions of the Mound Builder have not yet been adequately studied by the methods of ethnological comparison. The adult skeletons found by us here, and generally over this Bourneville site, have a size not much varying from that of average modern civilized humanity, but tending to inferior rather than to larger dimensions. Many of the male specimens, measured by us, did not exceed the length of five feet three or four inches. One almost gigantic figure, however, atoned for the brevity of his neighbors; his huge, naked skeleton, as it lay grimly composed with head resting on a polished stone slab, stretching, from crown to heel, the full six feet of manly proportions. In life he must have exceeded that stature by several inches, while in girth of ribs and massiveness of bone he was truly colossal — evidently from his size and distinction in burial a towering Saul among his race.

The skull of the Mound Builder, as it came under our inspection, if subjected to minute examination, would furnish a curious study and one far more fruitful in inference than has yet been made. The specimens upturned by us were apparently not of the Indian type with which we are familiar, there being both greater regularity and delicacy than mark that type. They were still further removed from the type of the yet lower savage races, distinguished by the prognathous jaw and heaviness in the occipital region. On the contrary, while the jaw of the Mound architect as here found is regular and massive, as became his carnivorous habit, there is a distinct tendency to elevation and symmetry in the cerebral parts, ranking him rather with the best of the Turanian types of men. Much, however, must be awaited to reduce speculation to scientific inference on this point.

Exhausting after a few days the limits of the some thirty-feet square graveyard, we proceeded in our excavations into the immediately adjacent dwelling sites.

The Mound Builder deposited his dead under two feet of earth, at his doorway; his habitation and sepulchre — possibly from lazy convenience sake — knowing little distinction. Life or death had for him little of the civilized panorama. The necessities of both were pressing and imperative. Sentiment and imagination, or even considerations of health, were not his masters. Unquestionably, in spite of his mounds and his pots and his somewhat equivocal military fortifications, he was not greatly superior in habits to the Indian who succeeded him. His burials, his stone tools, his crude art and his reckless care of his babies attest this. But he was clever in the ways of the semi-barbarian. His dwelling sites, which we now entered, revealed something of his methods and status. To us delving and creeping amid these day after day the atmosphere of the primitive life and time stole with curious effect over the imagination, the impression verging at times on the weird and uncanny. Here were the penetralia, the Lares and Penates, the home and current life, of the ancient race. The Mound Builder, outside of his mound, was not an architect. Beyond his primitive implements, he wrought neither in wood nor in stone. His home was probably a wigwam of skins and twisted boughs. There are no remains or evidences to the contrary — only here and there a still existing earth hole or socket, into which he thrust the stake or pole that propped his dwelling. The inference, subject to correction, may do him vast injustice; but the Mound Builder, barring his zealous proclivity for heaping his huge barrows, was a lazy son of the soil. The testimony is against him. He carried his dead only beyond his door lintels; and here, around and underneath his immediate habitation, he dug circular holes, from three to six feet in depth, into which to empty his ash pots and toss the remnants of his broken food and other refuse from domestic uses. In vulgar parlance, they have "given him away." Through them, like the Indians in the comic opera of "Columbus," he has been "discovered" — in his habits, his tastes and his indolence. His reputation for industry, so laboriously wrought up in his stupendous monuments over the surface of the earth, has disappeared in these discreditable apertures beneath it. As to his dealings with the soil, the Mound Builder, prudent for his fame, should have limited his efforts to the superior direction. But history has been served. As has been intimated, within these circular pits, clearly defined by the softness of their soil against the hard wall of the untouched neighboring clay, are to be found the true vestigia of the home life of the early American. As with the minute trowels we painfully disemboweled these cavities of their contents, the fruits of our labors became intently curious. Remnants of food, broken and entire implements of stone or bone for household use, shells of the native river mussel and land tortoise, flint quirts, fish hooks and arrowheads — all flung with careless hand into these convenient domestic abysses — were found in plethoric abundance. Ashes, in layers or heaps, most frequently intervened between these more significant finds of family débris. The Mound Builder cooked his victual.

The mode of clearing these waste pits was grotesquely and, at times, comically uncomfortable; their limited circular area requiring the delver, with his tiny spade, to squeeze himself into cross-legged sitting posture and sink gradually, in the process of the evacuation, from the sight of his fellows. The slowly-vanishing vision of one bald-headed member of our party, as he thus disappeared from the surface, was the unfailing signal for merriment.

These cavities were uniformly prolific in their yield of the customary finds in flint and stone, such as hammers, hatchets, knives, chisels, wedges and similar instruments. But additionally significant of the industries of the mystic people were the implements and utensils in bone and shell. Notable among these were needles fashioned from the delicate bones of birds and the so-called "scrapers," sharply and curiously carved from the bones of the elk and deer and, inferentially, used in the cleaning and preparation of the skins of these and other animals. The articles in shell, quite commonly from the favorite and ornamental land tortoise, were the more than inferential cups and ladles and spoons employed in the distribution of the family soup. Still added to these were the constantly abundant fragments of the earthen pot, indicating a varying size of the vessel from two inches to nearly as many feet in diameter. Indeed, from the everywhere profuse remains of this family receptacle over and underneath the soil hereabouts, it must have been nearly as plentiful with the tribes as modern crockery with their civilized successors.

The taste and supply in ornament of these strange folk was evinced in our frequent discoveries of bone beads and diminutive specimens of copper, together with other articles of decorative gear, not infrequently fashioned from material transported from remote sections of the country.

But most significantly characteristic of all in the contents of these pits were the varied and literally massive remains of animal life, the relicts of food of the human inhabitants here. The shells of the river mussel were found in literal heaps, while every thrust of trowel or shovel threw to light the bones of deer, elk or bear; the accumulation of these being sufficient to make a respectably impressive mound by the side of each pit. The remains, indeed, of not less than twenty species of animals, mostly native to the region, were found not sparingly in these excavations, including the elk, deer, bear, panther, wolf, wildcat, squirrel, rabbit, coon, wild turkey, opossum, polecat, dog, and many others, most of which had been apparently utilized in the way of subsistence. The succulent marrow of the bones of the deer and kindred animals had been cleanly extracted or carved, in every instance, from its investment. With every hour and step of the investigation there grew the overmastering impression of the carnivorous voracity of these ancient denizens of the soil. In whatever else the primal American may have been lacking, he had in our modern vernacular his "appetite always with him." He evidently lived close to nature in his struggle with her here. He was a tickler, if not a rude cultivator, of the earth and a hunter among men. His weapons for the largest game were obviously ample. His pots were capacious, and he filled his stomach. But beyond his specialty of the towering mound, neither his art nor his ornament was high or elaborate. From the contents of these curious earth cavities adjacent to his hearthstone, it may not be quite fair, indeed, to conclusively judge of the ancient inhabitant of the soil — to construct the imaginary temple of his civilization from the fragments of his domesticity, by himself rejected. Even civilized man would not elect to be so deduced by his successors.

His gigantic barrows and crude fortifications in the ultimate verdict make for the Mound Builder measureable amendment. His cranium is not unpromising; the discovery of an occasional grotesquely-carved pipe or copper ornament may elevate him toward the rank of the Zuni or Aztec; but it stands to reason that these tell-tale cavities, fecund with the broken paraphernalia of his daily existence, are the true memorabilia and evidence of his half-barbarous, evanished race. Taking the case as it stands, at least, it is disconcerting to acknowledge how barely he is rescued by his mound and his pot from the status of the familiar Indian, of whose arts and habits he so abundantly partook.

THE CAMPAIGNS OF THE REVOLUTION IN THE OHIO VALLEY.

Their Effect on the Growth of the United States.

JULIETTE SESSIONS.

[In 1903 the Ohio Society, Sons of the Revolution offered a prize of $100 for the best essay which might be submitted upon the subject heading this article. Miss Sessions, a member of the teaching corps of The Columbus High School entered the contest and was awarded the prize. The essay is herewith made public for the first time through the courtesy of the awarding committee. — EDITOR.]

The American Revolution was, unquestionably, in its chief movements a struggle for independence, but, on the other hand, it was a war of conquest. While the colonists, truer to the English ideals than George III. and his friends, were fighting for the principles of English liberty, some of their number were at the same time taking from England a territory more than equal to their own and subduing the land and its savage inhabitants. This conquered territory, extending from the heigths of the Alleghanies to the Mississippi, has as its center the Ohio Valley, and the events that took place there during the war make most of the story of this first conquest of the United States.

At the close of the French and Indian War, while the outcome of Pontiac's conspiracy was still uncertain, a royal proclamation was issued which defined the policy of the English government with regard to the lands just acquired from France. After arranging for governments for Quebec and for West and East Florida, the proclamation declares it "to be our royal will and pleasure . . . that no governor or commander-in-chief of our colonies, or plantations in America, do presume for the present to grant warrants of survey or pass patents for any lands beyond the heads or sources of any of the rivers that fall into the Atlantic Ocean from the West or Northwest; or upon any

lands whatever which have not been ceded or purchased by
us," etc.[1]

The first object of this proclamation was, undoubtedly, to
pacify the Indians by assurances that their hunting grounds were
not to be invaded by settlers. Another object probably was to
maintain the Mississippi Valley a wilderness for hunters and
traders, where business would languish as advancing colonists
cleared the land and exterminated game. From several sources
it would appear, also, that the proclamation reveals the intention
of the English government to annul the "from sea to sea"
clauses of the colonial charters, and keep the settlements along
the seaboard. So thinks a writer in the "Annual Register for
1763.[2] The same restrictive policy is revealed in the refusal, in
1765, to grant permission to plant a colony in the Illinois country, Dr. Franklin finding four objections made to the plan:
(1) The distance would render such a colony of little use to
England; (2) The distance would render it difficult to defend
and govern the colony; (3) Such a colony might, in time, become troublesome and prejudicial to the British government;
(4) There were no people to spare in either England or
the other colonies, to settle a new colony.

When also, in 1772, the Lords Commissioners for Trade
and Plantations made a report upon the petition of the so-called
Walpole Company for a grant of land south of the Ohio, on
which to establish a new government, they found that to grant
the petition would be to abandon established principles. The
"confining of the western extent of settlements to such a distance
from the sea coast as that those settlements should lie within
reach of the trade and commerce of this kingdom . . . and also
of the exercise of that authority and jurisdiction which was conceived to be necessary for the preservation of the colonies in due
subordination to and dependence upon the Mother country" were
declared to be the two capital objects of the proclamation of
1763.[3] The refusal of the Lords of Trade was made, too, right

---

[1] Annual Register 1763.

[2] Hinsdale, p. 124.

[3] Poole, p. 687 in Chap. IX, Vol. VI, Narrative and Critical History
of America.

in the face of the Treaty of Fort Stanwix of 1768, by which Sir William Johnson had secured from the Iroquois a cession to the British crown of the very lands that the petitioners asked for and which the crown would be perfectly free to grant out if the proclamation were only to protect the Indians.

Washington, however, and other Americans looked upon it as only a temporary expedient which would lapse when the Indians were ready to give up their lands.[4]

But whatever the motives of the British government, the prohibition came as a real and immediate grievance to the colonists along the frontier. They had already, as Burke says, "topped the Alleghany Mountains," from which they beheld "before them an immense plain, one vast level meadow; a square of five hundred miles." Just as the men of the seaports refused to use the stamps of 1765, and on principle evaded the provisions of the Townsend Acts, so the frontiersmen went forward into the new land, spying it out, building hunters' lodges and occupying in defiance of the proclamation. While they did not grow into "the hordes of English Tartars," which Burke pictures, they became a sturdy power and rose in instant sympathy with their brothers of the coast lands.

Their frontier settlements were all south of the Ohio, the strength of the Iroquois and Algonquins of the lakes making an effectual barrier to the hunting grounds of the north. Into the western parts of Virginia the most considerable advance was made by Virginians and Pennsylvanians and groups of cabins were dotted all the way from Fort Pitt to the Kanawha before the Revolution began. In 1769 the first settlements were made about the head waters of the Tennessee in the Watauga Valley and Daniel Boone explored East Kentucky the same year.

The restrictive quality of England's land policy culminated in the Quebec Act in 1774, which made the territory north of the Ohio part of the Province of Quebec, thus disposing of any charter rights the colonies might later assert. The further statements of the act that the Catholic faith and the old French law should be established and that the latter was the only kind of government proper for a colony, placed the Quebec Act among

---

[4] Butterfield's Washington-Crawford Letters 3, quoted by Hinsdale.

the chief grievances of the Colonies and it is mentioned in the
Declaration of Rights, of October, 1774, in the Articles of Association and again, though in veiled terms, in the Declaration
of Independence. As late as 1782 Madison in a report says.
"The Quebec Act was one of the multiplied causes of our opposition and finally of Revolution." But what the colonists com-
plained of was not so much the destruction of their charter
rights to the ·territory as the extension of arbitrary government and religion. The charters were brought forth in the
peace negotiations of 1782 and 1783 to support the American
claims, but our right to receive the land west of the mountains
was plainly a right of conquest.

Before going into the events of the war it will be well to
review the situation at its opening. Fort Pitt, at the head of
the Ohio Valley, was in the hands of the Americans; Detroit
and other lake posts, in the hands of the British. In the northern
side of the Ohio Valley there were practically no English settlements. On the Mississippi, at Kaskaskia and Cohokia, and at
Vincennes on the Wabash were French communities now under
English control. In Eastern Ohio a few Moravian Missionaries lived with Christian Indians in the Tuscarawas Valley.
With a few such exceptions the control of the red-man was undisturbed from Fort Pitt to the Mississippi. Delawares, Shawnees, Miamis and the Wabash tribes bordered on the Ohio, while
Wyandots and others lived north of them along the Erie water-
shed. Indian territories were always vaguely bounded and overlapping, but the country directly south of the Ohio was not
claimed by any one tribe. It was a rich hunting ground, a great
buffalo pasture, and was used in common by tribes to the north
and south. The southern side of the valley of the Tennessee
river was the home of the Cherokee tribes, who during the
Revolution and long after made precarious the life of the pioneers
of Tennessee and Kentucky. On the west side of the Mississippi, a little above the mouth of the Ohio, stood the Spanish-
French town of St. Louis, and further south on the east side
was Natchez, in control of the English.

⁸ Poole, p. 715

In all the years of the war the Indians, with the exception of tribes temporarily subdued, were on the side of the British. The reasons are many and plain to see. In the first place, the tribes of the Mississippi Valley had been for generations the allies of the French and with the French had passed under English influence. Second, the Proclamation of 1763 had convinced them that the English intentions were friendly to them. Third, the English and the French of Canada came into the Indian country only as hunters and traders, while the Americans all the way from the Green Mountains to King's Mountain were pushing into their hunting grounds to settle and despoil. And last, and perhaps most potent of all, the English adopted the plan of enlisting these savage warriors in their behalf and sending forth the scalping knife and tomahawk against the frontier settlements. [6]The American used savage allies sometimes, also, but knew the horrors of savage warfare too well to employ them extensively.[7]

The undertakings of the British in the Ohio Valley were to send expeditions of Indians and white rangers from Detroit southward with these purposes in view; to secure and hold the Illinois country, to attack and drive settlers out of the Kentucky country and to cut off communication by the Ohio between Fort Pitt and New Orleans. On the southern side of the valley the Indians were incited against the whites of Tennessee and Kentucky in the hope of destroying settlements and also to prevent any aid going from the mountaineers to the men of the coast.

The work of the Americans in the valley was threefold. First, some few operations, conducted by militia or continental forces, from Fort Pitt; second, a steady battling against the Indian allies of England by the backwoodsmen of Kentucky, Tennessee and Western Virginia; third, the campaigns of George Rogers Clark, who was backed by Virginia and the backwoodsmen, which secured the Illinois country, kept the Ohio under American control and seriously threatened Detroit.

---

[6] Roosevelt I, p. 276-280. Hinsdale, p. 149.

[7] Winsor, p. 87.

As there was no extended or continuously pursued plan of war in the Ohio Valley, the only way to relate the facts will be to take them year by year, indicating the important movements as they come in order. One of the most famous Indian wars in our annals, Lord Dunmore's war, began while the Quebec Act was still under discussion and ended in the Battle of Point Pleasant, at the mouth of the Great Kanawha, after the Continental Congress was in session in the fall of 1774. This cannot properly be called a part of the Revolution, but has such important bearings on later events that it must be reviewed. It was conducted by a royal governor of Virginia and yet was in defence of 'Virginians who had gone beyond the sources of eastward flowing rivers into the land forbidden them by the Proclamation of 1763. This advance of the whites into the land south of the Ohio was viewed with hostile eyes by the Northwest Indians, the Shawnees and Mingoes in particular. Trouble had been brewing for a long time and Virginia had found it wise to keep a considerable force upon the frontier. Finally, the unwarranted murder of the people of Logan, a Mingo Chief, heretofore friendly to the whites, fired him and soon the natives of Southeastern Ohio were on the war path under the lead of Cornstalk, one of the bravest and best of his kind. Lord Dunmore himself took to the field, having one Andrew Lewis as second in command.

Dunmore at once took the offensive, going down the Ohio to Hockhocking and thence across country to the vicinity of the Indian town of Chillicothe. His instructions to Lewis were to join him there, but Cornstalk ferried about a thousand warriors across the Ohio and engaged the force of Lewis on the south shore at the mouth of the Great Kanawha. There followed "the most closely contested of any battle ever fought with the northwest Indians" and one of the most decisive victories for the whites. The spirit of the Indians was completely broken and Cornstalk and his fellow chiefs went to Dunmore's camp and made a treaty which restored all prisoners and gave up all claims to land south of the Ohio.

In this war figured many who were to be the leaders in the campaigns we are to study. Clark and Simon Kenton were with Dunmore; Boone was in charge of some of the forts, and with Lewis, whose force was chiefly of backwoodsmen, some of whom had come all the way from the Watauga settlements, were the Shelbys, father and son, and Sevier and Robertson. Before going to their homes the officers met and passed resolutions in which they professed their devotion to the king and the British empire, but extended their sympathy to the people of Boston and to the Continental Congress. They gave assurance that, although for three months in the wilderness they had no news of how the struggle for American liberty was progressing, they were not indifferent to the cause and called attention to the endurance and fighting ability of their troops.[8]

Into the much disputed question of Dunmore's motives and intentions we may not enter here, but the outcome of the war, by securing quiet and occasional alliances of the Northwest Indians for the next two years, made safe the navigation of the Ohio and opened the way to the settlement of Kentucky and thus to the establishment of an Ohio River garrison of "Long Knives," as the Indians called the Virginians, and leads us to believe that but for Dunmore's war, the treaty of 1783 might have left the colonies with the Alleghanies as their western boundary.[9]

In the spring of 1775 the systematic movement forward into the valleys of the Kentucky rivers began. The most pretentious undertaking was that of Colonel Richard Henderson of Virginia, who, early in March in the Watauga Valley made a treaty with the Cherokees in the presence of full twelve hundred of their tribe by which he acquired their title to land between the Cumberland and Kentucky rivers.[10]

Henderson's plan was to establish a feudal or proprietary state of Transylvania but the plan did not take with the pioneers and was declared against by the governments of Virginia and North Carolina and his state never materialized. But settlers went into the land and protected now by treaties with both northern and southern Indians Kentucky had a rapid growth.

---

[8] Roosevelt I, p. 240.
[9] Roosevelt I, p. 239.
[10] Winsor, p. 83.

Under warrant from Henderson, Boone blazed a trail from the Holston and Watauga valleys through the Cumberland Gap to the valley of the Kentucky — "Boone's Trace" or "the Wilderness Road," which became the great highway from Virginia and Carolina into the Ohio country.

In June, 1775, the Continental Congress, among its other preparation for the war already begun, arranged three Indian departments: the northern, embodying the Six Nations and other northern tribes; the southern, including the Cherokees and others in the south; and the middle which centered at Pittsburg. Commissioners were appointed to treat with the tribes and counteract the influence of the royalists. The same year Colonel Henry Hamilton was put in charge of the British post at Detroit. He was under orders from the London war office to enlist the savages and personally was strongly in favor of the plan. In the south John Stuart, who had long served as agent among the Southern tribes, received fresh instructions. Thus at the opening of the war both sides saw the importance of Indian alliances.

Hamilton began actively sending out war belts and calling councils, but through memories of the battle of the Great Kanawha and the influence of Zeisberger, the Moravian missionary, in the Ohio country, the northwest tribes maintained neutrality through the year 1776. Stuart was more successful and early in June the whole Cherokee nation was on the warpath. With this war as it affected the southern and seaboard colonies, we have nothing to do, except to note that the Cherokees were generally defeated, but the Watauga and Holston settlements, the southeast border land of the Ohio Valley, were attacked and their gallant defense under the lead of Robertson and Sevier marks one more step by which the whole Ohio Valley became American territory. These settlements were at the head of the Wilderness Road, and had they been annihilated Kentucky would have been open to attack and probably have been abandoned. The Cherokees made little trouble for several years after this and by that time the southern side of the Ohio country was strong enough to take care of itself.

The year 1777 was a dark one for the Americans of the frontier. Hamilton, by means of war talks and council fires, gifts of arms, firewater and trinkets, had established his influence among the northwest Indians. He won the title of "hair-buyer" among the backwoodsmen and there is certain evidence that scalps were paid for at Detroit.[11] Tories of the border flocked to that post and McKee, Eliot and Girty, fleeing thither from Pittsburgh, became leaders of bands of white rangers and Indians which Hamilton was organizing. The most notable attack of the year was made in September at Wheeling, then called Fort Henry. About three hundred Indians with some Detroit Rangers, flying the British colors, attacked the stockade. Many of the men were lured out by stratagem and slain, but those left, with the help of the women, repelled the attack. This fight is famed for the exploit of Major Samuel McCulloch, who rode his old grey horse down a three hundred foot precipice, the only way to evade the savages and reach his friends in Fort Henry. A hill above Wheeling is still known as McCulloch's Leap.

Fortunately for Kentucky, Hamilton seems not to have realized the importance of the settlements there and most of the efforts of the year were directed against the region of Fort Pitt. Small bands of Indians, however, crossed the Ohio and fell again and again on the Kentucky forts. The backwoodsmen, though they and their families were in constant peril, held tenaciously to their ground, once during the year encouraged by the men of the Holston settlements who marched north to help their neighbors. But the dangers about Pittsburg compelled Hand, in command there, to call in some of his outposts and that, with the news of Washington's loss of Philadelphia, left the trans-Alleghany pioneers very much alone in their struggle.

Early in 1778 the Kentuckians were weakened by the loss of Daniel Boone, who was captured with a party who had gone to the Blue Licks to make salt for the garrisons. He was taken by the Indians to Detroit where he was well treated by Hamilton, who offered to ransom him. But the Indians liked him, refused to give him up, and took him back to Chillicothe and adopted him into their tribe. Here he remained some months, but in June war parties of British and Indians began to gather, and finding his own village of Boonsborough was to be the object

---

[11] Roosevelt II, p. 3.

of attack Boone managed to escape, and taking a bee line through the forests, reached home in four days, having traveled one hundred and sixty miles and had one meal on the way. So fearful were the settlers of traitors even among their best, that Boone was at once tried by court martial for the capture at the Blue Licks, [12]but was acquitted, made a major and became the leader of the defense. Boonsborough was strengthened and then impatient waiting, in August, Boone led a foray across the Ohio, but learning a great force of Miamis was on its way south made a race with them for Boonsborough and got there in time to call in the people and successfully defend the fort. This makes the last serious troubles the people of that part of Kentucky had, but the doings of the border in the years following, the dangers and the darings, in which Daniel Boone and Simon Kenton were chief actors, would fill many a chapter and have made them the center of gathering traditions which in an earlier age would have grown into a national epic like the Cid, or the Story of King Arthur and knights of the Round Table.

Mention has been made of George Rogers Clark in Lord Dunmore's war. He was a Virginian who explored in the Kentucky country in 1775, and in 1776 had finally cast his lot with the backwoodsmen. By that time Henderson's claims as a proprietary ruler were fading and at the suggestion of Clark the settlers gathered at Harrodstown in June and chose two delegates, one of whom was Clark, to go to Williamsburg, the capital of Virginia. They carried a petition asking that Kentucky be organized as a county of that state and promising that its people would do their part in the struggle in which all Americans were engaged. The journey was accomplished after much suffering and danger and the petition presented. Clark's request for five hundred pounds of gun-powder, of which the settlements were in great need, was refused at first, but granted when Clark announced that Kentucky would have to assume her independence if she had to bear her burdens alone. The powder wast taken safely down the Ohio to Kentucky and the next session of the Virginia legislature organized the county of Kentucky.

---

[12] Roosevelt II, p. 21.

But the work of Clark had only begun. While aiding in repelling Indian attacks of 1777 he conceived the desirability of a forward movement by the colonists and with that idea in mind sent two young men as spies northward to find out the strength of the British posts in the French towns of the Illinois country and to ascertain the temper of the French inhabitants. His emissaries reported small garrisons and but little interest in the struggles on the part of the French, who were much impressed by the stories of the prowess of the backwoodsmen.[13]

Knowing that the Kentuckians could not furnish a sufficient force to leave their homes for this offensive movement, Clark went to Virginia, in the fall of 1777, journeying over the Wilderness Road, the shortest and safest way. The news of Burgoyne's surrender had reached Williamsburg and Clark went with patriotic enthusiasm to lay his plans before Governor Patrick Henry. The governor was responsive enough, but Virginia was exhausted. The matter could not be publicly discussed and volunteer contributions secured and all that Henry could do was to authorize Clark to raise seven companies of fifty men each, to act and be paid as militia. Some money was advanced and he was given on order for boats and supplies at Pittsburg. Three Virginians, Jefferson, Mason and Wythe, gave him their written promise to try to persuade the Virginia Legislature to give each of his men three hundred acres of the conquered land, should they be succcessful. The open instructions of the governor ordered Clark to the relief of Kentucky, a secret letter bade him attack the Illinois region. So, it will be seen, success or failure of the expedition rested solely on Clark as an individual.

Great difficulty was experienced in enlisting men, but by May, 1778, he had secured four companies in Western Virginia and started down the Monongahela to Pittsburg with a hundred and fifty men, and some other adventurers and settlers with

---

[13] Roosevelt II, p. 33. For the events of this campaign and the others, I follow largely Winsor and Roosevelt, both of whom, but particularly the latter, give exact references to original sources, the Haldimand MSS., State Department MSS., and so forth, which it has been impossible for me to verify.

their families. At Pittsburg and Wheeling he got his supplies
and then the rude flat boats started on their long and dangerous
journey down the Ohio. A landing was made at the Falls of
the Ohio on May 27th. Most of the families moved off into
the interior of Kentucky, but a few settled near the falls and
made the nucleus of that city which was later given the name
of the King of France, whose alliance with the colonies Clark
first heard of at that time and place. Here some Kentuckians,
Kenton among them, joined him, and a company from the Holston. When Clark announced his plan there were some mur-
murings and most of the Holston men deserted. He then weeded
out all weakly men and on June 24th his boats shots the rapids
bearing less than two hundred men, all told, none of the four
companies being up to its full strength of fifty.

Of the well known story of this campaign, which reads
like a mediaeval romance, only the most salient facts can be given
in this paper. Fearing interference on the Mississippi, Clark
left his boats a little below the mouth of the Tennessee, and the
expedition marched overland to Kaskaskia, guided by a party
of American hunters who had just come from the French settlements. Clark got valuable information from the hunters, and
convinced that he could take Kaskaskia only by a surprise attack, he led his army forward with all the stealth of Indians.
The final advance upon the town was made after dark. The
fort was found gaily lighted, a post ball being in progress
and everybody was off guard. Clark was himself inside the
fort quietly watching the dance before the alarm was given by
an Indian who saw the strange face in the flickering torch light.
In the confusion that followed with what grim humor Clark
bade them go on with the dance, but to remember that it was
now under the flag of Virginia, not of England!

The town was easily secured and the French passed a night
of abject terror, for the appearance of the backwoodsmen was
quite in keeping with the tales they had heard of their strength
and brutality. When morning came the chief inhabitants came
humbly asking the dear boon of life. Then Clark showed himself a master diplomatist as well as a keen warrior. He told
them he came not to enslave, but to set them free; told of the al-

liance between the French government and his nation and when questioned by the priest, Gibault, as to whether the Catholic church could be opened, made his master stroke by saying that under the laws of his Republic one religion had as much protection as another. The mercurial spirits of the French rose and all went home to rejoice after taking the oath of allegiance, while Gibault became from that time on a useful champion of the American cause.

The news of what had happened at Kaskaskia brought the immediate submission of Cahokia, to which town Clark sent a small force of his men with some French volunteers. Gibault on his own motion went to Vincennes and secured its adherence by his own arts of persuasion. Thus with practically no fighting Illinois passed into American control.

But the real difficulties of Clark's undertaking now began. He was in the midst of a great savage country with only a handful of men and no near base of supplies and reinforcement. The French of the villages were his friends and he found sympathy in the Spanish posts across the Mississippi, but the attitude of the Indians was still unsettled and a force might be sent against him from Detroit at any time. Moreover, the time of enlistment of his men expired and only about one hundred re-enlisted, though a few young Frenchmen filled up the companies. Crowds of Indians, representing all the tribes of the Northwest, began to gather at Cahokia to hear what had happened. There went on days of "talk," of negotiation, of conciliation and cajolery, during which Clark had to keep every sense alive to guard against sudden stealth and cunning. But he understood Indian character perfectly and finally in speeches of real Indian imagery convinced the gathered hordes of his power and that of the people he represented, as well as of their good intentions toward the redmen. A solemn peace treaty was entered into with full Indian ceremonies and the safety of the American garrison then secured. Clark was ever after a great figure in the Indian minds and it was reported that in later wars they would treat with no other American officer if Clark was present.[14]

---

[14] Roosevelt I, p. 57.

Hamilton at Detroit was planning an expedition against Fort Pitt when news of Clark's expedition reached him, and he immediately gave up that enterprise to go to the Illinois country. The Indians near at hand were rallied and the posts on Lake Michigan notified to stir up their savages. An expedition was promptly prepared at Detroit and in October (1778) started down the river for Vincennes. From Lake Erie they rowed up the Maumee, then had a nine-mile carry to the Wabash, the water of which led directly to Vincennes. Hamilton went in person and had in his commands only one hundred and seventy-seven whites, but gathering Indians as he went secured a force of about five hundred. It was a hard journey and Hamilton gained opinions as to the difficulties of the Illinois country which did Clark good service the following winter. The American force was so small that Clark had not dared divide it, and Captain Helm, whom he put in command at Vincennes had only a handful of men. Scouts sent out by Helm were captured, so news of Hamilton's approach did not reach him and the town passed easily into English hands on December 17th.

The British commander now felt perfectly secure, for spies had told him that Clark had but one hundred and ten men, and, besides, the route from Kaskaskia was one of the great difficulty in winter. If he had moved on at once it would seem that he might easily have crushed Clark, whose base of supplies at Fort Pitt was really cut off, while his own was comparatively accessible. But he dreaded a winter campaign and settled down to wait for spring.

When Clark learned through Francis Vigo, an Italian trader, that Hamilton had only eighty men in his garrison and that he planned to gather a great force to overrun the country in the spring, the terrors of winter weather and swampy wilderness faded away from before the Americans and preparations were at once begun for retaking Vincennes. An armed row-boat was sent down to the Ohio to watch the mouth of the Wabash. The French came gladly to his aid and young men volunteered until he was able to march out of Kaskaskia on February 7th (1779) with a force of one hundred and seventy. The march of two hundred and forty miles was accomplished against ordinarily insuperable obstacles. Cold and hunger were expected difficulties, but to this march was added the necessity of moving forward over plains flooded with ice-cold water, often to a man's waist, and sometimes deeper. Canoes or dug-outs were built to carry the weaker men and scanty baggage and occasionally the whole force was ferried where the water was over head in depth. It took all of Clark's ingenuity to keep his men alive, to keep up their spirits and prevent desertions. But he succeeded, and surprising Hamilton completely, secured Vincennes after a very little fighting, and the whole garrison of seventy-nine men, including Hamilton, as prisoners of war. A valuable load of supplies and goods of all sorts on its way from Detroit, was captured just above Vincennes and distributed among the soldiers, who were gladdened at the same time by messengers from the Virginia government bringing thanks and promises of pay.

The Americans were now in complete control of the Illinois country and all the Indians of the region were neutral through the rest of the war. Then French and Spanish across the river were Clark's enthusiastic friends. Virginia shortly organized the new territory as a county with John Todd as County Lieutenant. The great trouble now for both Clark and Todd was to secure funds with which to take care of their charge. Pollock, an American trader at New Orleans, and Francis Vigo stepped in here and honored Clark's drafts again and again.[15] The Ohio River was now perfectly safe, and before the summer of 1779 was over the Spanish from New Orleans took Natchez and supply boats could pass from Fort Pitt to New Orleans and back. Toward the end of the year Clark himself took up his post at the Falls of the Ohio where he might serve as a shield to both Kentucky and the Illinois country and from which point he hoped to be able to move against Detroit. Clark's great services to his country end here, but probably no single man ever did so much on his own personal responsibility to enlarge the territory of the United States as he had done.

The same season of Clark's campaign in Illinois, 1778, the Congress and Washington had decided to strengthen the forces at Fort Pitt, and General McIntosh was sent to take charge.

[15] Hinsdale, p. 155. Winsor, p. 131.

With an enlarged army of Continentals and militia, he was to move across country against Detroit. The start was made, but McIntosh moved with such caution and built forts with such care that winter set in when he had advanced only to the Upper Muskingum valley. He left a small force to hold that post, retired to Pittsburg, and sent his militia home.

The year 1779 saw some trouble for the Kentucky settlements, but Clark's work disorganized their foes and two great streams of emigrants poured into the territory, one by the Wilderness Road and one down the Ohio. It was this year that James Robertson, of Watauga fame, went to the Kentucky River by the Wilderness Road, and then struck across to the great bend in the Cumberland, where he made ready for a large party of his friends under Donelson, the father of the future Mrs. Andrew Jackson. Donelson's party, his daughter among them, came by water all the way down the Tennessee to the Ohio, and thence up the Cumberlanl. It was a perilous undertaking, but was really no part of the war except that each advancing colony made more secure the claims that America could make to trans-Alleghany territory.

In May of 1779 Indian forays stirred up the Kentuckians, and a party of about one hundred under John Bowman, a county lieutenant — for Kentucky was now divided into several counties — went against Chillicothe. The town was burned by the Indians, who rallied and drove off the whites. It was a humiliating defeat, but it had a disastrous effect upon an army just starting from Detroit, under Captain Henry Bird. His entire force of Indians fled from him, panic-stricken, when they heard of the attack on Chillicothe, and Kentucky was spared an attack.

In 1780, DePeyster, a New York tory, took command at Detroit, and a determined and systematic attack on the American positions was begun. Efforts were made to send bands against Vincennes and against Clark at the Falls, but the Indians of the region were now hard to rouse against the Americans, and made most uncertain allies. In May, a force of six or seven hundred Indians and a few Canadians started for the Ohio, aimed against the villages of Kentucky, where DePeyster correctly thought was the strongest hold of the Americans on the

Ohio Valley. Bird was in command again, and this time succeeded in passing down the Miami, crossing the Ohio and taking
two small stockades near the Licking River. Satisfied with this,
he began his retreat to Detroit, but his Indians became unruly
and stole and plundered, and he could not even get his little
cannon back to Detroit.

Stirred up by this small British adventure, Clark, disguised
as an Indian to prevent attack by strolling savages, hurried
through the forest to the panic-stricken Kentucky settlements.
Many recent arrivals were all ready to flee the country, but
Clark sent a force to drive them back from the Wilderness Road,
and, appointing the mouth of the Licking as a rendezvous, prepared for a counter foray. About nine hundred men responded
to his call. They went up the Ohio some distance, crossed it,
and marched against old Chillicothe. That town had been deserted, but a Piqua town, containing Girty and several hundred
Indians, was attacked. Clark's party was successful, drove out
the Indians and destroyed their property, and seized the stores
of some British traders. There was no more trouble in 1780.

In the winter of 1780-1781, Clark went to Virginia to secure forces and supplies for an attack on Detroit. Jefferson,
their governor, did all in his power, and both men appealed to
Washington. The commander-in-chief had more work than he
could take care of as it was, and could only instruct Colonel
Brodhead, at Fort Pitt, to do what he could to help Clark. The
latter was empowered to raise troops, but went up and down the
Ohio from Fort Pitt to the Falls and to Illinois, without getting
a sufficient response. One small party of Pennsylvanians, coming down the Ohio to join him, was attacked by a force of Indians under the famous Joseph Brant, and all killed or captured.
The news of Clark's intended attack on Detroit caused the collection of war bands to oppose him. One under McKee and
Brant attained considerable size, but fell to pieces when they
heard Clark had abandoned his plan, and only some small forays
took place.

The surrender of Cornwallis, in October, 1781, did not
bring quiet to the frontier. The winter following witnessed the
wanton massacre of the Moravian Indians, by a party from Fort

Pitt. The Moravians had been neutral all through the war, but between two fires, and suspected by their brother Indians and the Americans. It is a dark page in our annals, but cannot detain us here. The following spring a force of Pennsylvania and Virginia militia was sent against Sandusky, was worsted, and retreated with considerable loss. Some of the men had shared in the Moravian massacre, and captives were put to death by the Indians with peculiar torture; the chief sufferer, Colonel Crawford was, however, innocent of that crime.

The summer of 1782 was almost a repetition of that of 1781. Caldwell and McKee started from Detroit with some rangers, and speedily gathered over a thousand Indians, the largest force west of the Alleghanies during the Revolution. They planned an attack on Wheeling, but turned aside because of a rumor that Clark was intending to attack the Shawnee towns.[16] Finding it was a false alarm many of the Indians deserted, but three or four hundred were retained, and with them the Ohio was crossed and an attack made on the forts in Fayette County, between the Ohio and Kentucky Rivers, then the feeblest and most exposed part of Kentucky. Several stations were destroyed, and the party began a leisurely retreat to the Blue Licks, where they were overtaken by a hastily-gathered force of backwoodsmen. Boone was with them, and advised that an attack be postponed until other troops known to be on the way could come up. But rasher councils prevailed, and an attack made, which ended in a wild rout of the whites. "He that could remount a horse was well off; he that could not had no time for delay."[17] This battle of the Blue Licks was the bloodiest Kentucky had known.

Clark was once more roused, and gathering forces at the mouth of the Licking, as before, started up the Miami Valley in November, 1782, with one thousand and fifty mounted riflemen. The Indians fell back before this force — towns and supplies were destroyed. McKee tried to come to the aid of his Indian friends, but his forces were scattered; Clark's dream might also have been realized, for McKee wrote that the severity

---

[16] Roosevelt II, p. 188.
[17] Levi Todd's Letter, Roosevelt II, p. 203.

of the blow left the road open to Detroit.[18]   But the war went no further.   By the opening of 1783 the news of peace reached the frontier, and the campaigns of the Revolution were over.

Just what had been accomplished by the war in the West can be briefly summarized: (1) The advance of settlers to the south side of the upper Ohio, and into the Watauga Valley, gave the colonists a footing west of the mountains.   (2) These settlements made necessary the battle of the Great Kanawha, in 1774, and the defeat of the Shawnees there opened the Ohio River as a route to the Kentucky valleys.   (3) The treaty of Henderson and Boone, in 1775, and the settlements made by them established a hold on the Kentucky country.   (4) The success of the Watauga men over the Cherokees, in 1776, made their own position permanent and placed a barrier between Kentucky and the South.   (5) In 1778 Clark's conquest was in itself the greatest advance made and besides cleared the northern horizon so that, (6) the growth of Kentucky increased, and in 1779, especially, a new frontier was established by Robertson and his company in the Cumberland Valley.

It is well said that the last contest for the Western country was the diplomatic battle fought by John Jay, at Paris.   Though France and Spain had been our allies during the war there was nothing that either of them desired less than a free republic, extending from the Atlantic to the Mississippi.   In the negotiations that took place it was fortunate that the American Commissioners had a liberal English ministry to treat with, rather than that of Lord North.   It was a help to their claims that a shadow of a right to the Western lands had come down from the old charters, but the weight of argument rested upon the actual conquest and occupation of the country asked for.   As Livingston wrote to Franklin, in January, 1782, "This extension to the Mississippi is founded on justice, and our claims are at least such as the events of the war give us a right to insist upon," while the settlements in the West "render a relinquishment of the claim highly impolitic and unjust."[19]   Even France

---

[18] Roosevelt II. p. 209.

[19] Winsor, p. 209.

and Spain recognized the right that lies in possession, and one line was proposed by them, which would have given to the Republic the territory that had actually been settled by her people.[20] What the United States really got was only what had been conquered, for, though the treaty of 1783 gave the Great Lakes and Florida as the northern and southern boundaries, it took a good many years and at least one treaty more to obtain actual possession of it all. So the first result of the campaigns in the Ohio Valley was unquestionably the acquisition of that valley by the United States.

Further, this acquisition made sure the future growth of the territory. Count d'Aranda, the Spanish commissioner at Paris, "predicted the enormous expansion of the Federal Republic at the expense of Florida, Louisiana and Mexico, unless effectually curbed in its youth."[21] His prediction has been more than fulfilled. The possession of half the Mississippi Valley made essential the control of its mouth, hence the Louisiana purchase. The holding of the interior gave a need for the gulf coast, and we acquired Florida.

These campaigns were carried on chiefly by men who were coming into the land to possess it, and each advancing victory drew after it a fresh wave of immigration; colonization and conquest, mutually cause and effect. But the stress of danger brought forth united action of the frontiersmen, and developed a feeling of common interest which drew them together under some form of civil regulations; whereas, in less stirring times they might have remained much longer free bands of hunters and woodsmen, and the civilization and growth of the interior been much delayed.

The acquisition of the western lands appeared at first as an enormous advantage to certain States holding the ancient charters, but when their titles were quit-claimed to the United States a national domain was created, interest in which and care of which did a great deal to hold the States together in the perilous days of the Confederation and to lead to the stronger union of the Constitution.

---

[20] Hinsdale, p. 176. Map opposite p. 180.

[21] Roosevelt II, p. 376.

Furthermore, at the close of the war, a vast immigration into the new lands began. Some came to redeem soldiers' bounties, some from ruined homes along the coast sought to renew their fortunes in the rich soil of these river valleys. New sources of wealth were opened up and the opportunities of the great West drew to our shores throngs of Europeans to multiply our population and add to our wealth and power.

Finally, it may not be going too far to say that this Ohio Valley conquest developed a race of pioneers who have formed the forward moving element all through our history. Pioneers are men who keep ahead of civilization as long as there is a wilderness to conquer, and then turn to subdue the evils that grow out of civilization itself. Daniel Boone died west of the Mississippi, still pursuing the wilderness; Andrew Jackson was a product of East Tennessee in Revolutionary times, while his wife, the daughter of Donelson, went to the Cumberland Valley with her father in 1779; the younger brother of Clark shares with Lewis the credit for the exploration of the Oregon country, and Sam Houston, a product of the Tennessee frontier, was the founder of the United States power in Texas. As the first backwoodsmen went forward and took the land in the face of British and Indians, so it has been their sons or the inheritors of their spirit who have led the advance of the United States all the way to the Pacific. And Lincoln, "the first American," was essentially a backwoods product, whose pioneer instinct turned back to destroy the weeds of human slavery and in the tangles of State and party enmity to prepare the way, to make straight the paths, for a new and greater nation than the world had yet known.

Principal authorities for the facts related in the foregoing Article: *Hinsdale* — The Old Northwest. *Winsor* — The Westward Movement. *Roosevelt* — The Winning of the West. *Poole* — The West, in Narrative and Critical History of America, Vol. VI, Chap. IX. *Jay* — The Treaty of 1783 in Narrative and Critical History. *English* — Conquest of the Country Northwest of the Ohio River. *Fiske* — American Revolution. *Fiske* — Critical Period of American History.

BENTLEY'S LAKE.

A. J. BAUGHMAN, MANSFIELD.

Secretary of the Richland County Historical Society.

The Bentley Lake, seven miles east of Mansfield, was created in 1846, and had a peculiar origin. In 1821, Jonas Ballyet entered the northwest quarter of section 15, Mifflin township, Richland county, and near the center of this tract there was a circular marsh of eight orten acres, surrounded by a rim of elevations of gentle slope, giving a bowl-like appearance in the place. At the east side or end there was a depression in the rim, as though the marsh had at one time been a lake, and that this depression had been its outlet to the Blackfork of the Mohican river, a mile distant. Between the marsh and the river, and extending from the one to the other, is a stretch of boggy land called the "Black swamp," lower than the marsh. And "Uncle Jonas Ballyet theorized that to cut a ditch through the depression would drain the marsh through the swamp to the river, and thus add to the tillable acreage of his farm. The theory seemed so plausible that men were employed to dig a trench, the bottom of which was six feet below the surface of the marsh. The job was completed July 25, 1846. Through this ditch water flowed quite copiously, and the prospects seemed to be favorable for the marsh to be drained in a short time. But a condition existed which "Uncle Jonas" had not considered in his philosophy, for beneath was a lake, and the marsh was but a fenny cover — the accumulation of a century — over its deep waters. The night after the opening of the ditch, the waters underlying the morass having been lowered about six feet, the cover sank, and the next morning a lake was seen where the marsh had previously been.

The sinking of the bog-covering caused the earth to quake and tremble for miles around, and alarmed the people, some thinking it was an earthquake, others that "the end of the world" was coming, as had been prophesied by the Millerites.

The time set by the Rev. William Miller for the "second coming of Christ" was the year 1843, but as it did not occur at that time, nor at later dates, and the people were admonished to say not in their hearts, "My Lord delayeth His coming."

The lake covers an area of about nine acres, and has an average depth of seventy feet. It presents a lovely appearance in its frame-setting of hills, with a beautiful grove to the southeast. The water when viewed in the lake is of 'a green tint, but when dipped up in the hand is pure and clear.

In the camping party in the view given, is Gen. R. Brinkerhoff, president of the Ohio Archaeological and Historical Society;

BENTLEY'S LAKE — PRESIDENT BRINKERHOFF SEATED ON THE LOG.

the Hon. M. B. Bushnell and members of their families. Mr. Bushnell and the wife of General Brinkerhoff are grandchildren of Gen. Robert Bentley, for whom the lake is named. General Bentley was one of the pioneers of Richland county. He settled in the Bentley lake vincinity in 1815. He built the first brick farm house in the county. He was judge of the court in 1821-8, served two terms in the state senate and was a major-general of militia. History and historical associations are interestingly woven about the lake and its locality.

SONG WRITERS OF OHIO.

ALEXANDER COFFMAN ROSS.

AUTHOR OF "TIPPECANOE AND TYLER, TOO."

"I am a Buckeye, from the Buckeye State." This was the proud declaration of the author of *Tippecanoe and Tyler, too,* as he faced a large and enthusiastic audience in New York City, just before he gave to fame that political campaign song — the most effective ever sung in the history of the Republic.

Alexander Coffman Ross first opened his eyes to the light in Zanesville, O., May 31, 1812. His father, Elijah Ross,[1] born in Brownsville, Pa., November, 1786, located in Zanestown, (Zanesville) in 1804, and died there February 29, 1864. He was a soldier of the War of 1812, and, being a gunsmith, was ordered to remain in his home town to repair guns, swords and accoutrements. His wife, whose maiden name was Mary Coffman, was born at Fredericktown, Pa., September 10, 1788, and died in Zanesville December 29, 1862. Their family numbered twelve

---

[1] In 1804, Elijah Ross came to Zanestown (Zanesville) and prospected through the Muskingum and Miami valleys. He was a gunsmith by trade, the first of this section, and soon after his arrival in the new country settled in the village and erected a cabin, which served as dwelling and shop, on what is now the northeast corner of Locust alley and Second street. At the beginning of the War of 1812, he entered the service as third corporal, and was detailed to remain at home and repair arms for the soldiers. In 1816 he moved to West Zanesville. In 1823 he returned to the east side of the river, where he continued to work at his trade. He bored his own gun barrels, made the first blow-pipes there used for blowing glass (1815), and sometimes aided the glass-blowers in their work. He was especially fond of fox hunting, and seemed never happier than when following his hounds over the Muskingum hills. A genial, unassuming man and a total abstainer from intoxicants, he lived to the ripe age of seventy-nine years, and died respected for his industry and honesty.

children, two of whom, Mrs. Daniel Hurd, of Denver, Col., and Mrs. George W. Keene, of New York City, still survive.

The parents were of the sturdy pioneers of the new state. They began life on the frontier in a typical log cabin of the period. Here the subject of this sketch passed his boyhood in the midst of healthful home influences and the not unfortunate environment of this growing and ambitious western town, located on the banks of the Muskingum, and directly in the line of the great overland thoroughfare along which the tide of civilization was moving to regions more remote. At the close of the second decade of the last century, the "town of Zane,,[1] ranked second among the incorporated places of Ohio and stood without a rival north of the "River Beautiful" in thrift, aspiration and progressive spirit. The old road, known in history as "Zane's Trace," leading backward toward the base of American culture and expansive energy in the East, and downward southwesterly to the realm of forests primeval, was an avenue for the exchange of ideas as well as merchandise. The youth who in "that elder day" dwelt at the junction of the waterway and the highway, though surrounded by the wilderness, felt that he was still on the line of communication with the cities of the far-away Atlantic coast.

Especially was this true of young Ross, who seems to have been from early years studious, industrious and prompt to make the best of his opportunities.

His daughter, Ellen, writing interestingly of his social qualities, says:

His grandfather was a canny Scotchman, and I think it must have been from this ancestor that Alexander inherited his social traits and love of dancing, for one of the sisters, Margaret, used to say that the only recollection of her grandfather was seeing the old gentleman, on one of his visits to his son in Ohio, come dancing into the room in his black velvet knee breeches and silver shoe buckles, as gay and active as any young dandy of his day.

From his father he doubtless inherited and acquired a fondness and aptness for mechanical pursuits. In the little shop at home he witnessed the repair and manufacture of guns, and early

---

[1] Including Putnam, now a part of Zanesville.

learned to handle tools. Though he did not have the opportunity to attend free public schools, his education was not wholly neglected. Under private teachers and at home he gained a knowledge of the common branches, which he greatly extended by reading with avidity the best literature that he could get. He found greatest pleasure in the perusal of scientific works, and became an expert in demonstrating by experiment the principles set forth in what he read. "He was fortunate in having, toward the latter part of his school course, two very excellent teachers, Allan Cadwallader and his brother, members of a good old Quaker family."

At the age of seventeen years, he was apprenticed to a watchmaker and jeweler of his native city. In 1831-32, he completed preparation for his chosen trade in New York City.

To such a youth, two years in the metropolis was in itself no mean education. Here he enjoyed rare opportunities for reading and investigation. Nor was his leisure devoted to study alone. Music and art invited to occasional entertainment and recreation.

. Returning home at the close of his apprenticeship, he applied himself industriously to his trade and was soon recognized as a master in his chosen vocation. His chief interest was in the latest scientific discoveries, which he interpreted and applied with the ease of a trained specialist.

In 1838 he married Caroline Granger, who was in hearty sympathy with his various enterprises and "recreations." Their home attracted the young people of Zanesville who were fond of music and art. At the age of eighty-five years she manifests a lively interest in current events and finds a pleasant residence with her two daughters at the old homestead.

From its founding he was an enthusiastic patron of the Athenæum, the local library, one of the first in the state to have a home of its own. This building he rendered famous by using it as the object in testing a wonderful invention announced from across the sea.

In the year 1839, Daguerre's process of developing and fixing upon a plate the image of external objects, or, in other words, of making the daguerreotype, was first published in this country. Ross read the description and proceeded at once to construct a

MRS. ROSS AND CHILDREN.
(From Daguerreotype taken by A. C. Ross, 1848.)

camera, using telescope lenses, and transferred to a chemically prepared plate a counterfeit presentment of the Zanesville Athenæum, the first picture of the kind made in this country outside of New York City and perhaps the first in America:[1]

Following is Ross's account of the successful experiment. It illustrates his simple and direct exposition of a scientific process. No apology is made for reproducing it in full:

"On the 29th day of August, 1839, Daguerre gave to the French government the process which was proclaimed by Porfessor Arago. It was not until the following November that I saw a notice of it, and then a newspaper account of the process fully described. I concluded to make an attempt to produce a picture, although I had no camera or silver plate. I procured two nice cigar boxes, cut one down so that it would slide into the other; Master Hill loaned me the object lens from his spy glass, the lens having a focal length of eighteen inches.

"The lens was secured in a paper tube some six inches in length, and one end of this tube was fitted into the end of the largest cigar box, and a ground plate (which I also made) was fitted so as to slide in and out of this box; — this was my camera. The silvered plate was my next consideration, and here I had to rely on my knowledge as a silversmith; I took a piece of planished copper about three by four inches, and having dissolved some nitrate of silver in distilled water, I applied the fluid with a broad hair pencil to the surface of the plate until it was darkened, and then immediately rubbed it over with bitartrate of potash, and repeated the process until I secured a good deposit of the silver. Contrary to instructions I had a 'buff' — but more of this hereafter — and finished up the plate until I had what silversmiths call a 'black polish.' The next thing was to coat the plate with iodine; for this I placed some iodine in the bottom of a saucer, took it into a dark room, and by the light of a tallow dip in one hand, holding the plate over the saucer with the other, I watched the process for about twenty minutes, when I found it coated to suit me; I afterwards learned that this first coating was admirably done.

"Having progressed thus far, I set my camera out of the front window in the building now occupied by the Union Bank, then by Hill & Ross, and directed it to the Atheneum. The focus of the lens being so long,

---

[1] Dr. Draper was experimenting concurrently with Ross, and made daguerreotypes about the same time. As exact dates have not been preserved, it is impossible to say who may claim precedence in the application of the art. Dr. Draper took a picture of his sister, the first *portrait* made by the process in this or any other country. To produce this it was necessary for her to sit in a bright light with closed eyes for half an hour.

MAIN STREET, ZANESVILLE, OHIO, 1846. ON THE LEFT IS THE OLD COURT HOUSE, BUILT FOR OHIO STATE HOUSE AND ONCE USED AS SUCH. THE LEFT WING WAS THE ATHENÆUM. ON THE OPPOSITE SIDE OF THE STREET IS THE BUILDING IN WHICH ROSS HAD HIS JEWELRY STORE. IN THE OLD COURT HOUSE THE EPISCOPALIAN CHURCH CONDUCTED ITS SERVICES FOR A TIME. HERE "TIPPECANOE AND TYLER, TOO," WAS WRITTEN AND FIRST SUNG.

I could only take in about half the building. I focused the camera, took out the ground glass and inserted the prepared plate, covering the end of the camera with my hat lest the light might get in at the sides. I let in the light when all was ready, and left it exposed for over twenty minutes; it was a bright sun light. At the end of the twenty minutes I carried camera and all into my darkened room, took out my plate and expected to be able to see some outline of the building. I was disappointed, but soon I remembered that there was another process to be gone through, and that I had neglected to make any preparation for it — the plate must be exposed to the vapor of mercury. I soon got a spirit lamp, put a few drops of mercury in a tea cup, applied the lamp under the bottom of the cup and held my plate over it. Soon the fumes rose, and by the light of my tallow-dip, I watched the result in breathless anxiety; the picture began to appear and I witnessed my success with joy unspeakable. I called my wife and Master Hill and there in that little darkened room I showed them the first daguerreotype ever made in Ohio, or west of New York City, to my knowledge.

"But my picture was not yet finished; the iodine had to be removed before I dare expose it to the light; the chemical agent to be used to remove the iodine was hyposulphate of soda, and that I could not obtain. I thought I would try salt water — I made a strong solution in a tin dish, put the plate into it, warmed it over a spirit lamp, and in a short time found my picture clear. You may believe that I was not long in covering it with glass and showing it to my friends. It was noticed in the papers that day as the first daguerreotype ever made in Ohio.

"In February, 1840, I took a view of the Putnam Seminary, which I kept for many years. During the summer of 1840 I did nothing at picture taking; the political storm was upon us, and every ordinary employment seemed as nothing.

"In the winter of 1840-41, I got up a set of good instruments and turned my attention to taking likenesses, which was then being experimented upon by Professor Draper, Morse, Walcott and Dr. Chilton. I met with many difficulties in not having an achromatic lens, which at that time was hard to get. I ordered two planoconvex lenses (four inches in diameter with combined focal length of eight inches) from Paris, for which I paid $60 to a friend in Philadelphia. In the non-achromatic lens there was a certain focus to get which was not only my difficulty, but a difficulty with all others as well. Light has two kinds of rays — the chemical and luminous — and these rays have different foci, the focus of the chemical rays being within that of the luminous. You can, by sight, adjust the camera to the focus of the luminous rays, but, to get a well defined picture you must get your plate into the focus of the chemical or actinic rays. This I did not know, and I worked many a day experimenting.

"I had no trouble in getting a picture, but it was always taken in the luminous focus and was indistinct. My wife would sit for me for ten and even fifteen minutes in the sun, still the picture was blurred. I could get no information on the subject; I was almost in despair. One day I had been using some tea cups in my room, and had placed them on the edge of the window sill, just in front of where my wife sat. I had made some change and was trying to focus the camera on her, as usual. I could also see the cups, but not nearly so sharp in outline. I took the picture, developed it, and, to my great delight, found that the cup nearest the instrument was perfect, even showing the small flower on it. I felt as if I had made a great discovery, and to me it was one. After reflecting over the matter, I concluded to mark the tube of the camera as it was then adjusted. I then looked through the camera at the cup, and moved the tube until the cup was in the luminous focus, and then again marked the tube; the distance between the two marks thus made was about the one-eighth of an inch.

"I then prepared a good plate, placed my wife again, got the luminous focus, then pushed the tube in one-eighth of an inch, took a picture and found it an excellent one. My delight was unbounded. I felt that I had overcome a great difficulty, and solved a mystery. I was not long in letting it be known, and many a poor devil did I help out of difficulty, without reward. Visitors from Springfield, Marietta, Cincinnati, Cleveland, and other places, called upon me for information and got it free of charge. A Professor Garlick, however, insisted upon making some compensation, and gave me a splendidly bound book of steel engravings of the London Art Gallery.

"I will finish this by stating that, except those made by myself, I never saw a daguerreotype until the fall of 1841. I was frequently told by persons who had seen other pictures, that mine were far superior to any they had seen, although not so sharp in the outline as those taken with the achromatic lens. Mine were strong and bold, and could be seen in any position. I received the first premium at the Mechanics' Institute exhibition at Cincinnati in June 1842. I will now refer back to the buff. I found the superiority of my pictures was altogether in the manner in which I polished my plates.

"All others at the beginning followed Daguerre's process to the letter, and being a silversmith I knew that with the buff was the only possible way that a silver plate could be brought to a high polish, and as Daguerre said, 'the higher the polish the better.' I kept it no secret; it soon came into general use, and some few years after some one got out a patent for the buff wheel. If I could see you I could tell you many little incidents about the daguerreotype flattering to me, but I do not care to write them out.'"

Judge James Sheward, late of Dunkirk, N. Y., formerly of Zanesville, wrote a number of articles for the *Courier* of the latter city and signed them "Black Hand." In one of these he included the foregoing extract from a letter written to him by Ross, but not intended for publication. The two were life-long friends.

The details of Daguerre's procees seem to have been published in London, August 26, 1839. As there were no regular steamship lines across the Atlantic at that time, it must have been several weeks later when publication was made in America. Ross may therefore have been the first to make a daguerreotype on this side of the Atlantic.

Col. R. B. Brown, of Zanesville, who was intimately acquainted with Ross, in a letter to the writer says:

"You will note that Mr. Ross's pictures were made in November, 1839, following the publication of the description of the Daguerre process in a French journal the latter part of August of that year. The translation was printed in New York as soon as the mail could bring the article, and I am sure that you will make no mistake in the claim that A. C. Ross made the first daguerreotype in the United States. Of this I know Mr. Ross never had a doubt, but I have heard him say, as he has been quoted, 'I made the first west of the Alleghanies.' To me he always claimed, 'I made the first in this country.' I believe it, and I do not believe that the statement can be disproved."

As first practiced, the process required long exposure, and was applied successfully only to inanimate objects. Dr. Draper introduced many improvements. Ross followed these closely, and soon made excellent pictures, with apparatus of his own manufacture.

No sooner had the Morse system of telegraphy been announced than he began to test it experimentally. When the first line reached Zanesville, in 1847, he was so familiar with the practical working of the invention that he took charge of the office and became the first telegraph operator of the city.

In a similar manner he constructed from written descriptions the telephone, and even the phonograph, before either was brought to the city. When the latter was finally put on exhibition there, a friend called and invited him to see and hear it.

"It is not at all necessary or worth my while," said he. "I have had for some days a machine of my own make that works very satisfactorily."

As his father had followed the chase with keen zest, the son found interest in the study of natural history and taxidermy, and choice specimens usually adorned the windows of his jewelry store.

In his later years, he devoted a part of his leisure to water-color painting, and did work that might well have been the envy of the professional.

His scientific reading led him early into the investigation of gas lighting. He organized the first company to offer this illuminant to the city, and, as its president, conducted this business venture with marked success.

When an express office was opened in Zanesville he was chosen agent. He retired from the jewelry business in 1863. Four years later he withdrew from the management of the express office, to devote his entire time to the gas company and the insurance business. He was the guiding spirit in these interests until a few days before his death.

His was a fervent patriotism. He was president of the War Association of Muskingum County in the early sixties. He thoroughly understood military tactics, was an officer in a local independent company, and at the outbreak of the Civil War drilled numerous members of the "awkward squad," General M. D. Leggett among them. His son, Charles H. Ross, served the Union cause in the field till the flag waved over a united country.

Modest and unassuming in his demeanor, he was blessed with a large degree of public spirit, and was ever ready to lend his valuable aid to the industrial and moral upbuilding of the community.

This versatile son of Ohio was a lover of music, too. "He used to tell how, when a little boy, the young men of the town sent him to the circus to learn the popular airs, which, in those days, were always sung by the clown. The visit to the circus answered two purposes, as he always reproduced the best features, such as tight-rope dancing, vaulting and tumbling, for the benefit of the school, as well as singing the songs till the young men learned them." At the age of fifteen he began to play on the clarionet. He had a good voice, became a member of the local church choir, and was later in demand on occasions requiring the services of an entertaining vocalist.

Of his experience in New York City, his daughter writes:

"When a boy of twenty he became a member of one of the first orchestras organized in New York City—led by Uri Hill—playing 'by ear' the first clarionet. Music was always his passion, and he had opportunities when in New York on business to hear all the best musicians. When he returned to Zanesville to reside, the citizens reaped the benefit, for through his individual efforts all the first troupes traveling came to Zanesville and he made many warm friends among them."

The wave of Whig sentiment that swept over the country in the later thirties rose to tidal height in the memorable campaign of 1840. To the movement, Alexander Coffman Ross contributed a service that helped to swell the enthusiasm for "Old Tippecanoe," and carried the fame of the "Buckeye boys" and the Buckeye State to every home in the Union.

Though the theme might warrant the digression, space will not permit a general survey of the great uprising in support of William Henry Harrison — unfortunately designated in history as the "log cabin and hard cider campaign." If the political foes of that grand old patriot helped to their own immediate undoing in derisively referring to him as the "log cabin, hard-cider candidate," in the long run they would seem to have accomplished something of their purpose, to have detracted from the movement and the man, when a twentieth century historian can sit down and calmly write:

"In the campaign referred to a log cabin was chosen as a symbol of the plain and unpretentious candidate, and a barrel of cider as that of his hospitality. During the campaign, all over the country, in hamlets, villages, and cities, log cabins were erected and fully supplied with barrels of cider. These houses were the usual gathering places of the partisans of Harrison, young and old, and to every one hard cider was freely given. The meetings were often mere drunken carousals that were injurious to all, and especially to youth. Many a drunkard afterwards pointed sadly to the hard cider campaign in 1840, as the time of his departure from sobriety and respectability."

Doubtless drunken brawls sometimes attended the big demonstrations of the campaign. It is not true, however, that they

were peculiar to it or that the uprising was a wild, bacchanalian
orgie in honor of the fermented juice of the orchard and kindred spirits.

General Harrison had lived in a log cabin. He was for a
number of years a poor farmer. But it was not because of this
that he was nominated for the presidency. He was simple,
direct, hospitable and kind, but he was more. He was courage-
ous, he was honest, he was a man of affairs. On the field and
in the forum he had proven his patriotism and statesmanship.
Though surpassed in constitutional lore and forensic power by
Webster and Clay, he was an orator of no mean ability, prepared
his own addresses, and delivered them with an effectiveness
rarely surpassed by a candidate for the presidency.

The personality of General Harrison, however, was not the
occasion of the political upheaval of 1840. It was the rising of
the people in their might to smite the ruling autocracy. For
twelve years the Republic had been ruled by one man. General
Jackson will ever be honored for repelling the invader at New
Orleans and suppressing nullification in South Carolina, but it
is putting it mildly to say that in his administrations he levied
upon the American people a heavy tribute for his services. He
played politics to the limit. By profession and practice he was a
spoilsman. Entering upon his duties with the declaration that the
President should be ineligible for re-election, he did everything
in his power to pave the way to succeed himself in office.

At the close of his second term, he used the political machine
that he had built up to dictate the nomination of his successor.
Not satisfied to pause here, he had Van Buren renominated for
a second term. Every appointive office was filled by a man whose
first duty was to Jackson. The public service exhibited the inevitable results of the spoils system — insolence and incompetence.

The Jacksonian regime dominated the body politic. It dic-
tated nominations, national, state and local. Governors, judges
and country " 'squires" bowed to its sway. At length its fruit
began to ripen. Defalcations were frequent; "leg treasurers"
were numerous. "Business generally was at a standstill; the currency was in such a confused state that specie to pay postage
was almost beyond reach; banks had been in a state of suspen-

sion for a long time; mechanics and laboring men were out of employment or working for 62½, 75, or 87½ cents a day, payable in 'orders on the store;' market money could be obtained with difficulty, and things generally had reached so low an ebb as to make any change seem desirable."

The people, goaded to desperation, resolved to dethrone the dictator and restore the republic to the ideal of the fathers. Preparatory to their supreme effort to dislodge a desperate and thoroughly organized foe from the places of power, the Whigs and independent voters of the country chose Harrison as their leader, and they chose well. Those who have read his speeches, especially the one delivered at Dayton, and his inaugural address, can but regret that he did not live to carry out the reforms to which he gave eloquent approval.

The campaign opened with a burst of enthusiasm that surprised the Whig leaders almost as much as their opponents. On the 22d of February, 1840, twenty thousand people from all parts of the state met in convention at Columbus, O., to ratify the nomination of Harrison and Tyler. From places near and remote they came. Some had spent days on the journey. An eye-witness thus describes the scene presented in the capital city on that memorable occasion:

"The rain came down in torrents, the streets were one vast sheet of mud, but the crowds paid no heed to the elements. A full-rigged ship on wheels, canoes, log cabins, with inmates feasting on corn-pone and hard cider, miniature forts, flags, banners, drums and fifes, bands of music, live coons, roosters crowing, and shouting men by the ten thousand, made a scene of attraction, confusion, and excitement such as has never been equaled. Stands were erected, and orators went to work; but the staid party leaders failed to hit the key-note. Itinerant speakers mounted store-boxes, and blazed away. It was made known that the Cleveland delegation, on their route to the city, had had the wheels stolen from some of their wagons by Locofocos, and were compelled to continue their journey on foot. One of these enforced foot-passengers was something of a poet, and wrote a song descriptive of 'Up Salt River,' and was encored over and over again. On the spur of the moment, many songs were written and sung; the pent-up enthusiasm had found vent."

The spirit of the movement pervaded every rank. The business man, the recluse and the scholar touched elbows with lusty farmers, waded in the mud ·and helped to swell the universal shout.

In the procession was a cabin on wheels from Union County. It was made of buckeye logs, and in it was a band of singers discoursing, to the tune of *Highland Laddie,* the famous Buckeye song, written for the occasion by perhaps the first Ohio poet of his time, Otway Curry:

Oh, where, tell me where, was your Buckeye cabin made?
Oh, where, tell me where, was your Buckeye cabin made?
'Twas built among the merry boys that wield the plow and spade,
Where the log cabin stands, in the bonnie Buckeye shade.

Oh, what, tell me what, is to be your cabin's fate?
Oh, what, tell me what, is to be your cabin's fate?
We'll wheel it to the capital, and place it there elate,
For a token and a sign of the bonnie Buckeye State!

Oh, why, tell me why, does your Buckeye cabin go?
Oh, why, tell me why, does your Buckeye cabin go?
It goes against the spoilsmen, for well its builders know
It was Harrison that fought for the cabins long ago.

Oh, what, tell me what, then, will little Martin do?
Oh, what, tell me what, then, will little Martin do?
He'll "follow in the footsteps" of Price and Swarthout too,
While the log cabin rings again with old Tippecanoe.

Oh, who fell before him in battle, tell me who?
Oh, who fell before him in battle, tell me who?
He drove the savage legions, and British armies too
At the Rapids, and the ·Thames, and old Tippecanoe!

By whom, tell me whom, will the battle next be won?
By whom, tell me whom, will the battle next be won?
The spoilsmen and leg treasurers will soon begin to run!
And the "Log Cabin Candidate" will march to Washington!

"But," said Judge Sheward, of Zanesville, "the song of the campaign had not yet been written." He then proceeds with the following account of its origin and progress to popularity:

"On the return of our delegation a Tippecanoe Club was formed, and a glee club organized, of whom Ross was one. The club meetings

BADGE OF ZANESVILLE TIPPECANOE CLUB.
Engraved by Ross.

were opened and closed with singing by the glee club. Billy McKibbon wrote 'Amos Peddling Yokes,' to be sung to the tune of 'Yip, fal, lal,' which proved very popular; he also composed 'Hard Times,' and 'Martin's Lament.' Those who figured in that day will remember the chorus:

> Oh, dear! what will become of me?
> Oh, dear! what shall I do?
> I am certainly doomed to be beaten
> By the heroes of Tippecanoe.

"This song was well received, but there seemed something lacking. The wild outburst of feeling demanded by the meetings had not yet been provided for. Tom Lauder suggested to Ross that the tune of *Little Pigs* would furnish a chorus just adapted for the meetings. Ross seized upon the suggestion, and on the succeeding Sunday, while he was singing as a member of a church choir, his head was full of 'Little Pigs,' and efforts to make a song fitting the time and the circumstances. Oblivious to all else, he had, before the sermon was finished, blocked out the song of *Tippecanoe and Tyler, too.* The line, as originally composed by him of

> Van, Van, you're a nice little man,

did not suit him, and when Saturday night came round he was cudgelling his brains to amend it. He was absent from the meeting, and was sent for. He came, and informed the glee club that he had a new song to sing, but that there was one line in it he did not like, and that his delay was occasioned by the desire to correct it.

'Let me hear the line,' said Culbertson. Ross repeated it to him.

'Thunder!' said he, 'make it — Van's a *used-up man!*' — and there and then the song was completed.

"The meeting in the Court House was a monster, the old Senate Chamber was crowded full to hear McKibbon's new song, *Martin's Lament,* which was loudly applauded and encored. When the first speech was over, Ross led off with *Tippecanoe and Tyler, too,* having furnished each member of the glee club with the chorus. That was the song at last. Cheers, yells, and encores greeted it. The next day, men and boys were singing the chorus in the street, in the work shops, and at the table. Olcot White came near to starting a hymn to the tune in the Radical Church on South street. What the *Marseillaise Hymn* was to Frenchmen, *Tippecanoe and Tyler, too,* was to the Whigs of 1840.

"In September, Mr. Ross went to New York City to purchase goods. He attended a meeting in Lafayette Hall. Prentiss, of Mississippi, Tallmadge, of New York, and Otis, of Boston, were to speak. Ross found the hall full of enthusiastic people, and was compelled to stand near the entrance. The speakers had not arrived, and several songs were sung to keep the crowd together. The stock of songs was soon exhausted, and the chairman (Charley Delavan, I think) arose and requested any one present who could sing, to come forward and do so. Ross said, 'If I could get on the stand, I would sing a song,' and hardly had the words out before he found himself passing rapidly over the heads of the crowd, to be handed at length on the platform. Questions of 'Who are you?' 'What's your name?' came from every hand.

'I am a Buckeye, from the Buckeye State,' was the answer. 'Three cheers for the Buckeye State!' cried out the president, and they were given with a will. Ross requested the meeting to keep quiet until he had sung three or four verses, and it did. But the enthusiasm swelled up to an uncontrollable pitch, and at last the whole meeting joined in the chorus with a vim and vigor indescribable. The song was encored and sung again and again, but the same verses were not repeated, as he had many in mind, and could make them to suit the occasion. While he was singing in response to the third encore, the speakers, Otis and Tallmadge, arrived, and Ross improvised:

> We'll now stop singing, for Tallmadge is here, here, here,
>   And Otis, too,
> We'll have a speech from each of them,
>   For Tippecanoe and Tyler, too, etc.

The song, as originally written, was as follows:

TIPPECANOE AND TYLER, TOO.

> What has caused the great commotion, motion, motion,
>   Our country through?
>   It is the ball a rolling on,

CHORUS.

> For Tippecanoe and Tyler, too — Tippecanoe and Tyler, too;
> And with them we'll beat little Van, Van, Van.
> Van is a used-up man;
> And with them we'll beat little Van.

> Like the rushing of mighty waters, waters, waters,
>   On it will go,
>   And in its course will clear the way
>   Of Tippecanoe, etc.

> See the Loco standard tottering, tottering, tottering,
>   Down it must go,
>   And in its place we'll rear the flag
>   Of Tippecanoe, etc.

Don't you hear from every quarter, quarter, quarter,
    Good news and true,
     That swift the ball is rolling on
        For Tippecanoe, etc.

The Buckeye boys turned out in thousands, thousands,
    Not long ago,
    And at Columbus set their seals
        To Tippecanoe, etc.

Now you hear Van Jacks talking, talking, talking,
    Things look quite blue,
    For all the world seems turning round
        For Tippecanoe, etc.

Let them talk about hard cider, cider, cider,
    And log cabins, too,
    'Twill only help to speed the ball
        For Tippecanoe, etc.

The latch-string hangs outside the door, door, door,
    And is never pulled through
    For it never was the custom of
        Old Tippecanoe, etc.

He always had his table set, set, set,
    For all honest and true,
    And invites them to take a bite
        With Tippecanoe, etc.

See the spoilsmen and leg treasurers, treas, treas,
    All in a stew,
    For well they know they stand no chance
        With Tippecanoe, etc.

The fourth stanza was frequently changed to adapt the song to the different states. Other stanzas were added to suit particular localities and special occasions. A modern historian, who evidently did not know who wrote it, speaks of it as the "most popular song of the campaign," and says that it had, "by the inventive song-genius of Horace Greeley and scores of other less famous poets been extended to every incident and sentiment of the day." The following final stanza was frequently used in the Ohio campaign:

Now who shall be our next governor, governor,
      Who, tell me who?
      Let's have Tom Corwin, for he's a team
ForTippecanoe and Tyler, too — Tippecanoe and Tyler, too,
And with him we'll beat Wilson Shannon, Shannon,
Shannon is a used-up man,
And with him we'll beat Wilson Shannon!

It has been said that the song is poor poetry, and judged by literary standards this is certainly true, but the alliteral chorus is remarkably musical and "catchy" and the stanzas abound in homely truth and telling hits. It is needless to say that it was readily understood by all classes. The composition probably surpassed all others in popularity, because it more nearly met the demands of the hour.

The reference to the "ball that's rolling on" is worthy of notice in passing. Just when the "ball" began to roll in American political literature has perhaps not yet been definitely determined. Thomas H. Benton has been given the credit of starting it. Its origin probably dates some years prior to the Harrison campaign. It must be admitted, however, that the "ball," like the "buckeye," was invested with a new significance and a wider currency in the year 1840, and the song written by Ross was probably the first that "set the ball in motion."

In an account of the Young Men's Whig convention, at Baltimore, May 4, 1840, is found the following description of one of the features of the Maryland section of the procession:

"A curious affair followed here, which was immediately preceded by a flag announcing that 'Alleghany is coming.' It was a huge ball, about ten feet in diameter, which was rolled along by a number of the members of this delegation. The ball was apparently a wooden frame covered with linen, painted divers colors, and bearing a multitude of inscriptions, apt quotations, original stanzas and pithy sentences."

At the convention in Nashville, Tenn., August 17th, one of the leading attractions was described as follows:

"The great ball, from Zanesville, Ohio, which came safe to hand on the steamer Rochester, on Saturday night, occupied a conspicuous place in the procession. It was given in charge of the Kentucky delegation, and was hauled on four wheels, under the immediate care of Porter, the Kentucky giant. The ball is in the form of a hemisphere, moving upon its axis and representing each of the individual states of the Union."

Ross's daughter gives the following additional information:

"There was a real ball that illustrated the song. It was an immense thing made at Dresden, Ohio, and at great political meetings it was drawn in the procession by twenty-four milk white oxen. It was afterwards taken to Lexington, Kentucky, but not by oxen."

The Annapolis Tippecanoe Club, on August 18th, celebrated the progress of the cause in a song entitled "The Whig Ball." It began as follows:

> Hail to the ball which in grandeur advances,
>   Long life to the yeoman who urge it along;
> The abuse of our hero his worth but enhances;
>   Then welcome his triumphs with shout and with song.
>   The Whig ball is moving!
>   The Whig ball is moving!

The big ball started from Zanesville was probably the inspiration for the foregoing and similar effusions that broke forth about this time. At other great meetings throughout the country the ball literally "went rolling on."

It is perhaps needless to say that there have been rival claimants for the honor of authorship of *Tippecanoe and Tyler, too.* Fortunately, their pretentions, with a single exception, have not been sufficiently serious to merit attention. Henry Russell, the famous English singer, who seems in his later years to have developed a *penchant* for claiming pretty much everything that has been written in his line, in his autobiography, gives the following account of the initial launching of the song on its voyage to popularity:

"About this time, (1841) the presidential election was causing great excitement in America. The rival candidates for the presidency were Martin Van Buren, Democrat; and General Harrison, Whig.

*   *   *   *

"I was one day sitting in the office of the *Boston Transcript,* and to beguile the time while waiting for my friend, Houghton, the editor and proprietor, I sat idly turning over the pages of some of the numerous exchange journals with which the office table was littered, when my at-

Vol. XIV— 6.

tention was attracted by a poem on the subject of the forthcoming election. The name of the paper it appeared in has escaped my memory, but the poem was called "Tippecanoe," after the famous battle fought and won by General Harrison.

"I only remember now the chorus, which ran as follows:

For Tippecanoe and Tyler, too, for Tippecanoe and Tyler, too —
    With them we'll beat little Van
    Van! Van! Van! a used up man,
    With them we'll beat little Van.

"I had a singular remembrance of an old Irish song, known by the poetic title of "Three little pigs lay on very good straw," the chorus of which ran thus:

    Lila bolara, Lila bolara, Lila bolara, och hone,
    For my dad is a bonny wee man, man, man, man!
    My dad is a bonny wee man.

"Almost unconsciously I put the words of the poem before me to the melody of the old Irish song, and when Houghton came in I sang them over to him.

"He appeared delighted, and at his suggestion, I sang the song from the window of the *Boston Transcript,* to an enormous crowd which had assembled in the street below. The song was hailed with enthusiasm by the Harrison party, and it spread like wildfire through the States, where it is sometimes sung even to this day.

"Such is the true origin of this at one time popular election song. There has been much discussion about it from time to time in the American press, and while I do not claim to have written either the words or the music, I do claim to have adapted the one to the other — wedded them together, as it were — and giving the song its start in life by singing it from the window of the office of the *Boston Transcript.*"

It is scarcely necessary to observe that the song had become popular before it was printed, that it was written to the tune of *Little Pigs,* and that Russell did not see it until long after it had been sung. It will be noted that he has made a mistake of one year in the date of the campaign and that he is very indefinite in regard to the time of his rendition of the song in Boston. He does not state the occasion of the assembling of the "enormous crowd" in the "street below," so opportunely after he "sat idly turning over the pages of some of the numerous exchange journals." One might infer that the people just happened around in order to be convenient when the song was sung. It is entirely probable, however, that on some occasion Russell sang the words to the melody. The peculiar measure would naturally suggest the air.

It is not necessary to dwell on the results of the remarkable political contest that called forth the song. The thoroughly trained Jacksonian organization, under the skilful leadership of the "Little Magician," was overwhelmed by the spontaneous uprising of the country. The enthusiastic hosts, with music and song, inducted victorious "Old Tippecanoe" into office. Shortly afterward, the new President was laid low by the hand of death. There was mourning throughout the land, and the fruits of triumph turned to dust on the lips of the victors.

Alexander Coffman Ross continued to apply himself assid-uously to the jewelry business and to devote his leisure to sci-ence and music. He composed no airs, but wrote the words of a number of songs, some of which were published in the local papers.

He addressed the local medical society, of which he was an honorary member, on scientific subjects; lectured on the latest applications of electricity and magnetism before the students of Putnam Seminary; corresponded with Louis Agassiz and Professor Joseph Henry. He was an ardent admirer of the latter and insisted that to him rather than to Morse belongs the honor of having invented the electric telegraph. Among his letters is one from Spencer F. Baird, the famous naturalist and secretary of the Smithsonian Institution, thanking him for a contribution on "Flint Ridge." This was published in the Smithsonian Report for 1879. As an early contribution to this branch of Ohio archæology, it is appended to this sketch.

One of his daughters, Elizabeth B. Ross, was a good singer, studied harmony and wrote the words and music of a number of songs, some of which have had a wide sale. We here reproduce the words of two:

LITTLE BIRD, WHY SINGEST THOU?

Little bird, why singest thou,
   So merrily, so blithe and gay,
Hast thou ne'er a care to mar

At age of seventy years.

The pleasure of the passing day?
I sing, for ah! my heart's so light,
  No care or thoughts oppress me;
And this my song from morn till night,
  I warble free.

Little bird, where dwellest thou,
  Thro' chilling winter's icy reign;
Dost thou fly from bough to bough
  And warble forth thy glad refrain?
Oh yes, I fly to warmer climes,
  When first I feel cold winter's breath,
And there amid the southern pines,
  I warble free.

LIST TO THE NIGHTINGALE.

Come, come with me, dear one,
  Where moonbeams are glancing
And stars beaming brightly,
  Oh! come, then, with me.
Come, then, and we'll wander
  Where waters so sparkling
Are laving the green earth,
  Oh! come, then, with me.
List, to the nightingale singing o'er meadow,
Trilling a vow to the one that he loves.
  Then come, oh! come, my dear one,
    And, like the bird of night,
  Give thy heart to the one
    Who now sues for thy love.

Ross was very popular with the large German element of
Zanesville, and one of the last occasions on which he sang in
public was at a banquet given by the German citizens in the
autumn of 1869 in celebration of the centennial anniversary of
the birth of Von Humboldt. He requested his daughter Ellen
to write him some words to the *Marseillaise Hymn.* These he
sang to the delight of those who heard him. One stanza was as
follows:

We sing to-day a nation's glory,
  Germania hails her honored son!
But not to her belongs the story,
  In every land his fame was won.

From Asia's sunny mountain peaks
    To Mexicana's scorching plain,
    His natal day is kept again;
O'er all the world his voice still speaks.

CHORUS.

Then swell the choral song
    To hail Von Humboldt's name!
Rejoice! Rejoice! The nation's throng
    To celebrate his fame.

HOME OF ALEXANDER COFFMAN ROSS, NOW THE RESIDENCE OF CAROLINE
GRANGER ROSS, ZANESVILLE, OHIO.

The author of the famous campaign song of 1840 passed the
allotted three score years and ten. He was, first of all, a public
spirited citizen and systematic business man. His recreations
were the pursuits that brought him local fame along the lines
already noted. Of him it was truly said, "There were few things
that he had not done, and done well, and fewer that he cared to
do except as a pastime."

After a brief illness, he died February 26, 1883. His loss
was keenly felt by the city with which he had been identified

through his entire life. The local military company and other organizations expressed a desire to attend the funeral in a body, but the family, while appreciating the kind intentions, obeyed the wishes of the departed in dispensing with all parade and display.

Of his family, his wife and three children, Misses Elizabeth B. and Ellen, of Zanesville, O., and Major Charles H., of Milwaukee, Wis., are still living.

His memory is fondly cherished by those who knew him. Though not endowed with what is called "creative genius," he wrote a song that became national in celebrity and influence, and acquired enduring fame in his *Tippecanoe and Tyler, too.*

FLINT RIDGE.

Flint Ridge lies in Licking and Muskingum counties, about three miles south-eastward from Newark, and twelve to fifteen miles west-northwest from Zanesville. It extends eight miles southwest by north-east and is from one-fourth of a mile to one mile wide. The ridge is cut by hollows, ravines and gorges. Portions of the highest land are comparatively level, and this plateau is underlaid by a stratum of flint rock from fifteen inches to three feet in thickness. Besides this stratum are numerous flint bowlders standing up several feet above the surface of the ground. On the exact level of the flint are the "diggings" hundreds of which may be seen, which range in depth from one or two to thirty feet, their depth depending upon the relation of the flint stratum to the surface of the earth. The very deep diggings are from the top of a hillock on the summit of the Ridge. The trenches are from a few feet to thirty feet across at the top, all sloping so gradually that it would be easy to walk down them. From the deeper cuts the earth appeared to have been carried out; the one from the top of the hillock is still very deep, and was about forty feet in perpendicular when completed, with proportional width. In one portion was a drift sixty to eighty feet in length, six to eight feet wide, and four to five feet high. The excavation was pursued with the same diligence when there was no flint as when the stratum was found, and was of the same character, to the same level. Of course, when the earth is below the flint level there is no evidence of digging, but when the earth is above that level the work extends to the flint. These works follow the dip of the flint towards east-northeast until the hills became too high above the stratum. In a meadow, and near a stream of water on land very much lower than the ridge, occurred a bed of crumbled flint and sandstone. This bed was about fourteen inches in depth, seven feet across, and fifteen to eighteen feet in length. The sandstone was near the north part and had been subject to great heat. A quantity of ashes was mixed through the whole bed. Several such beds are reported in that vicinity, and were generally near the water. No arrowheads or other objects made of flint occurred. Old, gnarly, full-grown oaks, some of them three hundred years old, have sprouted and grown since these excavation were made. There has not been any sign of a workshop discovered in the last sixty years, but at the point usually sought by visitors and curiosity hunters flint spalls cover the ground for acres. Only one arrow-head has been found there for years.

A. C. Ross in Smithsonian Report for 1879, page 440.

ROSS FAMILY.

Following are the names of the children of Elijah and Mary Ross in the order of dates of birth: Theodore, Elizabeth, Alexander Coffman, Mrs. Anne Fox, Mrs. Margaret Boyd, Mrs. Ruth Hurd, James, Mrs. Jane Stewart, George, Mrs. Harriet Brown, Mrs. Elvira Keene and Thomas.

Alexander's immediate family, whose names occur in the preceding sketch, are all still living.

Mrs. Ross was the daughter of Oliver Granger who, with his brothers, Ebenezer, Henry and James, came to Ohio from Suffield, Connecticut, where their ancestors had lived since 1640.

EDITORIALANA.

VOL. XIV. No. 1. *E. O. Randall* JANUARY, 1905

PROCEEDINGS OF THE SOCIETY.

On September 19, 1904, a meeting of the Executive Committee of the Trustees of the Ohio State Archæological and Historical Society was held in the rooms of the society, Page Hall, O. S. U., with the following members present: Mr. George F. Bareis, Col. John W. Harper, Mr. W. H. Hunter, Prof. B. F. Prince, Secretary E. O. Randall, Hon. D. J. Ryan, Hon. S. S. Rickly, Prof. G. F. Wright and Mr. E. F. Wood.

The Secretary presented the resignation of Professor J. P. MacLean as Trustee of the Society and also as a life member. Professor Mac-Lean since his connection with the Society dating back to the annual meeting of April 26, 1901, when although not even being a member of the Society, he was elected a Trustee, has taken great interest in the progress and. success of the Society, having written several articles of historical value which have appeared from time to time in the Quarterly and having especially devoted himself to the gathering of material concerning the history and literature of the Shaker Societies particularly those in Ohio. He has made numerous donations to the Society of books published by or pertaining to the Shakers and has also collected for and delivered to the Society a considerable number of historical Shaker articles in the shape of household utensils, articles of dress, implements of farming, manufacture and so on. All this material the Society received, catalogued and prepared to properly arrange and preserve. On August 10th, during a visit to the museum and library of the Society, Professor MacLean requested one of the assistants in charge to send him a complete list of all articles and books delivered by him to the museum and that receipts of all donations be sent to the various donors. This was during the time when the curator of the museum and library was absent in Saint Louis having in charge the exhibit of the Society at the Louisiana Exposition and unusual duties devolved upon the assistants in charge. On September 1st, Professor MacLean wrote the Secretary, complaining that he had not received the requested list from the museum. In explanation of the delay the museum assistant wrote Professor Mac-Lean as follows:

"COLUMBUS, OHIO, September 6, 1904.

PROF. J. P. MACLEAN, *Frankin, Ohio.*

My Dear Sir:—

The list of Shaker pamphlets and books was forwarded to you some time ago. Mr. Mills has not been home in the meantime and I have had other duties besides making the list and answering receipt of the Shaker material so that the delay was unintentional. If you have not received the list please let me know and I will make a duplicate at once.

Very truly yours," etc.

To the expression in this letter, perfectly harmless and proper, "Shaker material" Professor MacLean at once took offense and in the face of attempted explanations by the Secretary to the effect that nothing was farther from the intention of the writer than the casting of any reflection upon the Shaker Society in the term "material," Professor Mac-Lean insisted upon an immediate resignation of his Trusteeship and after waiting only a few days for action upon it by the Executive Committee which had not yet met, he followed up his resignation by returning his ,life certificate and the peremptory demand that his name be erased from the list of membership. His resignation was dated September 13 and his demand for removal from the list of members was dated September 17.

The Executive Committee after making itself fully acquainted with the facts in the premises unanimously accepted the resignation of Professor MacLean as Trustee and also by the same formal vote ordered the Secretary to remove the name of Professor MacLean from the list of membership as per his request. In both of these actions the expressions on the part of the Committee and the Secretary were general that Professor MacLean had rendered admirable and valuable services to the Society in his studies and investigations of the history and various phases of Shakerism in Ohio and that they sincerely regretted that he felt compelled to discontinue his relationship with the Society. A committee consisting of three was appointed by the chair to present at the next meeting of the Executive Committee a name or names of candidates for the trusteeship to fill the vacancy caused by the resignation of Professor MacLean.

Mr. W. H. Hunter presented to the Society a handsome framed photograph of the medallion of Ohio's first Governor, Edward Tiffin. The medallion being the one which was placed in the Court House at Chillicothe with fitting ceremonies at the time of the Ohio Centennial held in May, 1903. The photograph was accepted by the Committee with thanks to Mr. Hunter and with directions to the Curator that it be hung on the walls of the Society's library.

Secretary Randall and Assistant Treasurer Wood on September 6-10 made a trip in behalf of the Society to the Saint Louis Exposition to inspect the exhibit being made by the Society in the Anthropological Building. They found the same in every respect highly creditable to the Society and the management and efficiency of Curator W. C. Mills. It was the favorite quarter of visitation for the thousands of spectators who daily sought entrance to the exposition. During their visit, in company with a party of archæologists including Curator Mills and Professor Starr, the eminent archæological scholar of Chicago University, Messrs Wood and Randall made a trip to the famous Cahokio Mound located in Illinois on the Mississippi opposite Saint Louis. This is the largest mound now remaining constructed by the mound builders. The trip proved to be a most delightful and profitable one as the party were the fortunate auditors of informal dissertations, by the various scholars present, upon the antiquity and purpose of the great mound, and the surrounding ones, of which there are more than one hundred in number.

On nomination of Colonel John W. Harper, the names of many prominent gentlemen, resident in Cincinnati, were elected to active membership in the Society.

* * * * *

On November 28 a meeting of the Executive Committee was held in the reference rooms of the Public Library, Columbus, with the following members present: General R. Brinkerhoff, Mr. George F. Bareis, Col. J. W. Harper, Prof. B. F. Prince, Secretary E. O. Randall, and Mr. E. F. Wood.

Explanations of absence were received from Hon. M. S. Greenough, Mr. W. H. Hunter, Hon. D. J. Ryan and Hon. S. S. Rickly.

The Secretary submitted for the consideration of the Committee some letters which had passed since the last executive meeting between the Secretary and Professor MacLean and also between Professor MacLean and General Brinkerhoff, President of the Society. The only portion of this correspondence worthy of attention was the request by Professor MacLean that the Society return to the Shakers any of the material which it had received through Professor MacLean and which the Society did not desire to retain. Without dissent it was decided by the committee that the Society would return none of the Shaker gifts as these donations had come properly into the possession and ownership of the Society and there was no legitimate cause for the return of any. Indeed, the Society had been at some expense in their reception; moreover these donations were regarded as of great interest and value by the Society and their acquisition had been duly appreciated. Indeed, the Secretary was requested to inform the Shakers that the Society would be very much pleased to receive further donations from them and would properly place and care for such gifts in its museum.

The committee appointed at the previous meeting of the Executive Committee to nominate a successor to Professor MacLean reported in favor of Hon. R. E. Hills of Delaware and he was unanimously elected to fill out the unexpired term which will terminate at the next annual meeting of the Society to be held in the Spring of 1905.

The Secretary reported to the Committee that on October 11, he had been invited as a representative of the Society to be present at the dedication of the Soldiers' and Sailors' Memorial Hall now being erected on East Broad Street, Columbus, under the auspices of a commission appointed by the Governor. He had accepted the invitation and was present at the open air exercises in the afternoon when the cornerstone was laid with fitting ceremonies. Captain N. B. Abbott presided. Addresses were made by Governor Herrick, Ex-Governor Nash, both life members of The Ohio State Archæological and Historical Society. General Eugene Powell on behalf of the commission made the chief address. In the evening an open campfire was held under the auspices of the Wells Post and McCoy Post, G. A. R. in the auditorium of the Board of Trade, at which the speakers were General H. A. Axline, Hon. J. Y. Bassell, Hon. D. C. Badger, E. O. Randall, Col. W. L. Curry and others.

Col. John W. Harper reported to the Committee an account of a visit made by Messrs. Harper, Martzolff and Randall of the Executive Committee to Serpent Mound on Saturday, November 5, 1904. The party met at the Pennsylvania Depot in Cincinnati on the morning in question and proceeded by the Norfolk and Western train to Peebles whence they were driven by private conveyance to Serpent Mound, arriving there about 11 A. M., and remaining till 2 P. M., dining at the custodian's house in the park. They were received by Daniel Wallace and conducted over the property of the Society. The inspection revealed that the park and the serpent were in most excellent condition; Mr. Daniel Wallace, the custodian, having continued in his faithful and efficient care of the property. Various suggestions were made by the members of the committee to the custodian in regard to details in the method of his protecting the property and preventing any injury being done by improper intruders. Mr. Wallace, the custodian, petitioned the visiting committee for the privilege of erecting at the expense of the Society a summer kitchen and a chicken coop, the cost of both not to exceed $110.00. The visiting committee reported in favor of this request to the Executive Committee and the Secretary of the Society was instructed to notify Mr. Wallace that he might proceed with the erection of the buildings in question.

The Secretary reported that he had received from Professor Mills, the curator, the following letter:

"SAINT LOUIS, U. S. A., October 19, 1904.

My Dear Mr. Mills:

This is to apprise you formally of the action of the International Jury of Awards in voting The Ohio State Archæological and Historical Society a grand prize on the admirable exhibit in this building, with a gold medal to yourself as collaborator. The certificates of award will probably be issued in the course of the month, though the medal will not be ready for delivery until some time later.

Yours cordially,   W. J. McGEE, *Chief.*"

This is a great honor to our Society as it places it foremost among the various competitors at the exposition. Several of the states and some of the foreign countries, particularly of South America, having made very elaborate archæological exhibits. This award places the Ohio Society at the head of the list in so far as its exhibit is to be compared with the other exhibits. The Jury of Awards was as follows: Prof. M. H. Saville, Columbia University, Chairman; Dr. De Lima, Brazil, Vice-Chairman; Dr. George G. McCurdy, Yale University, Secretary; Madam Zelia Nuttall, Mexico; Prof. F. W. Kelsey, University of Michigan; Prof. Mitchell Corrall, Columbia University.

The exposition was closed at noon, December 1.

Professor W. C. Mills, curator of the Society has been the recipient of many complimentary attentions during his stay at the exposition. He was invited to address the Congress of Arts and Sciences, The National meeting of Anthropologists, The Missouri Historical Society, Central High School of Saint Louis and other bodies.

Prof. Mills was also made honorary Superintendent of Exhibits, as the following letter will testify:

St. Louis, U. S. A., November 15, 1904.

Dr. Wm. C. Mills, *Ohio State Exhibit, Anthropology Building.*

My Dear Sir:— With the approval of the Director of Exhibits under authority vested in him by the President of the Louisiana Purchase Exposition Company, and in recognition of the confidence reposed in your abilities and training, I have the honor to designate you Honorary Superintendent of Archæology in this department. This action is inspired largely by the desire to convey to you some token of appreciation not merely of the high value of your special exhibit in the Anthropology Building but of the scientific and scholarly character you have constantly aided in giving to this Department.

In case you find it consistent with your duties toward the institution and state you have so efficiently represented to prepare a general report on the archæologic exhibits of the Department, I should greatly appreciate the favor and should take much pleasure in incorporating the same in the general report of the Department for publication by the Exposition Company.

With assurances of consideration, I remain,

Yous respectfully,

W. J. McGee, *Chief.*

Mr. Mills has also been made Consulting Editor of the *Records of the Past,* of which Prof. George F. Wright is editor-in-chief.

The Secretary announced that he had received a communication from Reuben Gold Thwaites, Secretary of the Wisconsin Historical Society, and a member of the Executive Committee of the National

American Historical Association, requesting that our Society be represented at the forthcoming annual meeting of the American Historical
Association to be held in Chicago, December 28-30. The Executive
Committee selected Secretary Randall and Mr. A. J. Baughman, life
member of the Ohio State Archæological and Historical Society and
Secretary of the Richland County Historical Society, as representatives
of the Ohio State Archæological and Historical Society at said meeting
in Chicago.

The Secretary reported that on the evening of Friday, November
18, the famous Liberty Bell passed through Columbus on its return trip
from Saint Louis to Philadelphia. It was on a special train accompanied
by the Mayor of Philadelphia and a committee of fifty citizens as its
escort. It stopped at the Columbus Union Depot from 7:00 to 7:30 P. M.
Arrangements had been made by Mayor Jeffrey and Superintendent
Shawan of the public schools to receive the bell with fitting ceremonies.
At the request of the Mayor a committee of thirteen each was selected
to represent the Daughters of the American Revolution, Sons of the
American Revolution, Ohio State Archæological and Historical Society,
Grand Army of the Republic, Ladies' Auxilliary to the Grand Army of
the Republic and the Schools and Universities of the city. The follow-
ing committee from the Society had been chosen as its representatives
on that occasion: Hon. C. B. Galbreath, Mr. O. C. Hooper, Mr. W. A.
Mahony, Mr. F. B. Pearson, Mr. A. H. Smythe, Hon. H. C. Taylor,
Gen. J. L. Vance, Dr. D. H. Gard, Rev. I. F. King, Hon. O. A. Miller,
Dr. G. S. Stein, Miss Anna E. Riordan, and Mr. E. O. Randall.

This committee met at the Chittenden Hotel at 6:00 P. M. on the
evening in question and with the other committees proceeded to the
depot to await the arrival of the bell train. Thousands of school children
and citizens were present. There were appropriate exercises consisting
of music by the Columbus Glee Club, patriotic tunes by the G. A. R.
drum corps and a speech by Mayor Jeffrey on behalf of the Columbus
welcoming committees.

Dr. Newell Dwight Hillis, Pastor of Plymouth Church, Brooklyn,
was elected an honorary member of the Ohio State Archæological and
Historical Society in recognition of his being the author of a book just
published by the Macmillan Company, being a story founded upon the
career of John Chapman known as "Johnny Appleseed," one of the unique
and original characters in early Ohio history. Dr. Hillis in his preface
to this book acknowledged his indebtedness to the Secretary of the Society
for valuable assistance in securing the historical material upon which his
book was founded. There were elected to life membership in the Society,
Hon. Jeptha Garrard, Cincinnati; Hon. E. V. Hale, Cleveland; Prof.
G. A. Hubbell, Berea College, Berea, Kentucky; Prof. John D. H. Mc-
Kinley of Columbus; Judge James B. Swing, Cincinnati; Dr. C. E.
Slocum, Defiance; Miss Martha J. Maltby, Columbus, and Mr. Stephen
B. Cone, Hamilton.

ENCYCLOPEDIA AMERICANA.

The latest and one of the best encyclopedias to appear is that known as the Encyclopedia Americana, published under the auspices of the Scientific American Company and edited by Frederick Converse Beach and a corps of competent assistants. It comprises sixteen large volumes and is produced in the best mechanical and typographical form with copious illustrations, maps, tables, etc. One of its excellent features is that the articles on leading subjects are written by well-known and acknowledged authorities over their subscribed names. This gives the topics thus treated an unusual attraction and value. The article on Ohio is contributed by the Honorable Daniel J. Ryan, Ex-Secretary of State and trustee of the Ohio State Archæological and Historical Society. It goes without saying that Mr. Ryan has produced a most scholarly, readable and comprehensive chapter. The article would occupy some fifty pages of an ordinary 12 mo. book and treats tersely of the typography, hydrography, and geology of the State, its natural resources; material, industrial, agricultural and other productions, its educational and charitable institutions; its development and government. The portion devoted to the history of the Buckeye State from earliest pre-state times to the present is a recital particularly satisfactory and interesting. Few, if any, students are better versed in the history of Ohio than is Mr. Ryan and in the compass of a few thousand words he has given in clear and logical sequence the brief events in the remarkable and romantic narrative of the emerging of the great and powerful Ohio Commonwealth from the early days when La Salle (1669) on his journey of adventure discovered the Ohio River and ascended its waters from the Mississippi to the site of Louisville. Mr. Ryan's chapter is the best sketch of Ohio "in a nut shell" we have yet seen in any publication.

GOVERNMENT OF OHIO.

The Government of Ohio, its history and administration is a new volume just issued from the press of the Macmillan Company of New York and written by Wilbur H. Siebert, professor of European History at the Ohio State University; author of the Underground Railroad from Slavery to Freedom. This little volume is an admirable and reliable compendium of the history of the State and the structure and machinery of its government. It deals with the growth of the government, beginning with Ohio as a part of the Northwest Territory and following the events that led to the organization of Ohio as a state. Chapters follow in logical order concerning the character of the state constitution, citizenship, suffrage, local **governments** of the state, the administration of justice, control of economic interests, management of public finances and so on. Professor Siebert is a careful and painstaking student and has exercised discriminating judgment as to what is necessary for the proper educidation of his subject. He gives under each chapter the list of authorities which he has consulted or which may be further examined by those who desire more exhaustive study of the various topics. The book is accompanied by an excellent appendix giving a chronological outline of the historical events incident to the development of the state, beginning with the land grant of King James in 1609 and leading through to the last event of importance in 1904 when the new school code was enacted by the legislature. There is also a complete text of the ordinance of 1787 and the enabling act of 1802, constitution of 1851, etc. The book is thoroughly indexed and will be of incalculable interest not only to the historical and economic student of Ohio but particularly to teachers. It comprises one of the series of handbooks of American government; 308 pages with map of Ohio giving counties, railroads, etc. Macmillan Company. 75 cents.

THE QUEST OF JOHN CHAPMAN.

John Chapman, known as Johnny Appleseed was an eccentric and unique character who first appeared on the Ohio River about 1790 in a boat filled with appleseeds. His plan was to go in advance of the settlers planting orchards through the wilderness. This strange and philantropic vocation he followed for some 25 or 30 years. His earlier career is shrouded in mystery but is made romantic with the tradition that he was early disappointed in love. He was a character of much ability in some directions and exercised in his peculiar way a serviceable influence upon the forest pioneers among whom he wandered.

Rev. Newell Dwight Hillis, the eloquent pastor of Plymouth Church has chosen John Chapman as the hero of a fascinating and beautiful narrative entitled "The Quest of John Chapman." Says Mr. Hillis in his preface: "Save Col. Clark, he (Chapman) is the most striking man of of the generation that crossed the Alleghanies." Sir Walter Scott thought it a matter of moment to his countrymen that some one should preserve the story of that old man who went through the cemeteries rechiseling the names of dead heroes. But this scarred old hero of our republic is a thousand times more fascinating than Old Mortality or the heroes of the Nibelungen Lied." Mr. Hillis with a vivid and artistic imagination and in the most felicitious and charming English initiates his narrative in the Town of Redham, New England, at the time of the departure of Mannasseh Cutler and his party for their journey to the Ohio wilderness. John Chapman is the son of the village minister and has given his heart to Dorothy, a daughter of Col. Durand. The latter is a prowd, high-spirited, influential gentleman who objects to the alliance of his daughter with John. Col. Durand and Dorothy are members of the Ohio Company. Subsequently John Chapman seeks in adventurous wanderings through the western country, the home of his plighted love. There is, of course, a rival, fascinating and chivalrous, but unworthy. Mr. Hillis has with rare gifts of pen portrayal pictured the simple but perilous life of the New England pioneers who sought their fortunes and amid the Indian inhabited fastnesses beyond the Alleghanies. It is a beautiful story, pure, idyllic, poetic and through the entire volume runs a delicate vein of moral and elevating sentiment such as renders the story at once a prose poem and an eloquent sermon. Amidst the flood of trashy and demoralizing novels of the day Mr. Hillis' "Quest of John Chapman" is like a draft of sparkling and refreshing water from some mountain spring. It should be read by every lover of a thrilling story told in the choicest language. It is published by Macmillan & Company, New York.

FIRST OHIO BATTLE IN 1812 WAR.

The *Van Wert Bulletin* of October 1, 1904, is responsible for the following:

The first trial of arms in Ohio, in the war of 1812, was a skirmish on Marblehead peninsula between Indians in the employ of the British and early white settlers in the Ottawa County firelands. The whites were principally from Trumbull and Ashtabula counties. Among them was Joshua R. Giddings, then aged sixteen years, and who later stirred the halls of Congress as one of Ohio's senators.

The skirmish resulted in the flight of the whites across Sandusky Bay. After going but a short distance, however, they met a relief party from their former homes bound for their own new settlement. The entire party returned, and succeeded in dispersing the erstwhile successful invaders. But it was only after a terrible conflict, and after many whites lost their lives, that the redskins were forced to retreat.

A number of years after this memorable conflict the survivors of the battle met on the spot where the conflict took place. It was agreed that they should meet at stated periods, but the few who assembled in later years dwindled until finally in 1864, but one was left. That person was Joshua R. Giddings, and, visiting the scene of the conflict for the last time, as fate destined it to be the last, he erected a monument to the memory of the hundred brave men who fought the skirmish and resisted the siege which was Ohio's debut in the war of 1812.

A short time after the placing of this little stone, and in the same year, 1864, Giddings died. The monument was placed by Giddings at Meadowbrook, a beautiful spot near Sandusky Bay, and but a short distance from Johnson's Island, another place which became a location of history as the federal prison for southern prisoners captured in the War of the Rebellion.

Vol. XIV — 7.

STORY OF THE FIRELANDS.

The following interesting account of the "Firelands" is taken from the *West Liberty Banner*:

Unnumbered native Ohioans, not to speak of hundreds of thousands of residents of the state from foreign lands and other states of the union, must have wondered why a fertile and productive tract in northern Ohio, a district which in no way hints of the ravages of fire, should be called the "Firelands." Among all the vicissitudes of Ohio's early history great conflagrations were known for their absence. No such terrible forest fires swept this state as ravaged large areas in Michigan and Wisconsin seventy or eighty years later.

The fires to which the name refers raged in Connecticut, not Ohio, and they were the work of British or Tory soldiers instead of the result of accidents or natural causes. In 1781, when the long struggle for independence was nearly ended, Benedict Arnold commanded an expedition which ravaged the Connecticut coast of Long Island Sound. He burned New London and other towns and left behind misery and destitution as well as a greater hatred himself than he had earned before the outrage upon his native state.

This and other cruel and senseless attacks upon Connecticut's towns left so strong a feeling of sympathy and injustice behind that in disposing of Connecticut's rights in lands now forming part of Ohio, 781 square miles in the extreme western edge in the Western Reserve were reserved to reimburse those who had suffered by the British raids. Five ranges of townships running north and south were included in this tract.

Sandusky Bay and Lake Erie extend so far southward at this point that the five ranges of townships contained only about 500,000 acres of land. The tract measured some twenty-seven miles by thirty. The Connecticut sufferers from the torch of the enemy lived chiefly in New London, Norwalk and Fairfield, and it was from these towns that many of the settlers of the "Firelands" came to build in the Ohio wilderness settlements bearing the same names and having like civic ideals and character.

OHIO COLONIAL WAR SOCIETY.

On November 25, 1904, at the tenth general court of the Society of Colonial Wars in the State of Ohio, held at the Queen City Club, Cincinnati, the following officers were elected:

Governor — Perin Langdon, Cincinnati.

Deputy Governor — Charles Theodore Greve, Cincinnati.

Lieutenant Governor — Hiram Harper Peck, Cincinnati.

Secretary — Harry Brent Mackoy, Covington, Ky.

Deputy Secretary — Murray Marvin Shoemaker, Cincinnati.

Treasurer — Howard Sydenham Winslow, Cincinnati.

Registrar — Robert Ralston Jones, Cincinnati.

Historian — John Uri Lloyd, Norwood.

Chancellor — Herbert Jenney, Cincinnati.

Surgeon — Dr. Phineas Sanborn Conner, Cincinnnati.

Chaplain — Rev. Henry Melville Curtis, Cincinnati.

Gentlemen of the Council — Nathaniel Henchman Davis, Cincinnati; Edwin C. Gashorn, Cincinnati; Charles Humphrey Newton, Marietta; Harry Langdon Laws, Cincinnati; Dr. Gilbert Langdon Bailey, Cincinnati; John Sanborn Conner, Cincinnati; James Wilson Bullock, Williamstown, Mass.; George Merrell, Cincinnati; Roderick Douglass Barney, Wyoming; Benjamin Rush, Cowen, Cincinnati.

Committee on Membership — Achilles Henry Pugh, Cincinnati; Charles James Stedman, Glendale; Ward Baldwin, Cincinnati; Howard Barney, Wyoming; Michael Myers Shoemaker, Cincinnati.

Committee on Collection of Historical Documents and Records — Rev. Dudley Ward Rhodes, Cincinnati; Prof. Edward Orton, Jr., Columbus; Ethan Osborn Hurd, Plainville.

Following the election a banquet was held, after which speeches were made by the retiring officers and Gen. B. R. Cowen.

The flowers used on the occasion were sent as a remembrance to the widows of the two members who have died in the last year, Mrs. W. W. Seely and Mrs. John Bailey.

CLARK COUNTY HISTORICAL SOCIETY.

On November 15, 1904, the Clark County Historical Society, in its new rooms in the East County Building, Springfield, Ohio, held its annual meeting and elected the following officers for the ensuing year:

President — Prof. B. F. Prince.

Secretary — William M. Harris.

Treasurer — Charles H. Pierce.

Trustees — Oscar T. Martin, for five years; L. H. Fahnestock, for six years.

All of the officers elected succeeded themselves except Mr. Fahnestock, who succeeded Prof. A. H. Linn. The Board of Trustees, as at present constituted, consists of seven members. An amendment to the by-laws was proposed, increasing the number of trustees to nine. The meeting was well attended and great interest was manifested in the progress of the Society. Professor Prince, who was honored with the presidency, is a trustee of the Ohio State Archæological and Historical Society.

NOAH'S ARK.

The construction and voyage of Noah's Ark is not exactly material pertinent to Ohio history or archæology; but as a matter of universal curiosity we herewith republish from very recent popular press items the following:

M. V. Millard, archæologist and distinguished excavator along the Nile, who was recently at Indianapolis, declared that he had discovered the place where Noah built the ark. Millard for a year past was engaged in excavations at various places on the Nile, especially at Gizeh, in the neighborhood of the great pyramid of Cheops.

"I have discovered during the last three years," he said, "just where Noah lived, where the ark was built, and that Noah built the great pyramid of Khufu, known as the pyramid of Gizeh. Noah was the greatest king this world has ever seen. He was the greatest of the Egyptian Pharaohs, not excepting Rameses the Great.

"Noah was a millionaire. The biblical account of the flood gives no clew as to where Noah lived or where his ship carpenters were at work for 120 years constructing the ark. Noah was 600 years old when the flood came. He must have been a millionaire, and a man of great authority. He built the ark at his own expense. Such a boat in these times would cost more than half a million dollars.

"Noah built the great pyramid during the earlier part of the fourth Egyptian dynasty, and not more than 1,200 years after God had expelled Adam and Eve from the garden of Eden."

*　　*　　*　　*　　*

King Christian of Denmark will, in the near future, have a chance to experience the feelings of Noah during the flood.

A Danish engineer, M. Vogt, supplied with money by the large Carlsberg fund, left by the late millionaire brewer, Jacobsen, has built an exact copy of the ark in which Noah floated around until he stranded on Mt. Ararat. The new ark was built according to the description contained in the Old Testament and an ancient representation of the Biblical vessel on an Apamean coin, dating back to 300 B. C., which is on exhibition in a museum at Stockholm.

M. Vogt's ark is, however, only one tenth the size of the one built by Father Noah, but a number of Danish University professors and scientists declare it to be a fine craft, which behaves spendidly in the open sea, as they had an opportunity to see during a recent trip on the Oeresound.

King Christian has promised to make a trip in the unique vessel during next month, and later the builder of the vessel may try to take it across the Atlantic.

OHIO DAY AT THE LOUISIANA PURCHASE EXPOSITION.

On October 6, 1904, the Buckeyes from all parts of the United States celebrated Ohio Day upon the grounds of the Exposition, St. Louis, Missouri. The exercises were held in the afternoon and evening in the beautiful Ohio Building. The Ohio Commission, appointed by Governor Nash under authority of an act passed by the 75th General Assembly, consisted of Hon. William F. Burdell, President, Columbus, life member of the Ohio

OHIO BUILDING, LOUISIANA PURCHASE EXPOSITION, 1904.

State Archæological and Historical Society; Hon. L. E. Holden, Vice-President, Cleveland; Hon. D. H. Moore, Athens; Hon. Edwin Hagenbuch, Urbana; Hon. M. K. Gantz, Troy; Hon. Newell K. Kennon, St. Clairsville; Hon. David Friedman, Caldwell. Hon. S. S. Rankin, South Charleston, was the Executive Commissioner having personal charge of the building and the affairs of the commission during the period of the exposition.

After an opening selection by the Philippino Band, Reverend Naphtali Luccock, President of the Ohio Society of St. Louis, was introduced by Mr. Burdell and asked to invoke the Divine blessing.

REVEREND NAPHTALI LUCCOCK:

"Our Father's God from out whose hand,
 The centuries fall like grains of sand,"

We stand in this sunlit hour of privilege with grateful hearts for the splendid inheritance thou hast given us in the midst of the years. We thank thee for the happy memories which crowd our hearts, and for the great opportunities which open before us. Put thy blessing upon the commonwealth which we honor this day, and upon all the commonwealths of our Nation! The blessing of the Lord our God be upon us and the work of our hands establish thou it, through Christ! Amen.

OPENING ADDRESS DELIVERED BY WILLIAM F. BURDELL, PRESIDENT OHIO COMMISSION.

Ladies and Gentlemen — On behalf of the Ohio Commission to the Louisiana Purchase Exposition I bid you welcome to these

WILLIAM F. BURDELL.

Ohio day exercises. We are justly proud of our state and we like to get together and talk about her. The Ohio Commission with limited resources has done the best it could to provide a comfortable and hospitable meeting place for Ohio people visiting the Fair. I am delighted that such a goodly number of Ohioans lend their appreciative presence to this superb effort of this most progressive city. To mass the products of the whole world in one comprehensive grouping — to search the globe and find its rarest treasures — to place beside the best gifts of an indulgent Providence, the best efforts of intellectual man, is a work of stupendous magnitude. St. Louis has done this and has done it well. We look upon the world's eighth wonder, and the people of Ohio congratulate you of St. Louis upon your splendid success.

There is much in this land and much in our time that should make us grateful contemporaries. To live in an age of accumulated genius — to have the work of man transcend man and approach the unknowable — to see spread out before us this grand panorama of man's accomplishment, is a privilege we do not fully appreciate. By some propitious accident of time, *we* rather than our fathers, behold civilization's supremest triumph. I do not believe that those of our day will witness a duplication of this magnificent exposition. You, fortunate men and women, who visit St. Louis in this year 1904, see with your own eyes and feel with human senses this impressive revelation of man's highest attainment.

Ohio has had some share in the great national development which this exposition reflects. Ohio and her sons have not been in the rear of this splendid procession. She and they have been making records for political and industrial America. Some pages in our country's history belong to her. Even now the tiller of the Ship of State is warm with the hand of that beloved and gentle McKinley — of that masterful, yet humane, Napoleon of modern politics, Hanna — of that wise pilot of our blackest night of financial stress, John Sherman — with the hand of Hay, who makes precedent for the whole world's diplomacy, and Taft, who built out of chaos a government for the Philippine Islands.

Yes, Ohio has been and is conspicuous in the larger affairs of our country. There were times when she seemed to dominate and control them. Her sons were forceful leaders, their eloquence was persuasive, their judgment sound and stable. If, in the growing power of this great West — in the mutation of our national life — if, in the future, the man and the issues of another state should seem ascendent in the councils of the nation — if other men of other states nearer the great heart and brain of this grand republic, should seem better fitted for the responsibilities of government, there will be in Ohio no resentment — no heart burnings. We will sustain and strengthen them, will follow on with them, the splendid highway of our common glory. And, in the triumphal march of which this exposition is but a halting place, the

East and the West, the North and the South, proud of each other's
attainments, glorying in each other's triumphs, will go on together
in that undying love of a common country which, in surpassing
goodness, justice and power, is the central sun of this western
hemisphere.

We will go on together, not content with this splendid exposition that seems today the acme of human achievement, but with
the unsatisfied longing, the unquenchable desire for better things,
with faces towards the light, with hands ever guided by righteous
hearts, will raise stone upon stone — a mighty monument of
national greatness.

I have alluded to the glories of this great exposition. I now
have the pleasure of introducing to you the man who, more than
all others, is responsible for the success of this fair — the Honorable David R. Francis, President of the Louisiana Purchase
Exposition.

HONORABLE DAVID R. FRANCIS:

Mr. President, Your Excellency, Ladies and Gentlemen —
The exposition management is more than pleased to see this representative outpouring of Ohioans on Ohio Day. You know, the
Government at Washington has not been able to run for years
without Ohio's assistance; consequently, no great exposition could
be successfully held without the participation of Ohio. We are,
therefore, deeply grateful to the Buckeye State for the assistance
rendered to this international or universal exposition.

Ohio has a history of which every citizen of the state should
be proud. There are many links which bind Ohio to the Louisiana
Territory, and there are many reasons why Ohio should participate
in this exposition; why the people of the Louisiana Purchase
should feel grateful to Ohio. I believe it was the same La Salle
who discovered the Ohio River and went down that stream before
he went down the Mississippi and reared the cross near the mouth
of the Father of Waters and named the territory "Louisiana" in
honor of his King of France. From that time on the hardy
pioneers who blazed the way in that country have constantly forged
their way westward. They were instrumental in bringing about
the purchase of this Louisiana Territory and have been very

potential agents in building it up from the time it was brought under the dominion of the United States Government.

I believe that Ohio's organization, as a state, was about contemporaneous with the coming of the Louisiana Territory under the control of the United States Government. I remember that when this movement for the celebration of this purchase was first thought of, at the inception of the plan, it was said that Ohio was also preparing for a centennial celebration commemorating the one hundredth anniversary of the admission of Ohio into the Union. I think this was planned to be held in Toledo.

The people of that state, with marked and memorable magnanimity, when they heard of the plans made to commemorate this Louisiana Purchase, abandoned their plans for a centennial at Toledo, and most generously united with the people of the Louisiana Purchase territory to commemorate its transfer from France to the United States Government. That is additional cause for gratitude for which the exposition management cannot make too frequent acknowledgement.

Not only that, but the management of this exposition well remembers the very efficient aid given to this movement by a lamented son of Ohio, whose influence was potent in the national councils, and who, from the time this celebration was first mentioned, gave it encouragement. Upon every occasion, whether in the Senate of the United States or in the councils of the State of Ohio, he spoke a good word for this exposition. We joined with the people of Ohio in lamenting his untimely taking off, and upon this occasion, we desire again to pay our tribute of respect and affection to the memory of MARCUS A. HANNA!

The other Senator from Ohio was likewise friendly to this exposition movement — I refer to Senator Foraker — from the time the suggestion was first made in the National Congress. In fact, all of the representatives of your great state, if I remember rightly, have given their support, in critical times, to this work as it progressed.

The Chief Executive of your commonwealth, who favors us with his presence today, and whose acquaintance and friendship I have been proud to claim for a longer period than he has been your Governor, has ever been a friend to this Exposition from the beginning of his administration. His presence here to-day is the second or third visit he has made. He manifests what we trust he cherishes, and what we would like to see on the part of the Executives of all the states, a proprietary interest in this great Exposition. It does not belong to one state alone, but every member of the sisterhood has contributed to this international celebration.

Here Ohio has erected a home in which her sons and daughters feel as much "at home" as they could if they were upon the soil of Ohio.

Furthermore, many of the sons and daughters of Ohio who left the state of their nativity and came West years ago have been associated in the organization of this celebration. They are represented on its Board of Directors, and as I stated in the beginning, no movement of a national character in this country can be successful without the aid of Ohio!

The exhibits of your state in our Exhibit Palaces demonstrate more forcefully than I can explain, the resources of Ohio and the progress that your state has made in wealth, in culture, and in everything that goes to make a great commonwealth!

Your state has contributed Presidents to the United States! There is a long line of distinguished sons of Ohio to which every citizen of the state can point with pride! Their descendants are still exerting their influence throughout the land! They are representatives of that composite American character which has made this country what it is. And this Exposition, which brings together people of Ohio and people of Texas, the people of Washington with those of Maine, serves but to make our Union the stronger.

It is a beautiful sight to contemplate, looking at these state buildings, forty odd of them, erected upon these grounds, the locations here bearing no relation to the locations of the states in the country. Here, as you observe, is Ohio, further south than Missouri. It is but a step from Ohio to Mississippi! The strains of the music participating in the ceremonies of dedication on these sites reminded us of the fact that no differences exist between the various sections of our country. The strains of "Dixie" had hardly died out on the Mississippi site when we were saluted with the familiar notes of "John Brown's Body Lies Mould'ring in the Grave" from the Kansas site. This Exposition belongs to the people, and to the entire people! When the "Star Spangled Banner" is played upon these grounds every man within reach of the sound rises and doffs his hat! It is such practices as these which deepen and quicken the patriotism of the American people!

The educational advantages of this Exposition are not confined to any one section. I am glad to say that your state has been so generously represented here. We ask you to remain with us as long as your affairs will permit; to give the exhibits in these palaces as thorough an inspection as your time will allow; and upon your return home to say to those whom you left behind that there is installed in St. Louis an Exposition, held in celebration of a great event in our country's history, which every American should patronize and which will be of great benefit to all who visit it because it here brings together within a small area the best products of all the civilized countries of the globe; because it is the occasion of the assembling here of representatives of all the primitive races, and because it will be, in the judgment of most men, the last universal exposition which this generation will see! The only criticism has been that it is too big for any one individual to properly inspect or comprehend! But that should be no reason why people should not visit it. When the American people plan to hold an exposition, they take no second place in expositions, as they take no second place in any other line!

Furthermore, the great event which we are commemorating, and which was the greatest transfer of territory in the history of the world by peaceful negotiations, could not be properly celebrated by an exposition second to any which had ever been held! There will be expositions in the future, but, in my judgment, they will be expositions along special lines.

Permit me to thank you again for your attendance here; and on behalf of the Exposition management, I desire to make acknowledgement to the Chief Executive of Ohio, for the very able and faithful labors performed by his Commission.

This characteristic structure has not only been a home for the sons and daughters of Ohio, but here has always been dispensed that genuine Ohio hospitality without which it would be a misnomer to call it the Ohio building.

The exhibits installed by the Commission in our Exhibit Palaces speak for themselves. This Exposition, if it did nothing more than to inculcate into the people connected with it, — not only the local management but the people here representing the different states of the Union,— if it did nothing more than inculcate in them that patriotic spirit, that sense of national duty which prompts them to sacrifice personal interest, personal convenience, and also personal means, to promote the interests of our common country, that, indeed, would be compensation enough for all of the time, for all of the labor, all of the means, all of the sacrifice, which this International Exposition has entailed.

I thank you for your attention.

Mr. Burdell:

Ladies and Gentlemen — It is with the greatest pleasure that I introduce the Honorable Myron T. Herrick, Governor of Ohio.

Governor Herrick:

My Fellow-Citizens, Sons and Daughters of Ohio, and Governor Francis — I want first of all to express the appreciation

MYRON T. HERRICK.

of this audience, made up largely of Ohio people, for the kind words Governor Francis has said of Ohio. We are, indeed, proud of the history of Ohio — prouder than we dare to say to you, Governor Francis!

This is Ohio Day at the greatest of all expositions. We are assembled to add our testimony to the success of this wonderful exhibit, and to express our appreciation and devotion to the great event it is intended to signalize; and to pay tribute to the genius, energy, and superb nerve of the men and women of St. Louis who have made this the greatest of all expositions. Surely, there never was gathered in one place such an array of proof of the world's progress, such amazing omens of the triumphs of peace, as are seen on these beautiful grounds. The ancient civilization of the East is here in touch with the modern life of the West. Strange people from strange lands, mingle and view each other's advancement with amazement and mutual benefit.

President McKinley designated these expositions as "mile stones to mark a nation's progress!" The men of St. Louis have laid this "mile stone" to the everlasting credit of their country and themselves. We Ohioans extend to you our felicitations upon this splendid realization which is possible only for our country, and for few cities beside St. Louis.

The evolution of the race toward higher planes of life is here pictured in stronger lines than the imagination of artist or writer can portray. Who can view the Philippine exhibit of its people and its products without a better understanding of, and a greater pride in, our most humane work in the Orient? We gaze into each other's faces with hope and surprise when we look over the magnificent display of the arts of peace, and recognize the victories of intelligence, skill, and purpose that characterize every advance. A scene like this marks the trend of a fairer destiny. It is a promoter of optimism. It extends the horizon wherein human genius does its real work. Think of the former days of crude endeavor in all fields of human effort, and then of this exposition of inventive genius, and mark how far advanced are the standards of life. Each of us absorbed in his own "day's work," awakes in amazement here to find that the dream of yesterday is the realization of to-day, the hope of to-day is the fact of to-morrow.

Progress is harnessing the forces of nature and adapting them to the desires of men. The air, the sea, the earth, are filled with energies, that are utilized for the comfort and joy of the race. These forces are taken from their primeval relation, ordained by a wise Providence, and fitted to the service of home, of shop, of farm and every avenue of human activity. "Behold what God hath wrought!" heralded the first message of electricity, and now again behold. There in the laboratory, there the engine, the telephone, the trolley cars, the phonograph, these Alladin palaces, blazing at night with electric lights, everywhere, a step forward, and a promise of loftier triumphs still to come, and one exclaims: "Behold what God hath wrought," and again behold what Governor Francis and his valiant men have wrought.

This exposition is not only a realization, but an inspiration. Who can look on this scene and not catch the harmony which the Eternal Goodness has reposed in all things, or fail to recognize the potencies with which He has invested all matter. Here one sees them put into service, so perfectly, so grandly, that one is sure to ascribe it all to a Divine purpose from the very beginning.

Such an illustration of human progress as we have here is a fit demonstration to celebrate the event for which it was so happily conceived, and that event, the Louisiana Purchase, was the crowning work and glory of a great Democratic administration, presided over by a great Democrat. It was men like him, whose clear vision saw that an untrammeled democracy was absolutely essential to the first development of this empire of freedom, and who thus laid the firm foundation for this Republic's future greatness.

Within a century an empire has arisen from a wilderness. The tomahawk and scalping knife have given way to the steam plow and self-binder. Where the wigwam stood the schoolhouse stands. The free citizen of the town and farm has taken the place of the red man of the chase. No area on this planet has taken up the march of civilization with a steadier tread than that within the compass of the Louisiana Purchase. In civic attainment, in agricultural advancement, in educational outlook, in whatever adorns life with honor and duty, this populous region has stood in the forefront of the republic in its onward march. If there could be a miracle in the evolution of natural destiny, this great transition would be one.

When one looks into the future, and extends the progress of the past century forward, his mind fails to comprehend that were he to appear at the two hundredth anniversary of the Louisiana Purchase it would be with all the bewilderment of Rip Van Winkle. Here is the center of the republic, and it will be the center of civilization whence mechanics, invention, science, art and philosophy will abide for countless years.

The fact that there are one million eight hundred thousand square miles of arable land west of the Missisippi, and eight hundred thousand square miles east of the Mississippi, tells us that when these lands which are becoming so rapidly populated are occupied, the center of the voting power of the nation will be on this side of the Father of Waters. And what we see all about us is an earnest that those foundation principles of the Republic will nowhere hold happier sway than in this region beyond the Mississippi.

Ohio has not the honor of belonging to that grand galaxy of states born of the Louisiana Purchase, but it comes to rejoice with them in the achievement of a national spirit, which has made them the pride of the Union. We do not come as a neighbor, but as a member of the family, to exult over our own good fortune as well as yours. First-born of the Northwest Territory, dedicated to freedom by the Ordinance of 1787, imbued with the first fresh impulse of the Republic's highest hope and devotion to the task of transforming a wilderness into a commonwealth, Ohio comes to you proud of her past and inspired by a memory that inaugurated this drama of national glory.

Ohio is the most cosmopolitan of states. It indulges in no provincial whims. It is proud of itself for the same reason that it is proud of the other states. Its population began with a vigorous blend of Puritan and Cavalier, happily modified by the Connecticut Bourbon and Pennsylvania Dutchman, a composite that embraced the elements of sterling manhood, and formed the basis of self-reliant and aggressive citizenship. Thus endowed, and occupying the center of the Union, and being the highway between the East and the West, Ohio knows no section, only a common country, the principles of whose government respond to all the legitimate aspirations of mankind.

It is not surprising that in all this magnificent empire building Ohio should look on with a feeling of pride and kinship? I say kinship, for Ohio is the mother — and a mighty mother is she, of this great middle west. Why, my friends, do you know that there are living in Indiana more than one hundred and sixty thousand Ohio born people, more than one hundred and forty thousand in Illinois, ninety thousand in Iowa, ninety thousand in Kansas, and more than seventy thousand in this great state of Missouri! So, when I claim this maternal relationship with the West, I speak of recorded facts. I have no fear of contradiction when I say that there are living now in the great valley of the Mississippi, more than three-quarters of a million Americans, who first saw the light of day in my grand old State of Ohio. Our unusual diversity of resources has trained Ohio men in a broad, catholic university of life. She has sent her sons out into the world, not trained in narrow lines, nor with the idea that any particular staple is king, but that all the bounties of kind Providence are given to man for his benefit and for the benefit of his fellow men.

Nearly two centuries ago John Law located here his visions of wealth. It was a mirage of the brain spreading over the horizon far beyond. Modern spirit has pushed through that mirage to the solid shores, and changed that vaporous scheme into a glorious achievement. No longer do those wild and desolate scenes appeal to a laggard faith. What was then a daring vision is now a civilization, as lasting as the earth, a civilization rich with the resources of the soil, with the victories of commerce, with the growth of cities, with the increase of schools and churches, and with the happiness of homes.

Not with material blessings only is this mighty progress attended. Here, with jocund spirit of aggression that animates the western heart, will be solved, as nearly as this virile progressive race is capable of solving, those social problems that rest on the bosom of society like a frightful dream. It is to be the land of liberty, of opportunity, and of brotherhood. We philosophically accept, with the characteristic of light-hearted Americans, conditions as we find them, and with the instruments which we have we strive earnestly to improve them. There is so much in American life of materialism mingled with our higher ideals that inequalities will continue to exist. Periods of depression and discouragement will come in the future as in the past, when our patriotism will be severely taxed and the obligations of citizenship will rest heavily upon us; but the man of today gives promise that his progeny, like himself and his ancestors, will be equal to the strain; and this nation will not, therefore, die of material opulence, as did Greece and Rome. These sentiments of equality and justice, these ideals of opportunity and fraternity, will more strongly direct the new evolution, and make rights and duties inseparable.

This great Jeffersonian expansion carried with it more than an increase of territory; more, too, than the conversion of a barbarism into a civilization. The aggressive spirit of the republic required an outing ground, a breathing place, where, free from dogma and social bondage of the Orient, it could exploit itself along the lines of ultimate ideals. Horace Greeley's advice to the young man, "Go West," was given in a spirit of true philosophy — go west, grow, evolve, differentiate, and there, upon the broad plains, along the shining rivers, and on the liberty-loving mountains, set up the standards of a true, self-reliant, American manhood. That is the doctrine of the West. That is the secret of its wonderful development.

This is the first centennial in honor of the dedication of this vast domain to the cause of American liberty. The whole world comes here to lay down its tribute to the progress of a century. Our theory of government, instead of repelling any people, has won the respect, if not the admiration, of all nations. This has been the accomplishment of the century that has just passed.

The rich gifts brought here from all lands testify to an alertness of brain and a deftness of hand that is marvelous, and we rightly pride ourselves on these things; but they have a deeper meaning — they tell of the kinship of nations, of the sympathy among them, of a generous rivalry in those things that raise the standard of living; and they tell us that, in different ways, we are reaching out toward one object: the happiness and elevation of the race. This quest, involving the exercise of the brightest intellects and the warmest hearts, moves along the path of peace, which it ever proclaims as the trend of national duty. That is one lesson of this grand demonstration; and while we may consistently boast of our own advancement, we do not forget that the world moves with us and rejoices in our splendid development.

The mission of every wheel, fibre, energy, tint, and form, that betters itself in the evolution now going on, increases the lustre of national life, and promotes peace among nations. There is a moral advancement in every triumph of mind over matter, and its influence is felt in commerce, industry, politics, social and domestic life. This exhibit that now awakens our wonder is a protest against Goldwin Smith's prediction of gloom and ruin for American institutions. Our problem may not be completely worked out, but the omens along our path, like those we see all around us, fill our hearts with faith and hope that the happiest and grandest days of this republic are yet to come. To that faith our lives are devoted; in that hope we press on.

And to you, men of Missouri and of the Sunny South, at whose portals we are standing, speaking for the great mother heart of our dear old state, which lies but a day's journey beyond your great river— speaking for her, and for these Ohioans gathered here today — I tell you that not only have all the old wounds healed, but that the scars have been obliterated. We meet today in this border state of that gigantic disagreement, not as friends merely, but in a closer, holier kinship, under that flag that waves above us; and we thank God that it represents a united sisterhood of states, standing as it does, for the fairest opportunity that the world has ever known.

MR. BURDELL:

During the panic times of '93 and '94, there was one thing that always flourished in the West — The Ohio Society! They tell me that no severity of weather, no discouraging condition of crops or business, could prevent an Ohio Society from flourishing. I have the honor of presenting to you, a representative of the Ohio Society of St. Louis, a man who has rendered distinguished service to his country in both civic and military life. I name the distinguished and honored son of Ohio, the Honorable John W. Noble, of Saint Louis.

HON. JOHN W. NOBLE:

Ladies and Gentlemen — The purposes for which this mansion was erected by the State of Ohio are being satisfactorily met in all ways, but its use at no time will be more important or interesting than today. The presence of Ohio's chief magistrate, his staff, its civil officers and multitudes of its people mark this event as one gratifying to its pride and destined to be remembered in its annals.

When in 1901 the Auxiliary Committee of the Louisiana Purchase Exposition Company, which was composed of members

HON. JNO. W. NOBLE.

of the Ohio Society of St. Louis, was invited by the legislature to Columbus, to address it upon the proposition of making an appropriation for such building, the opportunity was gladly accepted. The money was voted. Governor Nash favored the measure, and the present beautiful house is the result. The site is also fortunately good and is due in great measure to the earnestness and judgment of the Ohio Executive Commissioner and his associates who demanded an advanced and prominent location. Indeed Ohio has received from the President, architect and officers of the Exposition Company as to its buildings worthy consideration at all times.

The suggestions made at the time the appropriation was urged, that seemed to be most germane to the subject and persuasive, and which are now being proven correct, were, that this Exposition, universal in name, would certainly prove to be all the name implied, and here would be exhibited the products of land and sea, and of every state and all nations; that here would come in vast multitudes the people of all sections and every clime, and among them all there would be none prouder of the land of their birth, because of its origin, of its progress and of its worth and power than the sons of Ohio; and none who would more enjoy meeting together on Ohio's ground, as it were, and there renewing old ties of affection and loyalty to her and our common country; that Ohio could not have become the great commonwealth she has grown to be, but by having bred a race which could not all be content to remain within her borders, but many by force of character had to seek and find place for their energy and intelligence elsewhere; that natives of Ohio were numerous in almost every other state, and nowhere were more abundant, proportionately to population, than in Missouri, the locality of the Exposition and the states adjacent thereto; that they would be all coming to the fair and quite as much to see what Ohio was doing or had to show and to say, as for any other pleasure. It was also apparent, it was urged, that a great commercial state would find it worth while to secure such world-wide notice as could be here obtained for the products of her fields and factories; and that such an enlightened and generous people, who had received much from the early pioneers who had come to plant the state and sustain it in its infancy and growth, would gladly give a hand to Ohio's sons and daughters struggling elsewhere with less advantage; and that she would be pleased to set forth her accomplishments in the arts, in her educational system and her scholarship; and present her worthy and ever increasing roll of men and women, distinguished, and many pre-eminent as statesmen, as teachers, as authors, as soldiers, as merchants and as farmers, and in every vocation and station of life.

These were the purposes advocated for the establishment of this beautiful house, the Ohio headquarters. Are they not being most gratifyingly fulfilled? What Ohioan can pass from the palaces of this Exposition with Ohio's exhibits of her manufactories, varied industries and the liberal arts; of her mines, of her electrical appliances, machinery, agricultural products and fine arts, and of her educational system; or view the names of the presidents, statesmen and soldiers in the United States Government Building, and not turn at last proudly to this central place, to this high seat from which Ohio seems to preside over all the world besides, and where she smilingly welcomes them, as she does, today, and not here gladly join in her praise, whether he resides in Ohio yet, or dwells in some other state? We feel that "our state" holds a high place throughout this great Exposition and one worthy of her history and her fame.

It is also peculiarly appropriate that we should have set apart a day for these exercises. The history of Ohio and that of the domain in the Louisiana Purchase are closely and interestingly related, and indeed the settlement of Ohio and the northwest caused our acquisition of the Louisiana territory.

The expeditions to, and conquests of, Kaskaskia, near St. Louis, and the British post of Vincennes, by George Rogers Clark, aided by Governor Patrick Henry, gave, at the negotiations for the treaty of peace at the close of the Revolutionary War, the support necessary to the claim of the United States, through the charters of Virginia, and of the other colonies, to obtain the relinquishment by the English Crown of all right to the domain west of the Ohio River. By the Ordinance of 1787 this was organized into the Northwest Territory extending to the Mississippi River. Upon the adoption of that ordinance the settlement begun at the mouth of the Muskingum, ("The River of the Elk's eyes"), and its junction with the Ohio, ("the beautiful river"), on April 7th, 1788, was so rapid that the wilderness soon was peopled to such degree, that the state with its present boundaries was admitted to the Union in 1802. Its people, with those of the other portions of the Territory bordering on the Ohio River and partly on the Missisippi, was of the stock of those who carried to a successful issue the war of Independence. An outlet for their products by the great waterways was essential to their prosperity, and they demanded in unmistakable terms that the National Government should free from foreign control the mouth of the Mississippi, or they would resort to any means within her power to remove all barriers there and enforce their natural claims to untrammeled intercourse with all parts of their own country and with other nations. There was no one more conversant with the needs of these people or more sympathetic with their sacrifices, or more appreciative of the justice of these claims, nor any more desirous, both from principle and the necessities of the young Republic to avoid war, than the then President of the United States, Thomas Jefferson. Washington had in his early military career been engaged west of the Alleghanies, and comprehended as well as, if not better than, any of his fellow citizens and made widely known the beauty and exhaustless resources of the great region so secured by the treaty of 1783. Jefferson had himself formulated, in great part, the Ordinance of 1787, which was only second to the Declaration of Independence in its announcement of principles essential to good government and to the peace and progress of a free people. And although the resolutions first adopted were enlarged and advocated by Nathan Dane, and the ordinance was passed while Jefferson was absent abroad in the service of the country, its principles had his hearty approval; and he was eager upon his return to coöperate in their support and extension by all means within his control. And when he became President and the West demanded free navigation of the rivers, commissioners were sent to France to negotiate for the free passage of the Mississippi, and succeeded, even beyond their expectations, in obtaining title to the vast region of which that great river formed the eastern border.

As the success of George Rogers Clark, the pioneer soldier, wrought out by such apparently insufficient means had secured to our country the great Northwest, so now the necessities of the greatest commander of European armies, Napoleon, led him to grant to the United States for a comparatively small pecuniary consideration the Louisiana Purchase. Thus the behest of the flatboatmen of the Ohio found result in the acquisition of the farther west, reaching from the Father Waters to the Rocky Mountains. The Northwest was to the purchase as cause to effect. The homogeneous particles of the whole gathered into coherence, solidity and strength as a star, a world, from nebulæ. The fiat of the divinity that shapes our ends, brought the two great regions of the west together at the Mississippi, that divides but does not separate them, and here today we feel the heart of the nation pulsating; beating in mighty rhythm, with the force of daily increasing health and strength. Ohio comes to this celebration with the consciousness of having with the purchase an almost coincident birthday, and certainly a united interest and common destiny with the states that have arisen and the one that is soon to come from this vast domain.

Ohio headed the column when the young Republic began its forward march to broader fields and greater endeavor. On each day's advance her force has been effective to clear the way to win the battles for the right. At each night's bivouac her presence has given assurance of response and safety, and her bugles send forth today no uncertain signals of her purpose to keep the faith of her own deliverance, and still higher advance for all men the principles of public education, religion, liberty and justice to which she even before her birth was dedicated by the wisdom and virtue of the fathers.

The history of the realms of the Northwest and of the Louisiana Purchase is replete with adventure, romance, sacrifice and success. The one whose soil was from the beginning by the votes of the southern states themselves, ordained to be free from slavery, has so supported the cause of human freedom that the other now likewise enjoys it; and all the states rejoice that they are united in heart and hand, and stand among the strongest and most influential of the nations.

We are one people, from New England, Virginia or Florida, the State of Louisiana and Texas to the Pacific, and Alaska and the lakes. Each succeeding territory that has been formed, each state as it has been admitted to the Union, from the days of the Colonies to this hour, has been inhabited and filled substantially with the same stock of American people. The Territorial Acts and the State Constitutions have each been molded and made in all essential particulars the same as those of the earliest ones. And the means of communication enable the Governor of Ohio or of the State of Washington to visit and participate in services such as these of today with as much convenience almost as to go from his own home to the capital of, or any other city within his state. Alike in language, in the constitutions, the laws and the pursuits of business, the customs of home, and the love of our common country, when now a new territory is suddenly thrown open as was Oklahoma, sixteen years ago, or the other great states admitted from 1889 to 1903, the population begins its career, it is true, with hardships and sacrifices, but with the immense advantages of rapid transportation; the postoffice at hand, the telegraph from the former home, and all the aid that an advanced experience and all the help that vast improvements in the means of living and a more abundant facility of education can bestow; and above all with the protection and support of our National Government, so generous and so powerful.

As a citizen of Missouri and of St. Louis it is a great personal pleasure for me to be associated with the representatives and people of Ohio this day. Missouri welcomes Ohio as sister, yes, even as mother. The memories of my life embrace an acquaintance with many who were the pioneers of these now great commonwealths, Ohio the fourth and Missouri the fifth in the Union in population. Let us not now forget our obligation to those brave patriotic men.

The pioneer, as has been written of the greatest of them all,

>   *   *   * went forth to battle, on the side
> That he felt clear was Liberty's and Right's,   *   *   *
> *   * The uncleared forest, the unbroken soil,
> The iron bark that turns the lumb'rer's axe,
> The rapid that o'erbears the boatman's toil,
> The prairie hiding the mazed wander's tracks,
> The ambushed Indian and the prowling bear,
> Such were the needs that helped his youthful train:
> Rough culture, but such trees large fruit may bear,
> If but their stocks be of right girth and grain."

The march by states from the west coming successively into the line of the Union is about complete and the advance into the field where nations are contending has begun, not for war, nor with jealousy, nor with greed for wealth, dominion or power, but for the advocacy of the liberty of the individual, the practice of humanity, the elevation of the people of all the world to greater comfort and higher thought, and to hold high to view and vindicate the principles of our American Christian Republic. Let us rejoice that to the duties of the past Ohio has been ever true, and resolve that to the demand of the future she will bring like full measure of morality, loyalty and justice.

HARRISON-TARHE PEACE CONFERENCE.

COL. E. L. TAYLOR, COLUMBUS.

On the 28th of June, 1904, the Columbus Chapter of the Daughters of the American Revolution did themselves and their organization great honor by placing in Martin Park in the western part of the City of Columbus, a large bowlder of igneous origin, bearing a very handsome designed tablet in commemoration of the important council or conference which General William Henry Harrison had with the chiefs of certain Indian tribes, near that spot on June 21st, 1813. By this act the Daughters rescued from the very brink of oblivion and gave a permanent place in the history of the War of 1812 to one of the important and controlling incidents of that war. But for this action on the part of this organization, that event would probably have soon passed into entire forgetfulness, as there was but one co-temporary report of the proceedings ever published of that conference or council, and that was in a weekly paper then published at Franklinton, called "The Freeman's Chronicle," which was edited and owned by James B. Gardiner. It was the first weekly paper, or paper of any kind, ever published in what is now the City of Columbus. The first number of this paper was dated June 24th, 1812, and the publication continued for more than two years, covering the entire period of the War of 1812. Mr. Gardiner was present at the council and in the issue of his paper of June 25th, 1813, he published an account of it. Mr. William Domigan, at that time a resident of the Town of Franklinton, had the thoughtfulness to preserve a full file of that paper as it was issued, and had the same bound in substantial form, which sole copy has been preserved to this time and presents the best picture of the condition and life of the young village that is in existence to-day.

Mrs. Edward Orton, Jr., Regent of the Columbus Chapter of the organization before mentioned, in her very appropriate address in presenting the memorial tablet to the City of Columbus,

(121)

said: "We are assembled here to-day to commemorate an event more than local in character, far reaching in its results, and of the greatest importance to the state as well as to the capital of Ohio."

Mr. Robert H. Jeffrey, Mayor of Columbus, in his remarks, accepting the tablet on behalf of the City of Columbus, said: "The value of this bowlder lies in recalling to our memory the high patriotism of our forefathers. In its ruggedness, its strength and its power to defy all time, it typifies the immutable principles

PEACE MEMORIAL, STONE AND TABLET, HARRISON-TARHE PEACE CONFERENCE.

of the great union of states, which these ancestors fought, bled and died for."

General Benjamin R. Cowen then delivered an historical address concerning the events, the monument and the tablet were intended to commemorate. This address as well as all the proceedings of the day have been published in booklet form by the Regent, Mrs. Orton, for private circulation.

In order to give further permanency to the record of this important event, we give in full the account of Mr. Gardiner, as it appears in the issue of "The Freeman's Chronicle" of June 25th, 1813:

"On Monday last Gen. Harrison held a council in this place with the chiefs of the Delaware, Shawanoe, Wyandot and Seneca tribes of Indians, to the amount of about 50. In the General's *talk,* he observed that he had been induced to call them together from certain circumstances having come to his knowledge, which led him to suspect the fidelity of some of the tribes, who had manifested signs or a disposition to join the enemy, in case they had succeeded in capturing Fort Meigs. That a crisis had arrived which demanded that all the tribes, who had heretofore remained neutral, should take a decided stand, either for us or against us. That the President wished no false friends, and that it was only in adversity that real friends could be distinguished. That the proposal of Gen. Proctor to exchange the Kentucky prisoners for the friendly tribes within our borders, indicated that he had been given to understand that those tribes were willing to raise the tomahawk against us. And that in order to give the U. S. a guarantee of their good dispositions, the friendly tribes should either move, with their families, into the settlements, or their warriors should accompany him in the ensuing campaign, and fight for the U. S. To this proposal the chiefs and warriors present unanimously agreed — and observed, that they had long been anxious for an opportunity to fight for the Americans.

"We cannot recall the precise remarks that were made by the chiefs who spoke — but *Tarhe* (The Crane) who is the principal chief of the Wyandots, and the oldest Indian in the western wilds; appeared to represent the whole assembly, and professed, in the name of the friendly tribes, the most indissoluble attachment for the American government, and a determination to adhere to the Treaty of Greenville.

"The General promised to let the several tribes know when he should want their services; and further cautioned them that all who went with him must conform to *his* mode of warfare; not to kill or injure old men, women, children nor prisoners. That, by this means, we should be able to ascertain whether the British tell truth when they say that they are not able to prevent Indians from such acts of horrid cruelty; for if Indians under him (Gen. H.) would obey *his* commands, and refrain from acts of barbarism, it would be very evident that the hostile Indians could be as easily restrained by *their* commanders. The Gen. then informed the chiefs of the agreement made by Proctor to deliver him to Tecumseh in case the British succeeded in taking Fort Meigs; and promised them that if he should be successful, he would deliver *Proctor* into their hands — *on condition,* that they should do him no other harm than to *put a petticoat on him* — "for," said he, "none but a *coward* or a *squaw* would kill a prisoner."

"The council broke up in the afternoon; and the Indians departed next day for their respective towns."

In order to understand and appreciate the importance and full significance of this conference, it is necessary to recall some of the chief events of the times relating to the war.

The battle of "Fallen Timbers" was fought August 20th, 1794, at which General Wayne obtained a complete victory over the Indians who had concentrated in the region of the Maumee. This defeat was followed the next summer by a general council held by General Anthony Wayne at Greenville, Darke county, Ohio, with the Indian tribes of the northwest, which resulted in the celebrated treaty, known as the "Treaty of Greenville," which was concluded August 3d, 1795, and was in its result the most important of all the peace treaties made between the United States and the Indian tribes northwest of the Ohio. The Wyandots, Delawares, Shawnees, Ottawas, Chippewas, Pottawattomies, Miamis, Eel Rivers, Weas, Piankeshaws, Kickapoos and Kaskaskias, became parties to that treaty.

This treaty was followed by comparative peace for a period of sixteen years, and until about the year 1811, although in the meantime turbulent, revengeful and evil-disposed Indians frequently broke away from the different tribes and from the control of their principal chiefs and formed marauding parties, which from time to time committed all manner of murders, thefts and outrages on the frontier settlers of the northwest.

For a few years prior to the declaration of the War of 1812 between the United States and Great Britain, the relations between these two governments had been very much strained and it was generally considered that war was sure to ensue. In the meantime the British maintained numerous active and powerful agents among the Indians of the northwest for the purpose of supplying them with munition of war and creating discontent among them and inciting them to make war on the white settlers. Thus encouraged there was assembled under Tecumseh and his brother, the Prophet, at their camp at the junction of the Wabash and Tippecanoe rivers, in northwestern Indiana, a large number of turbulent and desperate Indians drawn from most of the various tribes east of the Mississippi. It was the purpose and hope of Tecumseh and his brother, and the Indians under their influence, by a united effort with the British forces, to drive the white people out of the territory of the northwest. These Indians thus assembled on the Upper Wabash, became very threatening and endeavored to deceive and surprise General Harrison, who was then governor of the Territory of Indiana with headquarters at Vincennes. Their actions and numbers were such as to make it prudent and even necessary that General Harrison should make a demonstration against them for the purpose of discovering their purpose and strength. This resulted in the Battle of Tippecanoe November 7th, 1811, at which battle the Indians were defeated, but not greatly dispirited, as they still relied greatly upon the looked for war between the United States and Great Britain when they would have the powerful aid of the British forces.

Tecumseh was not present at that battle and the Indians were under the command of his brother, the imposter Prophet. By this defeat the power which the Prophet had been exercising over his Indian followers was largely destroyed, and he was never afterwards in much favor.

The war which had long been threatening between the United States and Great Britain suddenly flamed into activity and war was declared on the part of the United States against Great Britain on June 18th, 1812. This was the opportunity the discontented and turbulent Indians of the northwest had long been waiting for. Tecumseh had before that time and in anticipation of it, concluded his alliance with the British forces, and the forces under him were already well prepared to join in active warfare. He was at the head of all the Indian forces in the northwest, and was by far the ablest war chief of his times and the ablest war chief which the Indian race has produced of which we have any accurate knowledge, unless it may be the great Pontiac of a half century before. He at once commenced a vigorous onslaught on the frontier military posts and frontier settlers, and with terrible effect.

Affairs went badly against the American forces for the first year after the declaration of war. On July 17th, 1812, Lieutenant Hanks, in command of Mackinac, was compelled to surrender the garrison, consisting of fifty-seven effective men, to the forces under the British commander at St. Joseph's, a British post near the head of Lake Huron.

On August 15th following, the massacre of the garrison at Fort Dearborn (Chicago) occurred, at which time between fifty and sixty United States soldiers were mercilessly murdered and the fort destroyed. This terrible slaughter in which the treacherous and blood-thirsty Black Hawk was engaged, was followed the next day (August 16th) by the cowardly and ignominious surrender of General Hull at Detroit, of about fifteen or sixteen hundred troops, to a greatly inferior number of British and Indians under General Brock of the English army.

By the first of September, 1812, the entire northwest, with the exception of Fort Harrison on the Wabash, and Fort Wayne on the Maumee, had been overrun and was in possession of the British and Indians, and these two forts were both besieged by hordes of savages. Fort Harrison with but fifty or sixty men under Captain Zachariah Taylor (then a young officer in the United States army and afterwards President of the United States) was heroically defended and the Indian hordes repelled. A like brilliant defense was made of Fort Wayne. The garrison was small, the Indians were in great numbers, the captain in command of the garrison was dissipated and incompetent, and was summarily deposed from command, which then devolved upon one Lieutenant Curtis, then a young officer in the United States army, who, by his heroic defense of the fort during the two weeks of unremitting siege, has recorded his name permanently in the annals of his time.

It was just at this discouraging and perilous time that General Harrison was appointed commander of all the forces in the northwest. He at once took most heroic measures to raise the siege at Fort Wayne and strengthen that garrison, and also to strengthen the garrison at Fort Harrison on the Wabash. This he accomplished and thereafter was able to maintain the lines of the Wabash and the Maumee, as the frontier between the American forces and the allied British and Indians. All beyond to the northwest was in the possession of the enemy.

But disasters to the American forces were not yet ended. On the 21st of January, 1813, General Winchester, who was in command of the forces on the Maumee, was defeated at the battle of the River Raisin by the combined forces of General Proctor and Tecumseh, and about 700 of his troops captured or destroyed. many of them being massacred after they had surrendered.

General Harrison was at the headquarters of the army at Upper Sandusky when he first heard that General Winchester, who was in command of the forces on the Maumee, intended to make an important military movement, the nature of which, however, he could not learn. No important offensive movement was contemplated by him at that time. On receiving this information he at once ordered forward all the troops then at Upper Sandusky, about 300 strong, and took a horse and rode to Lower Sandusky (Fremont) in all haste. Such was the energy with which he pushed forward over the terrible winter roads that the horse of his aid-de-camp failed and died under the exertion. At Lower Sandusky he learned that on the 17th of January, Colonel Lewis had been sent forward from the Rapids to the River Raisin in command of over 600 troops which was almost the entire available force on the Maumee. General Harrison's mind was filled with forebodings, and ordering the troops at Lower Sandusky forward to the Rapids, he again pushing forward for that place, where he arrived early on the 20th. Here he learned that General Winchester had gone forward to join his command at the river Raisin. There was nothing that could be done but wait for the troops which he had ordered forward from the Sanduskies, which were floundering along as best they could through the swamps of the wilderness. He did not have to wait long before he received the appalling news of the battle at the river Raisin, which was one of the most disasterous of all our Indian Wars.

The battle was fought on January 21st, the defeat was complete and overwhelming and Winchester's army was practically destroyed. This left the region of the Maumee entirely open to be overrun by the victorious British and Indians, and it was expected that they would soon make their appearance at the Rapids. A council of war was at once held, and it was determined to withdraw the remaining troops to Portage river, about twenty miles east from the Maumee. Here a camp was established and the troops which were struggling forward as well as the remnant of General Winchester's command were concentrated. Within a few days such a force had been assembled as to enable General Harrison to move back to the Maumee. He did not, however, resume possession of the old camp, Fort Miami, which had been occupied before by General Winchester's command, but a better place was selected some distance up the river from the old camp, and on the south side of the river where a strong fort was erected, which was named Fort Meigs in honor of the then governor of Ohio.

It was the intention to concentrate a force at Fort Meigs sufficient to maintain it against all attacks which might be made, but on account of the terrible roads through the wilderness, the expected recruits from Kentucky and Southern Ohio, did not arrive until the fort was besieged by the entire forces under Proctor and Tecumseh.

On the 1st day of April, 1813, the fort was invested on every side and an active siege was at once begun. The siege was carried on with great vigor, the Indians being incited to bravery by the promise of the monster General Proctor to deliver General Harrison into their hands should the siege be successful and the fort taken. However, after nine days of constant bombardment and conflict the siege failed and the British and Indian forces withdrew.

Immediately after the British and Indians had withdrawn from the Maumee, General Harrison hastened in person to southern and central Ohio to urge forward the troops that were being collected to meet and repel the British and Indian forces and drive them beyond the boundaries of the United States.

It was under these anxious and harassing circumstances that General Harrison came to Franklinton and held the conference with the chiefs of the Wyandots, Delawares, Shawanese and Senecas. The principal chiefs of these tribes had remained true to their obligations of neutrality under the Treaty of Greenville, but so many had been lured away from their tribal obligations by British pay and British bribes and promises, and such was their strength when commanded and guided by that able and energetic warrior Tecumseh that it became necessary for General Harrison to know as exactly as possible what proportion of the military strength of the powerful tribes would remain neutral, or if necessary join with the American forces. The chiefs assembled not only assured him that they would remain true to their obligations, but if called upon would join with the American forces against the British.

They were not called upon to take an active part in the war, but as a matter of fact several of the chiefs of these four great tribes with a considerable number of their warriors of their own volition accompanied General Harrison in his campaign, which ended in the decisive battle of the Thames. Chief Tarhe (the Crane), Grand Sachem of the Wyandots, whose village was then near Upper Sandusky, Wyandot county, and who was spokesman for all the tribes at the conference at Franklinton, although seventy-two years of age, went with General Harrison on foot with a number of his warriors to Canada, and was present at the Battle of the Thames, although he took no active part in that battle.

This conference or council at Franklinton enabled General Harrison to know what he could depend upon as to these four neutral tribes, and greatly relieved him from uncertainty and anxiety and also greatly relieved the frontier settlers from the apprehensions and fears with which their minds and hearts were filled.

From the date of that conference the tide turned strongly in favor of the American forces. The English and Indians were again in force along the Maumee and in July, 1813, again besieged Fort Meigs, but it had been so strengthened and reinforced that they made no assault upon it but retired after a few days, Proctor by water to Sandusky bay, and the Indians through the forest to Sandusky river. This demonstration was quite formidable both by land and water. Fort Stevenson at the mouth of the

Sandusky river, where the City of Fremont now stands, was first besieged. On July 31st, 1813, the British approached Fort Stevenson by water and landed about 500 British troops with some light artillery, while Tecumseh with about 2,000 Indians besieged the fort on the land side.

It is not our purpose here to narrate the history of that assault. Suffice it to say here that Major Croghan, in command of the fort with but 160 men in the garrison, successfully repelled the assault of the British and Indians and compelled them to retire after heavy losses. This brilliant victory was succeeded on August 10th by the celebrated and world renowned victory of Commodore Perry, by which the British fleet on Lake Erie was destroyed. This enabled General Harrison to move his army across Lake Erie to the Detroit river and to invade Canada.

On the 5th of October he was able to bring the allied forces under Proctor and Tecumseh to issue at the battle of the Thames, where a complete victory was gained over the allied forces. Tecumseh was killed in that battle and Proctor ignominiously fled the field. His army was captured or destroyed. The battle of the Thames and the death of Tecumseh practically ended the war in the northwest, although the British still held a few small forts like Mackinac and St. Josephs around the head of Lake Huron; but these were powerless of any offensive operations.

The war, however, between the United States and Great Britain continued in full force and destructiveness for more than a year after the battle of the Thames, during which time the commerce of both nations upon the high seas was largely ruined. In August, 1814, the British gained possession of the City of Washington and burned and destroyed all the public buildings and threatened further serious destructions. A year had now elapsed since the battle of the Thames, during which time quiet had reigned among the Indians in the northwest.

The neutral tribes of the northwest remained favorable to the cause of the United States, and many of those who had served under Tecumseh a year before had become angered and embittered toward the British for want of their fulfillment of their promises so lavishly made before the war, and were anxious to assist in the war against their former allies.

In this situation the government authorized and directed General Harrison and General Lewis Cass to meet the Indian tribes in conference at Greenville, Ohio, where the "Treaty of Greenville" had been concluded nineteen years before. Accordingly the commissioners met at that place with the chiefs of the Wyandots, Delawares, Shawanese, Senecas, Miamis, Pottawattomies and Kickapoos and concluded a treaty of peace as follows:

Article 2. The tribes and bands above mentioned, engage to give their aid to the United States, in prosecuting war against Great Britain, and such of the Indian tribes as still continue hostile, and to make no peace with either, without the consent of the United States.

The assistance herein stipulated for, is to consist of such a number of their warriors, from each tribe, as the president of the United States, or any officer having his authority therefor, may require.

Article 3. The Wyandot tribe, and the Senecas of Sandusky and Stony Creek, the Delaware and Shawanese tribes, who have preserved their fidelity to the United States, throughout the war, again acknowledge themselves under the protection of the said states, and of no other power whatever, and agree to aid the United States in the manner stipulated for in the former article, and to make no peace but with the consent of the said states.

Article 4. In the event of the faithful performance of the conditions of this treaty, the United States, will confirm and establish all the boundaries between their lands, and those of the Wyandots, Delawares, Shawanese, and Miamis, as they existed previously to the commencement of the war." Thus the Franklinton conference was embodied in treaty form.

No call was made for Indian help under this treaty, as on December 24th, 1814, the commissioners of the United States and the commissioners of Great Britain concluded the Treaty of Ghent, putting an end to the war. This second Treaty of Greenville was the last peace or war treaty ever entered into between the United States and any of the Indian tribes within the boundaries of the State of Ohio; and with the exception of an unimportant treaty concluded at Detroit the following year, the last made east of the Mississippi.

TARHE—THE CRANE

EMIL SCHLUP, UPPER SANDUSKY.

Probably no other Indian chieftain was ever more admired and loved by his own race or by the outside world. He was either a true friend or a true enemy. Born near Detroit, Michigan, in 1742, he lived to see a wonderful change in the great Northwest. Being born of humble parentage, through his bravery and perseverence, he rose to be the grand sachem of the Wyandot nation. This position he held until the time of his death, when he was succeeded by Duonquot. Born of the Porcupine clan of the Wyandots and early manifesting a warlike spirit, and was engaged in nearly all the battles against the Americans until the disastrous battle of Fallen Timbers, in 1794. Tarhe saw that there was no use opposing the American arms, or trying to prevent them planting corn north of the Ohio river. At that disastrous battle, thirteen chiefs fell and among the number was Tarhe, who was badly wounded in the arm. The American generally believed that the dead Indian was the best Indian, but Tarhe sadly saw his ranks depleted, and at once began to sue for peace. General Wayne had severely chastised the Indians, and forever broke their power in Ohio. Accordingly, on January 24, 1795, the principal chiefs of the Wyandots, Delawares, Chippewas, Ottowas, Sacs, Pottowattomies, Miamis, and Shawnees met. The preliminary treaty with General Wayne at Greenville, Ohio, in which there was an armistice, was the forerunner of the celebrated treaty which was concluded at the same place on August 3, 1795. A great deal of opposition was manifested to this treaty by the more warlike and turbulent chiefs, as this would cut off their forays on the border settlements.

Chief Tarhe always lived true to the treaty obligations which he so earnestly labored to bring about. When Tecumseh sought a great Indian uprising, Tarhe opposed it, and awakened quite an enmity among the warlike of his own tribe, who afterward withdrew from the main body of the Wyandots and moved to Canada. The Rev. James B. Finley had every confidence in Tarhe, as evidenced in 1800, when returning from taking a drove

of cattle to the Detroit market, he asked Tarhe for a night's lodging at Lower Sandusky, where the Wyandot chief then lived, and intrusted him with quite a sum of money from the sale of cattle, and the next morning every cent was forthcoming.

From 1808 until the War of 1812, Tarhe steadily opposed Tecumseh's treacherous war policy, which greatly endangered Tarhe's life, and it is claimed he came near meeting the same fate that Leather

CHIEF TARHE—THE CRANE.

Lips met on June 1, 1810. He even went so far as to offer his services with fifty other chiefs and warriors to General Harrison in prosecuting the war against Tecumseh and the English under General Proctor. He was actively engaged in the battle on the Thames. So earnest was he in the success of the American cause, so sincere did he keep all treaty obligations, that General Harrison in after years, in comparing him with other chiefs, was constrained to call him "The most noble Roman of them all."

Tarhe never drank strong drinks of any kind, nor used tobacco in any form. Fighting at the head of his warriors in Harrison's campaign in Canada, at the age of seventy-two years, is something out of the ordinary. Being tall and slender, he was nicknamed "The Crane." On his retiring from the second war for Independence, he again took up his abode in his favorite town — the spot is still called "Crane Town," about four and one-half miles northeast from Upper Sandusky, on the east bank of the Crane run, which empties into the Sandusky river. Here surrounded by a dense forest, he spent his old age in a log cabin, fourteen by eighteen feet. Just south of the old cabin site are a number of old apple trees, likely of the Johnny Appleseed origin— the fruit being small and hard; a short distance south of the cabin is the old gauntlet ground, oblong and about three hundred yards long; to the westward from the village site, is a clearing of about ten acres, still known as the Indian field, and still surrounded by a dense forest. Here Tarhe died in his log cabin home, in November, 1818. In 1850, John Smith, then owner of the land, had most all of the cabin taken down for fire-wood. At that time a small black walnut twig, about the thickness of a man's thumb, was growing in the northwest corner of the cabin, and is quite a tree at the present writing — a living and growing monument to the memory of the great and good Wyandot chief.

Aunt Sally Frost was Tarhe's wife when he died. To them one child was born, an idiotic son who died at the age of twenty-five years. Sally had been a captive from one of the border settlements, and refused to return to her people. After the death and burial of Tarhe, the principal part of Crane Town was moved to Upper Sandusky, the center of the Wyandot reservation twelve miles square. Here the government at Washington paid them an annuity of ten dollars per capita until the reservation reverted back to the government in March, 1842.

Cabin sites are plainly discernable in the old historic town, which was usually a half-way place between Fort Pitt and Detroit. Here in the early days Indian parties found a resting place when on their murderous missions to the border settlements. This was one of the "troublesome" Indian towns on the Sandusky river that the ill-fated Col. Wm. Crawford was directed against in the Spring of 1782. Traces of the old Indian trail may be seen meandering southward through the forest, where the war-whoop was frequently given and the bloody scalping knife drawn over many defenseless prisoners. The springs, just westward from the town site, are cattle tramped, but still bubble forth a small quantity of water, but likely not nearly so active as when they furnished the necessary water for the nations of the forest a century and more ago.

On June 11, 1902, Mr. E. O. Randall, the able and efficient Secretary of the Ohio State Archæological and Historical Society, in company with the writer, gave the place a visit. Numerous locusts were chirping away at their familiar songs, quite loud enough to drown out the voices of the intruders.

Jonathan Pointer, who had been a colored captive among the Wyandots and who was a fellow soldier with Tarhe in the Canadian campaign under General Harrison, returned with that celebrated chieftain to his home and stayed with him until the time of Tarhe's death, always claiming that he assisted in the burial of Tarhe on the John Smith farm, about a half mile southeast from his cabin home. Logs were dragged over the grave to keep the wild animals from disinterring the body. Jonathan Pointer was engaged as interpreter for the early missionaries among the Wyandots; he died in 1857. No memorial marks Tarhe's resting place. Red Jacket, Keokuk, Leather Lips, and other chieftains have received monumental consideration from American civilization; but Tarhe, the one whose influence and activity helped to wrest the great Northwest from the British and the Indians, has apparently been forgotten. And how long shall it be so?

Colonel John Johnson, who for nearly half a century acted Indian agent of the various tribes of Ohio and who made the last Indian treaty that removed the Wyandots beyond the Mississippi, was present at the great Indian council summoned at the death and for burial of Tarhe. The exact spot where the council house stood is not known, but a mile and a half north from Crane town site are a number of springs bubbling forth clear water which form Pointer's run, that empties into the Sandusky river. They are still called the Council Springs and the bark council house was likely in this vicinity. Colonel Johnson, in his "Recollections," gives the following account of the proceedings:

"On the death of the great chief of the Wyandots, I was invited to attend a general council of all the tribes of Ohio, the Delawares of Indiana, the Senecas of New York, at Upper Sandusky. I found on arriving at the place a very large attendance. Among the chieftains was the noted leader and orator Red Jacket from Buffalo. The first business done was the speaker of the nation delivering an oration on the character of the deceased chief. Then followed what might be called a monody, or ceremony, of mourning or lamentation. Thus seats were arranged from end to end of a large council house, about six feet apart, the head men and the aged took their seats facing each other, stooping down, their heads almost touching. In that position they remained for several hours. Deep and long continued groans would commence at one end of the row of mourners, and so pass around until all had responded, and these repeated at intervals of a few minutes. The Indians were all washed, and had no paint or decorations of any kind upon their persons, their countenances and general deportment denoting the deepest mourning. I had never witnessed anything of the kind before, and was told that this ceremony was not performed but on the decease of some great man. After the period of mourning and lamentation was over, the Indians proceeded to business. There were present the Wyandots, Shawnees, Delawares, Senecas, Ottawas and Mohawks. Their business was entirely confined to their own affairs, and the main topics related to their lands, and the claims of the respective tribes. It was evident, in the course of the discussion, that the presence of myself and people (there were some white men with me) was not acceptable to some of the parties, and allusions were made so direct to myself that I was constrained to notice them, by saying that I came there as a guest of the Wyandots, by their special invitation; that as the Agent of the United States, I had a right to be there as anywhere else in the Indian country; and that if any insult was offered to myself or my people, it would be resented and punished. Red Jacket was the principal speaker, and was intemperate and personal in his remarks. Accusations, pro and con, were made by the different parties, accusing each other of being foremost in selling land to the United States. The Shawnees were particularly marked out as more guilty than any other; that they were the last coming into the Ohio country and although they had no right but by the permission of the other tribes, they were always the foremost in selling lands. This brought the Shawnees out, who retorted through head chief, the Black Hoof, on the Senecas and Wyandots with pointed severity. The discussion was long continued, calling out some of the ablest speakers, and was distinguished for ability, cutting sarcasm and research, going far back into the history of the natives, their wars, alliances, negotiations, migrations, etc. I had attended many councils, treaties, and gatherings of the Indians, but never in my life did I witness such an outpouring of native oratory and eloquence, of severe rebuke, taunting national anl personal reproaches. The council broke up later in great confusion and in the worst possible feeling. A circumstance occurred toward the close which more than anything else exhibited the bad feeling prevailing. In handing round the wampum belt, the emblem of amity, peace and good will, when presented to one of the chiefs, he would not touch it with his fingers, but passed it on a stick to a person next to him. A greater indignity, agreeable to Indian etiquette could not be offered.

The next day appeared to be one of unusual anxiety and despondence among the Indians. They could be seen in groups everywhere near the council house in deep consultation. They had acted foolishly — were sorry — but the difficulty was, who would present the olive branch. The council convened very late, and was very full; silence prevailed for a long time; at last the aged chieftain of the Shawnees, the Black Hoof, rose — a man of great influence and a celebrated warrior. He told the assembly that they had acted like children, and not men yesterday; that

The picture of Mr. Schlup shows him standing beside the little log cabin which he recently presented to the Ohio State Archæological and Historical Society and which is now placed in its museum at Page Hall, Ohio State University. This little log cabin, almost toy-like in its size, has great historic interest attached to it. It is constructed of fifty different and distinct species of forest trees collected from the region immediately surrounding the scene of the burning of Colonel William Crawford by the Indians, in Crawford township, Wyandot County, June 11, 1782. The little cabin has greased muslin windows and is also provided with the historic latch-string. It is a faithful representation of the cabin constructed in the Western country during the period in which Colonel William Crawford lived. Mr. Emil Schlup built this unique cabin in the year 1904. He is a life member of the Ohio State Archæological and Historical Society and has contributed much valuable historical material to its publications.

he and his people were sorry for the words that had been spoken, and which had done so much harm; that he came into the council by the unanimous desire of his people, to recall those foolish words, and did there take them back — handing round strings of wampum, which passed around and were received by all with the greatest satisfaction. Several of the principal chiefs delivered speeches to the same effect, handing round wampum in turn, and in this manner the whole difficulty of the preceding day was settled, and to all appearances forgotten. The Indians are very civil and courteous to each other and it is a rare thing to see their assemblies disturbed by unwise or ill-timed remarks. I never witnessed it except upon the occasion here alluded to, and it is more than probable that the presence of myself and other white men contributed towards the unpleasant ocurrence. I could not help but admire the genuine philosophy and good *sense* displayed by men whom we call savages, in the transaction of their public business, and how much we might profit in the halls of our Legislatures, by occasionally taking for our example the proceedings of the great Indian council at Upper Sandusky."

THE CONQUEST OF THE INDIAN.

BENJAMIN R. COWEN, CINCINNATI.

[Portion of an address delivered by General Cowen on the 28th of June, 1904, at the placing of the tablet in commemoration of the Harrison-Tarhe Peace Conference.]

We have heard the story of the historic incident this monument is designed to commemorate eloquently told by the Regent

of the Columbus Chapter of the Daughters of the American Revolution. That society has rendered a valuable service in the erection of this unique memorial which commemorates what is not only an interesting incident in local history, but an important epoch in the history of the great Northwest Territory, while being at the same time an enduring landmark of our progress.

I have heard it suggested that inasmuch as woman has ostensibly little or nothing to do with government functions or with the wars, the hardships and the sacrifices of the race under primitive conditions she has no business meddling with them in any manner. Never was a greater error. True, war and border struggles and sacrifices are generally regarded as peculiar to the stronger sex from which woman is exempt. Yet war and sacrifice and hardship have been woman's burden since our first parents turned their backs on Eden. So that the women who have erected this memorial were strictly in the line of duty, and privilege, for women should have a place of honor wherever the hardships and the sacrifices of the race are held in grateful memory.

BENJAMIN R. COWEN.

'Tis said the doting pyramids have long forgotten the names of their builders. Here we have a monument eons old before those buildiers were born, yet to the eye of science the glacial hieroglyphics carved thereon tell the story of its antiquity and its endurance. We, the ephemera of a day, will soon pass from memory, but let us hope that this monument, in its indestructible character, may prove a type of the imperishable recollection of the event it is intended to commemorate and of the form of government to the establishment of which that event contributed.

In the mighty changes which have taken place since Harrison erected here a bulwark against a threatening barbarism the people of Ohio have had much to be proud of; much to be thankful for. In the intervening years Ohio has grown from 40,000 population to four millions and the Nation from eight millions to eighty millions, a growth so remarkable as to be without parallel in the world's history.

It is so customary, however, to give thanks for visible and tangible mercies and blessings, rather than for the escape from possible evils which have been averted that our expressions of gratitude for the former are so absorbing as to leave little room for thought of the latter.

We are all proud of our State and of her name and all that it implies of history and endeavor and achievement. Could we have been equally proud, think you, had the name once sought to be fixed on it been allowed to stand? I have my doubts.

It is a historic fact little known, to-day, that a Committee of the Continental Congress, March 1st, 1784, reported a scheme for the organization of the Northwest Territory which contemplated its division into nine States and prescribing the boundaries and the names of each. The territory now embraced in the State of Ohio was to be made into two states, the Northern to be called Washington and the Southern Polysipia. The only redeeming feature of the last name was that it was less objectionable than some of the other names proposed. Those names were: Sylvania, Michigania, Cheronessus, Asenisipia, Metropotamia, Illinoia, Saratoga, Polypotamia, Washington and Polysipia.

In reckoning our mercies let us not forget to return thanks that we are neither Polypotamians nor Polysipians, but plain Ohioans. The name Ohio is good enough for us.

Yet I have no doubt the wonderful achievements of the sons of this State during the past 100 years would even have popularized the name Polysipia and made it a name to conjure with as the name of Ohio is to-day.

This monument is intended to perpetuate an event in which both white men and Indians took part on a plane of perfect equality. The part borne by the Indians was not only highly creditable to them; it was of great advantage to the whites at a most critical period in our history. So that it seems appropriate to the occasion that I divide my time between the two races.

As the Indian has disappeared from the stage of action, however, we can only tell of his past. As the white man — the American — the Anglo-Saxon, so called, approaches the zenith of his powers, we may in some measure speak of his future.

But, through the glowing story of our pioneer struggles and successes runs a dark thread of shame in our treatment of the Indians which cannot be ignored in any fair narration of the story of the contact of the two races.

It was long an accepted maxim on the frontier that "the only good Indian is a dead one." But had an Indian Thucydides, smarting under the wrongs of his people, arisen to write a truthful story of his race on this continent I imagine the verdict of history might be different.

To civilize a race it would seem a wise policy to offer it such models as are pleasing and attractive and by as much as those models are superior to and more desirable than existing methods in so much will they be accepted.

The three civilizations — Spanish, French and English — which first came in contact with the North American Indian had respectively bloomed and given to the world as the ripe fruit of their culture and their faith the Inquisition, St. Bartholomew and the Bloody Assizes. The crimson annals of Indian warfare furnish no names so execrated for inhumanity as Torquemada, Catherine de Medicis and Lord Chief Justice Jeffreys. The Indian could not conceive, much less execute any tortures so exquisite, any crimes against humanity so horrible and unnatural, as were perpetrated under the forms of law in the lands of the several Christian sovereigns under whose broad seals of authority those pioneers of the New World had come to convert and to save.

Inflexible, merciless and selfish, and little adapted to attract simple, primitive natures yet it was those forms of civilization to which our aborigines were first introduced and which inaugurated the Indian policy which substantially prevailed on this continent ever since.

"Welcome, Englishmen," was the cordial greeting of the pagan Indian Samoset, as with the open hand of friendship he met the discouraged band of Christian pilgrims as they stepped ashore at Plymouth one bleak December day in 1620. For nearly 300 years, with mailed hand and the robber's plea, those civilized Christian Pilgrim-Puritans, so called, and their descendants, by robbery, murder, enslavement, debauchery, and every form of wrong which the devilish ingenuity of perverted religionists could devise, have given the response of Christian civilization to that pagan welcome.

Through all the colonial times since the first treaty when the Plymouth governor made old Massasoit drunk and stole his land, Indian treaties were made but to be broken, and from the first treaty made by our government, that with the Delawares at Fort Pitt in 1778, when that nation was cajoled into active alliance with the infant republic by the promise of a State organization and a representative in Congress, down to the latest treaty with the tribes huddled together on the arid lands of the far West — in all over 900 treaties, every one of the number was broken in one or more important particulars by the whites. And the same is true of all the contracts made with our predecessors, the French, the Spanish and the British.

In the treaty of peace of 1783 with Great Britain no mention was made of the native tribes and their rights in the soil, and no demand or request was made by Great Britain in their behalf, though she had been greatly aided during our Revolutionary War by her Indian allies.

Let me cite some authorities on the subject of the relative reliability of the two races:

Gen. Harney, of the army, said: "I never knew an Indian to break his word."

Again he said: "I have lived on this frontier fifty years, and I have never yet known an instance in which war broke out between the tribes and the government, that the tribes were not in the right."

Bishop Whipple said: "I have traveled on foot and on horseback over every square mile of my diocese. I have known every Indian settlement in it. I have watched them for a dozen years. Some of them will drink and some of them will steal, and they are of our race for they have our vices, but in every difficulty that has occurred in the twelve years of my residence between the Indians and the government, the government has been always wrong and the Indian has been always right."

In 1867 a celebrated council was held with the Sioux at which were Major Generals Sherman, Terry, Harney and Auger. The report of that council contained the following language:

"In every case of complication existing with the Indians at the date of our appointment and for several years previous to that time and which was investigated by us the cause of the difficulty was traced to the wrong doing of our own people, both civil and military."

Thus do men of war and men of peace, looking at the subject from different standpoints, reach the same conclusion.

All that the Indian ever knew of the justice of the Anglo-Saxon was the sharp edge of its sword; the equal balance of its scales he never saw.

On one occasion, while visiting the Quaker City in charge of a party of Ute Indians, the gentleman who was acting as our guide, took special pains to illustrate the character of William Penn, and pointed out the spot where his historic treaty was made, emphasizing his uniform justice and fairness to the Indians. Ouray, the head chief, a man of few words, listened quietly, and when the guide had finished said grimly: "Yes, Mr. Penn seems to have been a good man, and you say treated the red man right. His children are many and rich, and their lodges are crowded like the leaves of the forest; but where are the Indians?"

The battle of Little Big Horn where General Custer and his command were exterminated is cited as an evidence of Indian cruelty in war, but which was the attacking party, and where was the battle field? That fight was in broad daylight, and far within the lines of the Indian reservation. It was horrible in the result — only less so than some other incidents I shall cite. The army under Custer had followed the Indians to their homes and made the attack, resulting in the total destruction of the army.

"You defend yourselves savagely," said Alexander to the barbarians of India.

"Sir, if you but knew how sweet freedom is you would defend it even with axes," was the reply.

But acts of cruelty are not confined to the red men in their contact with the whites.

King Philip, of Pokanoket, was killed after a long and stubborn resistance. His body was quartered and his head exposed on a gibbet at Plymouth for twenty years.

In the rear of General Hancock's army in Kansas, an Indian woman was found scalped.

I have myself seen Indian scalps displayed as trophies of war by our soldiers and frontiersmen.

In a fight between our soldiers and the Cheyennes in 1878, one man and thirteen women and children were killed.

In the same year a great many horses and all the women and children were killed by our soldiers in a fight with the Bannocks.

In April, 1871, at Camp Grant, in Arizona, 118 women and children and eight men, peaceable, unarmed, and under government protection were murdered and mutilated by a band of white men from Tucson.

At Sand Creek, Colorado, in 1864, Indian men, women and children were butchered in cold blood, infants were scalped in derision, and men were tortured and mutilated in the most horrible manner. The result was an Indian war that cost us 30 million of dollars.

In January, 1870, 173 men, women and children of the Piegan tribe in Montana, suffering severely with the smallpox, were butchered in cold blood by our troops under Colonel Baker, of the 2d Cavalry. But 15 of the victims were men of fighting age.

This disgraceful affair was ostensibly to avenge the killing of a white man in a drunken brawl at Fort Benton, some time before, but the murder was found to have been committed by an Indian of another tribe.

It was my official duty to investigate some of these cases, so that I speak as one having knowledge. Is it strange that Indians should imitate such example?

"The villiany you teach me I will execute," said Shylock, "and it shall go hard, but I will better the instruction."

It is a fact, however, that the origin of our serious troubles with the Indian in later years was almost uniformily traceable to the encroachments and the impositions of the white settlers. After the trouble was precipitated by those encroachments the protection of the army was invoked and the natural result was that the punishment was swift and terrible. But the army was only the avenger never the instigator.

On the other hand, in Minnesota, in 1862, during the massacre, every Christian Indian remained friendly to the whites.

One Indian conducted a large party through the worst part of the massacre to safety. Another conducted 25 men and 42 women and children to St. Paul.

During the hearing of the celebrated Cherokee case in the U. S. Supreme Court Wm. Wirt made use of the following language: "We may gather laurels on the field of battle and trophies on the ocean, but they will never hide this blot on our escutcheon. 'Remember the Cherokee Nation,' will be answer enough to the proudest boast we can make."

Thus did the Anglo-Saxon civilization manifest itself through the passing years of our history. It has been the same old robber plea, that —

> "He shall take who has the power,
> And he shall keep who can."

During the years from 1869 to 1877 I visited, in an official capacity, every important Indian tribe in the country, both in the interior and on the Pacific coast, including some that were considered hostile, without military escort or armed guard, and was never disturbed or threatened. I passed in and out among them with impunity, and was never conscious that I was in any special danger.

If I have dwelt too long on this branch of my subject in defence of the Indian character attribute it to my pronounced conviction derived from personal contact and varied experience, and to the fact that there are few left to say a word in that behalf.

He is as amenable to fair treatment as any race of which I have knowledge.

It was a stereotyped phrase in Indian treaties for many years that the lands named therein were solemnly guaranteed to the Indian to be his home "While grass grows and water runs." The ground we walk to-day was thus granted, and every tender blade that meets the quickening breath of spring and every drop in your beautiful river as it runs to the sea are silent but eloquent witness of our perfidy toward that unfortunate people.

What has been said relates to events and policies of the past which may not be changed. The story of the vanished race can interest us now chiefly as it marks our progress. We are too busy striving to reach "the regions beyond" to pause beside its dishonored graves long enough to drop a tear.

Barbarism could not be allowed to occupy this fair domain forever. My criticism on the policy which prevailed in respect of the Indian is that it was a war against barbarians rather than against barbarism. The latter has no rights civilization is bound to respect; the former may have.

The effort to elevate and assimilate came too late, and never had a fair trial. Our policy and our contact brutalized and degraded the race before any real effort was made to elevate it.

Ninety-one years ago this place was the remote frontier, the skirmish line of our civilization. Since the day of Harrison's council that frontier has been pushed westward until it has disappeared from the continent. With it have gone those men of blood and iron who conquered the wilderness. Heroes of an heroic age were they, so grim and stalwart and unyielding they might have stalked from out the age of chivalry and romance; from ancient tombs in dusty crypts of old world cathedrals, to greet the sun of this New World with eager eyes, the lurid light of battle on their brows.

Yet the type is preserved in our magnificent youth who are battling on other frontiers. Wherever they go with their modern equipment of zeal and knowledge and skill and courage, battling for modern ideas, there is their frontier, and there they are already winning new victories.

What is the significance of this progress — this attitude — these conditions?

Before the 20th century shall have filled out its first decade this continent will in all human probability, have changed front, so to speak, and the busy human ambitions which now make Europe an armed camp will be transferred, or at least duplicated in the Far East — in Asia and Africa. Those continents are rapidly breaking to pieces. Their long centuries of stagnation are to be replaced by a healthier and more vigorous moral atmosphere. There a field offers for the wholesome civilization, the boundless resources, the commercial courage and the high moral purpose of the Anglo-Saxon. And by Anglo-Saxon I mean that composite product which controls this continent to-day and which should be called American.

The same spirit which drew our forebears to the fulfillment of their destiny during that stirring and picturesque era as they skirmished and battled with the wilderness and the savage, writing the nation's epic, is drawing the splendid young men of to-day to other and far distant fields where they find something to conquer — that is their Frontier.

THE ORDINANCE OF 1787.

SOME INVESTIGATIONS AS TO THE AUTHORSHIP OF THE FAMOUS SIXTH ARTICLE.

COL. W. E. GILMORE, CHILLICOTHE.

Senator Roberts, of Pennsylvania, in the great debate over the bill for the admission of Missouri to the Union, in 1820, characterized the Ordinance of 1787 as "that immortal Ordinance which, with its elder sister, the Declaration of American Independence, will shed eternal and inextinguishable lustre over the annals of our country."

Daniel Webster, in a speech upon the Foote Resolution (1829), said: "We are accustomed to praise the law-givers of antiquity; we help to perpetuate the fame of Solon and Lycurgus; but I doubt whether one single law of any law-giver, ancient or modern, has produced effects of more distinct, marked and lasting character than the Ordinance of 1787."

Salmon P. Chase, in his preface to his Statutes at Large of Ohio, says of it: "Never in the history of the world did a measure of legislation so accurately fulfill, and yet so mightily exceed, the expectation of the legislators."

"Whatever," said Senator George F. Hoar in his magnificent oration at the Marietta Centennial Celebration, "whatever of these gifts nature has not given, is to be traced directly to the institutions of civil and religious liberty the wisdom of your fathers established; above all in the great Ordinance of 1787. 'The spirit of the Ordinance pervades all these States' (of the Northwest). Here was the first human government under which absolute civil and religious liberty has *always* prevailed. Here, no witch or wizard was ever hanged or burned. Here, no heretic was ever molested. Here, no slave was ever born or dwelt.

"When older States and nations, where the chains of human bondage have been broken, shall utter the proud boast, 'with a great sum obtained I this freedom'; each sister of the imperial group — Ohio, Michigan, Indiana, Illinois and Wisconsin — may lift her queenly head with the yet prouder answer, 'but I was free-born!' "

The rays of the resplendent glory of having originated and pushed into legislation the Ordinance of 1787 illuminate many names, but chiefly concentrate upon those of Thomas Jefferson, of Virginia, Rufus King and Nathan Dane, of Massachusetts; and in lesser degree, William Grayson, of Virginia, and Timothy Pickering, of Pennsylvania. To make a just, equitable and truthful partition of this glory is the object of this paper.

It is wonderful, and it excites curious reflections upon the reliability of history, that there has been so much and such various assertion upon a matter as yet but a little over a century old, and which concerns *national* legislation!

Not only have Jefferson, King, Grayson and Dane, in turn, in Congress and otherwise, been glorified as *the one* to whom *all* the honor belongs — particularly for the VIth Article of the Ordinance; the article which forever prohibited slavery in the Territory northwest of the river Ohio, and the States to be carved out of it — but Rev. Dr. Manasseh Cutler is now, in 1888, vehemently asserted to have been the great benefactor of all the Northwest, in that he wrote that article and secured its passage through the Old Congress, through Dane.

And this latest, and too late claimant for the honor, finds supporters in such reputable writers as Dr. Hinsdale (in his "Old Northwest"), Hon. Daniel J. Ryan (History of Ohio, 1888), and Dr. William E. Poole, President of the American Historical Association, (Address of December 26, 1888, at the Fifth Annual Meeting of the Society), and a number of others.

Well may the Hon. Rufus King, of Cincinnati, in his recently published volume Ohio, of the American Commonwealth series, exclaim: "This subject seems to have fallen under that morbid infirmity in literature which delights in denying Homer and Shakespeare their works; and has not spared even the Holy Scriptures!"

Several of the original thirteen States claimed ownership in lands outside of their present State lines, in 1780. That Congress might legislate for the government of these Territories, it was necessary these States should quit claim them to the National Government. This was done in the following order:

In 1781, New York limited and defined her northern and western boundaries and ceded all her claims to lands outside of the lines so established.

In 1784, Virginia likewise ceded all her claims to territory northwest of the Ohio river.

In 1785, Massachusetts ceded all her claims to territory to the west of her prescribed boundaries.

And in 1786, Connecticut ceded her claim to a portion of the territory west of the Ohio river.

It is to be noted that the subject of negro slavery was so little considered in those times, that no one of these deeds of cession contained any exclusion of that domestic institution, or even any restriction of it whatever. Nevertheless, there were individual men, both North and South, as we will see, whose consciences were awakened and impressed by the moral wrongfulness and political impolicy of slavery, and the inconsistency of maintaining it in this country, in the face of the grand democratic doctrines of the Declaration of Independence.

First, in point of time, and most famous of these, was Thomas Jefferson, of Virginia, himself a slave owner.

On the 19th of April, 1784, immediately after the cession of Virginia's claims to the territory, he, as chairman of a committee appointed for the purpose, of which committee Mr. Chase, of Maryland, and Mr. Howell, of Rhode Island, were the other members, reported to Congress a "Plan of Government" for the Territories. In this plan for the first time appeared a clause intended, first, to limit and restrict, and then extinguish and exclude negro slavery from the Northwestern Territories and States to grow out of them. It has always been accepted as a fact that Jefferson was the author of that clause.

Upon the motion of Mr. Speight, of North Carolina, these words were stricken out of the reported plan: "That after the year 1800 of the Christian era, there shall be neither slavery nor involuntary servitude in any of the States" (to be organized thereafter under the provisions of the 'Plan') "otherwise than in punishment of crime whereof the party shall have been convicted to have been personally guilty."

Much controversy occurred in after years as to whether the legislation which ultimately excluded slavery from the Northwest had been attained despite the opposition of the old slaveholding States, or by their willing assent and co-operation. Therefore I give the vote by individuals and States upon the motion of Mr. Speight to strike out the above clause, noting the fact that it required two votes to have a State counted, and therefore New Jersey, then represented on this vote by Mr. Dick only, did not count, nor did North Carolina, whose vote was divided.

The question was presented by the formula "Shall the words moved to be stricken out, stand?" And the vote was:

New Hampshire — Foster, aye; Blanchard, aye. The State, aye.

Massachusetts — Gerry, aye; Partridge, aye, The State, aye.

Rhode Island — Ellery, aye; Howell, aye. The State, aye.

Connecticut — Sherman, aye; Wadsworth, aye. The State, aye.

New York — DeWitt, aye; Paine, aye. The State, aye.

New Jersey — Dick, aye. Only one vote.

Pennsylvania — Hand, aye; Mifflin, aye; Montgomery, aye. The State, aye.

Maryland — McHenry, aye; Stone, aye. The State, aye.

Virginia — Jefferson, aye; Hardy, no; Mercer, no. The State, no.

North Carolina — Williamson, aye; Speight, no. The State, no.

South Carolina — Reed, no; Beresford, no. The State, no.

And so the necessary number of States (at that time seven) not having voted to retain the clause, it was stricken out.

It is only fair to say that Southern statesmen always insisted that it was stricken out only because not accompanied with a provision for the rendition of fugitive slaves, as provided for afterwards in the Constitution of the United States.

In the next year Timothy Pickering wrote to Rufus King, of Massachusetts, (March 8th, 1775), "For God's sake, then, let one more effort be made to prevent so terrible a calamity"— (*i. e.,* as the introduction of slavery). "It will be infinitely easier to prevent the evil at first than to eradicate it, or check it at any future time."

Moved by such appeals, and his own opposition to the institutions of slavery, Mr. King accordingly moved to commit the consideration of the subject of Jefferson's rejected clause to a committee for report. The motion was seconded by Mr. Ellery, of Rhode Island, and prevailed. Mr. King, Mr. Ellery and Mr. Howell were appointed to constitute the committee, and on the 6th of April, 1785, made their report to Congress.

This report, which was in the handwriting of Mr. King, recommended the adoption of a resolve or ordinance, in the nature of a supplement to the "Plan of Government," by Mr. Jefferson — which had passed Congress after the elimination of the slavery restriction clause — and was in the words following: "That there shall be neither slavery nor involuntary servitude in any of the states described in the resolve of April 23d, 1784, otherwise than in punishment of crime whereof the party shall have been personally guilty; *and that this regulation shall be an article of compact, and remain a fundamental principle of the Constitution between the thirteen original states, and each of the states described in said resolve of April 23, 1784.*"

This proposition, so far as we can ascertain, was never voted upon by Congress. Bancroft's History of the Constitution says that it was never called up. (Vol. 1, pp. 179-180). It is to be noted that it differed from the clause of Mr. Jefferson's "Plan," in that it made the exclusion of slavery *immediate* as well as perpetual; and asserted the regulation to be a compact between the future states and the original thirteen.

Southern members of Congress in the debate on the Missouri Bill afterwards scouted the idea of a compact made between a tract of territory having, as yet, no inhabitants, with the thirteen states.

Mr. King's motion to raise the committee of which he was chairman, was made in March, and upon that motion, of course, a vote was taken; the report of the committee was made on April 6th, as stated. This explanation will untangle the confusion of statements which have been made in regard to the "vote upon King's proposition," and also of dates.

But although Mr. King's report was not acted upon at the time, the subject was not forgotten. The Indian titles to parts of the territory northwest of the Ohio river were being rapidly extinguished, and that fair region was being made ready for the occupation of white settlers. By the treaty of Fort Stanwix — 1784 — the six nations quit-claimed to the United States all their right to territory west of the Ohio river.

In January, 1785, the Wyandots, Delawares, Ottawas and Chippewas did the same, as to all the lands they respectively claimed, bordering on the Ohio river.

And finally, the warlike and dangerous Shawnees yielded to the United States all their claims to lands lying east of the Great Miami river.

The "Ohio Company of Massachusetts" was organized in Boston, in March, 1786. A year was allowed within which to obtain the necessary amount of subscriptions to the stock of the company; and on March 8th, 1787, at a meeting of the stockholders held in Boston, Samuel H. Parsons, Rufus Putnam and Rev. Manasseh Cutler were chosen to be directors of the company and charged to make application to Congress — the "Old Congress" — for the purchase of lands to suit the purposes of the company.

On the 9th of May, the memorial of Mr. Parsons, bearing date the 8th, was presented, and referred to a committee consisting of Edward Carrington, Rufus King, Nathan Dane and Egbert Benson. From the 11th of May to the 4th of July, there was no quorum of Congress present, and consequently no action upon any subject. On the 5th of July Manasseh Cutler arrived in New York, where the Congress was then holding its session, to urge the business of the company. On the 10th, the report of the committee appointed on the Parsons memorial, on the 9th of May, was made, submitting a plan to meet the wishes of the Ohio Company, and it was made the "order of the day" for the 11th. It is not my purpose to follow the history of the Ohio Company, but have stated this much of it, firse because the agents of that company, by their urgence of its business, hastened the action of Congress in passing the ordinance of 1787; and secondly, for the purpose of inquiring into the claim now made, that Manasseh Cutler proposed the VIth clause of that ordinance.

On the 9th day of July, 1787, the subject of forming a government for the territory northwest of the Ohio river was again taken up. It must be remembered that Mr. Jefferson's "Plan of Government" had, except the slavery clause, been adopted, and was still an ordinance in force; and that Mr. King's report of April 6th, 1785, had as yet, not been acted upon. On the 9th, when the subject was again taken up, the whole subject was referred for report to a new committee, or reformed committee, consisting of Carrington, of Virginia; Dane, of Massachusetts; R. H. Lee, of Virginia; Kean, of South Carolina, and Smith, of New York.

They were, of course, familiar with all the precedent discussions of the matter, and were therefore able to submit their report of an ordinance as early as the 11th, upon which day it was read for the first time; its second reading on the 12th; and its third reading, and enactment on July 13th, 1787.

It repealed the Jefferson "Plan" of 1784. There were eight states present — it is to be remembered that all voting in the old Congress was by states — and the vote upon the passage of the bill was as follows:

Massachusetts — Holton, aye; Dane, aye, As a State, aye.

New York — Smith, aye; Harring, aye; Yates, no. As a State, aye.

New Jersey — Clark, aye; Sherman, aye. As a State, aye.

Delaware — Kearney, aye; Mitchel, aye. As a State, aye.

Virginia — Grayson, aye; R. H. Lee, aye; Carrington, aye. As a State, aye.

North Carolina — Blount, aye; Hawkins, aye. As a State, aye.

South Carolina — Kean, aye; Huger, aye. As a State, aye.

Georgia — Few, aye; Pearce, aye. As a State, aye.

And so, "It was resolved in the affirmative," says the annals of Congress, volume 4, page 754.

It will be observed there were four states from the north of the Potomac, and an equal number from the south of it, represented by this vote. Yet every state voted for its passage, and every delegate but one, and he was from the northern state of New York.

At this point I quote from the journal of Rev. Manasseh Cutler, asking that the dates be observed:

"July 10th, 1787. As Congress was now engaged in settling the form of government for the Federal territory, for which a bill had been prepared and a copy sent to me with leave to make remarks and propose amendments, I thought this a favorable opportunity to go to Philadelphia." It appears from this journal that he did, on that day, leave New York, (where Congress was in session) and did not return until the 16th, three days after the adoption of the ordinance as it now stands.

Now, be it remembered, also, that the VIth Article — the anti-slavery clause for which the credit is claimed for him — was not contained in the bill until it was actually passed on the 13th, when Mr. Dane, joyfully astonished at the unanimous vote given to the bill, took instant advantage of the magnanimous mood which prevailed among the delegates, and added the VIth Article, which went through by the same vote by which the balance of it had just passed.

Mr. Cutler was then in Philadelphia.

It is very probable that Mr. Cutler had suggested, as his journal quite plainly asserts, the portion of the IIIrd Article which relates to "religion, morality and knowledge being necessary to good government and the happiness of mankind," etc. As a minister of the Gospel, he would be likely to make some such suggestions; but we think it clear that he was not the author of the VIth Article.

I am indebted to Hon. Rufus King, of Cincinnati, (grandson of Hon. Rufus King, of Massachusetts, so often herein mentioned) for leave to copy and use the following interesting letter, only recently discovered by Mr. King, in which Mr. Dane, writing to Mr. King, of Massachusetts, under date of July 16th, 1787 — only three days after the adoption of the Ordinance, says:

"When I drew the Ordinance (which passed as I originally formed it, a few words excepted) I had no idea the states would agree to the VIth Article, prohibiting slavery, as only Massachusetts of the Eastern states was present; and therefore omitted it in the draft. But finding the House favorably disposed on this subject, after we had completed the other parts, I moved this article, which was agreed to without opposition."

And long afterwards, when in 1830 he published the IX volume of his compilation of the laws of the various states, known as "Dane's Abridgement," in an appendix to his volume, he made an elaborate defense of his title to authorship of the Ordinance, as against the attacks of Benton, of Missouri, and Hayne, of South Carolina, made in the debate upon the "Foote Resolutions," in the course of which he says: "The VIth Article of the compact (the slave article) is imperfectly understood. Its history is, that in 1784 a committee, consisting of Mr. Jefferson, Mr. Chase and Mr. Howell, reported it as a part of 'the Plan' of 1784. This, (part) Congress struck out; only two members south of Pennsylvania supported it. All north of Maryland, present, voted for it, so as to exclude slavery.

"It was imperfect, too, first, in that it admitted slavery *until the year 1800;* second, in that it admitted slavery in very considerable parts of the territory forever; as will appear in a critical examination, especially in the parts owned for ages by French Canadians and other inhabitants. * * * In this ordinance of '87 slavery is excluded forever, from every part of the whole 'territory of the United States, northwest of the river Ohio.'

"The amended slave article, as it is in the ordinance of '87, was added upon the author's (Mr. Dane's) motion; but as the journals show, was not so reported.

"In the seventh volume (of the abridgment) published in 1824, full credit is given to Mr. Jefferson and Mr. King on account of their slave articles." * * *

Further on in Mr. Dane's statement, from which I am now quoting, he says:

"The author (Mr. Dane) took from Mr. Jefferson's resolve of '84, in substance, the six provisions in the IVth Article of the Compact. He took the words of the slave article from Mr. King's motion made in 1785, and extended its operation as to time and extent of territory * * * he (*i. c.,* Mr. Dane) furnished the provisions respecting impairing contracts, the Indian security and some other smaller matters; and the residue he selected from existing laws."

Such is Nathan Dane's own statement as to the history of this most important legislation. He says he took the VIth Article in substance from Rufus King — not from Manasseh Cutler. He claims as entirely his own, the provisions that neither the Territorial Legislature, nor the Legislatures of any of the states to be erected on the soil of the territory, should, by *ex post facto* enactments, impair the obligations of existing contracts; securing to the Indians their rights in their own lands and other property, and guaranteeing to them immunity from invasion and disturbance except during lawful war, "and some other smaller matters." He fully admits Mr. Jefferson's large share in forming or suggesting its most important provisions; and that much of the balance was selected from the code of Massachusetts.

Such is the true history of this important legislation. Daniel Webster was mistaken in his statement, made in the debate on Foote's resolution in 1829 to the effect that "this great measure was carried by the North and the North alone," for as the vote shows, as many Southern states voted for it as did Northern states.

Thomas Benton was disengenuous, when he asserted, in the same debate, that "that ordinance was first drawn by Mr. Jefferson, two years before Mr. Dane came into Congress;" as the foregoing narration fairly proves.

The truth is, that the great ordinance, like almost every important and permanent legislative enactment, grew; gradually accreting the best suggestions of Jefferson, King, Dane; and doubtless also Grayson, Carrington, R. H. Lee, Pickering, and other grand men of that day, whose noble natures would not allow them to claim for themselves, as God-given natural rights, "life, liberty and the pursuit of happiness;" and yet deny that these blessings were equally the rights of negroes and their descendants.

It is certain that the Northwestern states first, and then, consequently, the United States of America as a whole; including all the future commonwealth yet to be represented by stars in the blue field of "Old Glory," have reasons — abounding and ever increasing reasons — to be grateful to the statesmen who enacted the Ordinance of 1787; and so "may all the people praise them."

INDIAN BOUNDARY LINE.

W. S. HANNA, MILLERSBURG.

The Indian Boundary Line, sometimes known as the Greenville Treaty Line, or Wayne's Treaty Line, had its origin in the closing events of the Revolutionary War. As an historical land mark it has no equal in the early history of this country. Around its history cling many of the most stubborn and sanguinary conflicts and border outrages, that so distinctly marked the closing of the eighteenth century.

On every good map of Ohio it will be noticed that a line starts on the northern boundary of Tuscarawas county, and passes in a south of west direction through the county of Holmes and on across the State to the counties of Shelby and Mercer. What is this line? Why is it there? Who established it, and when, are the frequent inquiries made, and which have not been heretofore answered in such form as to come within reach of the general reading public. To briefly answer these questions, in such form as will reach the general public, is the sole apology for the preparation of this article.

At the close of the Revolution, by the treaty of Paris completed on September 3, 1783, Great Britain relinquished all her rights to the territory claimed by the thirteen original colonies, and recognized the sovereignty of the United States of America. The treaty of Paris did not extinguish whatever title the Indians claimed to have within the colonies. And in order to establish perpetual peace with the Indian tribes the Continental Congress appointed Oliver Wolcott, Richard Butler and Arthur Lee as commissioners to make such treaty with the Indians as would extinguish their title to the lands in the Northwest Territory. The commissioners proceeded to Fort Stanwix, New York, and there met the representatives of the Iroquois or Six Nations, who claimed to have conquered all the western tribes and on October 22, 1784, entered into a treaty whereby the Iroquois relinquished all their pretended claims and titles to the lands north and west of the river Ohio. This treaty was approved by the Continental Congress, but it was learned soon thereafter that the Iroquois had falsely made claim to title to lands in the Northwest Territory, and that their intrusion into said country had proved fruitless to them.

Thereupon the Continental Congress appointed George Rogers Clark, Richard Butler and Arthur Lee as commissioners to meet the Indians claiming title to the lands in the western country, and make, if possible, a treaty extinguishing their title to the same. The commissioners at once proceeded to Fort McIntosh, at the mouth of Big Beaver Creek, in western Pennsylvania. Here they met representatives of the Delawares, Wyandots and other tribes, who, on January 31, 1785, entered into a treaty with said commissioners whereby said Indian tribes relinquished all their right and title to all the lands situated south and east of a line commencing at the mouth of the Cuyahoga River, thence up said river to the portage between the Cuyahoga and the Tuscarawas, thence across said portage and down the Tuscarawas to the "Crossing Place" above Fort Laurens, near where Bolivar now stands; thence in a westerly direction to the portage between the Great Miami and Auglaize, near where stood Loramie's store; thence down the Auglaize and Maumee to Lake Erie.

This treaty was afterward confirmed by the Continental Congress under the mistaken belief that the Indian title to the lands had been completely extinguished, to the territory covered by the treaty. In pursuance to this belief, on May 20, 1785, Congress passed an act providing for the survey and sale of the lands northwest of the Ohio river, to which the Indian title had been extinguished. As soon as this work was commenced, the powerful Shawnee tribes appeared on the scene and contested the right of Congress to lay claim to the lands in which they had an interest. This resistance by the Shawnees caused Congress to appoint another commission consisting of George Rogers Clark, Richard Butler and Samuel H. Parsons, who met the Shawnee chiefs at Fort Finney near the mouth of the Great Miami, where, on January 31, 1786, a treaty was signed by the terms of which the Shawnees relinquished their title to all their lands lying east and south of the line established by the treaty of Fort McIntosh with the Delawares and Wyandots.

Again it was believed that peace had been permanently established between the western tribes and the United States. Emigration commenced to move rapidly toward the Ohio country, only to be again annoyed by Indian resistance and merciless butcheries. As an excuse for these depredations, the confederate tribes of the northwest joined in a powerful remonstrance to Congress in December, 1786, wherein it was claimed that the treaties above named were only partial treaties and did not bind the several tribes which took no part in the several conventions, and sought to justify their right to the whole country northwest of the Ohio, by virtue of the old treaty of Fort Stanwix, made in 1768 with the British Government.

The Continental Congress had now become exasperated at the unfaithfulness and treachery of the confederate tribes, and in order to meet the remonstrances squarely, determined to establish civil government in the Northwest Territory at the earliest time possible. The ordinance of 1787 was passed and Arthur St. Clair was appointed Governor. He arrived at Marietta on July 9, 1788, and on July 27 issued his proclamation establishing Washington county with the following boundaries: Beginning at the Ohio river where the western boundary of Pennsylvania crosses the same; thence north to Lake Erie; west to the mouth of the Cuyahoga river; thence up said river, across the portage to the Tuscarawas and down that river to the crossing place above Fort Laurens; thence west to that branch of the Great Miami on which stood the fort taken by the French in 1752; thence south to the Scioto river; thence with said river and up the Ohio to the place of beginning. Officers were appointed by the governor and an attempt to establish civil government in the county was made.

This attempt to establish civil government seemed to incite rather than allay the infractions by the Indians. And Governor St. Clair found it necessary to make a further attempt to establish peace, and called the chiefs of the various confederate tribes together at Fort Harmar, where on January 9, 1789, he succeeded in obtaining separate treaties confirming the treaties made at Fort McIntosh and Fort Finney.

These separate compacts were no more effective than those that preceded them. Indian depredations continued, even more cruel than before. Congress now realized that the only means left by which peace could be secured and the settlers protected, was by force of arms. An expedition was sent against the treacherous savages in 1790 under General Harmar which met with defeat; and another was sent out in 1791 under Governor St. Clair which met the same fate. General Wayne was then placed in command, and in August, 1794, at the "Battle of Fallen Timbers," he administered such a stinging rebuke to the Indian Confederacy and its British allies that they never recovered, and Indian conspiracy in the northwest came to an end.

As a direct result of the victory of General Wayne, he repaired to Fort Greenville in what is now Darke county. There the principal chiefs of the confederate tribes assembled, and on August 5, 1795, a treaty was consummated which extinguished forever the Indian title to the lands in the Northwest Territory situated south and east of the boundary line described as follows: Beginning at the mouth of the Cuyahoga river; thence up said river to the portage; thence across said portage and down the Tuscarawas branch of the Muskingum to the crossing place above Fort Laurens; thence in a westerly direction to that branch of the Great Miami at or near which stood Loramie's store; thence northwest to Fort Recovery; thence in a southerly direction to the mouth of the Kentucky river.

President Washington, on December 9, 1795, reported Wayne's Treaty by special message to the United States Senate, which afterward confirmed the same.

The gateway to the northwest was now open, and on May 18, 1796, Congress enacted a law providing for the survey of the outlines of the territory recently acquired from the Indians, and among other things provided for the appointment of a surveyor general, who was given power to appoint the necessary number of deputy surveyors and administer the oath to them. Another provision in said law was that the cost of surveying said outlines should not exceed three dollars per mile.

The surveyor general appointed one Israel Ludlow a deputy surveyor under said law, and he was assigned the task of surveying the line agreed upon by Wayne's Treaty, and which had been the subject of contention for so many years.

How Ludlow performed this task is herewith given, much of which has been taken from his report of the survey to the government.

The survey was under the personal direction of Israel Ludlow, Deputy Surveyor of the United States. The chain carriers were William C. Schenck and Israel Shreeve, both of whom were duly sworn by the deputy surveyor.

A random line was first surveyed in order to ascertain the true course of the Indian Boundary. This random line was commenced on Sunday, June 18, 1797, at a sycamore tree four feet in diameter standing at the fork of that branch of the Great Miami river near which stood Loramie's store, with the magnetic bearing of N. 4 degrees and 5 minutes E.; thence due east 131 miles and 50 chains to the Muskingum river, which was 8 chains wide; thence up said Muskingum river with the meanderings thereof 4 miles, 56 chains and 50 links to the confluence of the White Woman and the Tuscarawas; thence up the Tuscarawas branch with the meanderings thereof to a point opposite Fort Laurens; thence across said river to said fort; thence up said river about two miles to the "crossing place," above said fort, "which was the place named in the late treaty by General Wayne as a place from where a line is to run to that fork of the north branch of the Great Miami at or near where stood Loramie's store."

The courses and distances up the Muskingum and the Tuscarawas are given in Ludlow's notes. From the survey of this random line, Ludlow determined that the bearing of the line connecting the crossing place above Fort Laurens with that branch of the Great Miami at or near which stood Loramie's store and which is near the western line of what is now Shelby county was S. 78 degrees and 50 minutes W.

From Ludlow's report of the actual survey of the Indian Boundary Line the following quotation is made: "Sunday, 9th July, 1797, began a survey of Indian Boundary Line according to treaty of Greenville by General Wayne of August 5, 1795, at the crossing place of the Tuscarawas branch of the Muskingum river above Fort Laurens at a bottom oak 10 inches in diameter standing on the west bank of said fork, which tree is notched with three notches on the north and west sides with this inscription: 'Surveyed according to Treaty by Gen. Wayne, a line to Loramie's S. 78 degrees and 50 minutes W.' "

In tracing the boundary line southwesterly through what is now Holmes county, Ludlow entered among his notes the following, "19 miles, 32 chains, a water course running southwest, where a flat ridge divides the waters of Sugar creek and Killbuck creek," "26 miles, 30 chains and 50 links, Killbuck creek 2 chains wide, running south, 20 east current gentle." "40 miles, 17 chains and 50 links, White Woman creek (now called Mohican) runs south, 20 east, 4 chains and 50 links wide."

When Ludlow had surveyed the line to the distance of 119 miles and 59 chains, he ran a line south 480 chains when he found the trace of the random line he had run east. He returned to the camp on the treaty line and changed the course of the same from S. 78 degrees, 50 W. to S. 88 degrees, 50 W. and at 153 miles and 35 chains from the starting place, he came to a post 23 chains and 50 links above the forks of Laramie's creek on a course S. 10 W. This report is dated August 29, 1797, and is signed by Israel Ludlow, D. S.

The survey of the line from Loramie's to Fort Recovery, was commenced by Ludlow on Saturday, August 3, 1799, at Loramie's, and bears north 81 degrees, 10 minutes west, 22 miles, 51 chains and 50 links to Fort Recovery, which was situated in what is now Mercer county near the Indiana line.

The survey of the line between Fort Recovery and the mouth of the Kentucky river was commenced by Ludlow on Tuesday, 10 o'clock, August 8, 1799, at Fort Recovery, and bears S. 11 degrees, 35 minutes W. Six miles of this part of the line only is within the present limits of the State of Ohio.

A STATION ON THE UNDERGROUND RAILROAD.

MRS. FLORENCE BEDFORD WRIGHT, OBERLIN.

The Anti-Slavery agitation of the nineteenth century, called out the heroic qualities in many a quiet man in whom such attributes had never been suspected.

In no part of the country, did the friends of the fugitive slave make more personal sacrifices than those residing in southwestern Ohio.

·It was during this period that the name "under-ground railroad" was given to the manner by which the negroes were piloted to freedom.

Regularly routes were devised over which hundreds of slaves were sent on their way to liberty. These routes were known to but few, and those the persons actively engaged in the service.

While slaves could not be owned north of the Ohio river the owners had many warm friends in the north, who would have been glad to assist them in recovering their so-called chattels, and who used all their influence in making it uncomfortable and even dangerous for those engaged in relief work.

The phrase "having the courage of one's convictions" so often spoken with but little thought as to its meaning, had an intense force to those who were summoned before a judge who enjoyed inflicting the utmost penalty of the law. The truth of the poet's lines was unfelt by many.

> "Then to side with truth is noble
>   When we share her wretched crust,
> Ere her cause bring fame and profit
>   And 'tis prosperous to be just.
> Then it is the brave man chooses,
>   While the coward stands aside,
> Doubting in his abject spirit,
>   Till his Lord is crucified,
> And the multitude make virtue
>   Of the faith they had denied."

Added to the penalties of the law were the discomforts attending being out, always at night, often in storm, the nervous strain attending such experiences, and the enforced neglect of business. Cincinnati was of course the point first reached by the slaves, from there they were taken to Glendale, then to Foster's, on the Little Miami, and from there they were brought to Springboro, which was a village in Warren county, settled largely by "Friends" or Quakers, a people justly celebrated for their sympathy with the down-trodden. These stations were the homes of the various sympathizers and no questions were asked by the house-wives when well filled pantry shelves were mysteriously emptied. From Springboro they were taken to the home of a Dr. A. Brooks, near Wilmington, Clinton county, and from there to Oakland, a station near Xenia, Ohio, and so on towards Canada.

Among those acting as conductor was a Friend, William S. Bedford, by name, who had probably inherited his abhorrence of the system from his father, Thomas Bedford, who as early as 1786, shortly after his landing from England, threw up a lucrative position in Charleston, S. C., because his conscience would not allow him to direct or use slave labor, thereby so incensing his uncle, by whom he was employed, that he refused to pay him anything for the labor already done, upon which he started to walk to Philadelphia, stopping in Virginia and Maryland to teach school, thus helping himself forward. It is not surprising to find his children, later, showing strong feeling on the subject.

Only faint echoes from the past come to us now, but such as they are, they are worthy of preservation.

The manuscript containing the account published below was found among the papers of my father, the William S. Bedford above referred to, to which has been added the abstract of the court record.

In 1839 a citizen of Rockingham county, Virginia, by name Bennet Raines, started for Missouri, leaving his home hurriedly, he being seriously involved, financially. Accompanying his family were four slaves, an old woman, her daughter (a woman in the prime of life) and two small children belonging to the latter, one four years of age and the other an infant in arms. They passed through Springboro, Ohio, and pitched their tent one mile west. Word had been sent to the Abolitionists there of their intended arrival, and a hope expressed that they might manage to

free these slaves, — Springboro at that time being one of the regular stations on the under-ground railroad. The town was largely
composed of Friends or Quakers, most of whom were friendly
to the cause. We held a hurried counsel and agreed to meet at
his tent and inform him that he was violating our laws by passing
slaves through our state.

A goodly number appeared according to programme, Dr. A.
Brooks being appointed speaker. Raines said we might take them
if they were willing to go, the elder woman soon climbed into
our carriage, as would the younger, but a daughter of Raines had
secreted the boy, no doubt thinking she could sell him in Missouri. We felt the children could not judge, and that the mother
had the best claim to them so the search was continued until one
cried out: "I feel its kinky head," and within the next twenty
minutes they were all on the road to Canada. Raines was much
irritated and finally pushed his gun barrel out of the back of the
tent or wagon, some one told him "that was a game more than
one could play," and at once the noise of ramrods and gunlocks
was heard, the colored members having brought theirs without
our knowledge or consent.

Raines was shrewd and keen and found many sympathizers
in Franklin — a town near by, who advised him to prosecute.
He made oath that we had robbed him of $1,000.00 in gold and
$500.00 in paper. Sixteen of us in consequence were cited to ap-
pear before the court then in session in Lebanon, our county seat.
We engaged four eminent lawyers, Ex-Gov. Bell, Ex-Gov. Corwin, R. Schenck (later General) and Robert G. Corwin, who
agreed to see us through all the courts for $500.00, but before the
case was reached the old man died, and his son took it up. There
were three counts in the indictment: Abduction, grand larceny
and riot. The abduction would not bear handling, but fell
through at once; they then tried grand larceny. The mother and
son being examined separately, she on being asked from what
state she came, said she did not know, but thought it was Rockingham. She said the gold was put in a pasteboard box she supposed, but had never seen it, but the paper was in $100.00 bills.
The son then said there were no $100.00 bills, and all the gold
he had seen turn out was two or three $5.00 pieces, so the jury
let that drop, almost without leaving their seats; but they held us

on the last count, for they proved there were guns on the ground, and the unlawful manner of doing even a lawful thing was held by the court to constitute a riot. We were sentenced to five days in the dungeon, to be fed on bread and water and to pay a fine, some of $20.00 and some of $5.00. The dungeon proved too small, being but 8 feet by 10 feet, and one person already in it. They then made another room as dark as possible and placed us there. There were four of our company who were reported by the Grand Jury who were not tried in open court, but condemned with the rest. Our lawyers made a statement of the case and we sent it by a trusty messenger to the judge of the Supreme Court who ordered us all turned out by giving $500.00 bail for our appearance before the court when it should set in our county. Some of us had already given $3,000.00 bail on esquire's docket.

Judge Hitchcock cleared us in the Supreme Court in about 30 minutes, for he said we had a right to use as much force as was necessary to accomplish the object.

We learned long afterwards that the negroes settled among Friends and did not go to Canada.

WILLIAM S. BEDFORD.

COURT RECORD.

"State Record No. 5. Warren Common Pleas, March Term, 1840. The Grand Jury was impanneled, viz.: William Crosson, Joseph Smithers, James Hopkins, Spencer Hunt, Richard Taylor, Caleb Saterthwaet, William Hamilton, Joseph Edwards, William Miller, Walling Worley, Patrick McKinsey, Samuel Leonard, Amos Kelsey, Edward Robinson, and John M. Snook.

"Returned an indictment signed by J. M. Williams, Pros. Atty. of Warren Co., Ohio, and indorsed a 'true bill, William Crosson, Foreman,' against Abraham Brooks, James B. Brooks, Edward Brooks, Joseph Lukens, David Potts, John Potts, Lindley Potts, Perry Lukens, William S. Bedford, Ezekiel McCoy, John T. Bateman, Nicholas Archdeacon, Clarkson Bateman, Cyrus F. Farr, Jonas Wilson, Peter Lowe and Frederick Wilson, and divers other persons whose names are to the jurors aforesaid unknown, charging by the first count of said indictment that said defendants —

"On the 6th day of November, 1839, with force and arms at the township of Franklin, and county of Warren, aforesaid, unlawfully did conceal, advise and entice four colored persons, namely, Molly, Sarah, Adam and Mary, then and there being, and who by the laws of the State of Virginia did then and there owe labor and service to one Bennett Raines then and there, being then and there to leave, abandon and escape from the said Bennett Raines, to whom the said labor and service of Molly, Sarah, Adam and Mary, according to the laws of the said state of Virginia was then due and owing, contrary to the form of the statute," etc., etc.

The second count charges that said defendants "did unlawfully, did conceal, advise and entice four colored persons, etc., etc. They, the said (defendants) then and there well knowing that the said Molly, etc., etc., did according to the laws of Virginia, use, etc., etc. The third charges that said defendants did "unlawfully furnish a conveyance, to-wit: a carriage and two horses with intent and for the purpose of enabling four colored persons, viz., etc., etc., owing, etc., etc., to escape and elude the said B. R. They the said (defendants) well knowing, etc., etc.,

The fourth count is the same as the first except it charges that Molly, etc., etc., owed labor and service under the laws of Missouri.

The fifth count charges that the defendants, with force and arms, to-wit, with clubs, dirks, stones, guns, pistols, and divers other unlawful and offensive weapons, etc., etc., etc., unlawfully, notoriously, riotously, did assemble and gather together to disturb the public peace and with the intent with force and violence, to-wit, with clubs, dirks, etc., to tear down a certain tent the property of one Bennett Raines, and also to make an assault upon said Bennett Raines, Elizabeth Raines, Eliza Raines, and a colored person by the name of Adam, in the peace of the state of Ohio, and being so unlawfully assembled, etc., etc. They the said (defendants), with clubs, dirks, etc., etc., riotously, etc., did disturb the peace and also unlawfully, etc., and with great force, etc., did tear down the aforesaid tent and also then and there unlawfully, etc. The said Bennett Raines, etc., did strike, beat, bruise, wound and ill-treat the B. R., etc., then and there did contrary, etc."

The sixth count charges the defendants assault and battery on Bennett Raines. The indictment is signed J. M. Williams, Pros. Att'y, and endorsed a "true bill, William Crosson."

The defendants were arraigned and pleaded "not guilty." The case was continued to August term, when it was again continued to November term, when for trying the case, came a jury, viz., William Holcraft, Adam Bone, John St. John, William Hill, of the regular jury, and from the by-standers William Gregg, William Thompson, David Bone, Berkley S. Brown, Aaron Van Note, Robert M. Hull, Samuel Drake and John Pauley.

The jury being sworn, the case was tried before a full court, Benjamin Hinkston, President Judge, James Cowan, John Hart and William I. Mickel, associate judges.

The jury, by their verdict, found the defendants "not guilty," as they stand charged in the first, second, third, fourth and sixth counts of said indictment, and guilty as charged in the fifth count of said indictment.

The motion was made for a new trial, it was overruled by the court, and the defendants excepted. A bill of exceptions was prepared, signed by the court, but no proceedings in error had, and at the March term, 1841, "April 12th the defendants being present the court rendered judgment, viz., "That James B. Brooks pay a fine of $5.00 and be imprisoned in the dungeon of the jail of Warren county until 8 o'clock P. M. of this day.

That Joseph Lukens, Ezekiel McCoy, Cyrus F. Farr, Jonas Wilson, Frederick Wilson, John T. Bateman, Peter Lowe, Nicholas Archdeacon, each pay a fine of $5.00.

That Abraham Brooks, John Potts, Lindley Potts, William S. Bedford, each pay a fine of $20.00.

That Abraham Brooks, Joseph Lukens, John Potts, Lindley Potts, William S. Bedford, Ezekial McCoy, Nicholas Archdeacon, Cyrus F. Farr, Jonas Wilson, Frederick Wilson, John T. Bateman, Peter Lowe and Edward Brooks, "be imprisoned in the dungeon of the jail of Warren county for the term of 5 days, that is to say, until the 17th day of April, 1841, at 12 noon, and that during said imprisonment they be fed on bread and water only," and the state recover of said defendants, 17 in number (again naming them), the costs taxed at $261.38.

ROBERT WHITE McFARLAND.

FRANK S. BROOKS, COLUMBUS.

If all the men who have been so fortunate as to have come under the benign influence of Professor McFarland were each to

ROBERT WHITE M'FARLAND.

pay the tribute of laying one stone in his honor, no towering modern structure would overlook the pile. Such would be a fitting memorial; for, while indulgent toward many duller minds, patiently helping to mould the characters of boys and men, much of his incessant work has been among the stars.

Reluctantly I comply with the request to present a brief sketch of his busy life; not from unwillingness, but from a sincere feeling of inability to do justice to a polymathist so eminent. In an article brief as this must be, due measure cannot be given to a man so broad, a life so untiringly devoted to scientific inquiry and to the temporal and eternal welfare of others.

Astronomer and mathematician, an undisputed authority in scientific investigation, he has nevertheless ever been modest in his bearing, and at all times ready to guide and help the young. No student ever found him impatient or tyrannical. A prominent trait, for which many a man is better, has distinguished his career as instructor; a judicious confidence, amply sustained by common sense, that developed in his pupils honor and self-respect. Rarely was this trust abused. When abused, the case was hopeless.

Not lacking in the dignity required by his position, he is blessed with a rich and kindly sense of humor. Many a time the work of the class-room has been brightened by its illuminative ray. To Professor McFarland's happy sense *one* graduate at least of Miami University probably owes his diploma from that institution. Of that grave and reverend Faculty at that bygone day all others were fairly rigid with hard and solemn dignity, a veneer easily cracked.

Many a good and piquant story might be told of "Prof. Mac's" affable and kindly ways; of his forbearance under provocation; of his courage, as soldier and man — and he had the rugged physical ability to back it — but I must forbear, and turn to more essential lines.

Doctor R. W. McFarland is of Scottish descent; the family leaving the clan site on the west side of Loch Lomond, Scotland, about the year 1690, and living in County Tyrone, North Ireland, about fifty or sixty years. About 1745, the great-grandfather, Robert, came to America, settling in Pennsylvania. Not liking the style of land tenure there, he moved to Rockbridge county, Virginia; bought a tract of land on Cedar creek, close to the Natural Bridge, and lived there until his death, at the age of ninety-three, in 1796. Robert's son, William, the grandfather of R. W. McFarland, lived in the same vicinity.

Robert McFarland, the father of Robert W., was born there in 1782. Just one hundred years ago, December 27, 1804, he was married to Deborah Gray. His death occurred in 1863.

In 1796 the family located about two miles from the village of Lexington, Ky. Our Robert's grandfather, on his mother's side, in the same summer was killed and scalped by the Indians; the last white victim slain by them in that vicinity. In the course of two or three years the family moved again; settling five or six miles from Cynthiana, Ky.

In 1807, with several other families, the McFarlands moved to near Urbana, Ohio, under the leadership of the celebrated Simon Kenton. Here had come, shortly before, William, Simon Kenton's oldest brother, and others of that family; opening up several farms about three miles west of that village. A large proportion of these tracts is still owned by their descendants.

Subsequent to the death in 1814 of the elder McFarland's first wife, the present McFarland's father married a daughter of Philip, oldest son of William Kenton. Of the Kenton half-sisters to our R. W. McFarland, the issue of this marriage, one is now living, at the age of eighty-five.

After the death, in 1821, of the Kenton wife, Robert Mc-Farland was married the third time; this time to Eunice, daughter of Charles Dorsey, of Baltimore, Md.

Of these parents our R. W. McFarland was born near Urbana in 1825. He attended the district school in the county. At the age of fourteen he received a document that shaped his life work — his first certificate to teach; and, two months later, began in Miami county, Ohio, his career of fifty nearly consecutive years as instructor. His second quarter was taught in the summer of 1840 in Palestine (now Tawawa), a village in Shelby county. He was then in his fifteenth year. By March, 1843, he had taught eight terms.

Upon the solicitation of an itinerant Methodist, he then went to Westerville, Ohio; which proved a habitation with a name and one building; a two-story frame, "The Blendon Young Men's Seminary." Years afterward this became Otterbein University.

While at Westerville, in June, 1843, McFarland and four others availed themselves of a five days' vacation; and, just to see a COLLEGE, walked over to Granville, twenty-five miles away. Spurred by the sight, and the privilege of hearing a Latin recitation, McFarland and his roommate, Stillings, tramping back with the others, formed the resolution to go to college. Six weeks of the intense study of those days were put into Andrews's Latin Lessons. Algebra, Geometry, Trigonometry, Grammar, and Logic had been carefully studied.

So, in July, 1843, the two left Westerville, and returned to their homes; not by the rapid transit of modern days. On September 4, 1843, a brother's farm wagon carried our young aspirant and his modest trunk from near Urbana twenty-two miles to the Stillings place, near Marysville. From there another similar conveyance brought the boys twenty-eight miles to Columbus. On the 6th the adventurers embarked on a canal packet boat, and reached the old town of Chillicothe at daybreak of the 7th. Portsmouth was reached on the morning of the 8th. The sternwheel steamboat, boarded here in the afternoon, reached Augusta, Ky., about midnight. Five days of travel; one hundred miles! To-day we execrate a change of cars in a thousand miles!

At this time McFarland was eighteen; Stillings twenty. The latter had studied Greek and Latin six months; McFarland Latin a few weeks, and Greek not at all. But McFarland was a born mathematician, familiar at thirteen with Surveying, and at this time well up in Algebra, Geometry, etc.

Stillings fitted in partly with the Freshmen. But there was no class down to McFarland's apparent level; so he was put in the Cæsar class with the other. The master of the school quickly saw the burning earnestness of the new recruits, and asked the Faculty to allow them to enter the Freshman class. Proud of recognition, still working like beavers, the two sturdy Ohioans put in daily six solid hours on Greek; and in six weeks were allowed to read with the Sophomores as well; McFarland's absolute knowledge of mathematics standing him in good stead. At the close of the year at Augusta they were passed to full Junior standing.

After teaching at Westerville, near Urbana, Ohio, in the fall and winter of 1844, McFarland went to Delaware, Ohio, in the spring of 1845, at the opening of the second term of the college at that place. A public exhibition at the close of the term gave McFarland opportunity to deliver the first public address of this, The Ohio Wesleyan University. Mindful of her sons, this institution has since conferred upon him the titles, A. B., 1847; A. M., 1850; LL. D., 1881.

Making his own way, alternating teaching with college study, McFarland graduated August 4, 1847. After teaching a select school near Delaware for six months, he held an important position in Greenfield Seminary, Highland county; remained there from 1848 to 1851.

At Greenfield, March 19, 1851, he was married to Mary Ann, second daughter of the late Judge Hugh Smart of that place; old time Associate County Judge — an office abolished by the New Constitution about 1851. Truly esteemed in all circles refined by the charm of her presence Mrs. McFarland and two daughters, Elizabeth Eunice and Frances Smart (Mrs. Llewellyn Bonham), still grace the Professor's home life.

Judge Smart, having a nephew about to embark in business at Chillicothe, induced young McFarland to join in the undertaking. The great fire of April 1, 1852, burned out the establishment. After having charge of one of the three buildings of the new Union schools at that place for some time after September, 1853, McFarland for the following three years occupied the position of Professor of Mathematics in Madison College, in Guernsey county, Ohio.

Elected in July, 1856, to the chair of Mathematics and Astronomy in *Miami University,* Oxford, Ohio, his work there was especially successful, until the closing of that institution, in 1873.

At once, indeed in the same week, he was elected to a similar position in the Ohio State University at Columbus. Here he remained for twelve years in charge of Mathematics, Astronomy, and Civil Engineering; having most of the time an assistant in each department. (In recognition of his work and worth, the catalogue of O. S. U. bears his name: "Robert White McFarland, Emeritus Professor of Civil Engineering.")

This position of the highest consideration, and entirely satisfactory, was reluctantly relinquished, under urgent and persistent solicitation, for the presidency of Miami University; to which he was elected in 1885. After about three years, seeing the University again well under way, McFarland presented his resignation as President to resume, as agreed, his former chair of Mathematics and Astronomy. But owing to differences in doctrine and discipline, of which compulsory or optional attendance at prayers formed a part, by those then in authority a reorganization was effected, under which McFarland was omitted. This, however, without discredit — to McFarland. No man to-day believes that any of those destroyed long ago by the rabidly good people of Puritanic Salem were guilty of sorcerous error.

Later, for nearly eleven years, McFarland was Surveyor, Mining Engineer and Manager of Real Estate, at the mines in Hocking Valley of the Sunday Creek Coal Company. Concerning his services here, or rather, part of them, the former manager says:

"To be accorded the privilege of sending you a word regarding our good and honored friend, Professor McFarland, is almost as delightful as the rare man himself.

"The Profesor came to the Sunday Creek Coal Company first in the capacity of mining engineer; afterwards taking charge of the company's real estate (about 16,000 acres), also its 500 houses.

"Up to the time of his coming, the deeds to the several tracts of land had not been examined with regard to their accuracy of description, etc. He found that about forty were defective, in one way or another; indicating that the old time cabalistic 'E. & O. E.,' formerly placed at the bottom of statements and documents, really meant 'Errors and Omissions *expected.*' But his usual and correct methods soon triumphed, and in about a year and a half every tangle had been unraveled and every discrepency reconciled.

"I mention this because it illustrates the Professor's uncompromising standard of exactness and precision. These errors, which had been passed over by attorneys as being trivial, were to him utterly abhorrent; in one instance a certain piece of land was in reality situated six miles from the location given in the deed.

"Of his services during the entire ten or eleven years it will suffice to say, in general terms, that they were in exact consonance with his own lofty ideals of an upright and righteous commercial and moral life. Language offers but a poor and halt means of bearing witness to the high esteem in which, by his every action, he enshrined himself in the hearts of all who were fortunate enough to be associated with him.   J. F. STONE."

In 1862 the government called for three months' men, for positions then occupied by trained soldiers, to allow the latter to go to the front. The boys in college (Miami) formed a company, of which McFarland was made captain. This company organized in May, 1862, and served about four months, in West Virginia, between Clarksburg and Parkersburg.

In the spring of 1863 Governor Tod wrote to the captains of the disbanded regiment (86th O. V. I.) to reorganize if possible. McFarland secured thirty-eight of his old company. All others, officers and men, were new recruits. Colonel Burns, of the old 86th not intending to again go out; the lieutenant colonel being then in Libby Prison; and there being no other captain at once available, Captain McFarland, of Company A, was appointed lieutenant colonel.

This second 86th, mustered in about the middle of July, 1863, at once started in pursuit of John Morgan, then on his celebrated raid; and, after his capture in Eastern Ohio, escorted the 585 Confederate prisoners to Camp Chase, near Columbus. In the escorting detachment McFarland had four companies of the 86th.

The second 86th proceeded with Burnside to East Tennessee. The capture, September 9, 1863, of Cumberland Gap by "Mac's" Brigade — to use soldier and student parlance — in which about 2,500 Confederates yielded to 800 on the Union side, the latter short of rations and insufficiently equipped, but under Colonel DeCourcy making such skillful display of force as to give the impression of overwhelming numbers, is ably and accurately described by Lieut. Col. McFarland, in a pamphlet published in 1898. The 86th was finally mustered out in February, 1864.

As an officer his relations with his men were marked by the most unfailing solicitude. Their privations and exposure he generously shared; as, for instance, in the rain and mud of the trenches. On the march out of the Gap, the care of the regiment devolved upon McFarland. Seventy weary miles of this march were humanely plodded by the Lieutenant Colonel; his horse being resigned to one after another of the tired boys in the ranks, as with faltering step they reached the limit of endurance.

McFarland's busy pen (the time-honored quill, in the making of which he was an expert while his sight was good) has produced a vast number of historical and scientific and semi-scientific articles. Most of these essays have been for special occasions; and when printed usually suffered the fate of the Sibylline leaves of the Virgil story; carried away by the winds, they are not now to be found. A few are attainable in the valuable volumes of the Ohio State Archæological and Historical Society; such as (Vol. 1) "Ancient Earthworks, Oxford;" (Vol. VIII) "Forts Laramie and Pickawillany;" (Vol. X) (a) "Notes, Geographical," (b) "Historical Notes," (c) "The Chillicothes;" (Vol. XIII) (a) "Simon Kenton," (b) "Ludlow's Line."

For more than fifty years his essays on astronomical subjects have found place in various periodicals, chiefly "Popular Astronomy." They are notable for clearness and accuracy. His edition of Virgil (1849), six books of the Aeneid and three Eclogues, for many years was a valued text book in colleges and schools. He aided in a revision of Robinson's text books, and also a revision of Loomis's Algebra.

One of McFarland's widest known and most esteemed labors was during the four years of 1876-1880; averaging four hours per day, six days in the week, for the entire period, when he was engaged in the computation of the eccentricity of the earth's orbit, and longitude of its perihelion.

Croll had used the form of the earth's orbit, in his theory of the Ice Age. The late Dr. Orton asked McFarland if Croll's astronomical work could be relied on; if so, the presence of boulders over Ohio and other states could be fully explained. Croll had computed the form of the orbit at intervals of 50,000 years, over a period of 3,000,000 years. Meanwhile Newcomb, the Astronomer, had said that Croll's work could not be trusted; but that Stockwell's could.

McFarland computed the form, by both Stockwell's and LeVerrier's methods, for over 4,500,000 years; and at the short intervals of 10,000 years; and showed that the two were in substantial agreement for the entire time. When the two curves were platted they were very much alike — no difference for 70,000 years.

To us on the back seats McFarland thus shows that the Ice Age repeats itself after about 1,500,000 years. We can forgive him and not worry!

In the Smithsonian Report, (1889), in a translation by W. S. Dallas, F. L. S., of the work of A. Blytt (Sweden) "On the Movements of the Earth's Crust," appears in this connection the following:

"The curve of the eccentricity of the earth's orbit has been calculated from LeVerrier's formulæ by J. Croll ("Climate and Time") for a period of 4,000,000 of years; 3,000,000 of years backward, and 1,000,000 forward from the present time.

"The curve is also calculated according to the same formulæ by McFarland. (Am. Jour. Sci. 1880-3, Vol. XX, pp. 105-111.) His calculation extends from 3,250,000 years backward to 1,250,-000 years forward in time.

"He has calculated with shorter intervals than Croll, (Croll 50,000 McFarland 10,000) which, however, has had no particular influence in altering the curves. McFarland has in the same place calculated the curve for the same period of time from new formulæ of Stockwell's.

"The two curves taken in the gross, show a uniform course throughout their length, but as regards the first half LeVerrier's curve is thrown somewhat backward. Stockwell's formulæ are considered to be more accurate than LeVerrier's.

"Both curves are given by McFarland. If we compare these two together it appears —

"(1) The curves coincide with only a small essential difference from the present day until 1,000,000 years back.

(2) ————————————————

(3) A very remarkable consequence proceeds from these calculations. *The curve repeats itself* after the lapse of 1,400,000 years when it is calculated according to Stockwell's formulæ. In the period of 4,500,000 years for which McFarland has calculated it, it repeats itself in this way with remarkable regularity a little more than three times, etc."

James Croll (of H. M. Geol. Surv. Scotland) in his "Climate and Cosmology," (1885) — his and LeVerrier's conclusions having been questioned by Newcomb,— acknowledges the results of McFarland's justifying computations, and says: "I may here mention that Professor McFarland, of the Ohio State University, Columbus, a few years ago undertook the task of recomputing every one of the hundred and fifty periods given in my tables; and he states that, except in one instance, he did not find an error to the amount of .001. * * *

"In this laborious undertaking, Professor McFarland computed by means of both formulæ the eccentricity of the earth's orbit and the longitude of the perihelion for no fewer than 485 separate epochs. See Am. Jour. Sci., Vol. XX, p. 105, 1880."

Some critical reviews now under preparation under McFarland's tireless hands are to appear in the February or March number of "The Open Court" of Chicago, and in the February number of "Popular Astronomy." Though now eighty years of age, while dimmed are the keen and kindly eyes that so long read the most illimitable of Nature's books, and have flashed in appreciative merriment or truly penetrated the inner soul of youth, to-day our revered instructor is still cheerfully and intently *busy;* still contributing to the knowledge of mankind.

SONG WRITERS OF OHIO.

BENJAMIN RUSSEL HANBY.

Author of "Darling Nelly Gray."

C. B. GALBREATH.

A plain brick structure of ample size and pleasing proportions, rising on firm foundations from a well-kept campus; a
mute array of sentinel trees, guarding the shady silence of the
place and leading outward along the avenue in two noble ranks
that stretch forth their arms in salutation to the passerby; a beautiful stretch of lawn, facing the afternoon sun and sloping gently
toward the winding stream that with never failing current mur-
murs gladly on its southward journey; and, bordering all, the
neat and orderly village of Westerville, — such is the seat of
Otterbein, honored preceptress of a worthy student body, beloved
alma mater of numerous and devoted alumni, typical educational
institution of the middle west, in the strictest sense a denominational college, in which founders and faculty built broader and
better than they knew. In glorifying the Master, they ennobled
man; in advancing the interests of a sect, they made no mean
contribution to the world outside of the church; in preparation
for the hereafter, they achieved something of immortality here.

The visitor entering the spacious main building is impressed
with the fact that many of the excellent features of the old
time Ohio college are here retained unmarred by the innovations of later years; the chapel, where students and instructors
assemble daily; recitation rooms, where the traditional curricu-
lum, with its preponderance of pure mathematics and ancient
classics, is faithfully taught; the halls of the literary societies,
with richly carpeted floors, immaculate tinted walls and vari-
colored windows, admitting a softened radiance by day and
transmitting by night something of the mellow glory that glows
within; below, a carefully selected library, administered in accordance with modern methods and frequented by the student body,
whose clean-cut, thoughtful faces are at once a study and an

"That sweet, pathetic song,
"Darling Nelly Gray," written not
long before the Civil war, contained a sentiment which deep-
ened the feeling already aroused
for the oppressed and touched
a responsive chord, which though
many years have passed, still
vibrates. Who can, even now, sing
the touching lines without sympathy for the poor bondman
so cruelly separated from his love?

Alhambra, Cal.
Jan. 26-1905.   Kate Hanly.

inspiration. Even the modern conveniences of life enter unobtrusively. Natural gas and electricity blaze and beam silently,
and at the end of the avenue of trees the interurban cars come
and go without a rumble to disturb the student as he bends
over his books. Athletics are not excluded, but football, with
its glorious concomitants of stentorian hilarity and broken heads,
is still subordinate to music and debate.

But why dwell upon this institution unknown to fame and
unambitious to emerge from the delightful seclusion peculiar to
numbers of its kind? Again, we repeat that the founders built
broader and better than they knew.

It is worthy of note in passing, that one of the great universities of the East is even now considering the raising of an
endowment fund of two and one-half million dollars for the
avowed purpose of greatly increasing the teaching force and
"importing into the university the methods and personal contact between teacher and pupil which are characteristic of the
small college." It is refreshing to know that a great university
can learn something from such a source. It encourages the
hope that further investigation may reveal other features worthy
of imitation.

That the denominational college, with all its limitations, has
rendered an important service to the cause of education, is
attested by results — the men and women it has sent into the
world.

If a single alumnus of this particular institution should be
known as widely as his work, his name would be a household
word in America. When Otterbein was young, from her classic
shades he gave to music and to human liberty that sweetly pathetic song, *Darling Nelly Gray.*

Occasional comment has been made upon the fact that most
of the southern melodies have been composed by northern men.
It is a singular coincidence that the authors of *Dixie* and *Darling
Nellie Gray* were both born in the North and in the central part
of the same state. In the little village of Rushville, that nestles
among the picturesque hills of Fairfield County, O., Benjamin
Russel Hanby began life July 22, 1833. The same county gave
to Ohio and the Union Thomas Ewing, the younger, and the
famous Sherman brothers.

The subject of this sketch was the eldest son of Bishop William Hanby, a prominent minister of the United Brethren Church, who early espoused the cause of universal liberty in America and by word and deed supported the anti-slavery cause. His humble home was for a time a station on the "underground railroad," and in the family the wrongs of the sable bondman was frequently the absorbing theme of conversation.

In many respects the childhood of young Hanby did not differ from that of his fellows in the isolated hamlet of that day. The boy was prophetic of the man. Blessed with a happy temper and bubbling over with good humor, the pious teaching of his parents, to whom he was devotedly attached, usually kept him in his sportive hours well within the limits of harmless mischief and innocent fun.

Of a teachable nature, he early found engrossing interest in his books, and with advancing years he aspired to follow in the footsteps of his father.

The salary of the itinerant minister to-day is usually far from munificent. Sixty years ago it was meager and sometimes precarious. Bishop Hanby was a power in the pulpit and held in high esteem throughout his circuit; his good wife was careful and frugal, but his stipend was not sufficient to provide for the family of children and give to each a collegiate education. Young Benjamin, like many a youth of his time, went cheerfully and resolutely to work "to earn his way," with a baccalaureate degree and the ministry as his goal.

At the age of sixteen, he enrolled at Otterbein, the college of his church, in which his father was deeply interested, and in a short time was commissioned to teach in the common schools. This gave him thorough drill in the common branches, opportunity for study, and employment to earn his way through college. At the age of seventeen, he taught his first school at Clear Creek, in his home county; later he had charge of the schools of his native hamlet. He formally united with the church before the close of his first term in college.

From childhood he manifested a fondness for music. His genial, sensitive nature found soul-satisfying expression in song. At the regular church service on the Sabbath day and through protracted religious revivals, his voice was heard in the choir.

In his first school teaching, long before he had received formal instruction in the art, he taught his pupils to sing. To his other gifts were added the graces of speech. In the school he was at once teacher and companion. He mingled with the children on the playground. With the older boys, outside of school hours, he roamed over the surrounding hills, through the lonely forests and along the murmuring stream. They followed where his spirit led, and many at that early day through his influence united with the church.

An event of first importance in the history of the family and the cause of general rejoicing among the children, who thoroughly appreciated the opportunities it would bring, was the choice by Bishop Hanby of a new home in the village of Westerville. Thither the family moved after many farewells, and soon the older children were enjoying the advantages of higher education in the little college, already launched on an auspicious career under the ambitious name of "University of Otterbein."

Here the natural gifts and winning personality of "Ben," as he was familiarly called, made him a leader among the students. True, he did not have the advantages of physical culture enjoyed by the college boy of to-day. His gymnasium was the wood-pile; his natatorium was Alum Creek; his stadium was chosen at will in the wide valley of meadow and woodland that stretched away on either side. In spite of the absence of trapeze and arena, he excelled in athletics, was fleet of foot, accurate of eye, a lithe, agile wrestler and an expert swimmer. On one occasion a student got beyond his depth in the stream and with a gurgling shriek sank from sight.

"Hanby, Hanby," shouted the affrighted companions. Hanby rushed to the water's edge, leaped in, dived, caught, raised and rescued the drowning boy.

In the college literary society he took a prominent part, participating in debate and always assisting in the arrangement and rendition of the musical program. He wrote a play that was acted with great success by a selected cast of amateurs. His enthusiasm in these diversions, however, did not cause him to neglect his regular studies, and he was graduated in due time with the degree of bachelor of arts.

DARLING NELLY GRAY.

As already intimated, the convictions of the father were shared by the son. In the troublous times before the war, Bishop Hanby from the platform and the pulpit sternly denounced the slave power. His milder mannered son, through the avenue of song, rendered more effective service to the cause. In 1856, two years before graduation, he composed *Darling Nelly Gray*.

Definite and trustworthy details in regard to the composition of a popular melody are usually very difficult to obtain. Especially is this true when the witnesses who were personally competent to bear testimony have passed away. Even when those who knew the facts are still living, the difficulty is not wholly removed, for memory is treacherous. Fortunately, in this instance, while the composer does not survive to relate the origin of his famous lay, friends and relatives qualified to speak with almost equal authority are still living, among them the cousin of the author who was present when the song was sung from manuscript and the announcement was made that it had been dedicated to the young lady who was then teaching music at Otterbein.

The song had its origin in the composer's sympathy for the slaves of the South. The immediate inspiration, if such it had, is not definitely known. Among the stories of its origin, one that gained considerable currency is to the effect that while on the cars, Hanby read in a newspaper an account of the separation of a slave girl from her lover in Kentucky. A planter from the far South bought her and took her to Georgia. After reading the article, Hanby took out some blank paper and wrote a part of the song. He finished it and composed the music on his return home. This story is plausible, but careful investigation has failed to reveal any basis for it in fact. It is quite probable that the words of the song suggested this origin to the imagination of a newspaper correspondent or his informant.[1]

---

[1] Dr. W. C. Lewis, of Rushville, O., contributes the following reminiscence relative to the writing of *Darling Nellie Gray:*

"Ben Hanby and myself were very intimate when boys, and well along into our young manhood. I think it was during the autumn of 1855, when he taught school here. His assistant was a young man he brought

This much seems beyond dispute. A number of young friends, including the cousin of the author, Miss Melissa A. Haynie, and the music teacher, Miss Cornelia Walker, were invited to the Hanby home, where as usual on such occasions,

---

with him from Westerville, Samuel Evers. They were then attending the Otterbein University, of that village. The same winter I taught a graded school about one mile from Rushville, but lived in town.

"Mr. Hanby and myself frequently spent the evenings together. We also attended a singing school, taught by Peter Lamb. Even at that early day Ben. Hanby was recognized wherever he was known as possessing musical ability of a very high order.

"It was in this winter when he first composed what afterward became the noted popular song, *Darling Nelly Gray*. He read the manuscript to me, and said at the time that when he was perfectly satisfied with the composition he would set it to music. I am not able to say how long it was before he did this, or how many changes, if any, he afterward made; but I very well know that I caught the following lines from his reading the manuscript:

> Oh, my Darling Nelly Gray, they have taken you away,
> And I'll never see my darling any more."

A well-known local historian of Hamilton, O., gives quite a different account. In a recent published article he says:

"When living in Sevenmile, the Rev. Hanby was a regular subscriber to the *Cincinnati Gazette*, and while reading this paper one day, on the train between Sevenmile and Cincinnati, his attention was drawn to an account of a slave sale in Kentucky. Nelly Gray, a beautiful mulatto girl, was among the list of slaves sold. She was to be taken to Georgia, far away from home, early scenes and kindred. This incident created an impression upon the mind of Rev. Hanby, and suggested the theme for his world renowned southern song, *My Darling Nelly Gray*. He drafted a skeleton sketch of this familiar air on the train, and when he returned home, that same night, completed the song. It was first published in the *Cincinnati Gazette*, and immediately became very popular."

In a letter the author of the above adds that he personally heard Hanby relate the circumstances under which the song was written.

It may be observed that the song bears the copyright date of June 17, 1856. Mr. Hanby did not go to Sevenmile until about four years afterward. He therefore could not have written it while a citizen of that village. There is nothing in Mr. Lewis's statement that conflicts with the accounts given by other friends and relatives. The song might have been commenced at Rushville. It was certainly completed and set to music in Westerville.

singing was the leading feature of the evening's meeting. Mrs. Cornelia (Walker) Comings of Girard, Kansas, distinctly recalls the evening in a recent letter to Mrs. Hanby, and we give in her own words her statement relative to the initial singing of the song for the entertainment of guests. She says:

"I well remember the first time I heard it. We were at a little gathering at the Rev. Mr. Hanby's one evening. We always had music at such

HANBY HOME AT WESTERVILLE, O., WHERE "DARLING NELLY GRAY" WAS
COMPOSED AND FIRST SUNG.

times. At last I was called upon to listen to a song by the Hanby family. I admired it *very* much, and then Ben. told me it was intended for me."

As explained elsewhere in the same letter, Mrs. Comings meant to say that it was dedicated to her. She urged the young author to send it to a publisher, which he did. Mrs. (Haynie) Fisher, cousin of the author, recalls that on this occasion Hanby made a few minor changes in the arrangement of the song. It is her impression that it was written very shortly before this gathering. Collateral testimony sustains this view. The song was composed in Westerville early in the year 1856.

As no response came from the publisher, the young composer supposed that the manuscript had been consigned to the waste basket and oblivion. He gave the matter no further consideration. He had written it without a thought of publication and he was not disappointed. In fact, the word disappointment had no place in the vocabulary of this optimistic youth. He and his family were genuinely surprised some months later on learning that it had been published and was already on the road to popularity. He procured a printed copy and saw that it bore his name, with the dedication to Cornelia Walker.[1] The words, which have a merit peculiarly their own, aside from the melody, are as follows:

There's a low, green valley, on the old Kentucky shore,
    Where I've whiled many happy hours away,
A sitting and a singing by the little cottage door,
    Where lived my darling Nelly Gray.

CHORUS.

    Oh! my poor Nelly Gray, they have taken you away,
        And I'll never see my darling any more;
    I am sitting by the river and I'm weeping all the day,
        For you've gone from the old Kentucky shore.

When the moon had climbed the mountain and the stars were shining too,
    Then I'd take my darling Nelly Gray,
And we'd float down the river in my little red canoe,
    While my banjo sweetly I would play.

One night I went to see her, but "She's gone!" the neighbors say,
    The white man bound her with his chain;
They have taken her to Georgia for to wear her life away,
    As she toils in the cotton and the cane.

My canoe is under water, and my banjo is unstrung;
    I'm tired of living any more;

---

[1] All printed copies bear Hanby's name. Only the first edition has the dedicatory imprint.

My eyes shall look downward, and my song shall be unsung,
  While I stay on the old Kentucky shore.

My eyes are getting blinded, and I cannot see my way.
  Hark! there's somebody knocking at the door—
Oh! I hear the angels calling, and I see my Nelly Gray,
  Farewell to the old Kentucky shore.

CHORUS.

  Oh, my darling Nelly Gray, up in heaven there they say
    That they'll never take you from me any more.
  I'm a coming, coming, coming, as the angels clear the way,
    Farewell to the old Kentucky shore.

It is very difficult to apply to a popular song the rules of literary criticism; it is nevertheless safe to affirm that the foregoing verses are not without poetic merit. What is said of Foster's songs is true of Hanby's first successful composition: "There is meaning in the words and beauty in the air." Indeed we may go further and aver that the author of *Old Folks at Home,* first though he be among the writers of southern melodies, never wrote verses more sweetly simple, more beautifully and touchingly suggestive, more sadly pathetic, than *Darling Nelly Gray.* Perfect in rhyme and almost faultless in rhythm, the words flow on, bearing their message directly to the heart. The tragic climax is delicately veiled behind the picture of the bondman pouring forth his sorrow for his lost lady love. Her vain appeal to the slave driver; the insult of the heartless new master; the burdens of the cotton and the cane fields; her comfortless grief, wild despair and pitiful decline to the merciful release of death, — these were too awful to find expression in song. We are spared the heart-rending reality; even the pain from what we see is relieved by the vision of a happy reunion. Darling Nelly goes to her cruel fate — and meets her lover in heaven.

It has been urged in criticism of the song that it idealizes the colored race. The sable twain are clothed with the refined sentimentality of the Caucasian. We are told that the bondman and his love are creatures of the imagination without counterparts in the realm of reality; that death from the pangs of separation is about the last thing that, under the circumstances, would have occurred; that the beautiful Nelly down in Georgia would have yielded gracefully to the new situation; that her dusky lover would soon have drifted again down the river and twanged his banjo to the delectation of another "lady of color"; that constancy was foreign to the slaves of the Southland.

That this was often true is one of the saddest commentaries on the brutalizing system that held the black man in a "debasing thraldom." Despite his unhappy condition, however, there is abundant evidence that home was held dear and that ignorance did not blunt the pain when love's ties were ruthlessly sundered.

A well known poetess, now a resident of Ohio, whose father and grandfather were slaveholders in Kentucky before the war, and who recalls vividly and relates entertainingly much that occurred on the old plantation, tells a story from real life that may not inappropriately be introduced here. Frederick Brown was the name of a slave who had grown up on the Brown estate. Physically well formed, tall and commanding, he was a natural leader among the slaves. Though gifted with a high degree of natural intelligence, he was, with his less favored fellows, forbidden the privilege of acquiring even the rudiments of an education. Of a somewhat fervid religious temperament, he frequently preached to the slaves on the Sabbath day, leafing over, as he did so, a Bible in which he could not read a word. Though popular among his people, by the master's family he was regarded somewhat impertinent. He had married, shortly before the events we are about to narrate, one of the most beautiful and gentle slave girls on the plantation. Finally the old master died and the slaves, sharing the fate of other property, were divided among the children. "Rev." Fred fell to the share of a daughter whose husband did not appreciate his worth and magnified his irritating delinquencies.

"I will sell the impertinent rascal," said the new master. "I will sell him and send him South."

The slave buyer, that ubiquitous person of shadowy repute, detested alike by the poor black whom he drove and the master with whom he bargained, hearing of the threat, presented himself one day and made an offer for "Rev." Fred, which was promptly accepted.

Consternation reigned among the cabins when the driver came to claim his purchase. Fred was overpowered and chained. Into the midst of the throng rushed the poor wife, and with pitiful tones pleaded not to be separated from her husband. The driver laughed at her. Fred was dragged away and his wife, shrieking wildly, was carried back half dead to her broken home. To the cabin sleep came not that night. At frequent intervals a plaintive moan was heard and then piercing shrieks that sent the tremor of despair through the darkness, penetrated the stately mansion and broke the slumbers of luxury and pride.

As a son of the late master heard the cries, he muttered, "Slavery is an accursed institution."

Day brought small comfort to the weeping wife. Nights came and went, but rest and dreamless sleep returned no more. For a time the stricken soul was buoyed up with the hope that Fred would find some one to write. No message came. In spite of kind attentions of mistress and friends — for she was a favorite with all — her sturdy frame succumbed beneath the weight of woe, the luster faded from her eye and after a few months of agony she sank into the grave. This picture was a reality. Witnesses of the tragedy still live.

Darling Nelly Gray was a protest against a wrong that was terribly real. The characters were not ideal; they were typical of the better slave element on the "old Kentucky shore." The song rendered a distinct service in the great movement that culminated in the emancipation proclamation and gave the Republic "under God, a new birth of freedom."

While it almost immediately became a great favorite in the North and was echoed back from lands beyond the sea, it brought neither fame nor fortune to the composer. In no work does the author so completely bury himself as in the lay that gains a measure of universality. The statesman and the warrior each goes down to posterity conspicuously associated with his immortal work. The world accepts the melody that nurtures the noblest sentiments of the human heart with scarce a thought of him who first with magic touch struck the chord of the soul's sweet harmonies.

Whence came the lullabies of childhood? Who first called forth the familiar strains of the flute and the violin? What was the origin of the repertoire of the sable knight of the banjo? What soldier soul launched the battle hymn? What saintly spirit framed the simple words and music that on the lips of rural choir and cathedral chorus raise the mortal into the visible presence of the Infinite? The throngs that are moved, uplifted and inspired know not, reck not. The singer is lost in his song.

Darling Nelly Gray was copyrighted and issued by one of the largest musical publishing houses in America. The author purchased his first printed copy from a dealer in Columbus, Ohio. He wrote to the publisher and asked why he had not been notified of the acceptance of the manuscript. The reply was to the effect that the address had been lost. One dozen copies of the song were sent to the composer and this was the only compensation that he ever received. The credit of authorship, however, was not taken from him, and this the publisher seemed to consider ample reward. In reply to a request for the usual royalty, Hanby received the following:

"Dear Sir: Your favor received. *Nelly Gray* is sung on both sides of the Atlantic. We have made the money and you the fame—that balances the account."

The song had a phenomenal sale. It was published in many forms and the tune arranged for band music. The publisher must have made a small fortune out of it; Hanby had the obscure notice accorded to the song writer, — and what to a man of his taste and sensibility must have been far greater — the satisfaction of knowing that he had reached the popular heart and conscience in the support of a worthy cause. This consolation was left to him to transmit to his for all time.

Of the many songs that were written to advance the anti-slavery cause, *Darling Nelly Gray* alone retains a measure of its old time popularity. The melody and words survive because of their intrinsic beauty. And if the words of the poet are true, the song shall live on, for

"A thing of beauty is a joy forever."

LITTLE TILLIE'S GRAVE.

After honorable graduation at Otterbein, in 1858, Hanby traveled in Pennsylvania, Virginia and Maryland as agent for the institution. He married Miss Kate Winter, a cultured young lady whom he met in college and who as a member of the first graduating class had completed her course one year in advance of her husband.

In 1860 he published *Little Tillie's Grave*, a composition that was well received.[1] It did not rise to the level of *Darling Nelly Gray,* though intended to be somewhat similar to it in character. Following are the verses as they originally appeared:

'Tis midnight gliding on her deep, dark wings,
　And the wind o'er my gentle Tillie sighs.
And my poor heart trembles like the banjo strings
　That I'm thrumming near the hillock where she lies.

CHORUS.

Weep, zephyrs, weep in the midnight deep,
　Where the cypress and the vine sadly wave;
I have taken down my banjo for I could not sleep,
　And I'm singing by my little Tillie's grave.

When they tore my Jennie from her sweet, sweet child,
　And her heart was withering with mine,
In my arms I bore thee to this island wild,
　Lest the fate of thy mother should be thine.

How sweet have the seasons glided by since then,
　How happy each moment of the year,
Save a sigh that the lov'd one might come back again
　We have known not a sorrow nor a tear.

But the swamp fever lighted on thy dark brown cheek,
　And I knew death was knocking at the door;

---

[1] A correspondent to a Hamilton, O., paper says: "The Rev. Hanby subsequently wrote and set to music a 'catchy' song along the same lines of his first production, entitled *Little Tillie's Grave.* This he dedicated to an old-time friend, Jacob A. Zellar, of Oxford, Butler County, O. *Little Tillie's Grave* was received with great favor, and had an immense sale."

How my full soul trembled with its bursting grief
    When I saw that my Tillie was no more.

Now the wildcat is wailing and the night-hawk screams
    And the copperhead is hissing in the shade;
They shall come not hither to disturb thy dreams,
    For I'll watch where thy sleeping dust is laid.

CHORUS.

Sleep, Tillie, sleep, in the midnight deep,
    Where the cypress and the vine sadly wave;
Let my fingers keep thrumming and my fond heart weep
    Till I die by my little Tillie's grave.

OLE SHADY.

Hanby again entered upon the work of teaching. He was chosen principal at the academy at Sevenmile, Butler County, O., a position that he held for two years. While traveling in the South he had opportunity to study more fully the character of the colored people. *Darling Nelly Gray* and *Little Tillie's Grave* represented their serious, sentimental characteristics. He now portrayed their exuberant jollity in the familiar dialect song, *Ole Shady*. There is humor and pathos in the liberated soul bent on breaking for "ole Uncle Aby," "an' the wife an' baby in Lower Canady."

Oh! yah! yah! darkies laugh wid me,
For de white folks say Ole Shady's free,
So don't you see dat de jubilee
        Is a coming, coming,
        Hail mighty Day?

CHORUS.

Den away, away, for I can't wait any longer.
    Hooray, hooray, I'm going home.
Den away, away, for I can't wait any longer.
    Hooray, hooray, I'm going home.

Oh, Mass' got scared and so did his lady,
Dis chile breaks for Ole Uncle Aby,
"Open de gates, out here's Ole Shady
        A coming, coming."
        Hail mighty day.

Good-bye, Mass' Jeff., good-bye Mis'r Stephens,
'Scuse dis niggah for takin' his leavins'.
'Spect pretty soon you'll hear Uncle Abram's
    A coming, coming,
    Hail mighty day.

Good-bye hard work wid never any pay,
Ise a gwine up North where the good folks say
Dat white wheat bread and a dollar a day
   , Are coming, coming,
    Hail mighty day.

Oh, I've got a wife, and I've got a baby,
Living up yonder in Lower Canady,
Won't dey laugh when dey see Ole Shady
    A coming, coming,
    Hail mighty day.

The title in full of this song as originally published in 1861, was *Ole Shady, the Song of the Contraband.* It antedated the emancipation proclamation and anticipated the freedom of the slave, "de jubilee," and "white wheat bread an' a dollar a day." It was introduced by the Lombards and soon attained great popularity with the negro minstrel troupes.

That it was a great favorite in the northern armies is attested by the reminiscences of many who wore the blue. The soldier's appreciation finds generous expression in an article[1] by General Sherman, published in the *North American Review.* In describing an incident connected with the siege of Vicksburg, he says:

"A great many negroes, slaves, had escaped within the Union lines. Some were employed as servants by the officers, who paid them regular wages, some were employed by the quartermaster, and the larger number went North, free, in the Government chartered steamboats.

"Among the first class named was a fine, hearty 'darkey,' known as 'Old Shady,' who was employed by General McPherson as steward and cook at his headquarters in Mrs. Edward's house, in Vicksburg. Hundreds still living, among whom I may safely name General W. E. Strong, of Chicago, General Hickenlooper, of Cincinnati, Mrs. General Grant, Fred Grant, Mrs. Sherman and myself, well remember 'Old Shady.' After

---

[1] Old Shady, with a Moral, North American Review, October, 1888.

supper he used to assemble his chorus of 'darkies' and sing for our pleasure the songs of the period, among them one personal to himself, and, as I then understood, composed by himself. It was then entitled the *Day of Jubilee,* but is now recorded as simply *Old Shady;* and I do believe that since the Prophet Jeremiah bade the Jews 'to sing with gladness for Jacob and shout among the chief of the nations,' because of their deliverance from the house of bondage, that no truer or purer thought ever ascended from the lips of man than did at Vicksburg in the summer of 1863, when 'Old Shady' sang for us in a voice of pure melody his own song of deliverance from the bonds of slavery.   .

"After the war I met 'Old Shady' on a steamboat on the upper Mississippi, when he sang for us on the hurricane deck that good old song, which brought tears to the eyes of the passengers; and more recently I heard of him far up in Dakota, near 'Lower Canady,' toward which he seemed to lean as the coigne of safety, where his wife and baby had sought and obtained refuge. I believe him now to be dead, but living or dead, he has the love and respect of the old army of the Tennessee which gave him freedom. 'Good-bye, Mass' Jeff., good-bye Mis'r Stephens,' was a beautiful expression of the faithful family servant who yearned for freedom and a 'dollar a day.' "

After paying a glowing tribute to the colored people in the article quoted, General Sherman adds:

"What more beautiful sentiment than that of my acquaintance, 'Old Shady': 'Good-bye, Mass' Jeff., good-bye, Mis'r Stephens. 'Scuse dis niggah for takin' his leavins'—polite and gentle to the end. Burns never said anything better."

Old Shady seems to have derived his name from the song. He was not the author of either the words or the music, as General Sherman learned and freely admitted soon after the publication of his article. When Mrs. Hanby read it, she wrote to the General, sending him a copy of the song which was duly credited by the publisher to her husband. She received promptly the following courteous reply:

"Mrs. Kate Hanby: Dear Madam—I have received yours, with enclosure, and note the exception you take regarding an article from my pen in the October (1888) number of the *N. A. Review.* Shortly after the publication of that article I received a long letter from the subject of your husband's song, 'Old Shady,' then living, I believe, at Grand Forks, Dak., in which he disowned the authorship of the song but claimed the distinction of the title. Should I ever have occasion to refer to the subject in a future article, I shall certainly correct the misstatement. The expression, 'Good-bye, Mass' Jeff.; good-bye, Mis'r Stephens,' was surely most appropriate for a run-away slave, and led me to the conclusion that such a one was the author, but you are perfectly right in claiming it for your husband. With best wishes to you and yours, I am,

"Very truly yours,"

"W. T. Sherman,"

The real name of "Old Shady," as he was called, was D. Blakely Durant. After the war he worked on the upper Mississippi. The letter to Mrs. Hanby explains that he was not dead in 1888, as the General had supposed. He moved to Grand Forks, Dakota, where he acquired a comfortable home and where one of his children afterwards was a student in the North Dakota State University. He died in 1896.

NOW DEN! NOW DEN!

Darling Nelly Gray aroused sympathy for the slave; *Ole Shady* portrayed his practical ideal of home and freedom, and inspired him to seek both in the North; another song entitled *Now den! Now den!,*[1] for years after the war heard in many a cabin of the South, and still a favorite in some sections, held up to the vision of the freedman an ideal of joyful labor and its sure reward in the land of corn and cotton, which in the dawn of the new era of liberty was to be to him indeed the "Land ob Canaan." A recent writer,[2] as he glides down the Chesapeake and cruises along the shore where verdant and fruitful undulations of valley and hill put him into a reminiscent and poetic

---

[1] On the second page of this song occurs the following note: "The object of OLE SHADY was to encourage the contrabands to escape from their masters to the Union lines, and was suggested by the correspondence between General Butler and the authorities at Washington, with regard to the status of escaped slaves. The song in a very short time became known all over the South as the 'Contraband Song,' and was sung by the slaves everywhere, though very few at the North had as yet heard it. In like manner it is hoped that this song, while furnishing amusement to the social circle, may subserve the further and more important purpose of inducing the freedmen to return to their homes and labor."

[2] In "By the Waters of Chesapeake," *The Century Magazine,* December, 1893.

mood, recalls other days when the freedman, in the first joy of his release, poured forth his soul in these words, and listens with delight, for the colored laborers on deck are still singing:

De darkies say dis many a day,
 We's far from the land ob Canaan.
Oh, whar shall we go from de white-faced foe,
 Oh! whar shall we find our Canaan?

CHORUS.

Now den! Now den! into de cotton, darkies.
Plow in de cane till ye reach the bery bottom, darkies.
Ho! we go for de rice swamp low,
Hurrah for de land ob Canaan.

Oh happy day de darkies say,
 For at last we've found our Canaan.
Old Jordan's flood rolled red with blood,
But we march'd right ober into Canaan.

No driver's horn calls de slave at morn.
 Jordan swamp'd him crossing into Canaan.
But at break ob day we're away, we're away,
 For to till the fertile fields ob Canaan.

Come, ye runaways back, dat underground track
 Couldn't neber, neber lead you into Canaan.
Here your fathers sleep, here your loved ones weep;
 O come home to de happy land ob Canaan.

(To be sung after chorus to last stanza.)

Oh! Canaan, sweet Canaan,
We's been hunting for the land ob Canaan.
Canaan is now our happy home.
--urrah for de land ob Canaan.

THE NAMELESS HEROINE.

This song was written in honor of the young lady who aided fleeing Union prisoners to escape from the South.[1] One of these afterward related the incident upon which it was based substantially as follows:

---

[1] In January, 1865. The "nameless heroine" was Miss Melvina Stevens.

"She led us for seven miles. Then, while we remained in the wood, she rode forward over the long bridge which spanned the Nolechucky River, to see if there were any guards upon it; went to the first Union house beyond, to learn whether the roads were picketted; came back, and told us the coast was clear. Then she rode by toward her home. Had it . been safe to cheer, we should certainly have given three times three for the nameless heroine, who did us such vital kindness. 'Benisons upon her dear head forever!'"

As will be noticed, the words and measure are modeled after Tennyson's *Charge of the Light Brigade*:

> Out of the jaws of death,
> Out of the mouth of hell,
>   Weary and hungry, and fainting and sore,
> Fiends on the track of them,
> Fiends at the back of them,
>   Fiends all around but an angel before.

CHORUS.

> Fiends all around, but an angel before,
> Blessings be thine, loyal maid, evermore!

> Out by the mountain path,
> Down through the darksome glen,
>   Heedless of foes, nor at danger dismayed,
> Sharing their doubtful fate,
> Daring the tyrant's hate,
>   Heart of a lion, though form of a maid.

CHORUS.

> Hail to the angel who goes on before,
> Blessings be thine, loyal maid, evermore!

> "Nameless," for foes may hear,
>   But by our love for thee,
> Soon our bright sabers shall blush with their gore,
>   Then shall our banner free,
>   Wave, maiden, over thee:
> Then, noble girl, thou'lt be nameless no more.

CHORUS.

> Then we shall hail thee from mountain to shore,
> Bless thy brave heart, loyal maid, evermore!

It was quite natural that he should manifest an appreciative interest in the best literature of the day. He was much impressed with Holland's "Bitter Sweet." A congratulatory letter to the author called forth the following response:

"SPRINGFIELD, MASS., September 3, 1860.

"B. R. HANBY, DEAR SIR: If my book has done you and yours any measure of good, I am glad, for I should not like to be indebted to you for the whole of the deep satisfaction your letter has given me. I thank you for your thoughtfulness, and I thank you for spending so much time in its demonstration. Such letters pay better than money. I was glad when Mr. Scribner paid me a generous copyright, but I didn't cry; and, next to laughing, I think crying is the most satisfactory exercise of a man's lungs. May God bless you and your wife, and all whom you hold dear.

"Yours truly,
"J. G. HOLLAND."

THE MINISTRY.

Endowed with a deeply religious nature, which was developed and confirmed by home environment and education, Hanby had looked forward to the time when he should enter upon the realization of his life's work in the ministry. His eldest sister, still a zealous worker in the church, bears loving testimony to his conversion, his disinterested service in bringing others to the Master, and the fidelity with which he responded to the call to preach the Gospel of Christ.

"The foremost business of his life, from conversion to the end," says she, "was the salvation of souls. . . . One day in church he rose and with pallid face, which none who saw it can ever forget, calmly said, 'Brethren, God is preparing me either for the charnel house or for greater service to Him.' After that all knew without further words that God had set his seal upon him." He had heard the call, and only awaited the opportunity to enter fully upon the great work of man's redemption. At the close of his second year at the head of the academy, he realized his fondly cherished hope and donned the clerical robes.

He entered upon his labors in the village of Lewisburg, O. Young, scholarly and eloquent; kind, genial and optimistic; direct, ingenuous and sincere; blest with a refined and intelligent face

OTTERBEIN UNIVERSITY, WESTERVILLE, OHIO.

and a poetic soul that found expression in song, it is needless to say that he became the idol of the little flock that gathered and grew around the pulpit under the spell of his personality and power.

As a minister, according to the testimony of an old time friend and companion, he had many excellent qualities. He was enthusiastic without being pedantic, full of emotion but calm and earnest. He never read his sermons, nor did he permit himself to write them. It must not be presumed, however, that he entered the pulpit without thorough preparation. The theme of his text was thoroughly thought out, and even the sentences, as he once remarked to this friend, were carefully formed before delivery. While at college he often served as critic in his literary society, where the ability, just discrimination and kindly spirit evident in the discharge of the delicate duties of that post made him a general favorite. His analytic and well worded report at the conclusion of the evening's exercises, was awaited with pleasure alike by performers and audience. He thought out his sermons with critical exactitude, after weighing with great care synonymous expressions to determine which most nearly expressed his idea. If from a doctrinal point these sermons were not profound, they were never dogmatical, always natural, sweet in spirit, messages from the Master.

His chief interest was in the young people of his congregation and the community. He mingled freely with them socially, and entered with zest into their innocent recreations and amusements. The sleigh rides of winter — usually taken in a large sled — the outing in quest of the first wild flowers of spring, and the harvest home picnic with all its simple but delightful and elevating attractions were dear to the young clerical friend of the children. He taught them drawing and music, and delivered special sermons and lectures for them. No wonder that they were affectionately fond of him and referred to him with fervor as "our preacher."

It followed, as a matter of course, that his church was the center of attraction to the young and that many should find their way to the Christian life under his inspiration and guidance. Of that number, one relates how after she and many others had united with the church, the good minister planned a pleasant surprise. He and the parents quietly contributed to a fund with which there was purchased for each new member a neat and substantially bound copy of the Bible, with the name of the recipient stamped on the back in gold. In many families these precious gifts are still fondly treasured in loving memory of the long ago and the dear teacher who was a beneficent part of it all.

His love of children, of course, antedated his entrance into the ministry. Mrs. Hanby, speaking of this characteristic, recently said:

"If 'to be a good story teller is to be a king among children,' he certainly deserved the title. His ideal life was the child life. He loved it for its unconscious sweetness. All the children who knew him were his friends, and would hasten to greet him when they met him on the street. Nothing was too difficult if it was for the little ones. He would go miles to entertain them. While he was with the John Church Company, the Friends of Richmond, Ind., collected into a school several hundred of the poorest children of the city. Although no singers themselves, they fully realized the sweetening and refining influence of music, and invited Mr. Hanby to come and sing for them whenever he could. He was glad of the opportunity, and frequently gave up other things for the sake of pleasing those poor little children. He taught them many little songs, and among others was *Chich-a-dee-dee,* which they particularly liked. By and by those good Friends rented the largest hall in the city and gave these children and their friends a banquet. It was in the evening, and the hall was beautifully lighted and decorated. Mr. Hanby was invited to sing. I accompanied him to the hall, and never shall I forget the greeting given him by the children. Their faces lighted up, they clapped their little hands and exclaimed: 'Oh, here comes Chick-a-dee-dee!' He sang to them, told them stories, and was a child with them all evening."

His advent was a distinct stimulus to the æsthetic development of the little village. The local schoolmaster found him companionable and helpful. There was a new interest in public entertainments, in which of course music was given a prominent place. Pianos and organs began to appear in the homes of the well-to-do, and much was added to the sum of happiness in the community.

To a careful observer it is scarcely necessary to say, however, that Rev. Benjamin Hanby was treading dangerous ground. The church of the middle west forty years ago was not the church of to-day. The austere element of the Puritan spirit was then still dominant. This was not in any measure, be it said, due to the peculiar doctrines of the United Brethren Church. For its day it was progressive, even liberal. It early took advanced ground against the institution of slavery, and within comparatively broad limits it gave conscience free range.

The barrier that loomed up in Hanby's way was not so much the spirit of his church as it was the spirit of the times. There was among the religious folk of almost every community a somewhat clearly defined opinion as to the minister's place and proper attitude toward the people. They had little faith in the conversion of those who joined church "because they liked the preacher." An impression prevailed that the minister should hold himself somewhat aloof from his people; as a pious soul once expressed it, they should feel, when they approached him, that they were "in the presence of a superior being." Public entertainments, with attendant features that even remotely sug- gested the stage, were objects of suspicion and alarm. And as for music — well, there were many among the devout and right- eous who thoroughly believed that it was one of the insinuating devices of Satan himself. These good people would naturally assume the interrogatory attitude toward the innovations of Rev. Hanby. That his affable manner and the genial sunshine of his smile melted away much of this incipient opposition there can be no doubt; it perhaps would be too much to expect that it should wholly silence criticism.

The leaders of the conservative element, however, had mis- givings of a more serious character. They noticed that the vicarious atonement and the resurrection had been somewhat slighted and that the doctrine of eternal punishment had been wholly eliminated from his sermons. Worse than all, the report gained currency that he had privately declared that he did not believe in the last of these. Matters moved quietly but promptly to a crisis. There was no dramatic scene. No outward struggle marked his progress at the parting of the ways. Without a word of complaint or a plea to shake the faith of any mortal, with a heart full of tenderness and love and hope, without an intimation of the new light that was leading to the broader way, he left the pulpit and soon afterward severed his connection with the conference.[1]

That the change of his views did not shake the foundations of his religious faith is attested by his subsequent life and the large number of sacred songs he composed and published after he left the ministry. He did not formally sever his connection with the church, to which he was bound by many happy associations. His experience, like that of Emerson, seems to have prepared him for larger service in a sphere for which he was peculiarly fitted.

MUSICAL COMPOSER.

He entered at once the employ of the John Church Music Company of Cincinnati, O., and remained with the firm about two years. He continued to compose occasionally, but the demands of the business in which he was employed did not leave him much leisure for other work.

He was a temperance advocate and wrote some songs dedicated to the cause, among which were *Revelers' Chorus* and *Crowding Awfully*. He contributed to Ohio political literature at least one effusion, with the refrain

> Oh, Governor Brough,
> It's terrible tough.

He was next transferred to the well known music house of Root & Cady, of Chicago, Ill. He regarded this change as in every way most fortunate. Here at last he seemed to have found the work for which he was especially equipped. He was employed to write Sunday and day school songs. This brought him again into contact with children. The echo of his soul might have found expression in the words of Dickinson:

> Oh, there's nothing on earth half so holy
> As the innocent heart of a child.

---

[1] In the proceedings of the conference of 1866 occurs the following minute:

"On motion, the credentials of B. R. Hanby were received back by the conference at his request, and his connection with the conference severed."

Of his work here, Mrs. Hanby says:

"He loved to write children's songs because he loved children. Teaching them, singing with them, and writing songs for them, was, I think, his real work. He was happier in it than in anything else that he ever did. His relations with George F. Root were of the most pleasant character. Mr. Root regarded him almost as a son, and their intercourse was that of very dear friends rather than that of employer and employed."

The two edited *Our Song Birds,* in which a number of Mr. Hanby's songs appear. These were days of joyful labor. He composed over sixty tunes and wrote the words for about half of them. At the same time he was preparing for publication a work in which he developed his system of teaching music. It included most of his songs and numerous selections from other composers. He was enthusiastic over the book and confidently expected it to yield him an ample return for his labor. The manuscript was almost ready for the printer when business called him to St. Paul in the summer of 1866. He took the work with him in order that he might employ the leisure hours of travel in putting on the finishing touches. Soon after reaching his destination, he was taken seriously ill and returned home at once. He checked and shipped the trunk containing his manuscript, but it never reached its destination. All efforts to locate it were unavailing. No trace of it was ever found.

He reached his home with a hectic flush on his cheek. His lungs were seriously affected. But hope, so native to his buoyant nature and characteristic of his malady, bore him on, his former self in everything but waning strength. Though confined to his home most of the time, mind and pen were still active. *Our Song Birds* claimed his especial interest. Following are the words of a few of his contributions:

DEVOTIONAL SONGS.

THE HOLY HOUR.

How sweet the holy hour,
　When at the throne of grace;
The friends of Jesus bend the knee,
　And angels fill the place.

Oh, haste, my willing feet,
　To join the happy throng;
Confess thy sins, my trembling lips,
　Or raise the grateful song.

The gentle Shepherd flies,
　(Oh, wealth of love untold!)
To hear, and help, and heal and bless
The humblest of His fold.

Oh, Shepherd, Savior, King,
Come, make this heart Thy throne;
Drive out Thy foes, Thou Mighty One,
And make me all Thine own.

GONDOLA.

We come in childhood's joyfulness,
　We come as children, free!
We offer up, O God! our hearts,
　In trusting love to Thee.
Well may we bend in solemn joy,
　At Thy bright courts above.
Well may the grateful child rejoice,
　In such a Father's love.

We come not as the mighty come;
　Not as the proud we bow.
But as the pure in heart should bend,
　Seek we Thine altars now.
"Forbid them not," the Savior said;
　But let them come to Me;
Oh, Savior dear, we hear Thy call,
　We come, we come, to Thee.

To Thee, Thou Lord of life and light,
　Amid the angel throng,
We bend the knee, we lift the heart,
　And swell the holy song.
How blest the children of the Lord,
　Who wait around His throne,
How sweet to tread the path that leads
　To yonder heavenly home.

COME FROM THE HILL-TOP.

Come from the hill-top, the vale, and the glen;
Lights now the Sabbath the landscape again;
Little feet patter like rain o'er the sod,
On in the path to the temple of God.

CHORUS.

On to the temple, on to the temple,
On to the temple, on to the temple.
Little feet patter like rain o'er the sod,
On in the path to the temple of God.

Who to the fields or the forests would stray,
Seeking their pleasure at work or at play?
Who, when that banner of love is unfurl'd,
Turn to the bubble-like joys of the world?

We from the service of Sin would depart,
Heeding Thy mandate of "Give me Thine heart;"
Suffer the children to "come unto me."
Savior, behold at Thy feet here are we.

Thus when our Sabbaths on earth are no more,
We shall be with Thee, and love and adore;
Singing in heaven, that bright world of bliss,
Songs that we learned on the Sabbaths of this.

NOW TO THE LORD.

Now to the Lord on high,
　　Ye saints your voices raise.
Let little children throng His court,
　　And sing the Savior's praise.

Here on this holy day,
　　Ye multitudes, repair,
And pour your swelling souls in song,
　　Or lift the humble prayer.

Rejoicing, or in grief,
　　Come, sit and hear His Word;
And thro' your smiles, or thro' your tears,
　　Look up and see your Lord.

His ear is quick to hear,
  His hand is open wide;
Each trusting soul shall surely find
  His ev'ry want supplied.

OCCASIONAL SONGS.

ROBIN SONG.

We are coming, sang the robins,
  For the woods and groves are gay;
Will you give us kindly greeting,
  Little Jessie, little May?
We will join your matin carols,
  We will chant your vesper lay,
While we wait your sweeter echoes,
  Little Jessie, Little May.

CHORUS.

We are coming, sang the robins,
  For the woods and groves are gay;
Will you give us kindly greeting,
  Little Jessie, little May?

There's a tree beneath your window,
  With a paradise of leaves,
We will build our robin homestead
  In the branches 'neath the eaves;
There will be the sweetest chirping,
  In the garden by and by,
When our pleasant toil is ended,
  And the nestlings learn to fly.

You will scatter crumbs, it may be,
  On your friendly window sill,
For each darling robin baby,
  Has an empty, gaping bill.
We will give our farewell concert,
  When the flowers pass away,
But will come again as they will,
  Little Jessie, little May.

EXCURSION SONG.

Ho! ho! ho!
Out to the beautiful groves we go;
This is our holiday now, you know.
Sweet shall our melodies float and flow,
　Out on the balmy air:
Bear them, ye breezes that gently blow,
　Scatter them everywhere.

Sing! sing! sing!
Heaven shall smile at the praises we bring.
Forest and meadow with music ring,
Echo the cadences gracefully fling,
　Out on the balmy air:
Bear them aloft on her silv'ry wing,
　Scatter them everywhere.

Play! play! play!
Run, oh, ye happy ones while ye may;
Roam thro' the forests at will to-day,
Pouring your shouts and your laughter gay,
　Out on the balmy air:
Sylvia beckons, oh, speed away,
　Scatter them everywhere.

BOAT SONG.

Row! row! row!
Over the beautiful blue we go!
Row! row! row !row!
Over the waters we go.
　Lightly every heart is bounding,
　Gay the voice of song is sounding,
　Sweet the light guitar resounding.
Thus we gaily row.

Row! row! row!
Over the beautiful blue we go!
Row! row! row! row!
Over the waters we go.
　Starry vaults above us beaming,
　Starry depths below us seeming,
　Silver wavelets 'round us gleaming,
Thus we gaily row.

Row! row! row!
Over the beautiful blue we go!
Row! row! row! row!
Over the waters we go.
   Heart to heart we'll sail together,
   Hand in hand for aye and ever,
   Naught shall change us, naught shall sever,
Thus we gaily row.

WEAVER JOHN.

Down in that cottage lives Weaver John,
   And a happy old John is he;
Maud is the name of his dear old dame,
   And a blessed old dame is she.

CHORUS.

Whickity, whackity, click and clack,
   How the shuttles do glance and ring!
Here they go, there they go, forth and back,
   A staccato song they sing.

Close by his side is his gentle wife,
   And she's twirling the flaxen thread;
Sweet to his ear is the low wheel's hum,
   It was purchased when they were wed.

Pussy is frisking about the room,
   With her kittens, one, two, three, four;
Towser is taking his wonted nap
   On the settle behind the door.

Soft as the hum of the dame's low wheel,
   Does the music of time roll on;
Morning and noon of a useful life
   Bring a peacefully setting sun.

  Our Song Birds was a musical periodical, each number named after some bird whose picture appeared on the cover. The last issue to which Hanby contributed was, by a touching coincidence, called "The Dove." Among the selections from this number are *Come from the Hill-top* and *Weaver John*, with the beautifully suggestive closing stanzas:

Thus when our Sabbaths on earth are no more,
We shall be with Thee, and love and adore.
Singing in heaven, that bright world of bliss,
Songs that we learned on the Sabbaths of this.

Soft as the hum of the dame's low wheel,
  Does the music of time roll on.
Morning and noon of a useful life
  Bring a peacefully setting sun.

His life had not reached the zenith of the allotted three score years and ten when it swiftly but silently declined, and the twilight shadows began to gather. One day in March, Mr. Cady, one of his employers, visited him and found him weak but cheerful and sanguine as of old. He said little about his condition; his conversation was all in the hopeful vein; his mind was full of plans for the future. His illness by subtle, painless stages bore him through waning strength, while the evening star to his raptured eye was radiant with the promise of the years stretching peacefully before. Behind were the snows of winter. From the frozen streets and blackened air of the great city, he turned in thought to the glories of reviving nature, as with enfeebled hand he had drawn them in his latest verse:

The morning is beaming, the morning is beaming;
  Oh, hasten the sight to behold!
The mountains are gleaming, the mountains are gleaming,
  With tintings of purple and gold.

The brooklets are dashing, the brooklets are dashing
  O'er pebbles of crimson and white;
The rivers are flashing, the rivers are flashing,
  Their arrows of silvery light.

Gone were the wintry blasts. He looked forward with eager anticipation to the coming of spring. While balmy south winds were whispering of her approach, he fell asleep and woke not with the coming day.[1]

---

[1] He died March 16, 1867.

BENJAMIN RUSSEL HANBY—PORTRAIT AND MONUMENT.

"He was just beginning to make a name for himself in the musical world," declares a writer, "when he was stricken down in the prime of young manhood."

"He was educated for the ministry," says Mr. Root, in his autobiography, "but was so strongly inclined to music that he decided to try to make that his life's work. But he died almost at the commencement of his career."

Backward to the old home in the college town were borne the mortal remains of this dear interpreter of the melodies of the human heart. On the campus, at the corners of the streets and in the study room, there was the pall of sadness that only the *alma mater* of that day could feel at the obsequies of such a son. Professors, students and citizens moved in silent procession to the little cemetery by the winding stream, and in the quiet southwest corner, where sunshine and shadow weave changing figures on the sward the whole year round, the bard was gently laid to rest.

He yearned for the return of the season dear to poetic souls. With warmth and fragrance and music, spring came to open buds and spread the living green above his grave.

Nor poet, nor minstrel in all this middle west has found in place more fitting his lowly mansion of dreamless repose. Among the little mounds, the dark cedar and the arching elm stand guard, while at the edge of the sharp declivity beyond the grave and shading it from the declining sun, rises a sturdy oak, that has stood through calm and storm while generations have passed away. Not far distant and seen distinctly through the intervening branches, the stream with circling sweep moves onward as of old. Around is the music of nature, pleasantly broken at intervals by the college bell as it calls the students to the lessons of the day.

Fair Otterbein! Blest are thy classic shades and hallowed thy memories. From these walls high-minded sons have gone forth to win laurels in the fields of honorable endeavor. Ministers and educators and jurists have acquired more than local fame, and one sweet singer found his way to the universal heart. The great world, in its mad rush for gain, may care but little who and what he was. But a better day will dawn — is dawning.

When vulgar wealth yields to intellectual culture; when to sway thousands through the magic power of song to the support of a righteous cause is as great as to move men by eloquent appeal or to lead them forth to battle; when to add to the world's happiness is to be the world's benefactor; when to touch and refine the heart is to be a savior of mankind; when greed shall not outweigh the things of the spirit; when self is less and love is more, the fame of this son of song shall have a wider range, and for his memory there shall be a resurrection in the land he loved so well.

ACKNOWLEDGEMENT.

In the preparation of the foregoing pages the writer has received helpful material from printed sketches by Mrs. A. L. Billheimer and Mrs. Kate (Winter) Hanby. He is also under especial obligations to The John Church Company who have kindly permitted him to use the words of the following copyrighted songs: *Little Tillie's Grave, Now Den! Now Den!' The Nameless Heroine, The Holy Hour, Gondola, Come from the Hill-Top, Now to the Lord, Robin Song, Boat Song, Weaver John and Excursion Song.*

EDITORIALANA.

VOL. XIV. No. 2.   *E. O. Randall*   APRIL, 1905

THE AVERY HISTORY OF THE UNITED STATES.

A philosophical essayist on the study of history tritely remarks that a historian should be possessed of industry, conscience and imagination.

ELROY M. AVERY.

Industry and patience to faithfully exhume the facts, conscience to truthfully and impartially exploit them, and imagination to vividly portray the scenes and events involved that the reader in his mind's eye may perceive them realistically reproduced. Such is the ideal historian. Such an one to a rare degree is Mr. Elroy M. Avery, author of "A History of the United States and Its People," published by the Burrows Brothers Company, Cleveland, Ohio—to be completed in twelve octavo volumes. The first volume is before us. As the proof of the pudding is in the eating, the test of the book is in the reading. It has long been our notion that the history of the United States has not yet been written. To be sure, many so-called histories have been put forth, but in the main written by eastern authors—provincial scholars, whose pens have been cramped by local pride or prejudices—a narrow range of historical vision—a vision bright and clear often till it reached the Alleghany Mountains, but beyond that lost in the vista of the great and overwhelming West. The vast and vital part played in the Ohio and Mississippi Valleys and beyond, in the formative period of our country, has usually been slightingly treated or practically ignored. The true history of the United States must be written by a Westerner; the entire sweep of the historian's realm can only be had from the center and not from one side of our vast domain. Mr. Avery was properly born, located and educated for this work. All hail to a recital of the origin and growth of the American Republic by a Westerner—an Ohioan. Mr. Avery is a typical American. Born in Erie, Monroe County, Michigan (1844), of the best New England stock and tradition, the best blood of our forefathers, and the best brawn and brain of our western self-made manhood. A descendant of Puritan ancestry, a son of the American Revolution, a

country farm boy, ambitious, industrious, indefatigable in his efforts for
the development of all that was best in him, an improver of opportunities,
a student in the school of experience and the academic course, a school
teacher, a printer and newspaper writer, a brave soldier boy in the war
for our nation's unity and preservation, college graduate (Michigan, '71),
professor, litterateur, scientist, lecturer, principal of high-school, author
of many standard text-books in scientific and literary subjects, a politi-
cian of the higher order and statesman in the Ohio Senate (1894-1898).
Rare combination of natural and acquired fitness for the work which has
engaged his attention for the past twenty years.

This first volume covers the period of the geologic formation of the
land, the first Americans, paleolithic and neolithic Americans, the North-
men, voyages of the early navigators, Columbus, Da Gama, the Cabots,
Vespucius, the Spanish, English and French pioneers, the American
Indians, etc. The chapters on the first Americans, the paleolithic the
neolithic man, are especially interesting and satisfactory. They deal with
subjects fascinating because somewhat nebulous—on the border between
myth and history. Mr. Avery has been unusually happy in treating these
topics—concisely and comprehensively giving what is known and what has
been guessed by the leading knowers and chief guessers. After stating
the geologic hypothesis of the formation of surface of our land, he says:

> "In the earliest archean age (Azoic), only dead matter
> existed on earth. Then life appeared: first the unconscious life
> of the plant, then, the conscious and intelligent life of the animal.
> After almost countless ages, man appeared. Upon matter, life
> had been imposed; now, mind was to crown the structure, stand-
> ing upon matter and life and dominating both. 'And the even-
> ing and the morning were the sixth day.' At what stage in this
> scene of development did man first appear in the world that
> Columbus found, and what sort of a being was he?"

He then discusses the earliest evidences of man's appearance—the
glacial man—the original "ice-man"—the paleolithic man, so-called because
of the "rudeness of the relics found in the quaternary gravels." He was
followed by the neolithic gentleman (?), also pre-historic, but of a higher
grade of intelligence and skill, residing in the stone age, but whose implements were ground or polished in a manner that set him above his paleolithic predecessor in the scale of civilization. The evidences of the neolithic race are very abundant and widely distributed. The third period
was called the ethnographic, lying partly before and partly within historical
times. "It began with our first knowledge of the red man, and is now
fading from the screen like a dissolving view that has been held up for
study for four hundred years." Then follow descriptions of prehistoric
monuments. The shell heaps, the bone heaps, graves, village sites, and
the innumerable and interesting remains of the cliff dwellers, mound
builders, and peoples who left their indelible and often vast and wonderful

works but no written records or continuing traditions. Fort Ancient, Serpent Mound and the incomparable and inscrutable earth structures near Newark and Chillicothe are described and faithfully diagramed. The researches and conclusions of the archæologist and ethnologist are admirably summarized. The testimony of the prehistoric remains as to the art, mode of life and warfare of the strange and lost race is set forth, briefly of course, but with skillful marshalling of facts and fancies.

"There are two widely held and antagonistic opinions concerning the builders of these mounds. One school of archæologists insists that the mound builders were far more cultured than any known North American Indians, that their earthworks were more complicated and better finished, that their arts of fashioning and polishing stone and of fabricating pottery, their agriculture and their architecture, were more advanced, and that their social and religious systems were of a higher order than 'were those of their successors. This theory leads up to the concept of an extinct civilization and a vanished race. The more modern school confidently insists that 'there is nothing found in the mode of construction of these mounds nor in the vestages of art they contain to indicate that their builders had reached a higher culture-status than that attained by some of the Indian tribes found occupying the country at the time of the arrival of the first Europeans.'

"At no time in the history of any of the older nations of the world has the whole population been removed to give place to another altogether different. Continuity is the law of history, and it is difficult to believe that that law has been violated here. It is hardly conceivable that a race should come upon the stage, act its part, and go away to give place to another company of players with whom the first had naught to do."

The chapter on the Indians of North America deals with the "red man" of our earliest historic knowledge. His origin, extent of his habitations at time of Columbian discoveries, his racial separation into tribes and groups of tribes.

"At the end of the nineteenth century, there were about one hundred and fifty officially recognized tribes in the United States, exclusive of Alaska, gathered upon more than fifty reservations, besides others that occupied state reservations or were scattered among the whites. We have no sufficient data for ascertaining the aboriginal population at the time of the discovery, but, after making all allowances for exaggeration in the early estimate, there can be no question that it has greatly diminished. The popular impression that the eastern tribes have simply been removed to the west is true in but a few cases. In most instances they have been exterminated by war, disease, and failure of accustomed food supply, consequented upon the advent of the whites."

The simple and primitive existence and the peculiar characteristics of these children of the forest are entertainingly depicted. This chapter is followed by a valuable and full appendix of statistics concerning the Indians—treaties of the United States with the tribes, the cost to the government in the case of these aboriginal wards, the reservations, their area, number of Indians in each, etc.

Mr. Avery's style is most felicitous. We know of no historian more readable in manner or more elegant in rich but simple English. One could easily be persuaded to read these pages for entertainment, no less than for information. Mr. Avery has the true historic temperament as well as the scholarly intellect; there is nothing mechanical, dull or common place in the pages of this recital; once entered upon the opening of this volume, the reader is borne along with an interest as unflagging as that imparted by the shifting scenes of some play.

The author has selected the material for his readers from an almost limitless store-house, with exact discrimination. The work is popular in form, it is, as the author declares, for the reader of general culture, rather than the professional student. The latter, however, is partially provided for by having placed at his disposal a bibliographical appendix, in which are given for this volume alone a list of over five hundred authorities arranged alphabetically and under topical heads, so that sources of information on any given subject may be readily found. The work is profusely illuminated with maps and illustrations. The mechanical execution of the work surpasses that of any history we have seen. The publishers have given the production of Mr. Avery's graphic and fascinating pen a setting worthy the theme and treatment. The volumes are most perfect and attractive specimens of the modern "art of arts." No history of the United States has been honored with such royal encasement. It is worthy the shelves of a sovereign.

THE AMERICAN HISTORICAL ASSOCIATION.

The twentieth annual meeting of the American Historical Association was held in Chicago, Wednesday, Thursday and Friday, December 28, 29 and 30, 1904. Members were present from nearly every State in the Union, representing nearly all the leading historical societies and the historical departments of the leading colleges and universities. The Ohio State Archæological and Historical Society was officially represented by the secretary, E. O. Randall, Columbus, and Mr. A. J. Baughman, Mansfield, life member of the society and also secretary of the Richland County Historical Society. There were also present Miss Martha J. Maltby, Columbus, Mr. Nelson W. Evans, Portsmouth, and Dr. C. E. Slocum,

Defiance, all life members of the Ohio State Archæological and Historical Society.

The meetings of the association were held in the Mandel Assembly Hall and the Reynolds Club Rooms of the University of Chicago. The first session of the association was held Wednesday afternoon, and was opened with a felicitous address of welcome by President William A. Harper, of the University of Chicago. During the several sessions that followed, various phases of historical work, both American and foreign, were presented and discussed. Among the topics considered were methods of collection of materials, the best means of organizing historical societies, mutual calendaring of manuscript collections, and the possibility of co-operation among societies in the matter of publications. Also the relation of state historical societies to the state government, the work of American historical societies, the historical congress at St. Louis, the material of American history in the English archives, and the teaching of history in the elementary schools and other kindred topics.

The names of some fifty professors of history in the colleges of the country were on the published program. Three foreign universities were also represented. Ettore Pais, professor in the University of Naples, gave an address on Roman History; Paul Milyoukov, professor of the University of Sofia, spoke on the subject of "Russian Historiography," and Friedrich Keutgen, professor in the University of Jena, gave a very useful and interesting talk on the necessity in America of the study of the early history of modern European nations.

Especially interesting was the "Round Table" conference, held by the representatives of the various state and local historical societies, at which Mr. Reuben G. Thwaites, Secretary of the State Historical Society of Wisconsin, presided. At this conference formal papers were read on the following subjects: "Forms of Organization, and Relation to the State Government," Thomas M. Owen, director of the department of archives and history, Alabama; Warren Upham, secretary of the Minnesota Historical Society. "The Possibilities of Mutual Co-operation Between the Societies, State and Local," C. M. Burton, president of the Michigan Pioneer and Historical Society; Benjamin H. Shambaugh, State Historical Society of Iowa. Director McLaughlin, of the Bureau of Historical Research, Carnegie Institute, gave an account of the indexing of manuscripts. W. C. Ford, chief of the division of Manuscripts, Library of Congress, read a paper on "Government Archives in Our New Possessions."

Many topics and phases of historical research, collection and collation were presented and considered. Reports show that there is a growing interest in the history of the country, and the consensus of opinion was that more work upon the lines indicated should be taken up by the colleges and other institutions of learning, and to this the two hundred professors and teachers present enthusiastically assented.

Among the social features of the meeting were a luncheon in Hutchinson Hall, Wednesday at 1 p. m.: a reception by the Chicago Historical

Society Wednesday evening, and a reception Thursday afternoon by President and Mrs. Harper, at their residence, corner of Fifty-ninth street and Lexington avenue. President Harper is an Ohio man, and was formerly connected with Muskingum College, at New Concord. His wife is also a Buckeye, and when a girl lived in Mansfield. She is the daughter of the Rev. David Paul, who was the pastor of the Mansfield United Presbyterian Church from 1858 until 1864, when he resigned to accept the presidency of the Muskingum college.

The American Political Science Association and the American Economic Association held their annual meetings at the same time, in the halls of the Chicago University buildings.

NEW YORK HISTORICAL SOCIETY BUILDING.

Apropos of the need for a building for the Ohio State Archæological and Historical Society, we note with much interest and not a little envy the announcement that the New York Historical Society is erecting a building for its future home on Seventy-sixth Street, opposite Central Park, New York. The site of the building was bought in June, 1891, at a cost of $300,000. Some difficulty was experienced in raising the additional money necessary to begin the work of the construction. Dean Hoffman, father of the present president of the society, was the leader and director of this undertaking. He induced several prominent New Yorkers—among them Archer M. Huntington, Miss Matilda Wolf Bruce, J. P. Morgan, F. Robert Schell, the late John Alsop King, Cornelius and George W. Vanderbilt—to contribute large amounts.

The building committee was appointed in June, 1901, to receive and report upon plans for the proposed building. This committee decided to erect the central portion, 135 x 115 feet, on the lines of American colonial architecture, from the plans of Messrs. York & Sawyer, at an estimated cost of $400,000. The cornerstone was laid by ex-Mayor Seth Low, November 17, 1903. The work has been going on with more or less interruption, but it is expected that the building will be completed as far as the first story this spring. The building when completed will be the finest of its kind in the country. It will be of pink Milford granite, three stories high, affording ample shelf space for nearly 500,000 volumes and several special rooms for exhibits of various sorts, and will contain an auditorium on the main floor, capable of seating 400 persons, a lecture room, reception, lounging and committee rooms. On the second floor will be a large museum, two large lecture galleries and a reading room. The plan of this central portion of the building is so drawn that at some future time extensive wings of the same general style of architecture may be added.

The New York Historical Society was founded on November 20, 1804, on which date Egbert Benson, De Witt Clinton, Rev. Dr. William Linn, Rev. Dr. John N. Abeel, Rev. Dr. John M. Mason, Dr. David Hoosack, Anthony Bleecker, Samuel Bayard, Peter G. Stuyvesant and John Pintard met in the picture room of the old city hall, in Wall Street, to organize this society, whose principal object should be to collect and protect materials relating to the natural, civil and ecclesiastical history of the United States in general and the State of New York in particular. The society was incorporated by an act of the legislature of February 9, 1809. It is now one of the richest historical societies of the country in its accumulation of books, pictures, manuscripts and objects of art. Its library comprises over 100,000 books, pamphlets and manuscripts. At present the society is housed in its own property, a small, unpretentious building, which it has occupied for a century, which is literally packed with the invaluable collections which the society has purchased or from time to time have been bequeathed to it by distinguished donors.

The securing by the New York Historical Society of such worthy quarters as it will soon possess is an object lesson which it is hoped the Ohio State Archæological and Historical Society may be able to follow at no distant date. With a home such as the life and work of our society now deserves it, too, would be the beneficiary of innumerable collections of books, manuscripts and archæological relics and endowment funds. Provided with proper permanent quarters the Ohio State Society would soon occupy the same relation to Ohio archæology and history that the New York Society now bears to the Empire State.

THE MAUMEE VALLEY PIONEER AND HISTORICAL ASSOCIATION.

The Maumee Valley Pioneer and Historical Association held its annual meeting at the court house, in Toledo, on February 22. The association is comprised of earnest pioneers and other loyal, patriotic citizens, living along the historic Maumee. They are endeavoring to keep alive the fires of patriotism and preserve the historic landmarks of the eventful locality in question. There was a good attendance of gentlemen and lady members. Mr. D. K. Hollenbeck, of Perrysburg, the president, called the meeting to order, and the Rev. N. B. C. Love, trustee of the Ohio State Archæological and Historical Society, delivered the invocation. The report of the treasurer showed a balance of $38.96 on hand. The following members were elected as trustees for thee years: D. K. Hollenbeck, J. L. Pray and C. O. Bringham. A committee of three, consisting of Julius Lamson, David Robinson, Jr., and J. Kent Hamilton, was appointed to confer with the electric roads, with a view of their contributing toward the fund for buying the unpurchased portion of Fort Meigs, which the association hopes to obtain entire, and, without destroying its historic character, transform into some sort of a public park. The association already owns nine acres, which is about one-fourth of the entire fort tract. The committee on Fort Miami reported that the association should no longer contemplate buying that property, as it had been purchased by Mr. A. M. Woolson, who they were glad to learn proposed to preserve the landmark, and, it was understood, would set off a portion to the Daughters of the American Revolution. There was also some discussion concerning the proposition that the association acquire possession of the old court house at Maumee, which building is located on the spot of the famous Dudley massacre. The court house would be a most fitting building for a museum of the relics of the pioneer days.

Rev. N. B. C. Love pronounced a fitting eulogy upon Mr. J. R. Tracy, a deceased member of the association. Upon adjournment of the association, the board of directors held a meeting and re-elected the old officers, as follows: President, D. K. Hollenbeck; Vice-President, William Corlett; Secretary, J. L. Pray, and Treasurer, A. F. Mitchell.

TO RAISE PERRY'S FLAGSHIP "NIAGARA."

The Cleveland *Plain Dealer,* of late date, in announcing that a movement is in contemplation of raising the Niagara from its watery grave, in Lake Erie, says:

"Whatever may be the objections to raising the hull of the battleship Maine from the mud of Havana harbor, none of them can hold in the case of Commodore Perry's flagship, the Niagara, which it is now proposed to raise from the bottom of Misery Bay, in Erie harbor, where she has reposed for three-quarters of a century. The ship was built in Erie, and when her day of usefulness was over was sunk out of sight, and for a long time almost out of memory. The house committee on naval affairs has ordered a favorable report on the bill, providing money for raising the Niagara and turning her over to the state home for disabled soldiers and sailors.

"The Niagara was the flagship of the man who performed off Put-in-Bay in September, 1813, the unprecedented feat of compelling the surrender of an entire British squadron, and as such she should fairly share that affection and veneration which the American people have long lavished on the Constitution and one or two other historic ships, none of which really performed such a glorious part in naval war as fell to the share of Perry's flagship.

"This national neglect can be attributed in great part to the fact that no gifted lyrist like the author of "Old Ironsides" has embalmed the Niagara's achievement in deathless verse and in part, perhaps, to the American tendency to forget the day of small things. The Niagara was little if any larger than one of the boats which a modern 16,000-ton battleship carries on her deck. In these days a 2,500-ton war vessel is not considered worthy of a place in a line of battle, and is used chiefly for sea police duty, yet the combined tonnage of Perry's squadron did not exceed 2,500 tons. An ordinary lake freighter is larger."

FIRST NAVIGATOR OF THE OHIO RIVER.

It is a most interesting but generally unknown fact (which we have verified by a letter from Mr. William Loeb, secretary to the President) that the brother of the grandfather of President Roosevelt was the first man to navigate a steamboat on the Ohio and Mississippi Rivers, says Mr. Charles C. Allen. Captain Roosevelt was a warm personal friend of Robert Fulton, the inventor of steam craft, and soon after Fulton's successful voyage on the Hudson conceived the idea of launching such a vessel on the Western rivers. A good deal of doubt was expressed as to the practicability of the undertaking, but Captain Roosevelt was enthusiastic, and along about 1810 made a personal survey of the Ohio and Lower Mississippi to determine its feasibility beyond all peradventure. The result of his survey was entirely to his satisfaction and, returning to Pittsburg, he began the construction of a steamboat from plans furnished him by Fulton and Livingston. In the spring of 1811 the vessel was launched, and, accompanied by his wife, who had the true pioneer spirit and refused to be left behind, the President's grandfather began his voyage down the Ohio. He entered the Mississippi during the throes of the earthquake which devastated so much of southeastern Missouri, but weathered the tumult successfully and continued his trip to New Orleans, where he arrived a short time after, the first man to build a steamboat west of the Alleghanies and the first to navigate one on western waters.

LIFE MEMBERS.

Since the issue of the January Quarterly the following have qualified as life members of the Ohio State Archæological and Historical Society:

Mr. Frank S. Brooks, Columbus, Ohio.

Hon. Ross J. Alexander, Bridgeport, Ohio.

Mr. George W. Vanhorn, Findlay, Ohio.

APPOINTMENT OF TRUSTEES.

On February 23, 1905, Governor Myron T. Herrick re-appointed Professor B. F. Prince, Springfield, and Mr. E. O. Randall, Columbus, as trustees of the Ohio State Archæological and Historical Society for the term of three years ending February, 1908.

WILLIAM ALLEN TRIMBLE.

UNITED STATES SENATOR FROM OHIO.

MARY MCARTHUR THOMPSON TUTTLE.

A woman's way of writing History, differs essentially from the conventional style and methods approved by great historians. It is well that this is so, for the student of history obtains thus now and then, a lighter, more transparent atmosphere; a more sympathetic view of a life, than could be presented by the massive outlines of the great scholars, who strive for the philosophy of life as well as the presentation of facts.

Several years ago while in Washington City visiting, we were taken by our kind hostess to the National Cemetery as we had expressed a wish to find the grave of our great uncle, William Allen Trimble. It was found to be near the entrance marked by a generously proportioned gray slab, whether supported by a low brick foundation or four short pedestals, we cannot now recall. The inscription was still clear and easily read — as clear as the inscription we find to-day in the old Trimble Bible, — written by Jane Allen Trimble, the noble pioneer mother of this worthy son. She wrote in honest Continental chirography "William A. Trimble, born April 4th, 1786, departed this life on the 12th day of December, 1821, at the City of Washington. His death was occasioned by a wound he received in the lungs during the late war from which he never recovered. He was in the 36th year of his age."

Just above one reads in this same record in the same hand writing, "James Trimble, our honored and beloved husband died on the Lord's day at 1 o'clock October 14th, 1804." Captain James Trimble, father of William Allen Trimble, had been a soldier of the Virginia line in 1776, who, after the Revolutionary war removed to Kentucky and settled in Woodford county in 1784. He had participated in the battle of Point Pleasant,

(1774), and was a captain in the Revolutionary war. His father, John Trimble, was killed in the Mountains of Virginia by the Indians. John Trimble with three brothers emigrated from the north of Ireland to America in the early part of the 17th century. Their ancestors were of Scotch descent, disciples of the great reformer, John Knox. This John Trimble settled in Virginia, the other brothers in Pennsylvania. The ancestors were of Scotch-Irish descent also on the maternal side, Allens, Anderson, Christies; Trimble, Trumbull, Turnbull and Pringle, on the father's side.*

The parents of William Allen Trimble lived near Staunton until 1784, when, as we have stated, they removed to Kentucky where they liberated their slaves. The woman who inscribed so carefully in her Bible the inevitable facts of her family history, was the oldest daughter of James and Peggy Allen. Her father had two brothers, John, the eldest was in the Virginia regiment that marched under General Washington in 1758, against the French and Indians, at Fort Duquesne, now Fort Pitt. In the battle called "Grant's Defeat," fought near this place, John Allen was killed. Hugh Allen the younger brother, fell at the bloody battle fought at the mouth of the Great Kanawha, now Point Pleasant. The Virginia detachment was led by General Lewis, and the Wyandot Indians, by that celebrated warrior, — Cornstalk. She thus knew how much fortitude, energy, and endurance, how much industry and economy the life the pioneers had undertaken, required; and as one of a party of five hundred emigrants, from Virginia and North Carolina to Kentucky, she consented to travel on horseback, with one child wrapped in homespun blanket, clasped in her arms and another placed on a "pillion" holding fast to her waist, Mrs. Erwin carried two negro children in a wallet thrown over her horse. These were washed away by the force of the current in Clinch river. Mrs. Trimble now in the midst of this "deep and dashing" stream, showed a decision which characterized her and her family. She turned her horse, but gave him the rein,

---

* The motto on the coat of arms is Servavi Regem — heads of animals and helmet. A young Yeoman turned the head of the animal who was about to gore the King. — *Turnbull.*

— then grasping firmly the bridle, and mane with her right hand, holding her infant son Allen in her left arm, and calling to her little boy behind to take sure hold, she committed herself to God's mercy.*   When she struck the opposite shore loud shouts went up from all who had beheld the danger.   General

WILLIAM ALLEN TRIMBLE.

Knox called out "henceforth she should be his Aid-de-Camp, and lead the women, as Captain Trimble led the men."

Allen Trimble always called himself a child of Providence, because of this incident, and William Allen Trimble the subject

* See Life of Jane Allen Trimble, by Rev. J. M. Trimble.

of this sketch, who was born two years later often heard through his boyhood of the perilous experiences of both father and mother. They gave their son William a liberal education at Transylvania College, Lexington, Kentucky, and allowed him to study law at Paris, Ky., under the late Judge Robert Trimble, United States Supreme Court, then one of the leading lawyers of the State.

John the oldest son died soon after the arrival in Kentucky.

In 1805 the Trimble family moved to Ohio, — at which time "William" was about nineteen years of age. He and his elder brother, Allen, had made a previous trip to Ohio, on horseback, toward Yellow Springs. As they journeyed through Cincinnati the beautiful black Kentucky horses upon which they rode, were observed, and Allen was offered the city lot where stood later Judge Burnet's home, for one of these horses, but he deliberately declined what would afterward have made for him a splendid speculation in real estate. As Captain James Trimble the father, died in 1804, just after his reconnoitering trip to Ohio, where he purchased land, and determined to bring his family, — the care of the family now fell upon Allen, the oldest son. William, the subject of this sketch, had aided his brother in opening up a farm near Hillsboro, Highland county, Ohio, — before settling as he did, in Chillicothe, then the capital of the State, where he entered the law office of Hon. William H. Creighton, member of Congress from that district.

In the summer of the year 1810, a Swiss gentleman at the head of a large boarding school, — Major Joseph Neef, — invited him to be his assistant. The school was situated at the Falls of the Schuylkill near Philadelphia. Two of his younger brothers "Cary Allen," and "John Allen," aged fifteen and nine,* accompanied him "crossing the mountains in a strong single gig, — constructed for the rough and fatiguing journey of five hundred miles." He remained one year with Mr. Neef, and then visited Litchfield, Connecticut, to complete his law studies, under Judge Story. He there met the late Judge Storer of Ohio — as a classmate. The brothers, Cary and John, remained

---

* The mother named the youngest son John in memory of the son who died.

at Mr. Neef's school. He wrote to Carey, the older, "to ascertain if he did not desire to study Medicine." He replied: "It may sound louder to be a Doctor, but I have about decided to be a School-master. The school here is flourishing, thirty-one pupils. The system is approved by the most literary people. Governor Clairborn has promised to lay a bill before the Legislature of Louisiana, to send ten boys of good capacity at the expense of the State and have them educated as teachers for that country. If similar plans were adopted by the several states of the Union it would be a means of establishing a system that would be of infinite importance. If I have it in my power I shall establish a school in the Western country on the same principles. It will be a great pleasure to help some of my hardy countrymen up the hill of Science." Falls of Schuylkill, 1811.

Like all young men the recital in letters to their brothers was not confined to the facts that they were learning French, Science and Mathematics, but the tailors' bills, and the watches, etc. had to be written of, and the bills reported. Boots, $12.00; Vests, $5.00; Coat, $28.00; Hat, $10.00; Watch, $40.00; the watch had to be purchased Carey remarked, because he was asked to assist Mr. Neef, and he must have a watch, and a seal and key, $15.00 extra. John stood high in his classes, and became later in life the Historian of the family. Carey was musical, played the flute, spoke French, was very handsome, chestnut hair and brown eyes and a great favorite. When thinking of establishing a school, on the Pestalozzian system as soon as he could learn the value of his property in Ohio, he heard that his brothers, William and Allen, were in Military service, — and he writes from Falls of Schuylkill, July 7th, 1812: — Dear Brother: — I received your letter dated Fort McArthur, which confirmed the report I had heard that you on your return to Ohio joined the Army. It was mentioned in the papers that a William Trimble was appoined Major in the neighborhood of Chillicothe. Public sentiment seems to be much divided in the North Eastern States, concerning the late measures of government, the people called federalists, (but who do not deserve the name), are loudly declaiming against the government, and late accounts say that the governors of Massachusetts, Rhode Island, here refused to

raise the quota of Militia required from their states. Great
enconiums are passed on the people of Ohio, for their patriotism." Later, Sept. 27th, 1812, "The surrender of Hull has
caused considerable anxiety. Popular opinion is very much
divided; some impute it to cowardice, others to treachery, — yet,
it seems to have been because of bad management. Many are asking me what you write on the subject?"—"I say, nothing at
all." But young Carey did not know that his brother William
had kept his oldest brother, *Allen*, informed of all his opinions
and movements."

Foot of the Rapids, Head Quarters, July 1st, 1812.

Dear Brother Allen : —

The Army arrived here day before yesterday evening, having opened
a road from Malden block house and built three block houses. General
Hull has chartered a small Schooner to take the heavy baggage round
by water. The Army commences the March for Detroit, by land, in ten
minutes, leaving twenty-five men at this place to build a blockhouse.
General Hull received letters from Detroit, dated the 29th inst. The
Indians are assembled at Malden, to the number of about two thousand.
They draw rations and every necessary accoutrements from the British.
The British force is not accurately known. If we do not have a fight,
we will get to Detroit about the 7th inst. Captain Barrerer and Captain
Jones' companies are more healthy than any in the Regiment. I have
tolerable health and much fatigue.

Your affectionate brother,
William A. Trimble.

General Harrison's orders for raising a Company of mounted volunteers , 21st of September, 1812 (St. Mary's), addressed
to Major William Allen Trimble, reads :

"You are hereby requested to proceed through that part of the State
of Ohio lying in the direction of the mouth of Scioto and endeavor to
prevail upon some of the organized Companies of Militia in that part of
the State to join me as mounted Volunteers, with as much expedition
as possible under the permission heretofore given by Governor Meigs.
Companies serving during the Expedition, which is not calculated to exceed 30 days and will not extend beyond 40, will be considered as having performed a tour of duty."

I am respectfully,
Your Humble Servant,
Wm. H. Harrison.

POSTSCRIPT — Those who have any disposition to accept the very favorable proposition contained in General Harrison's letter, will meet at Hillsborough on Monday the 28th inst., prepared to March to St. Mary's, where they will be supplied with bread, fresh provision, and forage, each man will carry as much bacon or salted meat as will last the Campaign, clothing, blankets, etc. Those who cannot conveniently furnish themselves with rifles, can draw market at Dayton or Urbana, Horses, guns, and equipage, and will be appraised and paid for at the rate of 50 cents per day for each horse.   WM. A. TRIMBLE."

The men in Hillsboro doubtless remembered how Major Trimble had left his other ambitions on his return from Litchfield, Conn., in 1811, and while on this trip to attend Court in West Union, met the first rider, the herald, with an order from General McArthur, calling on Highland County for a quota of one hundred volunteers; how he turned aside from his cherished profession, the law, and turning his horse toward Hillsboro, made his first speech the next day, in the public square. In two days two full companies were raised. That little army of the 4th United States Infantry with the brigade of General Finley, took up its toilsome march through the dense forests of four hundred miles through Ohio and Michigan, and shared the inglorious fortunes of Hull in his surrender of four thousand men to General Brock, at Detroit. Major Trimble as a prisoner of war, was paroled and returned to Ohio. He was ordered to attend the Court-martial for the trial of General Hull, at Albany. General Henry Dearborn as president of that Court. Major Trimble returned by way of Washington City, soliciting and procuring the appointment of Major for the 26th Infantry to be recruited in Ohio.* His younger brother, Carey, from whose letters we have quoted, then seventeen years of age, received the appointment of Lieutenant in the same Regiment. This young brother writes from near Fort George, Deputy's House, 9th of January, 1814, "I was taken on the morning of the surrender of Fort Niagara in attempting to make my escape from the garrison. I saved nothing except some money, which I luckily tied in my cravat; all my clothing and other luggage was taken. The garrison was completely surprised, was not in a state of defense, and its commandant absent,

---

* See Biographical Encyclopedia Ohio.

which I hope, the U. S. will bring him to strict account." Then the particulars are given with great care, and a postscript added, "The General will please seal this and send it by the first flag, to the United States and oblige

Your obedient servant,
CAREY ALLEN TRIMBLE. "

But to return to the record of William Allen Trimble : In the Spring of 1813, he was superintending the recruiting department, while General Harrison was at Dayton, Ohio, making preparation for a campaign to recover Detroit, and obliterate the inglorious Hull's·surrender. Major Trimble was not yet exchanged as prisoner and was not eligible to active duties in the field against the British. At Dayton, he waited on General Harrison, and procured for his brother Allen Trimble, a commission of Colonel. Allen Trimble was to raise a battalion of five hundred mounted men, armed, equipped for the relief of Fort Wayne, on the Maumee, then besieged by the Indians, under Tecumseh. Major Trimble gave the pledge and riding all night, fifty miles to Hillsboro, handed his brother the commission, and instruction from General Harrison. The march of Harrison to Fort Meigs, was protected by these brave Spartans, — the Indians were dispersed. Allen Trimble, later twice Governor of the State of Ohio, before starting on this trip, went into the "loom room," above the spring-house, where yards and yards of blanketing hung on ropes, woven by the weaver employed by him for such work. He cut off yard after yard and handed to the men, and then went down into the room of the spring-house, where on a swinging-shelf was placed some twenty cheese, the product of his wife's industry. He quartered these, giving one-fourth to each man, then bade his wife farewell, handing her one hundred and fifty dollars. When he returned she handed him two hundred and seventy-five dollars, as she was appointed Clerk of the Court, regularly sworn in—the young man fell ill who had been appointed—there being no one left to fill the office. This woman was Rachel Woodrow Trimble, different, as we shall see, from Jane Allen Trimble, but each perfect in type and nobility. Rachel W. Trimble was an ideal wife, mother, and daughter-in-law. She had charming tastes and was known throughout Governor Trimble's public career, as the beautiful home-keeper.

Thomas McArthur Anderson said in his Ohio Centennial address on the Military History of Ohio: "Hull was fifty-nine years of age at the time of his surrender. His age and Revolutionary service saved him a sad fate. He was the same age as Major Robert Anderson, when he defended Fort Sumpter. He was just the age of Admiral Dewey, when he sank the Spanish fleet, in Manila Bay."

When McArthur, Major General of the Ohio Militia, was directed by Governor Meigs, to call out all men capable of bearing arms, under the flag, of thirteen stripes and seven stars,—the last star being that of Ohio, — which from that time on, has led men of the Buckeye State from victory to victory.

We have before us letters from General Harrison to Col. Allen Trimble, Commander of the Ohio Volunteers, St. Mary's, one dated Head Quarters Fort Mary's, 6th Oct., 1812. Another from Franklinton, Nov. 18th, 1812, and one from Brig. Gen'l Foos, 4th Brgd, & Commandment of the 2d Division Ohio Militia; General Harrison says: "Your exertions on this occasion, Sir, as well as those belonging to your Command who were willing to do their duty, merit my thanks, and I beg you to communicate it to them in such manner as you may see proper." In fact they had not the least reason to complain against Major Trimble. They fared as well in every respect, as the six and twelve month Dragoons of the Army."

> With great regard and respect,
>
> I am, Sir,
>
> Your Hum. Servant,
>
> WILLIAM HENRY HARRISON.

Again in a letter of October 6th, "proceed immediately from Fort Wayne to the Potawatimee Towns about seventy-five or eighty miles beyond and about twenty or thirty beyond the towns on Elk Hart, lately destroyed by a Detachment of the Army under my command," etc., etc.,

> WILLIAM HENRY HARRISON.

In the Spring of 1814, Major William A. Trimble received his exchange and joined his regiment, which had consolidated with another and was the 19th, known so well at Chippewa, Lundy's Lane and Niagara. He commanded at the post of Buffalo and Black Rock, both considered very important.

On the Canadian side, General Gaines occupied the defense of old Fort Erie. The night of the 14th, 1814, history gives the following facts : " Under General Gaines, the whole British Army assaulted the American forces. Major Trimble, anticipating a battle, waited upon General Gaines and was permitted to take the command at Buffalo and his own regiment, the 19th, was taken charge of by another officer stationed in the bastions and block-houses of the fort. Major Trimble examined by lamp-light all the positions of his regiment, and its exposed situation. The night was stormy. The enemy's veterans, led by Col. Drummond and Scott, approached the parapets of the Fort, and with scaling ladders and great charge of bayonets, they carried the principal batteries of the Townson and Douglas, then pushed forward toward the 19th, under Major Trimble. Drummond started the watchword, which in these days of Arbitration and Peace, we decline to repeat. Drummond fell within six feet of Major Trimble, Col. Scott, of the 103rd Royal Regiment was also killed and his sword, a fine Damascus blade, Col. Trimble secured and wore during his subsequent military career."

General Brown took command of the army. Fort Erie was commanded by the British position, but on the 17th, the intrenched camp was assaulted. Major Trimble was in Miller's brigade and in the advance and after storming and carrying two redoubts, fell mortally wounded it was thought, within the British lines, shot through the lungs.

At the kind home of his friend, General Peter B. Porter, of Black Rock, he was cared for, for many weeks—after, he was removed from Fort Erie and the following letter to his brother, Col. Allen Trimble, tells of his wound in his own dignified, simple language :

BUFFALO, 18 Oct., 1814.

DEAR BROTHER:

"After storming the Center Battery, of the enemy, on the 17th ultimo and near the close of the action, I received a musket ball under my left arm which passed out near by back bone, where it fractured a rib. After dressing my wound bled freely, which in addition to about a gallon of blood the Surgeons drew from me, reduced me very low. I have now been some time on the recovery, have had a good appetite and am gaining strength as fast as could be expected.

I can walk about my room and my surgeon tell me I am out of danger. I am now situated with a very agreeable family, who take very good care of me, and William has always been very attentive.

(This was Bill Hackett, the colored man, in his service as body-guard many years. The surgeons thought he saved the life of Col. Trimble, for seeing there was no time to be lost, he drew a ram-rod from the Colonel's musket, and wrapping it with a large silk handkerchief, probed the wound, thus relieving it of the clot of blood.)

"You can hardly imagine the pleasure I enjoy in meeting brother Carey, whom I had not seen for more than a year. He stayed with me two days and then went back, took command of the 19th Regiment, with which there was in consequence of wounds, sickness, resignation, etc., no officer but Lieut. Nixon. Gen. Izard's army arrived here on the 12th, and crossed the Niagara at Black Rock, on the 13th, where it was joined by the left Division under General Brown, the whole proceeded that evening toward Chippeway. From the lateness of the season and some other reasons which I shall not now explain, I do not expect much will be done. The army amounts to more than 7,000 effective men and is perhaps the handsomest that was ever formed in the United States.

"The Army had not crossed the Chippeway on yesterday. On yesterday evening I heard from brother Carey who is with the Army. He desired his respects might be presented to the family.

"Tell Mother when I was not expected to live an hour that I was not afraid but perfectly willing to die. Give my respects to all the family.
Your affectionate brother,
WILLIAM A. TRIMBLE.

The paper upon which this letter was written, now ninety-one years ago, has turned almost as yellow in hue as the cloth waist-coat, through which the dreadful bullet went, on that awful night, at Lake Erie. It was our duty not long ago to destroy the time-honored waist-coat. Removing the buttons, and putting them aside as a memento, the white cloth vest, so yellowed by time, had finally found "the moths to corrupt." It lay in the trunk, covered with sheepskin, and fastened with brass tacks, amid other relics, of the War of 1812-1813, — but the day for the burial came; and the fumes which went up from its ashes were, indeed, solemn to our minds. We turned in contemplation to the portrait of the handsome face, regular features, olive complexion, dignity of pose, brilliant epaulettes, dark blue uniform, — and we promised ourselves to make a copy of the portrait for our own especial collection; but instead of the brush, the pen has been at work building up the life again from fragmentary MSS.

ERIE PENNSYLVANIA 4th October, 1814.

DEAR BROTHER ALLEN:

Brother William left Buffalo about the 17th November for Washington City. His wound has not yet healed on one side, but he intended travelling only in good weather by very easy journeys. He will go as far as Albany on horseback, from where he will go principally by water. I expect to be ordered on to Albany, or New York.

Yours,

CARY A. TRIMBLE.

Perhaps the digression can be made here as well as elsewhere to the import that Jane Allen Trimble had seven sons, and two daughters, the oldest son died young, the others were Allen, William, James, Cyrus, Cary, John, — daughters, Mary and Margaret, (Mrs. Nelson and Mrs. McCue). Allen was not only a statesman, but an Agriculturist; William not only a Soldier, but a Senator; James an owner and cultivator of land; Cyrus a Doctor; Cary a Soldier; John a historian and merchant. It was to the Hillsboro home that they all returned at intervals of time, — the mother lived to the age of eighty-seven, respected and beloved; the father, as we have seen, died in 1804. The Trimbles were men of integrity, industry, intelligence, and sobriety.

Major William A. Trimble, after his recovery, which was a great surprise to his Surgeon, Dr. Trowbridge, "was restored to active duties in the field." His friend and comrade, in the sortie at Lake Erie, General Peter B. Porter of Black Rock," was sorry indeed, to have him leave his home. In 1814, Sept. 17th, he was breveted to the rank of Lieutenant-Colonel for his gallant services and was retained in the Army with the same rank in the 8th Infantry, Colonel Nichols of Kentucky. A short letter from Cary A. Trimble of the 26th Infantry written from Beaupost, "a village in full view of Quebec," March 27th, 1814, says, "he, Cary, had the choice of remaining at Montreal or coming to

Quebec, when the general exchange took place; he had located himself in a French family to learn still more of the language, had subscribed to a circulating library in Quebec and so on. When Fort Erie was demolished by our troops, he remarks, the Batteries blew up with a terrible explosion. General Q's division was encamped on the sand beach opposite. All the movements of this great last man of the Alphabet show an unpardonable want of energy."

In 1815 Cary writes from Philadelphia to his brother Allen, — "Western paper is at 7% discount. Baltimore at 3½, Virginia and District of Columbia notes at 4 below par. There are many brokers who will not discount Western notes at any price, Silver fell from 17½ to 7, on the receipt of the news of Bonaparte's fall. Feb. 10th, 1806, he advises his brother Allen, "as to the Militia claims, not to purchase any more until it is ascertained the appropriations will be made this session for paying them off. They are pretty hard pushed for funds at Washington, and the Militia will always be served last."

Lieut. Col. William Trimble had been with his regiment in 1815 in St. Louis, Missouri, and had established the post at Fort Des Moines. He had also ascended the Red River in keelboats and barges, with his men when ordered to Natches. On the 30th April, 1817, he writes from there to Allen Trimble: "The first regiment of Infantry is at Baton Rouge; the 8th, is at Pass Christian. In a most business like letter to his brothers, interested in the purchase of goods, he says: "I have taken the liberty of forwarding two crates of queensware assorted and 500 bls. of copperas, — invoices will be forwarded by next mail. I have made arrangements with Barbour Dent and McClelland, commission merchants of this city, to furnish you with anything you may want from this quarter, which you may obtain by writing to them at any time. These gentlemen have sent a quantity of British Iron to Sumati Limestone. It will be delivered at that place to about 185 dollars per Ton french weight. They sold the Iron here at 110 dollars per Ton, and engaged the freight at 3½ cents per pound. I agreed for two Tons, but as the Iron had been put on board the boat and could not be conveniently assorted and weighed they say that when the Iron arrives at Limestone you may have any quantity you want at 110 dollars, per Ton, and carriage. This arrangement will be to your advantage as you will be at no risk in the freight.

There are some vessels in the river loaded with coffee should it sell low I can send you two or three barrels. Coffee of first quality is not easy to obtain and sells for 31 cents, — Sugar is from 11 to 12½ cents and cotton has fallen from 32 to 27 cents and will probably fall to 25 cents. There is now no demand for the produce of the western country; tobacco, beef, pork excepted, and beef and pork are so badly put up, and brought in such wretched order to this market that the sales are very much injured. Flour cannot be sold for six dollars. From the best information I can obtain beef and pork, if properly put up are the best articles which can be brought to this market. In my next letters I shall inform you how salt may be clarified. Pure salt is of the utmost importance to preserve from putrefaction of animal and vegetable substances. The Salt manufactured in the Western country is very impure. Give my love to the family and remember me to my friends.

WILLIAM A. TRIMBLE.

This letter shows the unselfishness of his life: always trying to help his brothers. From the time he rose before breakfast, at the school where Cary and John were taken, by himself, to be educated, in order to aid them in acquiring their lessons, that they might succeed the better, and so on, until the night he rode without rest to carry to his brother Allen — General Harrison's Commission, — nobility of purpose, was ever present with this man. His brother Cyrus wrote from No. 201 Walnut Street, Philadelphia, Pennsylvania, December 25th, 1818 : "I have just been admitted a member of the Philadelphia Medical Society, to which all the first Medical men, in the United States belong, and of which Dr. Chapman is President.

In 1818, Col. Trimble co-operated with General Jackson in the celebrated Florida campaign and the capture of St. Marks and Pensacola. But although only now thirty-two years of age, he became weary of the life of the army, in times of Peace, and decided to resign and return to Hillsborough, Highland county,

Ohio an ascending series in its arrangement of names: town, county, state were rising.

The Trimbles had located much land in this part of the state, and the land Warrants on Parchment, signed by the early Presidents, remain to this day relics of interest in Governor Allen Trimbles' old Secretary, where all of his important letters and papers were carefully filed away.

The Senatorial Contest, was on when Col. Trimble returned to Highland county. A letter dated Nov. 25th, 1818, from an influential man in Washington City says: — "Col. Jessup is in the City, and I have had a conversation with him. The Claims of William Allen Trimble are superior to any man's in your State; *all things considered,* and I am almost sure, would be elected. You may rest assured, that the members of your state, would be glad to have him associated with them here. If he can name any office which is at the disposal of the Executive, I am sure he could get it. — Because it is impossible for him to stand better than he does at Head Quarters, or be more respected than he is already. While others were working for him, he was acting the same unselfish part towards his brothers; to Dr. Cyrus Washington Trimble, at this date he desires his "regards to the ladies of Philadelphia, of their acquaintance in closing his letter, he remarks, 'that his brother Allen has gone to Richmond, Va. to purchase land. James will purchase 100 Spanish hides, at Philadelphia, but best Buenos Ayrean would be preferred. I enclose copies of the entries in the name of Samuel Bradford, No. 260 for 900 acres. Nine warrants of the Virginia state line. I was pleased to read in the National Intelligence Doctor Mitchel's address to the Agricultural Society, in which he recommends an investigation of the Medical properties of indigenous plants.

The Senatorial Contest was full of mettle, high-spirited and animated, for Governor Worthington and his adherents and friends, desired to see him continued in office; a man who had served his State so ably and was so highly informed on all the internal issues of the day, so that the success of Col. Trimble was the more surprising. The Civil Service idea had not permeated the minds of the people to the same degree it now has; they felt

that although Governor Worthington was undoubtedly highly informed about the interests of the State of Ohio, yet Chillicothe
had had sufficient éclat and Hillsborough would now like to see
one of her worthy sons brought forward. Personally, Col.
Trimble was greatly admired and trusted, he had served his country more, perhaps, than his State, but for this very reason, Washington City would receive him gladly—so unselfish a man in his
personal interests as he ! so gallant a soldier !

We find among his papers a small package of visiting cards,
from the following gentlemen: Mr. Stratford Canning, "His
Britannic Majesty's Envoy Extraordinary," etc., "The Minister
Plenipotentiary de La Majeste tres Chrétienne," the Russian En-
voy's card, Le Baron de Mallitz, the Secretary of the Russian
Embassy; cards of all the representatives of the French Embassy,
and the Consul General of France, Mr. Petry, General Jesup,
George Towers, Eugine Vail, Mr. Ogle Tayloe, W. A. Duer, S.
Ruggold; with many others and invitations, one of which reads
as follows :

"Gen. Van Renssalaer, requests the Honor of Col. Trimbles' Company
to Dinner on Monday next at 4 o'clock.
    "Saturday, 27."

These are all addressed to Col. Trimble, 66 Broadway, and
with them is placed the receipted bills for board at Mrs. Peyton's,
$12.00 per week, with extra charges for coach and horses.

While we are on the social side of life in Washington, 1820,
an extract from one of Col. Trimble's letters will be of interest :

"We have lost James Burrel Jr. from Rhode Island — in my opinion
one of the most able and useful members of the Senate. The question of
relative rank in Society, seems to be of great importance. If I were
competent to decide this question I should decline to engage in it. I claim
only the position of a stranger glad to receive calls, rather reluctant to
make them."

General Jessup tells him in a letter while he is absent from Washington for a few weeks, that gossip says, he is engaged to a certain lady
whose name he does not give.

The family had evidently persuaded him about this time to have their
cousin, Mr. Matthew Jewett, of Lexington, Ky., paint his portrait, for he
says, Dec. 23, 1820: "I have sent Jewett one hundred dollars for my
portrait."

There are letters to Col. Thos. Aspinwall, U. S. Consul, and replies dated from Bishop Gate Church Yards, 21st Feb. 1820, London, England.:

"We have sent the Maine and Missouri bill to the other house," Col. Trimble writes to his brother on the 21st Feb., 1820, "where it has been postponed until tomorrow. I suspect the Amendment of the Senate will be struck out and the bill for the admission of Maine sent back to the Senate, where it will be rejected. The Southern people are determined if possible to prevent the admission of Maine without Missouri is admitted at the same time without restriction. The Amendment attached to the Bill to prohibit slavery in the Territory North of Latitude 36″ 30′ I consider of little importance—because without any probability very few slaves would be taken North of that line. If the Senators of Indiana and Illinois would concur, slavery could easily be prohibited in the uninhabited territory of the United States. My time is so entirely occupied in my official duties and in attending to the private business of numerous correspondents that I have seldom a chance to write to you. It is reported here that the Spanish Government has refused to receive a note from Mr. Forsythe our Minister.

Your affectionate brother,
WILLIAM A. TRIMBLE.

GENERAL ALLEN TRIMBLE.

Later: "There will probably be a compromise to admit Missouri without restriction and prohibit slavery in the whole or much the largest part of the territory. I shall not vote for the Bill in any shape while connected with Maine.

12 FEB., 1820.

I have succeeded in getting an able Canal Committee appointed in the Senate on Roads, etc. He writes in Jan. 1821, from the Senate Chamber: — "My health continutes delicate, but I have not missed one day in attending to my duty in the Senate. The Canal bill came up when I was much indisposed. I defended it while I was able to speak, and I hope not without success. The Sketch of the debate in *The Intelligencer* does not by any means do justice to my remarks or even to ground upon which I supported the bill. Its fate in the Senate will probably be decided day after to-morrow." He sends a printed copy to Governor E. A. Brown, of the bill reported by Mr. King of New York, twice read by unanimous consent in the Senate — the bill to authorize the appointment of Commissioners to lay out a Canal in the State of Ohio. April 22, 1820. We got the bill through the Senate with great difficulty, giving the State the right of premption, a quarter Section of land in each of the new counties.

3rd MAY, 1820.

The Senate has just passed to a third reading by a large majority a bill for laying out a road through the states of Ohio, Indiana, and Illinois, and the committee of roads and canals of the Senate have just reported a bill to provide for laying out a canal through the lands of the United States, from Lake Erie to the navigable waters of the Scioto, or great Miami of Ohio. You can have no idea of the envy of the Atlantic and Southern countries of the rising prosperity of the North-western states. We shall probably have to rely upon our own resources and expect little from the federal government.

"A joint resolution has just passed both houses to adjourn on the 15th. The Tariff was reported this morning by the committee — with some amendments to reduce the duties on iron, hemp, and some other articles.

Three letters from Gov. Lewis Cass, dated March 31st, 1821, May 26th, and June 17th, to Senator Trimble containing earnest invitations for him to attend the treaty with the Indians. "The jaunt would be pleasant and useful to you, and through your exertions useful to the Community."

The time of holding the treaty shall be regulated as much as possible by your convenience. A journey on horse-back to the mouth of the Sandusky Bay is nothing. Five days from Chillicothe in Steam boat will bring you here. I trust you will come to my house and stay with me until your departure.

Ever your friend,

LEWIS CASS.

MAY 26th.

We have fixed upon Chicago as the place and upon the (15.), fifteenth of August. I shall be greatly disappointed if anything prevents your attending. I am, my dear sir,

Ever your friend,

LEWIS CASS.

JUNE 17th.

The Steamboat will touch Sandusky the 5th of August,—the treaty is fixed for the 15th. I shall give such instruction at Fort Wayne, as will ensure you a companionable escort, in case you should travel the whole distance by land. I hope nothing will occur to prevent you from coming. I am my dear sir,

Ever your friend

LEWIS CASS.

There is a brightness to these letters because of the big red seal, and they look remarkably well cared for — the Governor wrote a fine hand, which is still beautiful. Col. Trimble writes to his brother Allen as usual, telling him how well the journey went. The Indian agent, Mr. Hayes, furnished me with a guide at Fort Wayne. If you go to Kentucky soon, I will join you in the purchase of some of Mr. Mason's sheep and Clay cattle. Remember me to Mr. Clay and all my friends. Chicago is a flat Village one hundred and sixty-five miles from Ft. Wayne. It is built around a basin, in the rear of which a bluff rises abruptly on the summit of which stands old Fort Mitchel, — recently repaired, — from this we get a prospect of the whole Island. The surface is Limestone and gravel. Chicago is a small Indian Village. The white fish are said to appear in going down the Lake.

Mr. Stuart gave us a horse-back ride, — The Indians assembled in Council about One o'clock. Governor Cass told them that they had been invited to assemble at this place to receive a message from the Great Father, the President of the United States, which message would be delivered to them tomorrow; that Mr. Sibley had been associated with him, and that I was a member of their father's council. The next day they assembled and the commissioners delivered their message: that their Great Father desired to purchase the St. Joseph country, for which he would give them in goods which would be worth more to them than all the lands and game. One of the war chiefs, Mitia, answered for them, that they had sold to their Great Father the greater part of their lands and that they had reserved little upon which to lay the bones of their fathers, and that it was necessary to support their chief's women and children, and that they did not expect their Great Father would have asked them to sell."

"After this we took quarters with Mr. Ramsey and A. D. Stuart, Esq. the Collector. Many more details are given in this letter.

In September, sad news, indeed, reached Col. Trimble. His brother, Lieut. Cary A. Trimble, so much beloved by the entire family, now just 28 years of age, accomplished as a Flutist, as Linguist, as Soldier, betrothed to one of the loveliest young women in Philadelphia society, fell ill and suddenly died at Hillsboro, September 10th, 1821.

Senator Trimble evidently tried to distract his mind from this grief, for on his return trip to Washington, in October, he writes: — "I stopped at General Porter's at Black Rock. The Breckenridges were there, Robert, the son, and the Mother. Then I went to Niagara Falls, Lewiston, Rochester, Auburn, and seven miles north to Weeds basin on the *Grand Canal* now completed from Utica as far West as Montaganna, on Cayuga Lake. They leave Weeds Basin 8 A. M., arrive at Ithaca the same hour next morning, (92 miles), I also went to Schenectady, Albany, West Point. But the week at Saratoga did not agree with me. I have *not been well* since my return. I took cold on the return trip from Chicago. This little Indian bowl I send, is for Eliza.

It was a year of great anxiety for the Trimble family,— General Allen Trimble who had been Speaker of the House, at Columbus, now since 1818, began to feel that not alone must he experience the grief of his brother Cary's death, but that William's health was fast failing.

Letter addressed to Dr. Cyrus W. Trimble, by Dr. Powell, of Washington, D. C.

WASHINGTON CITY, 15th Dec'r., 1825.

MY DEAR FRIEND:—

You no doubt have heard ere this, of the death of your gallant and accomplished brother. His decline was gradual, and steady, and he was conscious long before his confinement, that his death was not far distant. He looked forward to his approaching dissolution, with all the firmness of a hero, and calmness of a philosopher: and during the whole course of his confinement, not a sigh, or murmur escaped his lips.

The funeral Ceremonies were grand, and imposing, beyond description. The body was removed from Mrs. Payton's, the late residence of the deceased, by the Committee of Arrangements, and placed in the Senate Chamber, directly fronting the President's Chair. The House of Representatives then entered the Senate Chamber; — preceding them, Speaker, Mr. Ryland, the Chaplain to the Senate, then raised his voice and in a peculiarly eloquent and pathetic manner, delivered an address upon the occasion and concluded by an affectionate appeal to the relatives of the deceased.

The body was then conveyed from the Senate and placed upon the Hearse, which was drawn by four elegant black horses. His coffin was covered with fine black velvet, elegantly trimmed with silver. From one side to the other was a plate handsomely formed, placed directly over the breast, on which his name, age, and time of decease, were engraven. He was buried with the honors of war which were eminently due to so gallant and distinguished an Officer.

The Procession then moved. It as exceedingly splendid, and solemn. There were at least One hundred private Carriages,—besides an immense concourse of citizens and strangers. The Marine Corps, commanded by Gen. Henderson, marched in front of the Procession, with full band playing those melancholy airs, which are calculated to suffuse cheeks with tears. Next came the Senators and Representatives from Ohio, as Mourners: then the Senate, preceded by their Sergeant-at-Arms: next the head of departments, foreign ministers, etc. The Procession then closed with a prodigious concourse of Citizens and strangers succeeded by a long line of two-hundred splendid carriages. When the body of the gallant man was consigned to the silent tomb, solemn silence reigned throughout this innumerable multitude, and the bosom of every individual seemed to heave with a sigh of regret for his untimely fate. To close the scene, the neighboring hills were made to reverberate by the marine corps firing volleys of funeral salutes with double charged cartridges, which at every heavy discharge seemed to say: "This tells the knell of a Hero!"

I beg you to believe that I sincerely sympathize with you upon the heavy sorrow which you have sustained.

Your brother's friends here are very numerous. In fact, he had no enemies, except they were enemies to his sterling honor, and integrity of character.   Yours most affectionately,

WM. L. POWELL.

To Dr. Cyrus W. Trimble.

THE FUNERAL OF COL. TRIMBLE.

Late of the Senate of the United States from the State of Ohio.— (Detroit.)

His body they bore to a warrior's grave —
　The morning sun splendidly beaming;
The hearse mov'd slow, and the War-plumes wav'd,
　And sabers and muskets were gleaming.

The cold winds blew, but he heeded them not —
　The sleep of the grave he was sleeping;
The wise and the great of the Nation were there,
　And his country around him was weeping.

The trumpets peal'd loud, and the death-drums beat —
　And the March was the March of devotion;
And deep as the musketry roll'd o'er his grave,
　Not a heart but throbb'd high with emotion.

For, Oh! he died in the glow of his years,
   In the pride and the bloom of his glory;
But long shall his memory emblazon with fame,
   The bright pages of our martial story.

The winter shall pass, and the Spring-flowers bloom,
   By the banks and the groves of his own native river, —
Weep, Parent of Trimble! He ne'er shall return!
   By the wave of Potomac he's sleeping forever.

   But he sleeps with the great; and sweet be his sleep,
   And hush'd be the requiem of sorrow;
His star has gone down, like the Sun hid in storms,
   To arise in new glory to-morrow.

In Ohio's Centennial address of *"Ohio in the Senate,"* by the Hon. J. B. Foraker, the following reference was made to Col. William A. Trimble. "Harrison and Garfield," said Mr. Foraker "were so conspicuous as soldiers that all are familiar with their achievements in that respect, while Trimble was noted among the men of his time for chivalric deportment and dauntless bravery. He died, when he had only fairly entered on what promised to be a most brilliant and distinguished career in the Senate, from the effects of a wound received in action at Fort Erie. He was the only one of all Ohio's Senators who died while holding office. He was buried in the Congressional Cemetery at Washington, and his untimely death was mourned universally by the people of Ohio and all his colleagues in public life."

CALEB ATWATER.

CLEMENT L. MARTZOLFF.

It is as Ohio's first historian that Caleb Atwater is best known. But had he never written his History of Ohio, his efforts to provide an educational system for the state and the record he made in Archæology might in themselves be sufficient reason for placing his name in "Ohio's Hall of Fame."

Caleb Atwater was a versatile, peculiar, eccentric and visionary individual. From the world's material point of view his life might not be reckoned a success. He never accumulated any property. He lacked that power of concentration which alone gives success in a pursuit. But he was not lazy. He worked hard on things that were congenial to him. He was a close observer of nature. He had his ideas and theories and it seems he spent much time in formulating them.

His versatility expressed itself in his being a minister, lawyer, educator, legislator, author and antiquarian. He was a pioneer in more senses than one. And since a pioneer is ever a brave man we can forgive Mr. Atwater his inclination to be a "Jack-of-all-trades."

It was on Christmas day in 1778 at North Adams, Massachusetts, that Caleb Atwater was born to Ebenezer and Rachel (Parks) Atwater. He was a direct descendant of David Atwater one of the original settlers of New Haven. On the maternal side he inherited Welsh blood. His mother died when he was five years old. The child was placed in the home of a Mr. Jones in North Adams, where he remained until his eighteenth year. About this time Williams College was founded and young Atwater was sent by his guardian to this school. He completed his studies here and received the degree of Master of Arts.

I wish to express my thanks to Miss May Lowe, Librarian at Circleville; Miss Wilder, Assistant Librarian; Mrs. L. G. Hoffman, of Circleville, and Rev. Dr. Brown, of Indianapolis, for courtesies extended in the preparation of this article.　　　　C. L. M.

Upon his graduation he went to New York City and opened a school for young ladies. While thus engaged he studied theology and in due time entered the Presbyterian ministry. He now married a Miss Diana who lived only about a year. On account of his health he gave up the ministry and began the study of law. His preceptor was Judge Smiley of Marcellus, New York. After a few months reading he was admitted to the bar. He married a second time. His wife was Belinda, a daughter of Judge Butler.

It seems that now he entered into some business arrangements that proved disastrous. What this business was is unknown but it left him impoverished.

He had determined to go West. It could hardly be said that he wished to "grow up with the country" for he was now thirty-seven years old. He came to Circleville, Ohio, in 1815, and there made his home until his death fifty-two years afterward.

The first six years of his residence in Circleville was devoted to the practice of law. In 1821 he was elected to represent the Pickaway-Hocking District in the Ohio Legislature. One of the great issues before the American people at that time was the question of "internal improvements." Governor De Witt Clinton of New York had begun his Erie Canal. Roads were demanded. Better facilities to get the produce of the land to market were asked for. As usual the people were divided.

Mr. Atwater upon his entrance into the General Assembly aligned himself with the friends of "improvement." He had not been a member long until he had an opportunity to defend his position. A bill had been introduced to abandon for a year the usual road tax. Mr. Atwater opposed the measure in the following speech.

"The people of Ohio are an enterprising people and they are as patriotic as they are enterprising and will not thank you for giving up the road tax. Does the public voice call for the abandonment of the road tax? Sir, the spirit of the age remonstrates against this bill in the strongest language and he must be deaf indeed who does not hear its voice and perverse indeed who disobeys it. There is not a single state over the mountains that is not up and doing. In New York besides a vast number of turnpikes running in all directions through the state the patriotic Clinton and his friends are cutting a canal, three hundred and fifty-eight miles in length connecting the Great Lakes with the ocean. Virginia and North Carolina have each their Boards or Public Works busily and successfully engaged in these improvements. Shall this young State lose all the benefit of example so praiseworthy? 'But the pressure of the times.' Great minds rise under every pressure. The sages who on the Fourth of July, 1776, declared us an independent nation did not sit down to inquire where our armies were, where was our navy, where our money was to be obtained, to carry on a war with the most powerful civilized nation in the world. Had they done so we had not been as now, here legislating for a respectable state.

"Shall we throw dollars and cents into one scale, against a great system of internal policy in the other? From such legislation I devoutly pray to be delivered on this and all other occasions."

Mr. Atwater was a friend to the Canal System. He was a great admirer of Governor Clinton of New York. That fact is evidenced when it is noted that he named a son after the great New York champion of canals. Many Ohioans, including Mr. Atwater, had kept in close touch with Governor Clinton during the years the Erie Canal was building. His advice to the Ohio people was valuable. Accordingly when the friends of "internal improvements" were ready to strike they were not entirely ignorant of the best methods to be followed. It is significant that the friends of roads and canals were also friends of public education.

On the 6th of December, 1821, the initial canal bill was introduced in the Ohio House of Representatives. Mr. Atwater supported the bill as a member of the Legislature but he did more than that. There was a popular opposition to overcome. The people had to be educated. During these years of debate and agitation the pen of Caleb Atwater was busy in writing for the press. The files of the Circleville newspaper of the time show many articles that are evidently his. While they are signed, usually, as was the custom of the time by a high sounding Latin pseudonym, yet to a person who is but meagerly acquainted with

Mr. Atwater's style, but little difficulty is found in recognizing the author.

These articles are vigorous and the arguments are telling. There is no doubt that they had considerable influence in molding the public opinion of the section.

But it is in the cause of popular education that Mr. Atwater deserves to be held in fond memory by the people of Ohio. Coming from the halls of an eastern college as he did he soon saw the need of an educated proletariat. In expressing his views of the stability of our Republic he said, "To effect this object universal education is the only remedy." He had full confidence in the function of the school master. He did not doubt the potency of an efficient system of education.

On the same day that the Ohio Canal Bill was introduced in the General Assembly, Mr. Atwater set the educational wheels revolving by presenting a resolution asking for a committee on "schools and school lands."

The part taken by Mr. Atwater is best told in his own words which are taken from his History of Ohio.

"The congress of the United States, by several acts, usually denominated 'the compact,' gave the people, of all the territory northwest of the Ohio river, one thirty-sixth part of the land, for the support of common schools. No small portion of these lands were occupied, at an early day, by persons who settled on them, without any title to them, than what mere occupancy gave them. These occupants, made no very valuable improvements, on these lands, but they contrived in time, to obtain various acts of our general assembly, in favor of such squatters. Such acts increased in number every year, until they not only had cost the state large sums of money for legislating about them, but some entire sessions were mostly spent, in such unprofitable legislation.

"In the meantime, scarcely a dollar was ever paid over to the people, for whose benefit these lands had been given, by congress.

"Members of the legislature, not frequently, got acts passed and leases granted, either to themselves, to their relations, or, to warm partisans. One senator contrived to get, by such acts, seven entire sections of land into, either his own, or his children's possession!

"From 1803-1820, our general assembly spent its sessions mostly, in passing acts relating to these lands; in amending our militia laws; and in revising those relating to justice's courts. Every four or five years, all the laws were amended, or as one member of the assembly well remarked in his place, 'were made worse.' At a low estimate, this perverse legislation, cost the people, one million dollars. The laws were changed so frequently, that none but the passers of them, for whose benefit they were generally made, knew what laws were really in force. New laws were often made as soon as the old ones took effect.

"During these seventeen years, there were a few persons, in different parts of the state, who opposed this course of legislation. And here we introduce to the reader, Ephraim Cutler, of Washington county, near Marietta, who was one of the framers of our state constitution. He had succeeded in his motion, so to amend the original draft of that instrument, as to make it the imperative duty of the general assembly, to support 'religion, morality and knowledge, as essentially necessary to good government.' And the constitution goes on to declare 'that schools and the means of instruction, shall forever be encouraged •by legislative provision.' This provision remained a dead letter until in December 1819, Judge Cutler, its author, being then a member of the general assembly, introduced a resolution for that purpose, and was appointed chairman of a committee on schools. He introduced a bill into the house of representatives, for regulating and supporting common schools. This bill after being much injured by amendments, passed the lower branch of the legislature, but, was either not passed in the senate, or so modified as to render it useless. This state of things continued, until, in December, 1821, the house of representatives appointed five of its members, to wit: Caleb Atwater, Lloyd Talbot, James Shields, Roswell Mills, and Josiah Barber, a committee on school lands. To that committee was referred a great number of petitions from occupants of school lands, in almost every part of the state. This committee devoted nearly all its time to the subjects submitted to its charge. All the acts of the legislature, relative to the school land were carefully examined, and this committee came to the conclusion, that, inasmuch as the legislature were the mere trustees of the fund set apart by congress, for the support of common schools, not a few of these acts were void, because they were destructive to the interests of the people whose children were to be educated by this grant. The trustee, the committee believed, had the power to so manage this fund as to increase its value; but, the trustee had no power to destroy the fund. The committee saw all the difficulties which surrounded 'the object of their charge; as well as the delicacy of their own situation, sitting as members with those who had possession of more or less of the school lands. They weighed in their minds all these things and finally adopted a plan and the only one which to them seemed feasible, which was, to recommend the adoption of a joint resolution, authorizing the governor, to appoint seven commissioners of schools and school lands, whose duty it should be, to devise a system of law, for the support and regulation of common schools. Their chairman who writes these lines, immediately after this decision, drew up, and presented to the house of representatives, the following report.

'The committee to whom was referred so much of the governor's message, as relates to schools and school lands, have had these subjects under their consideration, and now beg leave to Report,

"That in the opinion of the committee, the education of our youth, is the first care and highest duty of every parent, patriot and statesman. It is education which polishes the manners, invigorates the mind and improves the heart. If it has been encouraged even by despotic governments, how much stronger are the motives held out to induce the Republican statesman to promote this object of prime importance? Shall Louis XVIII of France, support from the national treasury, learned professors, in every branch of science and learning, in all the celebrated schools in his kingdom; and will the legislature of this young, rising and respectable state, neglect to provide for the education of her youth? The committee presume not.

"It will be recollected by the house, that many of the best scholars, warriors, philosophers, and statesmen, whom this nation has produced — men who have shone as lights in the world; who have been blessings to their own country and the world at large; who have been applauded by the whole civilized world, for their learning, their genius, their patriotism and their virtues in public and private life, were many of them when young, poor and destitute as to property, and yet through their own exertions, under the genial influence of the Republican institutions of our elder sister states, were enabled to raise themselves from the lowest circumstances, to the heights of fame and usefulness.

"The name of the illustrious Franklin will occur to every mind. Are there no Franklins, no Monroes, no Wirts in the log cabins of Ohio, who possess not even a cent of property, who have no knowledge of the rudiments of a common education, and are deprived of a father's advice and protection, and even without the benefit of a mother's prayers? Is it not the duty of the legislature, to lay, in season, a foundation on which to build up the cause of education? Ought not a system of education to be founded, which would embrace with equal affection the children of the poor and the rich?

"It has been said that 'a little learning is a dangerous thing.' This may be true in monarchical governments, where the extremes of wealth and poverty, power and weakness, exist, but never can be true in a republic like ours. Where universal suffrage is the birthright of every citizen, learning enough to enable the elector to become acquainted with his own rights and his ruler's duty is necessary for him to possess. In a moral point of view, learning enough to enable every rational being to fully understand his duty to himself, his neighbor and his Creator, is absolutely necessary. Without education and morality, can a republic exist for any length of time? The committe presume not.

"A great philosopher has said that 'knowledge is power.' It is that power which transforms the savage into civilized man, surrounds him with a thousand comforts, unattainable through any other medium, and exhibits man as he ought to be, at the head of this lower creation, and the image of his Maker. It is an acquaintance with letters which enables man to hold a correspondence and become acquainted with his fellow man, however distant they may be from each other. Through this medium all the ideas of the warrior, the statesmen, the poet, the philosopher and the patriot are conveyed from age to age and from country to country. Through this medium the treasures of learning and science are brought down to us, from the remotest ages past. Through this same medium, these treasures are accumulating, as they are borne along down the stream of time, will be conveyed to the remotest ages yet to come.

"Gratitude to those who have gone before us, for their labors in the field of learning and science, duty to ourselves and to those who are to come after us, call on us for a system of education for common schools, so framed that genius, to whomsoever given, by the all-wise and beneficent Author of our existence may be drawn forth from its abode however exalted or however humble it may be to enlighten mankind by a divine radiance.

> "Full many a gem of purest ray serene,
> The dark, unfathomed caves of ocean bear,
> Full many a flower is born to blush unseen,
> And waste its sweetness on the desert air."

"Is it not the duty of the legislature to explore the recesses of the ocean of distress and poverty and to draw forth the gems of genius and place them before the public eye? Ought not the field of learning to be so far extended as to enclose within its limits, those beautiful wild flowers of genius which are now wasting their sweetness on the desert air?

"But it may be asked, how shall we effect this desirable object? Where are our means of doing it? The committee answer, that nearly one-thirty-sixth part of our territory has been granted by congress, (for a fair equivalent it is true) to the state in trust for the support of common schools. Had this fund been properly managed, the committee are of the opinion, that a great permanent one would have been created, the interest of which would have done much toward the support of common schools. The committee deeply regret that the school lands have been in many instances, leased out for different periods of time, to persons who in numerous instances seem to have forgotten that

these lands were granted to the state (for a fair equivalent by
congress), for the support of education and for the benefit of
the rising generation.

"From all the committee have been able to learn it would
seem that more money had been expended by the state in legislation concerning these lands, than they have yet or ever will
produce, unless some other method of management be devised
than any hitherto pursued. The committee refer the house to
acts concerning these lands on the statute books and to the fact
in numerous instances, the lessees are destroying all the valuable
timber growing in these lands. The committee are impressed
with the belief that unless these lands are soon sold and the
proceeds thence to be derived invested in the stock of the United
States, or in some other permanent and productive stock, no
good and much evil will accrue to the state from the grant
of these lands by congress. Shall we proceed on, legislating
session after session, for the sole benefit of lessees of school lands,
at the expense of the state? Or shall we apply to the general
government for authority to sell out these lands as fast as the
leases expire or are forfeited by the lessees? Or shall we entirely surrender these lands to present occupants, with a view
to avoid in future the perpetual importunity of these troublesome petitioners? The committee are of opinion that in order
to collect information on subjects committed to their consideration, commissioners ought to be appointed to report to the next
general assembly, a bill to establish and regulate common schools,
accompanied by such information on the subject, as they may
be able to collect. Should the general assembly authorize the
governor to appoint such commissioners, a judicious selection
would doubtless be made, with a reference to the local interests
of the state, as well as to the cause of learning among us.

"Such commissioners ought to take into their consideration
the propriety or impropriety of obtaining leave of the general
government, of making such a disposition of the school lands
of the state, by sale or otherwise as may best comport with the
original intention of the grantors.

"It is our sincere wish to incite into activity the learning,
the talents and patriotism of the state, so that the attention of

our constituents may be immediately turned toward the subjects committed to us.

"The following resolution is respectfully submitted to the consideration of the house:

"*Resolved by the General Assembly of the State of Ohio*: That the governor shall be authorized to appoint seven commissioners whose duty it shall be to collect, digest and report to the next general assembly, a *system* of education for common schools, and also, to take into consideration, the state of the fund set apart by congress for the support of common schools, and to report thereon to the next general assembly.

"This report and this resolution being read, at the clerk's table, were ordered to be printed and on the 30th day of January, 1822, they passed the house without a dissenting vote. The joint resolution for the appointment of commissioners passed the senate, January 31st, 1822, without opposition.

"In the month of May following, Allen Trimble, Esquire, the then governor of the state, appointed seven commissioners of schools and school lands, to-wit: Caleb Atwater, the Rev. John Collins, Rev. James Hoge, D. D., N. Guilford, the Honorable Ephraim Cutler, Honorable Josiah Barber, and James M. Bell, Esquire. The reason why seven persons were appointed, was because there were seven different kinds of school lands in the state, viz: section number sixteen in every township of congress lands; the Virginia military land; United States military lands; Symmes' purchase, in the Miami country; the Ohio company's purchase, on the Ohio river; the refugee lands, extending from Columbus to Zanesville; and the Connecticut Western Reserve land.

"Caleb Atwater was appointed for congress lands; John Collins, for the Virginia military lands; James Hoge, for the refugee lands; James M. Bell, for the United States military district; Ephraim Cutler for the Ohio company's lands, N. Guilford, for Symmes' purchase, and Josiah Barber for Connecticut Western Reserve school lands.

"All the persons appointed commissioners, accepted of their offices, as it appears, by referring to Governor Trimble's message to the legislature, in December, 1822. Five of these commissioners, to-wit: Caleb Atwater, John Collins, James Hoge, Ephraim Cutler and Josiah Barber, entered on the duties of their appointment and assembled at Columbus the seat of government, in June 1822. They organized their board, appointed Caleb Atwater chairman, and inasmuch as N. Guilford and James M. Bell did not appear nor act, the five who were present and acting informally appointed Caleb Atwater, to perform the duty assigned to N. Guilford; and James Hoge was appointed to supply the place of James M. Bell.

"This board, thus organized, ordered their chairman, to address a circular letter, to all such persons as had the charge of the school lands in the state soliciting information as to those lands; what was their value, how they were managed, how, and by whom occupied, and finally, all the information necessary to be possessed by the commissioners.

"Each commissioner agreed to exert himself in obtaining all the information in his power relating to these lands. After an active session of seven days, the board adjourned to meet again in August the next.

"Five hundred letters were addressed to persons in various parts of the state and fearing that unless the postage were paid, these letters would not be attended to, by those to whom they were addressed, the author of them paid the postage. His time was devoted almost wholly to this business, until in August following, the board met again at Columbus. At this meeting, which lasted seven days, the chairman was directed to prepare three pamphlets for the press: first, a pamphlet showing the actual condition of the school lands; second, a bill proposing a system of law, regulating common schools; and thirdly, an explanatory one, of the school system to be proposed.

"The chairman was directed to collect all the school systems in use in all the states; and to consult by letter or otherwise, all our most distinguished statesmen, scholars, teachers and jurists on this matter. In pursuance of this order, he opened a correspondence with not a few such men, in all the old, and many of the new states. This correspondence occupied nearly all his time, during the three following months of September, October and November, and until early in December 1822, the

board again assembled at Columbus. During all this time not
a dollar had been advanced by the state to this board, nor was
there a dollar in the state treasury to spare for any object.

"Two of the commissioners had been elected members of
the general assembly, to-wit: Ephraim Cutler and Josiah Barber. The other three, Messrs Atwater, Collins and Hoge devoted up their whole time to this service. Occupying a room in
a public house, it became a center of attraction for all the lovers
of learning who visited the seat of government, during that session of the state legislature. In this legislature were many influential men who were opposed to a school system; to a sale
of the school lands; and to internal improvements. Calling
occasionally at the commissioners' room, these enemies of all
improvement, discovered the commissioners discussing the merits
of the different school systems which they had collected. These
opposers as it now appears, with the intention of swindling the
commissioners out of what would be justly due them for their
expenditures of time and money, requested the chairman to
let them see what the postage on his official correspondence
amounted to, and they would pay it. This being acceded to,
and that being found to be seventy dollars, these legislators
framed a report in the senate that it would appear that all the
services had been finished and paid for, nine weeks before the
commissioners concluded their session.

"The board proceeded in their labors, day after day, and
week after week, and prepared for the press and printed the three
pamphlets aforesaid, at the expense of printing and paper — paid
for by the chairman, and never fully remunerated to this day by
the state! Fifteen hundred copies of each, or four thousand
five hundred copies, after an absence from home on that business,
of eighty-two days, were printed and done up in handsome
covers. They were circulated over the whole state in the spring,
summer and autumn of 1823.

"On the assembling of the legislature in December, as soon
as that body were properly organized the report of the commissioners was presented to the general assembly which they
accepted, *thanking,* but not paying anything for their labors and
expenditures. This session had a majority in both houses, op-

posed to the school system and the sale of the school lands, and all that was done by them, was to quarrel about these subjects. They finally broke up in a row and went home. During the next summer and autumn, the contest about the sale of the school lands, the school system, the canal, and an equitable mode of taxation, was warm and animated, but the friends of these measures, triumphed over all opposition at the polls in the October election of 1824. Large majorities were elected in both houses, friendly to these highly beneficial measures. These measures were carried through the general assembly and the greatest revolution, politically, was effected that our history offers to the reader. That legislature was the ablest in point of talents and moral worth that we ever had in the state.

"They gave us a system of education for common schools; changed the mode of taxation; created a board of fund commissioners who were authorized to issue stock and borrow money on it, wherewith to make canals. They passed many other wise, morally, healthful and useful acts. These measures effected more for us than all others, ever originating with the people, and carried out into execution by the legislature.

"Our domestic policy thus established, has never varied since that time, and this new state has as fixed a policy as any other state in the Union."

In Mr. Atwater's term as a legislator a bill for the education of the deaf and dumb was introduced. Mr. Atwater opposed the measure in no uncertain terms. He said:

"When we have established a system of schools throughout the state; when we have respectable academies in every county and one college at least, well endowed and supplied with the necessary qualified instructors, then our means could not perhaps be better applied. But until provision is made for the proper education of those not deaf and dumb it would be dividing our attention and diminishing the means necessary for this object by applying them to other objects of much less importance."

In 1822 Mr. Atwater was a candidate for Congress. He was defeated by Duncan McArthur for whom he had a warm friendship. It was this friendship that prompted him to dedicate one of his books to McArthur, who had in the meantime been elected governor.

Mr. Atwater's ideas of education were not theories alone but he aimed to put them into practice. Naturally he began in his own town, Circleville. In 1823 he presided at a meeting of the citizens who had met to elect school trustees. He himself was elected to the board and it is to be expected that he was the most active member. The duties devolving upon these trustees were multiform. They included the examination and employment of teachers, erection of buildings and the supervision of the schools.

It was about this time that Mr. Atwater conceived the idea of editing a paper of his own. It was to be published in Chillicothe under the name of "The Friend to Freedom." In a notice published in a Circleville paper the editor advanced his platform. The paper was to promote the best interests of the country, internal improvements and a good system of education for common schools. It would contain nothing "unfriendly to religion or morality, and modesty will find in it nothing to condemn." There were to be essays both literary and scientific. For the benefit of the people living beyond the mountains," the editor himself who has for several years been collecting a mass of information on the antiquities and natural history of the Western states will present his essays on these topics. But three numbers of "The Friend to Freedom" were ever published. It failed for lack of support. For this failure Mr. Atwater was, to use his own words, "maligned by evil disposed persons." His financial condition was certainly not the best, for in a short time the sheriff levied upon his personal property to satisfy a creditor.

The presence of many prehistoric earthworks at Circleville was partly, at least, responsible for Mr. Atwater's interest in that class of Antiquities which he is pleased to call them. Already in 1820 he contributed to the American Antiquarian Society his observations. In 1833 he produced a volume on "Western Antiquities." This book contained all he had previously written with much additional matter. There is no doubt that he knew more on this subject than any other man of his time. His personal knowledge extended over many years of investigation from

New York to the Tennessee valley. Many of the places he personally visited, others he knew only by what he could glean
secondhand. Of course his methods would not bear the criticism
of modern scientific investigation. Yet his theories of the use
for which the various earthworks were designed tallies very well
with those of our "up-to-date" archæologists. In comparing the
generalized, superficial statements of Atwater with what has
more recently been produced we find that many who followed
him in point of time have also trod in the "beaten paths." Besides the descriptions of the principal earthworks at Newark,
Glenford, Marietta, Circleville, Paint Creek, Portsmouth, Fort
Ancient, etc., maps of the inclosures are also presented. They
were evidently not surveyed yet they show a decided degree of
accuracy. Throughout Mr. Atwater's descriptions he draws
his conclusions from his knowledge of Roman customs. For
instance the parallel walls at Fort Ancient suggest the probability
of their use for foot races. One thing Mr. Atwater did do for
archæologists and that is he furnished descriptions of many
mounds that were destroyed before a more systematic study
of them began. It is singular that the Serpent Mound in Adams
county is not mentioned. Certainly Mr. Atwater had never
heard of it or he would have included it in his descriptions.
Yet before he published the last edition of his work it is definitely
known that he passed within a few miles of the famous "Snake."
This was on the occasion of his journey to Prairie Du Chien
which was the next important event in his life.

It was in May, 1829, that President Jackson commissioned
Caleb Atwater as one of three commssioners to treat with the
Winnebago Indians concerning some land near the junction of
the Wisconsin and the Mississippi rivers. The start for Prairie
Du Chien was made at once. Mr. Atwater in a book published
in 1831 gives a minute account of this trip. His decriptions of
the mode of travel and the towns and country through which
he passed makes intensely interesting reading. His first description is of Maysville, Kentucky. After dilating upon the progress
of the town and the hospitality and general intelligence of the
people, he concludes by wondering why map makers had never
placed upon their maps such an important place.

Cincinnati with 30,000 people receives encouragement to the effect that it will easily reach 50,000; that it will continue to be the largest town in the state unless surpassed by Zanesville or Cleveland. A four days' stay in Louisville awaiting a boat gave Mr. Atwater ample time for a lengthy "write up" of the town. He went into details. After giving some of the history, he proceeded to tell the plan of the streets, the nature of the buildings, churches, schools, theater, market houses, and then at some length, the facilities for manufacturing. He appended a list of the various steamboats and tonnage of each. He recognized Kentucky chivalry and hospitality and believed the state to have been unjustly slandered.

The trip down the Ohio and up the Mississippi opened a new world to our traveler. For the first time he realized the great possibilities of the West. He anticipated the building of railroads and with words that are almost prophetic says:

"When locomotive engines are brought to the perfection, experience and ingenuity will soon bring them, goods and passengers can pass between the two seas in ten days. That this will be the route to China within fifty years scarcely admits a doubt. From sea to sea a dense population would dwell along the whole, enliven the prospect with their industry and animate the scene. The mind of the patriot is lost in wonder and admiration when he looks through the vista of futurity at the wealth, the grandeur and glory that certainly await our posterity."

"As he looks upon the map of this country where is the man whose mind is not expanded with the extent of this vast national domain? How is the heart of the patriot, the statesman, the philanthropist, the lover of liberty filled with joy unutterable, when he looks with prophetic eye over this vast field of future happiness, grandeur and glory, yet in reserve for the human race? Here one language will prevail over a great extent of country and be used by over three hundred millions of people."

A part of Caleb Atwater's prophecy has been fulfilled. It was one of his characteristics that wherever he went his mind penetrated into the potentialities of the region. He saw the possibilities of commerce, agriculture and manufacturing and in his judgment he was scarcely ever mistaken.

He remained in St. Louis for three weeks. During this time he was acquainting himself with his duties as Indian Commissioner. He also succeeded in getting well acquainted with St. Louis. One thing in particular attracted his attention; it was the democratic spirit of its people. This was so noticeable that he alluded to it in these words, "There was but one tinner in the city and he was noticed — taken into the best society in the place and was making a fortune by his business."

Of his trip up the Mississippi he has much to say of the country on both sides of the stream. His description is minute. He expatiates upon the beauty and fertility of the country. The trip was a long tedious one and he had plenty of time at his command for observation.

Arriving at Prairie Du Chien the work of treating with the Indians began. Several weeks were taken to reach a satisfactory agreement. On the 1st of August, 1829, the final treaty was concluded. The tribes interested were the Chippewas, Ottawas, Pottawotamies and Winnebagoes. The land ceded to the national government contained about eight million acres, and extended from the upper end of Rock Island to the mouth of the Wisconsin — from latitude 41° 30' to latitude 43° 15'.

Mr. Atwater in his book then proceeded to give his impressions of the Indians. He discusses the red man from every point of view. He inquires into his origin; he notices his language, customs and government; he looks at his social status and makes some interesting remarks upon family life. The character and influence of Indian women receives a fair share of attention. He discovers a propensity for gambling among the braves but he admires the eloquence and the poetic instincts of the forest children. He recognizes that there is an Indian problem and goes into a full discussion of the subject. The final extinction of the red man he suggests can be prevented only by making him a civilized man. The Indian must be taught to build houses, to give up the chase and cultivate the earth. The Indian youth should be taught the mechanical arts and schools for that purpose should be established.

Mr. Atwater was a deep sympathizer with the Indian and he already saw in the treatment accorded him that "Century of Dishonor."

"As the tide of emigration rolls westward our red brethren will be driven from river to river, from mountain to mountain, until they finally perish. My heart is sick of the idea. My poor veto against the wasteful and villainous expenditure of millions of dollars under the hypocritical pretensions of benevolence and piety and even charity is of no avail against the united efforts of a corrupt set of men who contrive to plunder the treasury every winter under the solemn sanctions of law. I feel ashamed of my country and I conclude by reminding our rulers and our people that the red man is on our borders — that he is wholly in our power, either to save or destroy him — that the whole civilized world of this day and all posterity, will judge us impartially."

A Dictionary of the Sioux language occupies some space in the book. Whether this was the result of original investigation on the part of the writer, can not be determined. Certainly it forms an interesting chapter on the Indian language.

Mr. Atwater's return trip to Ohio is described with the same degree of care as his outward journey. From Prairie Du Chien to Louisville he traveled overland. Sickness overtook him and he was obliged to halt for several days. His conveyance was by light wagon and by stage. Nothing along his route remained unnoticed. The Wisconsin snow-birds, the prairie hen, the Dodgeville lead mines, the pure atmosphere, the falls in the streams where mills might be erected, the soil, the species of fish, the flowers, the trees, — all are jotted into the omnipresent notebook.

Of the future of the country Mr. Atwater was optimistic. In speaking of the Northwest he says: "This vast region in its present state is of little value, but the time will certainly arrive when it will be covered with farms and animated by countless millions of domestic animals. There golden harvests will wave before every breath of air that moves over its surface; there great and splendid cities will rear their tall and glittering spires and millions of human beings will live and move and display talents that will ennoble man and virtues that will adorn and render him happy."

"The longest, the most durable and the best rivers in the world intersect and pass through this country, standing on whose banks there will yet be some of the largest cities in the world. Comparatively speaking but few persons in the world have ever beheld this country. No tongue and no author have described it, but it is there."

From Louisville to Cincinnati the trip was quickly made by boat and according to his own statement he was glad once again to set foot on Ohio soil. Anxious to get to Circleville, he started at once and completed the journey in three days. His route lay by way of Lebanon, Wilmington and Washington. The fertility of the soil and hospitality of the people of the Miami valley are not forgotten. Interested ever in education, he informs us that there is a University at Oxford, rising in reputation and usefulness but sadly in need of funds. Then he pauses long enough to say, "There is an unreasonable prejudice against our colleges. They are considered by ignorant people as nurseries of aristocracy; whereas they are exactly the reverse. These colleges furnish competent teachers to our common schools, located near every poor man's door in which his children can be well educated. The college is the poor man's best friend and I regret that they are not looked upon as such by every man in Ohio."

After visiting a few days with his family at Circleville, Mr. Atwater started for Washington to deliver his treaty to the President. The first day he traveled to Zanesville by way of Lancaster and Somerset, a distance of fifty-eight miles. He stopped long enough to discuss the geology of the country and then hastened on to Wheeling toward Washington. At a tavern he was compelled to remain some time. This gave him an opportunity to present his views on the Allegheny mountains which he proceeded to do at some length and since he had ample time and for fear he might forget it he even discoursed on the Rocky mountains also.

Upon his arrival in Washington he waits upon General Jackson and breakfasts with the President and his family. For several weeks he is in frequent consultation with the President and the Secretary of War. The details of the treaty were gone over apparently to the satisfaction of both officials. This was in October. The treaty could not be ratified until after the convening of the Senate in December. During this interim a visit was made to Philadelphia. Here many prominent citizens were met. They impressed themselves most favorably upon the visitor for he can hardly find words sufficient and adjectives strong enough to express his ideas in the superlative degree.

By the opening of Congress Mr. Atwater had returned to Washington and was present at the first session of the Senate. A committee was elected to consider his treaty and he met with it twice a week. A most favorable report was made. Then the Senate confirmed, the President approved and Mr. Atwater's official life was closed. Before returning to Ohio he attended the first levee of President Jackson. With much *Naivete* he tells how the Mrs. Donelson and Miss Easton of the President's family and Mrs. Eaton, wife of the Secretary of War were dressed "in American calico and wore no ruffles and no ornaments of any sort."

It appears that this dress was donned out of deference to the western idea of simplicity, for Mr. Atwater continues, "As a western man, I confess, I could not help feeling proud that they were born and wholly educated in the west. The simplicity of their dress, their unaffected manners, their neatness, their ease, grace and dignity, carried all before them. The diamonds sparkled in vain at that levee and western unadorned neatness, modesty and beauty bore off the palm with ease."

"Our western ladies had felt some uneasiness before the levee, about the result, but their friends of the other sex, assured them, correctly enough, that republican simplicity would triumph over all the crosses and diamonds that the east would bring into the field. No time and no circumstance can ever efface that night from my memory. It was a splendid triumph for the Mississippi Valley."

It was in 1838 that Mr. Atwater published his History of Ohio. He had planned the work twenty years before and much of the material was gathered when first originated. It was his intention to publish the work in two volumes but the author evidently changed his mind. The book was well received and hearty encouragement was given it by the best people of the day. Among the original subscribers are to be found state and county officials, ex-governors and men of all professions.

It is gratifying to see how well the geological formations are treated, when it is remembered how limited was the accurate information obtainable. The first Geological Survey of Ohio was published in 1837, but since much of Mr. Atwater's manuscript had been written years before publication it is quite probable that what he has to say of Ohio Geology are his own deductions from his own observations. In the treatment of this part of his work he is almost wholly utilitarian. It is Economical Geology that he discusses. What practical use can be made of a stratum of sand rock or clay or limestone is the important question. He saw the possibilities of Ohio River Freestone and Scioto Valley Limestone for building purposes; the iron ores of southern Ohio, the clays of Zanesville and the coal fields of the Hocking Valley.

The rivers of Ohio are described from an agricultural and a commercial viewpoint. He utters a faint prophecy of the Monroe county oil fields by observing that on Duck Creek in boring for salt water, petroleum was found; that many such springs were reported to be in existence and that the oil was being burned in lamps and used for lubricating purposes in manufactories. The chief utilization of the product, however was the bottling of "Seneca Oil" or "American Oil" and selling it for medicinal uses. Mr. Atwater thinks that if some "water doctor" would take hold of it a large fortune would be made as a result. Subsequent history in many ways is a fulfillment of Mr. Atwater's prophecy.

The fauna and flora of the state are not neglected. Especially is the botanical feature well discussed. Not only are the native trees and their habitat pointed out but their preservation is urged for economical purposes. It is interesting to note in these days when the cry of "Save the forests" is heard on every hand, that our author raised a warning voice almost seventy years ago. Mr. Atwater's position on the question is undoubtedly the correct one and had his words been heeded, there would not now be that periodical, sentimental wail of "Save the forests" when there are no forests to save.

"Most of our timber trees will soon be gone and no means are yet resorted to, to restore the forests which we are destroying. In many places even now woodlands are more valuable than cleared fields. It is true that in the northwest part of the state we have vast forests yet, but it is equally true, that their majesty is bowing before the woodchopper's axe, and will soon be gone. We do not regret the disappearance of the native forests, because by that means more human beings can be supported in the state but in the older parts of Ohio means should even now begin to restore trees enough for fences, fuel and timber, for the house-builder and joiner."

Unlike Irving who begins his History of New York with the creation of the world, Atwater begins his with La Salle's discovery of the Ohio River. The treatment accorded to the various events down to the close of the War of 1812 is full and vivid. His conclusions on the Dunmore War do not vary greatly from what more recent writers have concluded. The land claims, the first settlements, the organization and admission of the state, the various treaties with the Indians, come in for their share of attention. Ohio's attitude and share in the second war with England is especially well handled. Mr. Atwater was a genuine Ohioan. He was not a Jingo by any means but he loved his state and believed in its citizens. He knew what every other fair minded student of history knows, that the War of 1812 meant more to the people of Ohio than to the people of the east. That while the locked doors protected the participants in the Hartford Convention, there was little protection to the frontiersmen, from the tomahawk and firebrand in the hands of a ruthless savage, urged and abetted by English influence. It is for this reason no doubt, that Ohio's part in that war is described with such minuteness by Mr. Atwater.

The period subsequent to the War of 1812 is passed over hastily except those times when the schools and "internal improvement" agitations were at their height. The opening of the Ohio Canal was certainly a great event in the opinion of our author. Governor Clinton of New York had been invited to Ohio and his journey through the state was a continual ovation. Mr. Atwater has, most probably, given us the best and most authentic account of the ceremonies. Interested as he was, and also active in urging the digging of the canal, there surely was no one better qualified to leave the people of Ohio its history.

The book closes with a brief account of the condition of Ohio at that time. Schools and colleges with their respective faculties, churches, with the growth of religious denominations, trade and commerce, banks and banking, newspapers, societies and cities and towns are described in the most optimistic manner.

On the question of slavery Mr. Atwater's attitude was something of a compromise. He thought it impracticable and impolitic to interfere with the institution. He believed that slavery ought to exist at least, a hundred years. Yet slavery had passed away before he himself died.

It were fitting after Mr. Atwater's long career as agitator for a public school system or the establishment of one, that his last literary work should be done along the line of his favorite theme. It was an appropriate climax. At the time of its writing, 1841, our common schools had been established. Yet there was much to be done for their betterment. In "An Essay on Education," a plea is made for efficiency; better school buildings, better teachers and broader curricula are demanded. His ideal of what a school ought to be was years in advance of his time. His essay makes good pedagogical reading even at this time.

The subject of music he places as one of the requirements of a complete education. He argues for its place in the course of study both as a cultural and utilitarian branch. He believes in the education of women on the same equality as men; that the future wives and mothers should be conversant not only with the elementary studies but with the higher education as well. He is a champion of co-education. He believes that women should be trained for their duties as well as men and that this training should be the same in kind.

He pleads for better teachers. He emphasizes the importance of a teacher in a country and asks for a higher degree of professionalism. He has little sympathy for the teacher who makes his work a stepping stone to something else. He places a high moral responsibility upon the teacher. He wants him to be an example for good in a community.

He goes into the subject of text-books. The histories in vogue he unmercifully criticises. He asks for a better arranged text and then goes into detail on the value of history as a school study. His reasons breathe the highest degree of patriotism. He wants the rising youth to know how our nation has been built and the fundamental principles underlying our government. He thinks that the books ought to be written by an American and that American should be Washington Irving. He deplores the lack of authenticity in our geographies. They contain such meagre information concerning the New West. Their descriptions and maps are so indefinite. They are made by eastern book makers who evidently do not know their subjects, for they speak of "Missouri Territory" and "other districts" in a vague uncertain way.

Another argument Mr. Atwater cites for popular education is adduced from the fact of the foreign immigration to our shores. The people should become acquainted with American institutions. He speaks in a commendatory way of the many Germans and Irish who were then settling up the middle west. They were the kind of people wanted and it only needed the school house to make of them ideal citizens because of their industry and thrift.

Mr. Atwater's essay occupied high ground. It was in every way worthy of the man. It shows him to be of broad sympathies and a noble nature. While it was not the most popular it was certainly the best thing he ever wrote.

Mr. Atwater was an admirer of the classics. His writings show a thorough acquaintance with both the Latin and the Greek authors. He was fond of quoting from them and his allusions to the writers of antiquity are numerous.

The career of Caleb Atwater was an uneventful one. He worked hard for others and he deserves to be remembered for it.

He was the father of six sons and three daughters, all of whom are dead, except his youngest daughter, Lucy Brown, who lives in Indianapolis, with her son, an Episcopalian minister.

He died at the home of a daughter in Circleville on the thirteenth day of March, 1867. He had been a familiar character in the village for years, yet when he died the local paper barely mentioned the event. It added, however, that at one time he had been a prominent citizen. It might also have said, and said it truly, that he helped to give their city its first school and their state its first system of education.

In Ohio's "Hall of Fame," let us place the name of Caleb Atwater.

New Lexington, Ohio, April 25, 1905.

ORIGIN OF OHIO PLACE NAMES.

MRS. MARIA EWING MARTIN.

[Paper read before the Fifth Ohio State Conference, Daughters of the American Revolution, held at Toledo, October 29, 1903 — EDITOR.]

The Iroquois War on the Shawanese tribes along the Ohio gave white men in 1670 their first knowledge of that river; La Salle's expedition down its waters to the Falls promptly followed; but eleven years later, when he stood at the mouth of the Mississippi and took possession for the King of France of all the country watered by its branches, the Ohio was closed to the French by Iroquois hatred. Before many years by the same enemies the Shawanese were driven out, and fled east and south of the mountains.

French surveyors and traders followed up La Salle's explorations, but they made no attempt to form settlements, and the Iroquois sold the Ohio country to the English in utter contempt of other claims.

In 1750 the Ohio Company, an association of Virginia planters and English merchants, prepared to colonize it and sent Christopher Gist to explore it and report on the best lands. The Miamis refused to allow the company to settle north of the Ohio, though they made a friendly alliance with the English. Jealous of this friendship, the French sent Indian allies, who surprised and burnt the Miami towns, including an English stockade. A chain of French forts was then built from Lake Erie through the disputed territory to the Illinois. The result was the French and Indian war and the final loss of this region by France. Before the English could make any systematic attempts to colonize, they in their turn were compelled to transfer their title to the United States after the Revolutionary War.

The Americans received it with a heavy mortgage in the shape of its savage occupants. This they endeavored to extin-

(272)

guish; first, by a second purchase of the Iroquois claims through conquest, and then by treaties with the western tribes.

The nation of the Cat, or Eries, had ceased to exist a century before. The Lake which forms our northern boundary, a county of the Reserve, and several townships, are all the trace of them left in Ohio.

The Wyandots, or Hurons, who were nearly wiped out at the same time by the same foe, the Iroquois, were only preserved from extinction by absorption among their kindred, the Tobacco Nation, whose tribes were the ones known to Ohio as Wyandots. The United States acknowledged their claim to central and eastern Ohio and compensated them for it. Fifty years before, their chiefs had permitted the Shawanese and Delawares to come out from the Potomac and from Pennsylvania. At the time of the treaty, the Miamis, the strongest and fiercest of the western tribes, who had held undisputed possession from the Scioto westward had moved back to the Wabash and the Miami of the Lakes; the Shawanese were occupying their deserted towns along the Sciotos and the Miamis; the Delawares were on the Muskingum, while the Wyandots had their principal villages on the Sandusky.

The ease and frequency with which Indian towns were destroyed and rebuilt, the keenness shown in the selection of the sites, and the general tolerance that existed among the tribes in their appreciation of a common danger from the white settlements, led to a succession and juxtaposition of villages, which creates a lack of correspondence between the names of localities and their occupants. There is hardly an important town in the State that was not built on the site of an Indian village, though often not bearing the same name even when of Indian origin. Thus, there were six well-known Chillicothe towns of the Shawanese; but our Chillicothe is not on the site of any, though in a region peopled with Indian shades. Thus, also, Christopher Gist found a Wyandot town at the forks of the Muskingum, now Coshocton, from the Delaware word, Goschachgunk. He found a Delaware village at the "Standing Stone" called Hock-hockin. On a map of the time it is called "French Margaret's Town," from the daughter of that strange, forceful character, the half-

breed interpreter, Madame Montour. The first white settlers,
Pennsylvania Dutch, found Shawanese here, and two towns in
full swing, Tarhe town and Tobey town; but they built a third
and dubbed it New Lancaster. Piqua is on the site of the
Lower Piqua town of the Shawanese, with a Miami name. The
Pickaway Plains and Pickaway County are a mis-spelling of the
tribal name.

The oldest names in Ohio are borne by the water-courses,
and, excepting a few small streams, are all of Indian giving.
Following the north bank of the "beautiful river," (Seneca,
Ohio,) we come first to the Mahoning, " at the Lick," with its
branches, Shenango and the Big Bear. Shenango is a variation
of the Iroquois word Yanangue, "tobacco," and comes from
Wyandot occupation. Indian Cross Creek, now Battle Ground
Run, is where Buskirk's battle was fought in 1793. The Muskingum is Delaware for "elk's eye," with its forks, the Tuscarawas, "open mouth," and the Walhonding, or " White Woman's Creek," for the first white woman who dwelt in this wilderness. She was Mary Harris, the heroine of the Deerfield,
Mass., massacre in 1704. Ten years old at the time, she was
carried captive beyond the Ohio, and subsequently married a
French Mohawk. Whitewoman's town stood at the mouth of
the Killbuck. Mary was given a rival in a second white captive,
who was called " the Newcomer." One morning the chief was
found murdered and " the Newcomer " was gone. I will give
you Christopher Gist's account of her end.

" December 26th, 1750.— This day a woman who had been
a long time a prisoner, and had deserted and been 'retaken and
brought into the town on Christmas Eve, was put to death in
the following manner : They carried her without the town,
and let her loose, and when she attempted to run away, the
persons appointed for that purpose pursued her and struck
her on the ear, on the right side of her head, which beat her
flat on her face on the ground; they then struck her several times
through the back with a dart to the Heart, scalped her and threw
the scalp in the air, and another cut off her head. There the
dismal spectacle lay till the evening, and then Barney Curran

desired leave to bury her, which he and his men and some of the Indians did just at dark."

At this time there could not have been less than twenty white traders in the town. Apparently there was not a word of protest. Only the day before, the Indians had begged Gist to remain and instruct them in the principles of Christianity and baptize their children. Newcomerstown, in Tuscarawas County, is a reminder of this poor woman's story.

Killbuck, after the noted Delaware chief, and Mohican are branches of Walhonding. The latter is called from an emigration of Connecticut Mohicans. Their old enemies, the Mingoes, were not in force in Ohio; but Mingo Shaft, a coal mine at Steubenville, and Mingo Junction, three miles below, are reminders that they existed here. Jerome Fork of the Mohican was the home of a French trader with a squaw wife in 1812, and Jeromeville helps to perpetuate his name. Buckhorn and One Leg, from a one-legged Indian, are branches of the Tuscarawas. Licking comes from the salt licks in its course; the Indian form, Pataskala, is now applied to a town. The importance of such places to wild animals and man cannot be overestimated; and among the smaller streams Salt Licks and Sugar Creeks are numerous, with Buck, Bear, Wolf, Beaver and Duck Creeks in almost as great number.

In Guernsey County, Leatherwood Creek is from a bush with tough, stringy bark used for tying bundles of furs; Yoker, from the Yoker brush that grows along its banks; Little and Big Skull Forks mark the banks where a pursuing party found the remains of a captive mother and baby; Indian Camp Creek is from a deserted camp; there is a town of the same name.

Next comes the Hock-hocking, "the neck of a bottle," from its shape at the falls. Without its first syllable, it is applied to a county. Of its branches, Sunday and Monday Creeks were named for the day of their discovery ; and Lost Run, for the skeleton of a lost hunter found propped against a tree with his rusty gun by his side. Margaret's Creek bears the name of Mrs. Joseph Snowden, the first white woman in Athens County.

Next, the Shade, a narrow, gloomy stream of darkest memory, for many an Indian war party bound for Kentucky filed down its banks.

Scioto is Wyandot for "deer;" the two Darby Creeks were named for an Indian, as well as the plains watered by them. Mount Logan, once the home of the great Shawnee chief, is on the Paint. Pea-pea is a branch of Paint Creek. The first settlers found an old beech tree by a creek with the initials "P. P." cut in it, and named the run, the meadows drained by it, and subsequently a township in Pike County from the incident. Many years afterwards its origin was learned. Some emigrants from Redstone Old Fort came down the Ohio and, leaving their families at its mouth, the men ascended the Scioto to explore. One Peter Patrick cut his initials on the tree. Being surprised by Indians, and two of the party killed, they fled down the river, and pulled out with their families for Limestone, Kentucky. If there is any descendant of Peter Patrick present, I would like her to explain just why her ancestor wanted to leave the Redstone settlement the very year that my ancestor was laying out the town of Brownsville in it.

The Big and Little Miami are named for their first occupants—the Ottawa name for "mother;" and the Mad River, the largest branch of the Big Miami, from its torrent. Tecumseh Hill is on the Mad. Paddy's Run, on the Big Miami, is in honor of an Irishman who was drowned there.

The Maumee, or Omee, and the Auglaize unite to form the Great Miami of the Lakes; the first name is now applied its full length. Auglaize River and County take theirs from the valley at the junction called by the French traders "Au Glaize," or "Grand Glaize," an important trading center. We have adapted the French, "the Au Glaize," as some people are determined to adapt the name "the La Grippe." Blanchard's Fork of the Auglaize (Indian, "Tailor's River,") is from a domesticated Frenchman who plied the needle; also Mt. Blanchard and several Blanchard townships; while Tone-tog-a-nee (Tontogany) Creek and a town in Wood County are from an Indian chief; and Abanaka, in Van Wert County, has the name of an early French tribe of Indians.

It is in this region that the French have left the most traces. Presque Isle, a hill on the Maumee, and Roche de Bout, or Standing Stone, are noted in Wayne's battle. Turkey Foot rock where a brave Indian of that name made a last memorable stand, still shows the triangular marks scratched in his memory. Kelley's Island was once "Cunningham's Island," from a French (!) trader. Loramie's store was a noted landmark and appeared in all the treaties after 1769. It was fifteen miles up Loramie's Creek, a branch of the Big Miami. The stream, the post-office at its mouth and the Reservoir in Shelby County, still bear his name. Peter Navarre, a French trader and a gentleman, died some thirty years ago in Toledo. A town in Stark County is named for him.

Moving east along the Lake we come to the venerable Sandusky, "at the cold water." The name is now applied to a river and bay and the county containing them. Sandusky on the Bay in Erie County, is built on the site of an Ottawa town called "Ogontz's Place." Its distinguished chief is now remembered by a street in Sandusky, several civic associations, and the village of Ogontz. Upper and Lower Sandusky are at Indian towns of the same name on the Sandusky River; the latter about 1849, in a burst of enthusiasm for our great explorer, changed its name to "Fremont." The Tymochtee, "around the plains," and the Scioto surround Wyandot County. Next, Huron, from the French for "Wyandot," with its town and county; Cold Creek (Erie County) from its source in a deep, unfailing limestone spring, called by some scholar "the Castalian fount," hence the town of Castalia close by it. Vermillion River is from the red paint the Indians obtained here, with Vermillion at its mouth. It has retained its obsolete spelling. The Black River is from its deep romantic gorge crowned with hemlock; while at its mouth the "Black River Settlement," next "Charleston," is now "Lorain," from the county.

We next reach the Cuyahoga or "Crooked River," whose source is farther north than its mouth. The county and the village of Cuyahoga Falls are named from the river. The name of Chagrin River is older than the various explanations of its origin. Chagrin, at its mouth, is now "Willoughby."

with Chagrin Falls farther up.   The Grand River was called
Sheauga, or "Raccoon," by the Indians, hence, Geauga County;
Conneaut, "many fish," and lastly, Ashtabula, "fish," River, Town
and County.

The savages generally had stood by the English during the
Revolution, and were no mean foes to be reckoned with along
the border, and in all military movements towards the west.   The
galling aggressions on the settlements south of the Ohio, by the
Shawanese, led to successive expeditions from Pennsylvania and
Kentucky which repeatedly destroyed their towns on the Miamis
and the Mad River and in the Scioto Valley.   Such terrible vengeance was exacted that the region earned the name of "the
Miami Slaughter House."   The most noted leaders of these expeditions, Generals Clark and Logan, are honored by counties
near the scenes of their exploits.

Two of the Pennsylvania expeditions were less justifiable.
One under Col. Williamson, attacked the Moravian missions on
the Tuscarawas and murdered in cold blood 94 unarmed Christian Indians, non-combatants, and half of them women and children.   The same summer a second expedition under Cols. Crawford and Williamson, crossed the Ohio with the same end in view.
Finding the villages deserted, they attempted to follow the refugees to their new homes on the Sandusky, but were surprised by
overwhelming numbers, and after a fierce battle retreated.   The
Indians pursued, killing all stragglers.   Col. Crawford was taken
prisoner by a Delaware chief, carried back to a Delaware town
on the Tymochtee, and there burned with the most horrible tortures that fiendish ingenuity could devise.   Col. Crawford's high
character and his terrible fate have relieved his memory
from the obloquy that a successful expedition would have brought
upon it.   The place where he was taken prisoner is within the
former limits of the county that bears his name.

As the facts became known with regard to the first expedition, public sentiment demanded compensation to the Moravians
and their converts.   Congress gave them a large tract of land
on the Tuscarawas, and their villages were rebuilt.   There are
still some Moravians at the little town of Gnadenhutten, "tents of
grace," but the other towns and the Indians are gone.

By the first treaty with the Ohio Indians at the close of the Revolution the boundary line ran from the mouth of the Cuyahoga south to Fort Laurens on the Tuscarawas, west to Loramie's store near the Big Miami, along the Portage to the Maumee and down it to its mouth. The country south and east of this line comprised two-thirds of the present State, and was erected into Washington County. The original designation of the entire region was the "territory northwest of the Ohio;" but when it was divided into two territorial governments the first settled portion (Ohio) received the name of honor which the State was proud to keep.

The next step was to clear off the claims of the old colonies. New York surrendered hers; Virginia also, except a reservation between the Scioto and the Little Miami for bounties for her Continental troops, in case the State lands in Kentucky should not hold out. Connecticut reserved the property in 3,500,000 acres, but surrendered the jurisdiction.

Then was passed the ordinance of 1787, that greatest of charters of liberty, and immediately thereafter the New England Ohio Company purchased 1,500,000 acres of land on the Ohio River from the Muskingum west, and the black canvas-topped wagon started for the Ohio country. April 7th, 1788, the emigrants landed at the mouth of the Muskingum River, pinned a code of laws for the colony to a tree, and named the settlement Marietta, after Marie Antoinette, one of the last acts of reverence vouchsafed that unhappy queen.

Another large tract lying to the west was contracted for at the same time and given to the Scioto Land Company, who undertook to sell surplus shares in France in advance of payment. It was the beginning of the reign of terror; many of the middle and upper classes were glad to emigrate to a romantic wilderness, a nobler Bois du Boulogne—there were no savages marked on the advertisement maps. About 200 carvers and gilders, wigmakers, jewellers and gentlemen, with a very few farmers, landed at the mouth of the Scioto. Between incompetence and fraud the company failed, and the settlers lost both money and lands, becoming reduced to absolute penury. Some years later from a sense of national pride, Congress gave them a portion of their tract; but they gradually scattered or perished and have left few descendants in that region. Gallipolis, the first settlement, with Gallia County, are all the names left.

But before Gallipolis, the second group of settlements was made at Columbia, Cincinnati and North Bend, at the most northerly bend of the river. Judge Symmes, of New Jersey, laid out the last as "Symmes City," but nobody paid attention to that, and Cleves, in Hamilton County, is his only namesake. Cincinnati was originally "Losantiville," a truly American hodge-podge of Greek, Latin and French for "the city opposite the mouth" of the Licking River in Kentucky. The next year, to please Governor St. Clair, who was a member of the order of the Cincinnati, the name was changed. The patriotic enthusiasm of the early christeners has been somewhat curbed by the general post office which has limited the number of towns of the same name. Still there is Washington Court House, Washington, Washingtonville, and -burg, New, Mount and Fort Washington, and finally Mt. Vernon. In a lesser degree the other Revolutionary favorites have been honored. Fortunately the national authorities cannot interfere with our townships, and half of them in each of the southern counties are the same. Patriot, Liberty Center, Union, town and county, with its variations by compass and in compounds; several Columbias, and Columbus laid out the day war was declared against Great Britain in 1812, all attest the same spirit. Of the counties formed before 1833, thirty-three were named for Revolutionary heroes, almost all generals, many of whom had direct relations with Ohio; while the war of 1812 is represented by nine more, all but Jackson winning their laurels within our borders. Meigs, Lucas and Morrow were early governors; Vinton was a distinguished Ohio statesman, and Noble honored its first settler regardless of the lack of a national reputation.

The Virginia reservation comprised the greater part of thirteen modern counties. The first settlers naturally were from Kentucky and Virginia. Col. Nathaniel Massie, with a party of Kentuckians, making the first permanent settlement at Manchester on the river twelve miles above Maysville. The region is under great obligations to Massie for his enterprise, energy and daring in surveys and settlements; but its appreciation on the map is only shown by Massie's Creek, and Massie township, in Warren County. Such names as Williamsburg, Point Pleasant, Bainbridge, Frankfort, Lynchburg and Jamestown, all speak of their origin; while scattered through the State are Richmond, Alexandria, Loudonville, Moorefield, and several Court Houses that have a pleasant "Faginny" twang. There is a touch of romance in the naming of Bowling Green shown by a grizzled old mail-carrier who had carried mails between Kentucky and Tennessee in 1802; thirty-seven years later he was on the line between Findlay and Bellefontaine. A little settlement further on drew up a petition for a post office, but could think of no appropriate name. The postman, happening to ride up, learned of the difficulty and, seizing a glass of cider, he waved it from north to south —"Here's to Bowling Green!" A green clearing in the forest made by an army encampment in 1812, made the Kentucky name all the more fitting.

The Government did its best to protect its infant colonies. Forts Harmar, Finney and Washington were built along the Ohio River. The savages, paid and armed by the British, committed constant outrages on the settlements. Col. Hardin, sent on a mission of peace to them, was murdered where the town of Hardin now stands. Harmar and St. Clair led two unsuccessful expeditions against the Indians of the Maumee, the latter suffering a most disastrous defeat. The third was in charge of General Wayne, who routed the enemy in the Battle of Fallen Timbers, August 20, 1794, and laid waste a populous country for fifty miles around. Previous to and during Wayne's march a line of forts was built from Fort Washington, at Cincinnati, north—Fort Hamilton at the crossing of the Big Miami, Forts St. Clair, Jefferson and Greenville, Fort Recovery on the scene of St. Clair's defeat, as recovered from the Indians; Fort St. Mary's, in Mercer County, and Fort Defiance, at the junction of the Auglaize and Maumee. The towns of Hamilton, Greenville, Fort Recovery, St. Mary's and Defiance still show the line of march. Wayne named Shane's Crossing on the upper Wabash from a half-breed trader, and destroyed the trading house and stores of the infamous British agent, McKee, who has left his memory in Mc-

Kee's Creek, and the Ottawa River, sometimes called "the Hog," because, in seeking to save his property, he drove his hogs down the steep banks of the stream.

Wayne made a firm peace with but little accession of territory. Shortly after, Ebenezer Zane's trace was cut from opposite Wheeling to opposite Limestone, Kentucky, which opened up immigration to the central counties. Zanesville was laid out on one of his reservations. The Western Reserve of Connecticut was erected into the County of Trumbull, than which there is no better name in American history. It comprised twelve counties in the northeastern part of the State. With the exception of the Firelands, at the western end, which were not yet purchased from the Indians, the lands were sold in a lump to a Connecticut syndicate and resold in large tracts, frequently by whole townships; naturally many of these townships bear the names of their original owners. The first permanent settlement was made in 1796, at the mouth of the Cuyahoga, and named for General Moses Cleaveland, the leader of the surveying party. It is said to have had an "a" in its name until 1832, when the first issue of the "Cleveland Advertiser," owing to a lack of proportion between the type and the page, was obliged to leave the "a" out of its title, and it soon went out of general use.

The names of the towns in the Reserve show a decided remembrance of the settlers' early homes; as West Andover, Deerfield, New London. North Amherst, Danbury, Saybrook and Farmington; while other characteristic New England names show Yankee colonies all over the State. In many instances a township organization was completed and a minister chosen before the emigrants left home. The first act of the Granville colony was to hear a sermon. Such communities were more law-abiding than those that grew up hap-hazard, and their distinctly religious character has left its mark on the whole State.

Other Eastern States are remembered by Rome and Utica, from New York; New Philadelphia, Germantown, and Somerset, from Pennsylvania; Newark from New Jersey; Dover, Delaware; Wilmington, North Carolina; and Baltimore and Fredericktown, Maryland.

Next in importance is the German immigration, direct and indirect. The Hollanders and Germans known as "Pennsylvania Dutch," were early settlers, and such towns as Antwerp and New Holland probably came through them. German, Berlin, Berne and Bremen Townships are without number; while, of the cities, Leipsic, Dresden, Strasburg and many Berlins are the most important. A German emigration in 1832, from Cincinnati to Auglaize County gave a New Bremen, a Berlin and a Minster within six miles. There was a large emigration to Ottawa County in 1849.. In one township in Erie County are Berlin, Berlinville and Ceylon. Switzerland township in Monroe County, takes its name from Father Tisher's large settlement of Swiss from Berne in 1819.

Though Scotch-Irish descendants are all through Ohio, there are but few national names: Antrim township, in Wyandot County, Aberdeen, Edinburgh and Caledonia, are all. Guernsey County gets its name from about twenty families from that little island in 1806. The Welsh, probably, are of too recent immigration to affect our nomenclature; Welsh Hills, a town quarter in Granville; Radnor township, in Delaware County, and Venedocia, the Latin for "North Wales," being about all.

From the Scriptures we have numerous Goshens, Gileads and Canaans (usually by way of New England) Rehoboth, Sardis, several Bethels and Zoar, a Tuscarawas County settlement in 1817, of two hundred poor German sectarians, whose desperate struggle for existence finally forced them to adopt the Communistic plan with ultimate success. Quaker City and several Salems mark our numerous Friends; and Lebanon, the Shakers. Batesville is for an old Methodist preacher, the only town named for that grand group of men, one of the best types of muscular Christians that the world has ever seen. The first Bethel in the State was by Obed Denham in 1797, who freed his slaves when he founded the town. Other Kentuckians and Virginians in divers settlements did the same, and many more came to escape the air of slavery. It is indeed "holy ground" where men, after a hard won fight for their own liberty, will begin life over again to make the lives of others worth having.

Ancient history is still further represented in our towns by several Palmyras and Carthages, Sparta, Iberia, Delphos and Scio —which smacks of Wyandot—and our learning has provided us with Xenia, "gifts;" Kalida, "beautiful;" Neapolis, "new city;" and Eldorado, which has not kept its promise.

The Capitals of the modern world and of the old Italian republics are all sponsors for the future glories of our towns; while Poland township, Pulaski, Moscow, Marengo and Napoleon warn us of the fleeting nature of earthly grandeur; the knightly Sir Philip Sidney has a namesake; and Caesarville is on Caesar's Creek, but whether black or white Caesar, I am sure I cannot tell.

Our first college town, Athens, had a proper ambition to which Oxford makes a good second; Kenyon College and Gambier, the town where it is situated, were named for generous English nobleman who made the college foundation possible; while Oberlin is in honor of the noble Alsatian pastor whose deeds of philanthropy were ably seconded by the founders of this college.

It may not be familiar to all of you that, in 1814, a company of infantry was recruited at Athens College, and formed a part of General Meigs' large command which reached the scene of war only in time to disband. When the recruits were gathered in the college chapel for a farewell service, the old president prayed fervently for the souls of the British and Indians whom these young men were about to kill. My grandfather, who was one of them, used to say that the boys never felt positive whether or not the old gentleman was poking fun at them.

The names concerning the oldest human events in the State are those applied to the remains of the mound builders. Fort Ancient, in Warren County, Fort Hill, in Highland are famous fortifications; Serpent Mound in Adams County, and Alligator Mound, in Licking, religious edifices, the finest in the west. There was formerly a large circular earthwork in Pickaway County with fortified gates on which the town of Circleville was built with the court house in the center; but time wore away the mound, and a vandal council levelled it, rebuilding the center on a square; so the name is now but a reminiscence.

Our primeval forests are kept in rememberance by such names as Oak Hill, Oak Harbor and Oakwood, Locust Grove,

Cherry Valley, Hazelwood, Maplewood and Elmwood, Sycamore, Laurelville, Sylvania, Rushsylvania and Forest; while the Buckeye characterizes the people and the State. Three Locusts is from a group on the village green, but Magnolia must be more what was hoped than what existed. Cranberry township, in Crawford County, comes from a cranberry marsh once 2,000 acres in extent, and well known to Indians, trappers, wild animals and snakes.

Our mineral wealth is attested in the east and south by such names as Irondale, Galena, Ironton, Minersville, Coalport, Coalton, Carbon Hill and Mineral City; Syracuse and Salineville are named for their salt; Jobs is not connected with dishonest speculation, as the name might indicate, but with an energetic miner named Job, who has become a very capable operator. We are not without a poetic fancy in the mining region, and Glen Roy and Dell Roy indicate this, as well as the respect shown to a mining inspector; so does Coal Gate, which the maps are beginning to misspell, as if associated with soap.

Rockbridge, in Hocking County, is near a natural bridge 100 feet long and ten to twenty feet wide; Lithopolis (Fairfield County) is from a good grade of freestone; Hanging Rock, in Jackson County, which lends its name to an ore region 1,000 square miles in extent in three States, is a sandstone cliff 400 feet high whose top projects like the eaves of a house; Put-in-Bay, on Lake Erie, has an original and expressive name; Gibralter Island, at the entrance, is a rock eight acres in extent which rises forty-five feet above the Lake to support its ambitious name; Rattlesnake Island, from a succession of rocky humps, claims precedence among the once snake-infested islands; Carryall township, in Paulding County, is from the resemblance of a rock in the river to the old-fashioned carriage; Buckhorn Cottage is from the shape of a hill; Clifton, in Greene County, is from a wild and picturesque gorge of the Little Miami; Plain City is on the rich Darby plains; Pigeon Roost Ridges are no longer true to their name; while many valuable springs give various appropriate names to towns in their vicinity.

Summit and Portage Counties remind us of the water-shed in the center of our State, and the old eight-mile portage between the Cuyahoga and the Tuscarawas; Ridgeway, on that same water-shed, is where the time-honored house stands whose roof sheds its rain into Lake Erie and the Gulf of Mexico. Crestline was thought to be the highest point in the State when founded; Akron is the Greek for "elevation," while Flint Ridge provided the Indians from far·and near with their arrow-heads. Lockport, Lockington and Lockland are towns on canals, the last having four locks.

A very few town founders have been gallant enough to remember their daughters and wives : Aurora was named, in 1800, for the daughter of a surveyor; Athalia, Marysville, Clarington (from Clarinda) and Anna are all named for daughters of the founders. Amanda township, Allen County, perpetuates Fort Amanda and the wife of Col. Poague. There are many more Amandas, but I don't know their true knights.

We have our literary favorites, though not many; Waverly was named by an engineer, on the Ohio canal, who was addicted to Scott; Massillon, by Mrs. James Duncan for her favorite French author; we have Homer and Roscoe, and Murdoch, for the distinguished actor and reader who lived there twenty-five years, whom many of us will always remember with pleasure.

Many of our names are unique : Bucyrus was called for Busiris in Ancient Egypt with the spelling altered; Ivorydale, for the soap made there; Leetonia, for a member of its mining company named Lee; Elyria, town and township, for their owner, Heman Ely; through his efforts the county was admitted in 1821-2 and called "Lorain" from his pleasant recollection of time spent in the Rhine province; Amity, Tranquillity, Harmony township, Urbana (from "urbanity"), from the tempers and expectations of the settlers; Felicity is, perhaps, somewhat indebted to an early settler, William Fee; College Hill is named from two colleges; College Corner, with similar educational advantages, has one Indiana and two Ohio counties cornering in it. The town of Medina was originally called Mecca, but both town and county were later named for the rival Arabian town; Utopia, founded about 1847, by a Fouierite, was for a good while run on Utopian principles. Celina was named for Salina, N. Y., from a resemblance in the situation, but with the spelling changed.

Silas Wells, of Miami County, always wore a gingham coat, and went by the name of "Gingham." His eccentricity is kept in remembrance by the town of Ginghamsburg. At Junction City three railroads cross; at Gore, a little corner of Hocking County is neatly inserted into Perry; Stringtown may have suggested the title of a recent novel. Our most successful manufacture has been Columbiana County—a compound of Columbus and Anna. A waggish legislator, when the name was under consideration, suggested that "Maria" be added, to read "Columbi-Anna-Maria."

By a treaty at Fort Industry, now Toledo, July, 1805, the Indian title to the Firelands was extinguished, and Connecticut gave them to such of her citizens as had been burnt out by the British during the Revolution. They were erected into Huron and Erie Counties, and Norwalk was appropriately named for the town that had suffered the most. The Indians were quiet until about 1810, when, fomented by Tecumseh and his brother, the Prophet, aggressions began again. Harrison's victory at Tippecanoe destroyed the power of the Prophet, but Tecumseh joined the British in the war of 1812, and showed himself a better man than his associates. The latter part of that war is marked by some brilliant victories. several within our borders: the stubborn defense of Fort Meigs; Croghan's gallantry at Fort Stephenson, this fight commemorated by Croghansville and Ballsville, which, with the Fort, have long been swallowed up by Fremont; and Perry's victory off Ottawa County, which is marked by a southern county and the town of Perrysburg, just below Fort Meigs.

The war deprived the Indians of tne remainder of their lands in Ohio. In 1818, the northwest portion of the State was purchased, certain reservations being given to them. These were subsequently ceded to the United States, the latest by the Wyandots in 1842, and the last of the Ohio Indians were moved beyond the Mississippi.*

---

* Among the Delaware Indians who were moved to Kansas in 1829 was Chief Johnny Cake. At the beginning of the Civil War he was more than once a caller at my father's house in Leavenworth. On one occasion the baby shook hands with him and said, "How do you do, Mr. Patty-cake?" at which the Indian's gravity was overcome and he laughed heartily.

Eighteen new counties were now formed, mostly from this territory, and were opened up for settlement. Of these counties, Seneca, Wyandot, and Ottawa ("a trader") were named for the tribes having reservations therein. The Shawanese were given theirs in Auglaize County. (The town of Shawnee is near their old haunts in the Hocking Valley.) The region was largely black swamp covered with a heavy forest growth except for the clearings about the Indian villages. Cutting down the forests and draining the swamps has given some of the richest land in the State; it required very hard work from the settler, but without annoyance from the Indians.

Rising parallel with the Lake along almost the entire northern border are ancient lake beaches which have afforded the best natural roads in the State, and which have been used in succession by buffaloes and Indians, and for the wagons of white men, at a time when the region was elsewhere impassable. These ridges are called in Lorain County North, Center and Butternut Ridges, five, seven and nine miles from the Lake, the Central ridge running almost the length of the Lake. Sand, Oak and Sugar Ridge are local names. Near the town of Ridgeville, in Lorain County, there are four ridges; in other places they are broken up into knolls or disappear entirely.

These counties have the latest and the friendliest association with the Indians, and many interesting local traditions. Wauseon, "far off," and Ottokee, are towns in Fulton County named for two great chiefs, by a man who loved them as brothers. There are several Roundhead townships. Zanesfield was owned by Isaac Zane, a Virginia captive, raised and married among the Wyandots ; Wapakoneta, in Auglaize County, succeeded a Shawanese village of the same name, built by refugees from the Piqua towns. Lewistown, an Indian village, named for Capt. John Lewis, a Shawanee, was the center of the Seneca reservation. The Lewistown reservoir is his memorial to-day.

The last war known to Ohio soil, until the Morgan raid, which left no names behind it, was the Ohio and Michigan Boundary War in 1835. It was settled by a decision of Congress in favor of Ohio. Toledo was the center of activities and the victory named the county for Governor Lucas. It is largely due to the oratory of Samuel Vinton, in the House, and Thomas Ewing, in the Senate, that we can have to-day a State D. A. R. Conference in Toledo.

The time limit of this paper has compelled a bare recital of the naming of our early towns while omitting a description of their settlement. The dangers and privations of the pioneers in this State are well known to us, but the horrors are somewhat worn off by time. We have a feeling that if they did not exactly enjoy their hardships, at least they were constituted differently from ourselves. One who was scalped as a child, but lived to marry and settle on our frontier, would naturally be somewhat inured to suffering and immune from nervous prostration. But there were as tender and beautiful women who crossed the river in those early days as among the ones who are enjoying the civilization that their heroism won. They followed their husbands as Rachel followed Jacob—and what brought *them?* Poverty, restlessness, the call of the wild, which at times dim and far off we still can hear, a desire for a democracy purer and stronger than the old colonies could produce brought them here. We do well to honor our forefathers of the Revolution, but Ohio Daughters are twice happy, for it is a mighty poor pioneer that doesn't make a glorious ancestor.

Our knowledge of the French in the Ohio Country is spectacular and evanescent. The associations of the British produce neither admiration for their courage, nor respect for their humanity. But we had a foe, during forty years of the occupation of Ohio, whose savage virtues at times shone brighter than our civilization. It is our boast that every foot of soil was honorably purchased from the Indians; but they sold with the bayonet at their throats, or to get them rum which white men had made a necessity to them. The Shawnee chief's message to Governor Gordon when leaving the Potomac, was: "The Delaware Indians some time ago bid us depart for they was Dry and wanted to drink ye land away, whereupon we told them since some of you are gone to Ohio we will go there also; we hope you will not drink that away, too." Yet afterwards in Ohio the other tribes bitterly blamed the Shawanese, who were as guests in the land, for being the first to sell.   White men easily become savages, but the Indian has not been civilized.   Their tribes have all been honored in our nomenclature; some of the greatest chiefs have not; but there are many, like Tecumseh and Little Turtle, whose valour and high character would ennoble even a ridiculous name.   Their deeds, too, are our heritage.   But for us their tribes will pass away and leave not even the mounds of the earlier races.   Let us hold fast what we have of their memories in this State, and, especially, let us not dissever

"Old places and old names;" but
"Guard the old landmarks truly,
  On the old altars duly
    Keep bright the ancient flames."

SONG WRITERS OF OHIO.

WILL LAMARTINE THOMPSON.

Author of " Gathering Shells from the Seashore."

C. B. GALBREATH.

The world no longer takes things for granted. The days of "original research" are upon us. The strenuous quest for the eternal verities works results at once constructive and iconoclastic. It reveals marvels and dissipates old illusions. The method of the analyst is merciless,— as frigid as justice, as "uncompromising as truth." Woe to the tradition or the ideal that rests on sandy foundation.

Theories of beauty in the abstract are older than the science of ethics. Beauty in the concrete, if it be at all existent, is relative. We are variously impressed as we view the pages of art and nature. The things that to-day satisfy the soul with their sweet harmonies, may pall upon the aesthetic sense to-morrow. Rare indeed are the things attractive to all eyes and in all seasons beautiful.

The sentimental Frenchman, so runs the history or the legend, when his eye beheld the river that forms the southern boundary of our state, called it *La Belle Riviere,*— "The River Beautiful." The hand of man had not marred its banks; industrial civilization had not polluted its waters. It meandered in stately grandeur through the solitude primeval. We are told that the Frenchman was mistaken — that even then it was somber rather than beautiful.

Passing over the varied comments of early explorers and the fervid tributes of some of our later poets, it may be observed that the great English novelist, who first visited America in a somewhat critical mood, found the Ohio "a fine, broad river always, but in some parts much wider than in others; and then there is usually a green island, covered with trees, dividing it

into two streams." In a different strain he describes the shores
on either side:

"The banks are for the most part deep solitudes, overgrown with
trees. * * * For miles, and miles, and miles these solitudes are
unbroken by any sign of human life or trace of human footstep; nor
is anything seen to move about them but the blue jay, whose color is
so bright and yet so delicate, that it looks like a flying flower. At
lengthened intervals a log cabin, with its little space of cleared land
about it, nestles under a rising ground and sends its thread of blue
smoke curling up into the sky. It stands in the corner of the poor field
of wheat, which is full of great unsightly stumps, like earthly butchers'
blocks.. * * * The night is dark, and we proceed within the shadow
of the wooded bank, which makes it darker. After gliding past the
somber maze of boughs for a long time, we come upon an open space
where the tall trees are burning. The shape of every branch and twig
is expressed in a deep red glow and as the light wind stirs and ruffles
it, they seem to vegetate in fire. It is such a sight as we read of in
legends of enchanted forests; saving that it is sad to see these noble
works wasting away so awfully, alone."

Here we have an impression decidedly gloomy, but sixty
years have wrought changes. Whether our river to-day may
justly claim the title that has graced it so long in song and story
will probably remain an open question. After the critics have
had their say, however, there are stretches of the stream and its
shores that will still claim something of the tribute of old.

It is not wholly the partiality of early association that selects
as one of these that portion of the river which emerges from
Pennsylvania and flows a few miles westward to a point where
a semicircular sweep turns it toward the south.

While the waters are usually somewhat turbid, the rugged
banks on either side present a pleasing variety of jutting ledge,
sloping woodland, undulating meadows and confluent streams,
bearing from far-off spring-brooks, through narrow valleys,
their tributes of sparkling water.

Even in mid-winter, when fetters of ice hush ripple and roar,
the eye will fondly linger on the widening expanse and bordering
landscapes, robed in vestments of jeweled white. When day
looks down from a cloudless sky, bright tapers gleam and scin-
tillate among the rime-covered twigs of the leafless trees, and
the dark green spruce wears right royally his ermine of snow.

Underneath the quail comes in quest of food, while from the sheltering boughs the cardinal flits forth in his red glory, and with flaming crest proudly aloft, pours forth into the waste of frost and sunshine the challenge of his valiant melody.

When winter departs and the rain and melting snow pour into the river and its tributaries great volumes of muddy water, the desolate and gloomy scene revealed by day is wondrously transformed under the mellow light of the full moon. How the gilt waves shimmer through the intervening trees! How the silvery streams thread their way through meadow and ravine to join the larger flood, while a constant roar echoes through the chambers of the night like the myriad voices of the far-resounding sea!

When spring, "sweet prophetess of the resurrection," walks the earth, and through the waste reveals her power in the miracle of bud and bloom, this region feels the spell of her presence, for she lingers fondly here. From trailing arbutus to budding rose, there is no break in the procession of flowers. Spring beauty, violet, anemone, trillium, phlox and columbine nod at the edge of the wood, while garden and orchard don their garments of many colors. The deeper pink of the peach yields to a lighter tint, a more ample and pleasing array, for the world holds nothing in its flowery realm more beautiful or delicately fragrant than an apple orchard in full bloom.

Here the gentle breezes of June are redolent with the sweetness of locust groves and clover meadows. Her golden billows roll over fields of ripened grain. Here autumn comes with radiant glories, and orchards bend with fruit, the woodland glows with russet and gold and crimson; there is a rustle among the gray shocks of fodder, and the jolly huskers heap high the golden corn.

These are but a few random glimpses of the year's panorama on the banks of the "river beautiful," in the first stage of its course on the border of our own Ohio. With all seasons there is music from stream and meadow and wood. No marvel here, but much to inspire melody in a soul attuned to its environment.

In the midst of this region, on the north bank of the river, stands the flourishing city of East Liverpool. Rising from the

water's edge up a steep declivity, it commands a picturesque
view of three states. When it was yet a small village it became
the birthplace of a singer whose music has gone to all lands.
Here Will Lamartine Thompson was born November 7, 1847.

"A prophet is not without honor save in his own country,"
so runs the text, frequently verified. Failure to recognize home
talent and achievement is due to indifference rather than to intended slight. Especially is
this true in our own state.
Our pride has made Ohio
birth synonymous with greatness. The local orator never
tires of pointing to the "long
line" of "illustrious." This
pardonable bias in favor of
what is distinctively our own
makes it somewhat difficult to
observe conventional limits in
speaking of the work and
worth of one with whom we
claim neighborhood nativity,
— a friend who is among the
living, who has achieved
marked success and who is
still at the flood-tide of his
career.

WILL LAMARTINE THOMPSON.

Will Thompson, as he is
known among his acquaintances, was the youngest son of a family
of seven children. His father, Josiah Thompson, was a successful merchant, manufacturer and banker, and for two terms a
member of the state legislature. His mother, Sarah Jackman
Thompson, was devoted to social and charitable work. All the
family were lovers of music, but the youngest son alone made
it a serious study. As far back as he can remember he was
humming tunes. He readily learned to play on instruments and
even while a boy was in demand as pianist for local concerts.

When he was only sixteen years old he composed *Darling Minnie Gray** and *Liverpool Schottische,* both of which were published.

He was educated in the public schools of the village. Later he attended Union College, then as now the Mecca for worthy young men and women in eastern Ohio who aspire to a liberal education. In the years 1870-3, he attended the Boston Music School, where he took a course in piano, organ and harmony. Near the close of his work here he wrote a song which, when published, almost immediately attained great popularity.

GATHERING SHELLS FROM THE SEASHORE.

The circumstances under which this was written are related by the author substantially as follows:

"I was attending the Boston Peace Jubilee Musical Festival. It was gotten up by Gilmore in 1873 and was a wonderful affair. After it was over I, with a friend, went to Nahant Beach to spend a day, and while there I sat down on the shore and wrote the song."

The words are as follows:

> I wandered to-day on the seashore,
>   The wind and the waves they were low,
> And I thought of the days that are gone, Maud,
>   Many long years ago:
> Ah! those were the happiest days of all, Maud,
>   Not a care nor a sorrow did we know,
> As we played on the white pebbled sand, Maud,
>   Gathering up shells from the shore.

---

* The title of the former indicates a possible partiality of the youthful author for the famous song written by Hanby some years earlier, but the measure is different. Here is the first stanza:

> In a pretty little cottage by the seashore,
>   Where the ivy and the honeysuckle climb,
> Lives the sweetest, the dearest little darling
>   That ever deigned to charm this heart of mine.
> She's as fair and as pure as the lily
>   And as charming as the beauteous flowers of May.
> Oh, I never shall forget my darling Minnie,
>   I shall never cease to love sweet Minnie Gray.

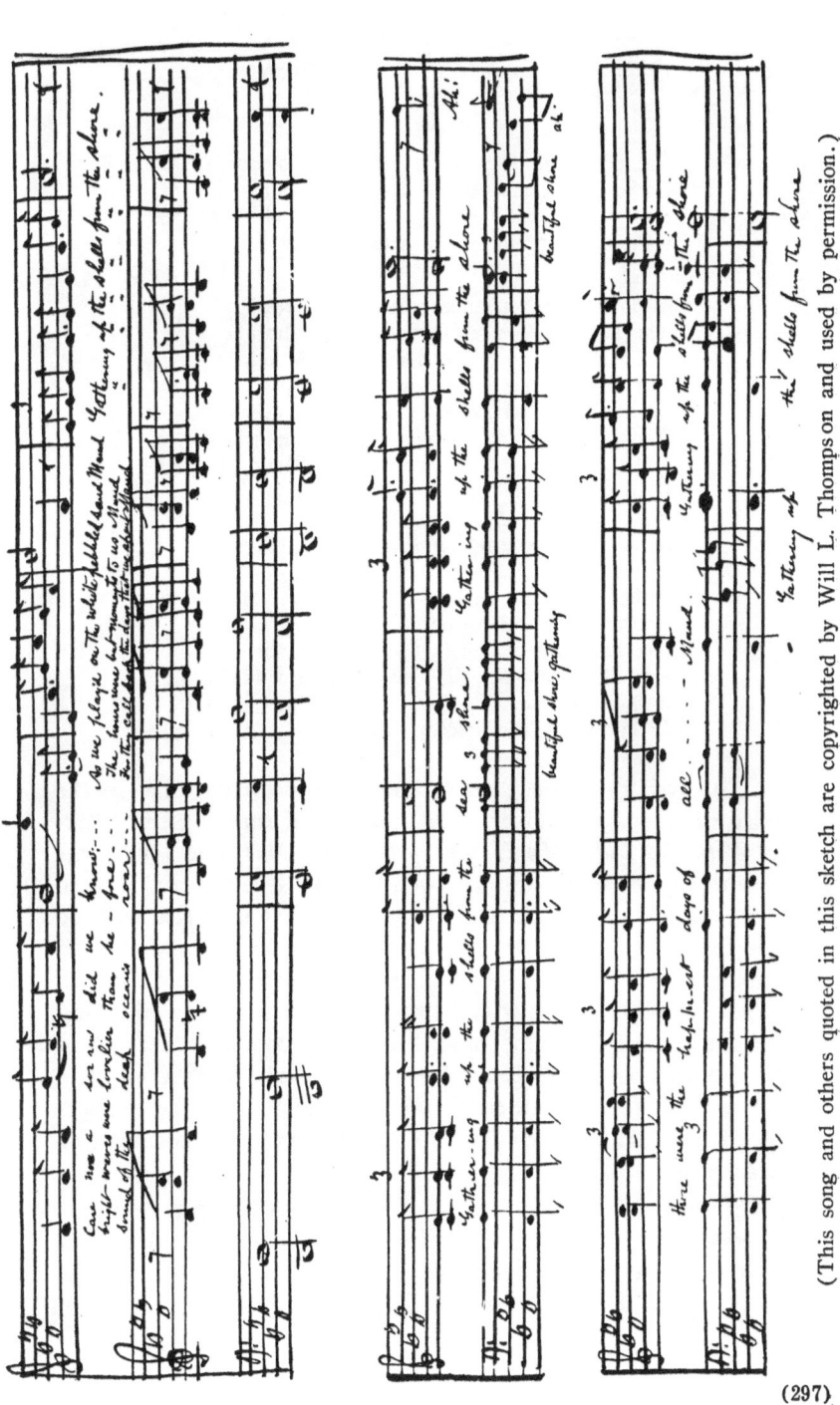

(297)

CHORUS:

Gathering up the shells from the seashore,
Gathering up the shells from the shore;
Ah! those were the happiest days of all, Maud,
Gathering up the shells from the shore.

Oh, don't you remember the day, Maud?
    The last time we wandered by the shore?
Our hearts were so joyous and gay, Maud,
    For you promised to be mine evermore:
Then the shells they were whiter than ever,
    And the bright waves were lovelier than before,
The hours were but moments to us, Maud,
    Gathering up shells from the shore.

But now we are growing up in years, Maud,
    Our locks are all silvered and gray,
Yet the vows that we made on the shore, Maud,
    Are fresh in our memories to-day:
There still is a charm in those bright shells,
    And the sound of the deep ocean's roar,
For they call back the days that we spent, Maud,
    Gathering up shells from the shore.

The writer of this composition was fortunate alike in the choice of words and music. He took it and three others, *Drifting With the Tide, My Home on the Old Ohio,* and *Under the Moonlit Sky,* to a well-known publisher in Cleveland and offered all for one hundred dollars. He was told that the price was too high for an unknown author; that such material could be had in abundance free of charge; that the four pieces were not worth at the outside more than twenty-five dollars. After thinking over the matter for some time, the young composer decided to hold his manuscripts. Later he went to New York City on a business trip for his father. Here he arranged for the publication of his songs, determining to undertake the management of sales himself.

His natural business tact was no small factor in the success scored by his earliest publications. Rightly concluding that *Gathering Shells From the Seashore* had distinctive merit, he sent copies of it to various minstrel organizations. From one of the best known in the country he received a large order.[1] He then sent copies to musical periodicals and newspapers. To each he attached a printed slip containing a brief notice of the song and the statement that it was used by the Crancross and Dixie Minstrels. This was so carefully and concisely worded, that it was usually reproduced in full. Soon orders began to come in from many sources. The presses were put in motion and for months they were kept running night and day to meet the demand. In less than a year the Cleveland publisher and dealer who had refused to pay one hundred dollars for the manuscripts had turned over to the author in profits more than a thousand dollars. *Gathering Shells From the Seashore* was sung almost everywhere. From this initial venture his financial returns were most gratifying.

DRIFTING WITH THE TIDE.

Another of his early songs was quite successful and still retains much of its former favor. The reader will readily recognize the words of *Drifting With the Tide*:

> We are floating on the ocean,
> Drifting, drifting with the tide;
> Far from home and far from kindred,
> O'er the boundless sea we ride.
> Giant waves, like wondrous mountains,
> Rise and fall with solemn sound;
> On we glide through foaming fountains
> On we're drifting, ocean-bound.

> CHORUS:

> We are floating on the ocean,
> Drifting, drifting with the tide;
> We are drifting on the ocean,
> Floating away, away.

> We are floating on the ocean,
> Drifting, drifting with the tide;
> Not a ray of cheering sunlight,
> Not a friendly hand to guide.

---

[1] John L. Crancross, of The Crancross and Dixie Minstrel Company, of Philadelphia, first introduced the song on the stage. Many other companies soon began to sing it.

Driving winds, with note of terror,
   Sweep across the maddened wave;
Soon we'll sink with plunge and quiver,
   For no earthly hand can save.

We are floating on the ocean,
   Drifting, drifting with the tide;
But a loving hand above us,
   Deigns our floating bark to guide.
Waves of trouble rise before us,
   But our boat goes safely o'er;
Trusting in our worthy Captain,
   Soon we'll reach the other shore.

MY HOME ON THE OLD OHIO.

Although not written while he was abroad, this lay reveals a dominant sentiment of the composer. Under all skies he has been a loyal Ohioan. In simple, unadorned measure he sings *My Home on the Old Ohio*:

Far away on the banks of the old Ohio,
   Down where the silver maples grow,
Where the river runs deep in the broad, green valley,
   Oh, there's where I lived, long ago.
Ah, well I remember the old cottage home,
   By the side of the long, grassy lane;
How oft I have wished for the moment to come,
   When I'll stand in my old home again.

CHORUS:

   Then carry me back to the old Ohio,
   Back to my own cottage home
   On the banks of the river,
   'Neath the green, weeping willow
   Let me linger, and nevermore roam.

Oh, 'twas there in the fields and broad, verdant meadows,
   I wandered with playmates that I loved;
'Mid the perfumes of flowers and sweet fragrant blossoms,
   Where the birds sing so sweetly, we roved;
But long, long ago all my playmates were gone,
   One by one 'neath the flowers they have lain;
On the banks of the river, 'neath the green, weeping willow
   I shall ne'er see their dear forms again.

Many long years have passed since I stood by the river,
  And said "Goodbye, my happy home;"
Oh, 'twas sad, sad to part with the scenes I loved dearly,
  And start o'er the cold world to roam;
Take me back, take me back to the dear old farm,
  Where the fields teem with ripe, golden grain;
For my heart is still longing for my home by the river,
  Take me back, and I'll ne'er roam again.

THE OLD TRAMP.

Who that lived through them does not recall the troublous times of 1876-7, when business was at a stand-still, the presidency in the air, the railroad men on a strike and thousands of the unemployed on the tramp. And who does not remember the song — on the lips alike of sturdy workman and street urchin — celebrating the sadly picturesque character to be met on almost every public highway? We were not a little surprised in looking over a collection of sheet music to find that this old favorite was written by our own Thompson. Here it is:

I'm only a poor old wanderer,
  I've no place to call my home;
No one to pity me, no one to cheer me,
  As friendless and sadly I roam.

CHORUS:

Only a poor old wanderer,
  I've no place to call my home;
No one to pity me, no one to cheer me,
  As friendless and sadly I roam.

I tramp, tramp along though I'm weary,
  No rest through the long, long day;
Through the rain and the snow, I must tramp to and fro,
  For I've no place in shelter to stay.

How I wish for a place by the fireside,
  For the night is so dark, cold and damp;
Vacant places I see, but there's no room for me,
  For I'm only a poor old tramp.

Long ago I was peaceful and happy,
  With dear, loving friends ever near;
But now they are gone, and I'm left all alone,
  With no one my pathway to cheer.

IN LIGHTER VEIN.

While our bard seldom essays the humorous, he has given us enough to show that he can be simply and exquisitely pleasant, if he so desires. One of the following selections will be remembered by many in connection with first efforts at the piano. The other, though not so widely known, will not, on that account be less heartily appreciated.

MY FIRST MUSIC LESSON.

My Ma she took it in her head that I should learn to play
On the organ and piano in the most newfangled way;
So to the teacher we did go, with lesson book in hand,
Determined I should music know, its mysteries understand.

CHORUS:

This exercise I then went through,
As all beginners have to do,
I sang so high that my voice broke down,
And I drove the neighbors out of town.

My teacher showed me A and B, and F sharp, G and D;
Said I, "Dear teacher, is that all? Don't we play on X and Z?"
He showed me clefs, and staffs and bars, I thought 'twould next be rails,
And the little things he called the notes, were like drum-sticks with tails.

I warbled high; said he, "You're sharp, just come a little down;"
My Ma chimed in and said, "You're right, she's the sharpest girl in town."
"Now, teacher, what's this little scroll?" "Why that, my dear's a rest."
I jumped up from my music stool (*Spoken*) and I've been *resting* ever
   since.

MY SWEETHEART AND I WENT FISHING.

My sweetheart and I went fishing,
   In the merry month of May;
Along the brook with bait and hook,
   We wound our happy way,
Till by and by we spied a place
   O'erhung with verdant boughs,
'Twas just the place for catching fish
   And making loving vows.

Then we caught the little fishes,
And we whispered loving wishes,
Along the brook, with bait and hook,
In the merry month of May.
Ah, happy the moments, all the livelong day,
Fishing with my sweetheart, in the month of May.

Said I, "Little sweetheart, listen,
　While I tell my happy wish!
I'd give my earthly riches all,
　If I could be a fish.
I'd turn aside from every bait,
　Until I came to thine;
Oh what a pleasure to be caught
　By sweetheart's hook and line."

The fish we caught that May-day,
　We shall ever dearly prize;
But sweetheart caught the largest one,
　In fact, 'twas just my size;
And now I am the happiest fish,
　That ever took the bait;
And sweetheart dear is ever near,
　My happy. loving mate.

PATRIOTIC SONGS.

Patriotism and politics often have little in common, but in Ohio they seem to flourish in close proximity. Even the most radical Democrat will forgive Thompson for writing a *Protective Tariff March* when it is remembered that he is a son of the city of East Liverpool, far-famed for Republican majorities and the manufacture of pottery. He will be forgiven freely when it is understood that personally he takes little interest in politics and that he has written songs that breathe the broader and deeper sentiment of patriotism. The second of those here given is one of his latest productions, having been published in 1904:

GOD SAVE OUR UNION.

God save our Union,
　May it ever stand;
　Watch o'er our happy land,

Through day and night,
Be thou our guiding star;
Protect us with Thy power,
Shield us, for Thine we are,
Oh, guide us aright.

God save our Union,
May truth and right prevail;
Tyrants and despots fail,
Bind treason's hand.
Father, we look to Thee,
Keep us forever free,
Our preservation be,
O God, bless our land.

God save our Union,
Prosper our glorious land;
One firm, united band,
Happy and free.
Angel of holy peace,
May wars and tumults cease,
Friendship and love increase,
Throughout land and sea.

SHOULDER TO SHOULDER.

Soldier, to arms, hear the country's call,
There's war in the air, we must fight or fall!
The trumpet is sounding, the battle is near,
But our gallant army has nothing to fear.

CHORUS:

Shoulder to shoulder, together, boys,
Musket to musket, with cheer and noise;
To arms! to arms! prepare for the war!
The call of the bugle comes from afar.

Good-bye, my sweetheart, good-bye, home,
Your soldier is off, he must march and roam;
We love you our darlings, more than you know,
But, when there is war, to the front we must go.

We fight not for empire, we fight not for fame,
We fight for our homes and our country's name;
Columbia, Columbia, the land of the free,
Our homes and our dear ones, we battle for thee.

The sun never shone on a land more free,
, This God given country's for you and me;
Beloved by our fathers, beloved by us all,
The soldier is honored who honors thy call.

OTHER SECULAR SONGS.

From a long list of secular songs of almost equal merit, the following have been selected:

THE MIDNIGHT FIRE ALARM.

'Tis midnight, and the sleeper
  Lies dreaming, free from care;
But anon his dreams are broken,
  By sounds on the midnight air,
Strange sounds like a hissing serpent,
  Or the roar of a mighty stream;
Then the fire alarm is sounded,
  And the sleeper awakes from his dream.

CHORUS:

Hark! Hark! do you hear those mournful cries?
See! see! yonder light across the skies!
Now the fire bells are ringing,
Now the loud alarm is sounding,
See, the lightning flames are flashing,
Sound the midnight fire alarm.

The fireman, quick to action,
  Like magic springs to his place,
The engines rush by madly
  Like dragons of fire at race, —
The sound of the wheels on the pavement,
  The noise of the swelling crowd,
The shouts of men at duty,
  And the ringing of bells long and loud.

The glaring flames grow hotter,
  And wave their wings on high;
The flying sparks grow brighter,
  And paint the midnight sky.
This demon of fierce destruction
  Knows naught but a tyrant's harm;
, Oh God, protect and save us
  From the midnight fire alarm.

UNDER THE MOONLIT SKY.

Under the fair moonlight,
When the bright stars are shining,
Wandering where the shadows gather,
Happy you and I.
Long, long ago in youth, Maud,
Happiest hours of life, Maud,
Under the moonlit sky.

CHORUS:

Oh, gently the moonbeams fall,
  Softly the night winds sigh,
Bright, happy hours of love and joy,
  Under the moonlit sky.

Under the quiet moon, Maud,
'Twas such a glorious evening,
When I spoke of love so tender,
Love for only thee.
Brighter the moonbeams fell, Maud,
Brighter the stars did sparkle,
Brighter my heart's high hopes,
Brighter my life to me.

Under the same old moon, Maud,
Under the same bright light,
Years roll on and still we wander,
Happy you and I.
Though we are old and gray, Maud,
Though we've not long to stay, Maud,
Still we'll be young and gay,
Under the moonlit sky.

I AM KING O'ER THE LAND AND THE SEA.

I am king o'er the land and the sea,
  My power reaches out o'er the realm;
The good ship of state never fears for her fate,
  When my hand rests secure at the helm.
My subjects are slaves to my own gracious will,
  I am king of the bond, and the free
Come and go at my call, for I'm ruler of all,
  Hail the king o'er the land and the sea.

I am king o'er the land and the sea,
  My power there is none to withstand.
I have only to speak or to sign a decree
  And my will is the law of the land;
I have treasures at hand and I've gold to command,
  What more could my heart wish to be;
My banner's unfurled, and I'm known o'er the world,
  As the monarch o'er land and o'er sea.

One is tempted to quote further. The words, of course, without the music, convey a very inadequate impression of the song. Especially is this true of the well-known *"Come Where the Lilies Bloom,* with its numerous and beautiful refrains. " I wrote it," says the author, "as I sat in my little boat one afternoon at Chautauqua Lake while my companion rowed through the lily beds. The surroundings generally suggest my themes." The Denman-Thompson Quartette in the "Old Homestead" sang this song for more than five hundred consecutive nights in New York City.

SACRED SONGS.

The list of sacred songs is a long one and includes several that have enjoyed more than national popularity. The first of the two here selected, *Softly and Tenderly Jesus is Calling* has gone to almost every land and has found expression in every language in which Christian music is sung. It has been published in the Hawaiian tongue and has enjoyed the favor of those sturdy latter-day Puritans — the Boers of South Africa.

SOFTLY AND TENDERLY JESUS IS CALLING.

Softly and tenderly Jesus is calling,
  Calling for you and for me.
See, on the portals He's waiting and watching.
  Watching for you and for me.

CHORUS:

Come home, come home,
Ye who are weary, come home;
Earnestly, tenderly, Jesus is calling,
Calling, O sinner, come home!

Why should we tarry when Jesus is pleading,
  Pleading for you and for me?
Why should we linger and heed not his mercies,
  Mercies for you and for me?

Time is now fleeting, the moments are passing,
  Passing from you and from me;
Shadows are gathering, death warnings coming,
  Coming for you and for me.

O for the wonderful love He has promised,
  Promised for you and for me,
Tho' we have sinned, He has mercy and pardon,
  Pardon for you and for me.

THE HARVEST TIME IS PASSING BY.

The fading flowers and autumn leaves,
  With all their wondrous beauty,
They tell us life is passing by,
  This life so full of duty.
Each falling leaflet tells us plain,
  As on life's road we're wending,
The harvest time is passing by,
  The summer days are ending.

O traveler through this busy world,
  One moment stop and ponder,
Was thy great mission here below
  For naught but gain and squander?
See how the wasted moments fly!
  Not one returns for mending;
The harvest time is passing by,
  The summer days are ending.

The days and months and years gone by,
  Should be to us a warning,
To point our faces toward the sky,
  Before the Judgment morning.
Then nerve the arm for glorious work,
  The grain is ripe and bending;
The harvest time is passing by,
  The summer days are ending.

Then turn to good the fleeting hours,
  Each duty now attending,
The harvest time is passing by,
  The summer days are ending.

HIS WORK.

Something remains to be said in regard to Thompson's aims and methods. He began with songs for the many. After completing his studies abroad, he wrote a few instrumental pieces of the "classic" order. "But," he says, "as I had already been before the public as a writer of popular songs, my business instincts told me I had better stick to writing music for the masses. Since then my aim has been to write good, elevating music, with words and melodies pure and clean, but not so difficult as to be beyond the ability of the masses." Here we have his purpose set forth very clearly.

His method he explains in his usual modest and direct way. "How do you go about writing a song?" asked a friend.

Opening a folio of manuscripts he replied:

"You see here perhaps fifty or more manuscripts in various degrees of completion. Most of them are unfinished, and some merely contain the idea or theme. Others, you see, are almost ready for publication. I carry with me always a pocket memorandum, and no matter where I am, at home or hotel, at the store or in the cars, if an idea or theme comes to me that I deem worthy of a song, I jot it down in verse, and as I do so the music simply comes to me naturally, so I write words and music enough to call back the whole theme again any time I open it. In this way I never lose it."

"But how do you get the music in your mind without going to the instrument?"

"That is hard to explain to any but a musician. The music comes to my mind the same as any other thought. As I write the words of a song, a fitting melody is already in my mind, and as I jot down the notes of the music I know just how it will sound. I write the different parts of the harmony and the whole piece is rehearsed in mind; I hear the blending of the different voices and know just how each part will sound in its harmonic relations to the other parts. Of course, to do this intelligently, one must have a knowledge of the science of harmony, as there are rules governing the harmonic relations of sounds just as arbitrary as the rules of mathematics."

About one year ago the writer met Thompson at his place of business in East Liverpool. The conversation drifted to his work. When told of a proposed sketch of his life he said:

"Certainly, I have no objection if you think the matter of sufficient importance to print. I shall be pleased to answer any questions, but I would prefer not to write anything in the nature of a personal sketch. I frequently get requests to do that, and while it would probably be all right to comply, I have an aversion to autobiography."

"Are you at present composing?" he was asked.

"Recently I have not done much. Perhaps I have been living a little too leisurely. I ought to be making use of my time, however. This thought has led me to take up the pen again."

Here he opened a table drawer, took out a few sheets of manuscript and said:,

"I am writing a military song, *Shoulder to Shoulder.*"

He read one of the stanzas and hummed a few bars of the music.

"I think, perhaps, it has some merit," said he, "but you cannot always tell. A little thing sometimes makes a song or spoils it."

BUSINESS CAREER.

This song writer, it is a pleasure to record, has made a goodly fortune from his work. Blest with rare business judgment, he has made every one of his compositions pay. Some, of course, have been much more profitable than others, but in the aggregate the returns have been large.

"Yes," he admitted, "the music trade papers sometimes speak of me as the 'millionaire song writer,' which, of course, is overdoing it," he added with a smile.

Inquiries directed to those whose judgment ought to be good, however, led to the conclusion that our friend in this, as in some other matters, was over modest. At all events, his work has brought him a fortune of which any composer or literary man might well be proud. It is doubtful if there is living in this country to-day a writer whose compositions have had so wide a sale. In addition to scores of songs published separately, he has issued in book form "Thompson's Class and Concert," "Thompson's Popular Anthems," and "The New Century Hymnal." Each of these has passed through a number of editions.

His music store at East Liverpool has little to distinguish it from like establishments in other cities. The volume of business is large, however. Thompson himself exercises general supervision only. The details are left to subordinates.

About fourteen years ago he married Miss Elizabeth Johnson, of Wellsville, O. He spends his time very pleasantly, migrating like the birds of passage, with the change of seasons.

RESIDENCE OF WILL LAMARTINE THOMPSON, EAST LIVERPOOL, OHIO.

The winters are passed in Savannah, Ga., where he enjoys the society of congenial spirits who have come to know and appreciate his pleasing and substantial qualities. Through the summer and early autumn months he resides in his native county. His country home near East Liverpool is a model of comfort and convenience. He frequently goes to the city and mingles freely with the people who are very generally acquainted with him, but who do not appreciate the fact that he is the author of many of the most popular songs of America.

He is an active worker in the church. His faith is broad and tolerant. He stands for temperance, order and all that constitutes good citizenship. Politics has no attractions for him, and he has never been a place seeker. He now fills most acceptably the only office that he ever held. He is president of the Board of Trustees of the local Carnegie Library.

Through the summer he visits the library frequently and delights to browse among the shelves and note the progress of the work. He is interested especially in the wide circulation of books and draws the attention of the visitor to the fact that they go to almost every family of the city.

And an interesting city this is, by the way. Here are the largest potteries in the United States. By water and rail finely decorated wares are shipped to all parts of the Union. The huge kilns, as they send their great columns of smoke into the clear sky, present an imposing scene. From shady lawns at places of vantage on the hill may be viewed an irregular array of roofs, with church spires proportionately numerous; busy streets, branching in many directions; the glittering river bordered on one side by rails over which the "iron horses" glide at frequent intervals, and crossed by a bridge that communicates with the beautiful farm lands beyond. Around is the music of industry, the rattle of machinery, the roar of transmuting fires, the shriek of factory whistles, a hoarse voice from the steamboat below, echoing among the hills. The local minstrel began by writing *Liverpool Schottische*. Will he not add to his rich repertoire a song that shall fittingly celebrate his native city?

TARHE, THE WYANDOT CHIEF,

AND THE HARRISON-TARHE PEACE CONFERENCE.

DR. CHAS. E. SLOCUM, DEFIANCE.

It is the desire of this writing to add somewhat to the mention of Tarhe, the Wyandot Aborigine[1] Chief, and to the mention of the character of the Aborigines, that appeared in the last number of the QUARTERLY, although this addition shows their character different from that there mentioned.

Tarhe grew to adult life in very troublous times. He was reared to savagery, and to inebriety, like all Aborigine youths of his range and time — first, in addition to the habits of his people, under the tutorship of the French against the British and later under the yet more savage policy of the British against the Americans. If he was born in the year 1742 (there is always doubt connected with alleged parentage and date of birth of the children of earlier Aborigines) he was eighteen years of age when Sandusky, Detroit, Fort Miami (at the head of the Maumee River) and all of this western country were surrendered by the French to the British; and he was thirty-three years old when Lieutenant Governor Hamilton began to send war-parties of savages from Detroit, with British outfittings and leaders, through Ohio, Pennsylvania and Kentucky, against American settlers. We may rightfully presume, therefore, that it was during these many savage raids, which continued throughout the Revolutionary War, that Tarhe, liberally supplied by the British and under their direction, demonstrated to the British and to his savage followers the worthiness of his claim to their chieftaincy. His tribe continued marauding excursions as allies of the British, with but little intermission after the close of the Revolutionary War, until General Wayne's crushing defeat of them at Fallen Timber.

---

[1] The writer desires to discourage the parrot-like use of the misnomer 'Indian' to designate an American Aborigine.

The Wyandots were a warring tribe — an offshoot from the Iroquois of the East — and consequently were quarrelsome, and brave in battle. But they, in common with all other Aborigines, were quick to desert their allies when the tide of battle turned against them. General Wayne took advantage of this phase of the character of the tribes and, after his signal success at Fallen Timber, he diplomatically drew them all to the most important treaty at Greenville in 1795. To his prestige as conqueror was added his very important overbidding of the British in supplies, and the discoursing of his agents on the growing power of the United States.

For several years after Wayne's treaty at Greenville the Aborigines were satisfied with the American annuities according to the terms of that treaty, and with their unrestricted hunting grounds. During this time we catch glimpses of Tarhe's ignoble character, including his inebriety and his disposition to make Americans his slaves. The Society of Friends had, from their first coming to America in 1656, taken great interest in the civilization of the Aborigines and had done much for them with this end in view. The Baltimore Yearly Meeting of Friends in 1795 appointed a large committee to consider the condition and needs of the western Aborigines; and the influence of this committee was felt at the first treaty at Greenville where General Wayne, who was reared a neighbor to the Friends, took occasion to commend their good offices to the Aborigines. The Wyandots, always ready like other tribes to enter upon anything that promised an increase of their supplies, sent a "speech with a large belt and ten strings of white wampum" to the Friends' Yearly Meeting at Baltimore the latter part of the year 1798, inviting them to visit the chiefs at Upper Sandusky. To this invitation were appended, by the white man who did the writing, the name of the chiefs Tarhe (Crane), Skah-on-wot (Adam Brown), and Mai-i-rai (Walk-on-the-Water). Seven Friends started westward on horseback May 7, 1799, to accept this invitation. After suffering many hardships in their tortuous way through the forest, through the mud and through flooded streams, they arrived at Upper Sandusky the third day of June to be witnesses of shocking scenes of drunkenness among the Aborigines, and to be subjected to many indignities by them. From his intoxicated condition Tarhe was unable to meet the Friends until late the next day; and then, with three other chiefs, the meeting was brief and unsatisfactory. The Friends with difficulty understood that the council would not meet until the middle of the month when Tarhe would present to those assembled the subject of the Friends' desire to instruct the people generally in religion, agriculture, mechanical arts, domestic economy, etc., and as soon as a decision was obtained they would send a 'speech' to Baltimore announcing it. The presents then given by the Friends and the efforts they offered, were not of the character to appeal to the dissolute inclination of the Aborigines; and request for the return of the Friends was not made. Being unable to obtain food for themselves and their horses, the Friends were obliged to immediately start homeward.

In the winter of 1803-04 Tarhe, and near one hundred other Aborigines mostly Wyandots, went to the upper waters of the Mahoning River to hunt bears. Snow fell to the depth of about three feet which, with their previous improvident use of their United States Annuity receipts and their established habit of beggary, quite incapacitated them in their opinion for any action but appeals for help to some families of Friends who lived about twenty miles distant. The first appeal, written by a lounging white man in their camp, reads in part as follows after being straightened out: . . . Brothers, will you please help me to fill my kettles and my horses' troughs, for I am afraid my horses will not be able to carry me home again. Neighbors, will you please to give if it is but a handful apiece, and fetch it out to us for my horses are not able to come after it. [Signed] Tarhie. Their needs were supplied by the nearest Friends, and then came another writing, viz.: . . . Brothers, I want you to know I have got help from some of my near neighbors. Brothers, I would be glad to know what you will do for me, if it is but little. Brothers, if you cannot come soon, it will do bye and bye, for my belly is now full. . . My Brothers, Quakers, I hope our friendship will last as long as the world stands. All I have to say to you now is, that I shall stay here until two moons are gone. Tarhie. More food was taken to them by these

Friends and members of the Redstone, Pennsylvania, Quarterly Meeting.

The United States Annuity gifts to these shiftless people, large as they were relatively, were overbid by the British during their collusion with Tecumseh and the 'Prophet' previous to the declaration of War of 1812, and then, as has even been the case with these wretched people, the side that bid the highest in sensual indulgences, including savagery, obtained their aid for savage work. The exceedingly lavish gifts of guns, ammunition, intoxicating liquors, food and gaudy raiment, at Malden (Amherstburg, Canada) to the Wyandots and other tribes of this western country by the British long before war was declared, attracted and allied to the British support during the War of 1812 practically all of the active warrior Aborigines. The old and decrepit like Tarhe, and many women and children, were left behind — and the United States continued to feed and clothe these non-combatant remnants, and to treat with them, in the hope thereby to win back to neutrality the warriors from the British ranks. To hasten this result General Harrison sent some old Wyandots to the hostile camp at Brownstown, Michigan, soon after the British withdrew from the first Siege of Fort Meigs, but the savage cannibals were yet cloyed with the flesh and booty obtained at the Dudley Massacre — and the ever alert British agents were at hand to neutralize the first appearance of dissatisfaction in the savage camp.

The British were somewhat less successful in allying the Shawnees and Delawares to their army for the War of 1812 than with other tribes. This was due in part to the influence for peace exerted on them by the Society of Friends, but principally to the chastisements given these tribes by United States soldiers and the liberal increase to them of the United States Annuity. The following table of United States Annuity gifts shows in its blanks which tribes went fully to the British (including Tarhe's own tribe), but it cannot show the number of warriors which deserted the Americans from other tribes on account of the relative increase of annuity to the remnants of tribes left behind in Ohio, Indiana and Illinois — and on this account the Senecas of the Sandusky River cannot be included in this table, viz.:

ANNUITIES DUE, PAID AND DELIVERED TO THE DIFFERENT ABORIG-
INE TRIBES FROM MARCH 3, 1811, TO MARCH 3, 1815.

Tribe.	Annual Amount Appropriations by Different Acts of Congress.	Amount Paid, 1811.	Amount Paid, 1812.	Amount Paid, 1813.	Amount Pair, 1814.
Miami	$2,300 00	$2,948 89	....	....	....
Eel River	1,100 00	1,100 10	....	....	....
Shawnee	1,000 00	1,000 75	$1,500 00	$1,500 82	$1,500 00
Pottawotami	2,400 00	1,000 54	400 00	....	....
Delaware	1,800 00	1,799 24	1,800 00	1,393 04	1,300 00
Wea	1,150 00	750 00	....	....	....
Kickapoo	1,000 00	500 00	....	....	....
Piankeshaw	1,000 00	1,000 00	....	....	....
Kaskaskia	1,000 00	900 00	1,000 00	400 00	1,000 00
Wyandot	1,400 00	1,400 00	1,010 28	....	....
Ottawa	1,800 00	1,800 00	1,800 00	....	....
Chippewa	1,800 00	1,800 00	1,800 00	....	....
Six Nations	4,500 00	4,500 00	4,410 00	4,500 00	2,300 00
To more distant Tribes		28,239 45	21,033 83	19,631 88	20,451 00

In addition to these amounts $496,647.14 was expended by
the United States at Sandusky, Fort Wayne, Detroit, Mackinaw,
Vincennes, Kaskaskia, Chicago, at the seat of government, and
other points in effort to keep these wretched people neutral during the war; but the British appealed to and gave free rein to
their savagery and thereby readily won their alliance.

The "Harrison-Tarhe Peace Conference" at Franklinton
(Columbus) could not keep the Wyandot warriors from the
British. It only resulted in adding a few worse than useless old
men to the Northwestern army at its advance into Canada. This
action, however, was insignificant for good; as they had no part,
even in remote influence, in turning the tide in favor of the
American arms. The repulses of the British and their savage
allies at Fort Meigs, at Fort Stephenson, and on Lake Erie, were

more than enough to dishearten all the hostile Aborigines and to turn many of them from the British before and during their flight from Amherstburg. They at once sought favor with the victors, and fully attended the numerous magnanimous treaties to which the United States invited them.[2]

---

[2] See *History of the Maumee River Basin* by Charles E. Slocum, pages 309, 312, 365, 385, 442 passim, for reference to authorities and evidence against other misconceptions.

COLONEL JOHN O'BANNON.

NELSON W. EVANS.

It is and has been utterly impossible to fix, with absolute certainty the date, or place of the birth of Colonel John O'Bannon. It was not later than the year 1756, and may have been several years previous. The place, as near as can be determined, was called Neville, Virginia. John Presley and Morgan Neville, prominent officers in the Revolutionary War, were her kinsmen, and likely brothers. We are not certain as to her father's name. From the best information obtainable, we are led to the conclusion that the O'Bannon family was of prominence in Virginia, and that John O'Bannon had a fair education. Among his other acquirements, he learned the art of surveying. We find that on April 14th, 1784, Thomas Jefferson wrote him

JOHN O'BANNON.

a letter on the subject of a military commission as Major. It was addressed to Captain John O'Bannon. It speaks of his men being in the field and of the expected resignation of Major Buckner. From the fact that Captain John O'Bannon is not found in Heitman's Register, we infer that his service must have been in the state line. Mr. J. H. O'Bannon, public printer at Richmond, Va., is sure that the Captain addressed by Thomas Jefferson, April 14, 1781, is the same one we describe. We are unable to account for John O'Bannon between April 14, 1781, and April 1786. In that

(319)

period he probably married. His wife was a daughter of Minor Wynne, of Loudon County, Virginia. In April, 1786, he was in Kentucky, and in an expedition against Indians, composed of ten persons. His party overtook the Indians and fired upon them. The Indians returned the fire and wounded Col. W. Christain. Alex. Scott Bullitt and John O'Bannon fired on the Indians, and two of them fell. One Kelley, a member of the party, approached one of the fallen Indians, believing him to be dead. The Indian raised on his knees, fired on Kelley and killed him. The Indian then fell back and expired. Some time in the summer of 1787, John O'Bannon was appointed a Deputy Surveyor of the Virginia Military District of Ohio, by Col. Richard C. Anderson, then at Louisville, Kentucky. The Virginia Military District of Ohio, had been ceded by Virginia to the United States, March 1, 1784, but Congress did not open the District to location until August 10, 1790. Notwithstanding this fact, John O'Bannon began making surveys in the District. The first he made, or rather which the record shows that he made was No. 386, for Mace Clements, which lies just east of Ripley, on the Ohio River, and was for 1,000 acres out of a 7,000 acre warrant. The record shows that on the same day he made a survey for his relative, John Neville, in Washington Township, Clermont County, Ohio, for 1,400 acres on Warrant 937 for 7,777⅔ acres. The record shows that one John Williams was a chain carrier on both surveys, and that he chained around 2,400 acres in one day, and that James Blair was a marker on both surveys. When we reflect that the locations were an absolute wilderness at that time, and that the parties might expect the crack of an Indian rifle at any moment, we see the absolute impossibility of these two surveys having been made in one day. The records show that John O'Bannon, Deputy Surveyor, continued to make these surveys right along until May 29, 1788, when he stopped work.

In that time he had surveyed along the Ohio River, between the mouth of the Scioto and Little Miami Rivers, 163,548 acres, and that it was distributed among the counties afterward formed, as follows :

The Surveys from 1 to 386 had been made in Indiana, opposite Louisville, Kentucky, and near that vicinity. The record shows that on November 17, 1787, John O'Bannon surveyed 5,000 acres of land; Survey 459, at the mouth of Ohio Brush Creek, on the right bank, for 1,000 acres; Survey 436 for 1,000 acres just above Vanceburg, Kentucky; Survey 496 for 1,000 acres for Byrd Hendricks in Sprigg Township, Adams County, Ohio, and 1,000 acres for John McDowell, in Liberty Township, Adams County, Ohio; Survey 418 for 1,000 acres on Warrant 386, for James Page, embraces the site of Ripley, Ohio.

Here were 5,000 acres purporting to be surveyed in one day and Sylvester Moroney was certified as a chain carrier on four of these surveys. When it is stated the Survey 496 is just above Maysville, Ky., and 386 opposite Vanceburg, Ky., and Survey 418 is at Ripley, Ohio, and when we reflect that the entire country north of the Ohio River was then an unbroken wilderness, without a single settlement of white men, we realize the utter impracticability of 5,000 acres of land between Vanceburg, Kentucky, and Ripley, Ohio, being surveyed in one day. 640 acres of land in one section is only one mile square, but 1,000 acres on a warrant was a favorite number to be entered by O'Bannon in the warrants he held. On November 19, 1787, he certifies to have surveyed 3,600 acres, all in Adams County, Ohio, in three surveys, lying close together and the same chain carriers and markers are used to each of the three surveys, which were some seven miles back from the river. On Christmas Day, 1787, he surveyed 4,239 acres of land in seven different surveys, in Clermont County, Ohio.

Evan Shelby, father of Isaac Shelby, afterwards Governor of Kentucky, was put down as a marker in four of the different surveys. George Marshall was put down as chain carrier in four of these different surveys.

To think that anyone would survey on Christmas Day is bad enough, but to survey 4,239 acres of land, over six square miles in a wilderness in one day, is more than human nature could stand. But there is worse and more to come. 839 acres of these 4,239 acres were for the immortal George Washington. The latter had a warrant for 3,000 acres of land, which could not be located in the Virginia Military District of Ohio, and yet O'Bannon had it there and not only located the 839 acres of it on

Christmas Day, but located the remainder of it, 1,235 acres in Miami Township, and 977 acres in Union Township, Clermont County. The one in Union Township lies partly in Hamilton County.

General Washington's Warrant was founded on a certificate issued to John Rootes, on December 7, 1763, by Lord Dunmore, under proclamations in the name of King George.

Washington, who was always around buying claims, bought this certificate, the basis of a land warrant. On December 14, 1784, the House of Delegates of Virginia, passed a resolution that certificates of this class owned by persons who purchased them prior to May 1, 1779, and who served in the Revolution from May 1, 1779 to the close of the war, could have them changed into warrants, which could be located on the lands reserved by Virginia north of the Ohio River. The Senate concurred in this resolution January 7, 1785, and on February 14, 1785, Washington had his warrant issued to him for 3,000 acres. This he gave to Col. O'Bannon, who located it in full and 51 more acres of another in the three surveys, 1775, 1765, and 1650, in Clermont and Hamilton Counties. This warrant numbered 3,753, could not legally be located in the Virginia Military District in the Northwest Territory.

The resolution of the Virginia Legislature was passed after the delivery of the deed of cession by Virginia to the United States, which was on March 1, 1784, and the claim under this warrant was not in the class of claims for which the land was reserved. The United States never extended the class of beneficiaries and hence this warrant could not be legally located in the Virginia Military District, which afterwards became a part of Ohio. Col. O'Bannon had located the Mayo Carrington Survey of 1,000 acres opposite Vanceburg, Kentucky, on a state line warrant issued to one Edward Williams, and which could not be located in Virginia Military District of Ohio. General Washington wrote in the year of his death as to the ownership of these 3,000 acres. He said he had owned them for 12 years, and that they were near Judge Symmes' grants, on the opposite side of the Miami River, in the neighborhood of Cincinnati and Fort Washington; that he had never seen them, but that the Surveyor had reported them valuable.

By using the calendar, we find that some of these large surveys were made on Sunday. From January 7 to February 2, 1788, Col. O'Bannon did no surveying. From February 7 to April 1, 1788, he did no surveying, but on April 1, 1788, he began and continued busy till May 29, 1788, when he ceased operations. He made no more surveys in the Virginia Military District, in the Northwest Territory, till 1792, when he made one or more. Col. John O'Bannon had no right or authority whatever to make these 199 surveys. He was a trespasser in so doing. He never, in point of fact, made them himself, and it was physically impossible he should have done so. He, no doubt, had not less than six parties of surveyors, and they did the work. He certified all the 199 surveys as Deputy Surveyor, and put down the names of the chain carriers and markers as occurred to him.

COLONEL JOHN O'BANNON.

O'Bannon claimed to have made these surveys under a law of Virginia, passed in October, 1783, which required the surveyor to actually run the lines and mark the corners. This law required chain carriers to be sworn.

The Continental Congress, at its last session, became alarmed at this wholesale surveying of Col. O'Bannon, and, on July 17, 1788, passed a resolution declaring these surveys void, and this resolution remained in force until August 10, 1790, when the act, opening the district for location was passed, and the resolution repealed. The act of August 10, 1790 incidentally referred to these 199 locations as to be approved, but never directly confirmed them. However, most of them were afterwards patented. But the business of locating in the Virginia Military District of Ohio, was stopped and not resumed again until about December 1, 1792.

Some lawyers claim that the patents issued on the 199 surveys of O'Bannon are void because the surveys were made without authority of law and were expressly declared void by the resolution of Congress of July 17, 1788. These lawyers claim the Act of August 10, 1790, opening up the district, did not confirm these surveys, and that the latter being void, the patents are void, but if such were the case, the parties could confirm their titles by deeds from the Board of Trustees of the Ohio State University, and in that case, the new title would relate to March 14, 1868. The Cincinnati Waterworks, east of the Little Miami, is on one of these O'Bannon surveys. In the celebrated McArthur will cases, which involved two or more of these O'Bannon surveys, the distinguished counsel on both sides assumed that the patents to these surveys were valid, and did not raise any question as to their validity.

As to the three Washington Surveys, they were never sent to the United States Land Office and never patented. It seems they were sent to the Virginia Land Office, in Richmond, and grants issued on them there. On May 20, 1806, some one in the name of Col. John Neville, who had died July 30, 1803, made a survey 4,847, which completely covered the Washington survey 1650, in Pierce Township, Clermont County, Ohio. On May 20, 1806, some one in the name of the same John Neville, covered Washington's Survey 1765, in Miami Township, Clermont County, for 1,235 acres. On the same day, a survey in the name of Major Henry Massie, the founder of Portsmouth, Ohio, was made, overlying the whole of General Washington's Survey 1775 for 977 acres in Union Township, Clermont County, and Anderson Township in Hamilton County. The Deputy Surveyor who made these three overlying surveys was Joseph Kerr. Congress, however, got alarmed at this kind of business and on March 3, 1807, enacted the famous proviso, which forbade the making of any surveys over previous locations. This famous proviso of March 3, 1807, was construed in Jackson vs. Clark, 1st Peters, 666, by the great Chief Justice Marshall.

No doubt Joseph Kerr, Deputy Surveyor, knew that Washington's Warrant was not locatable in the Virginia Military District of Ohio, and he took care to locate them on Virginia Military Continental Warrants, though two of the surveys were made in the name of a person who had been dead over two years.

The value of a survey made in the name of a dead man, I leave to the lawyers. I have no information as to whether the overlying surveys 4847, 4848 and 4862 have ever been patented. After the resolution of July 17, 1788, Colonel John O'Bannon returned to Woodford County, Kentucky, where he became an extensive land owner. The Virginia Military District had rest from any locations after his 199 surveys till 1792. In 1795, John O'Bannon was trustee of the town of Versailles, Kentucky. In 1808, he was sheriff of Woodford County, Kentucky, and George T. Cotton, his son-in-law, was his deputy. He had two daughters, Elizabeth, who married George T. Cotton, and Eliza, who married a man named Bucham. In the preparation of this article, I was unable to find any descendants of the latter. George T. Cotton, a son of Mrs. Elizabeth Cotton, was a Lieutenant Colonel of the 6th Kentucky Regiment of Infantry (Union), in the Civil War, and was killed at the battle of Shilo. The titles of John O'Bannon, Major and Colonel, were acquired after his location in Kentucky. He made his will on January 7, 1810. He recites that he is much afflicted with rheumatism, but is of sound mind. He was an extensive slave holder and land holder. He devised his wife seven slaves with his home plantation, and his lot in Versailles. He gave his daughter, Elizabeth Cotton, a plantation and five slaves by name. He gave his daughter Eliza, 500 acres of land in Hopkins County, and several slaves. He devised lands and slaves to his grandsons by the name of Cotton. He gave his brother, Presley O'Bannon, 1,000 acres of land in Clermont County, Ohio, a slave and a horse. He gave a slave each to his niece, Margaret O'Bannon and his nephew, George O'Bannon.

He gave to his brother William, two slaves and a plantation. He was an extensive owner of horses, cattle and live stock, and disposed of them by will. He directed certain of his slaves to be hired out and the hire to be applied in certain directions. His residuary estate, after the death of his wife, was to be sold and divided into eight parts, two parts to his daughters and the other parts to go to collateral relatives named by him. He appointed a committee of three friends, named in his will, to decide all questions arising under that instrument, without going to law. He made Robert Alexander and his son-in-law, George T. Cotton, his executors. He departed this life February 17, 1813, and his will was probated at Woodford County Court, in April, 1813.

Of his political or religious views, we know nothing. He evidently enjoyed the acquaintance and respect of Jefferson and Washington. He also had the complete confidence of General Richard Clough Anderson, who appointed him a Deputy Surveyor of the Virginia Military District, in the North West Territory. He was the only Deputy Surveyor who made any surveys in the District before it was legally opened by Congress. From the number of surveys made by him in Hamilton and Clermont Counties, it is apparent that he operated with Fort Washington as a base, and none of his surveys were made over five miles back from the Ohio River, except in Clermont or Hamilton Counties. All were made in peril of Indian attacks and no doubt three or more parties of surveyors traveled together. The lowest number of surveys made by O'Bannon was 386, made at Ripley, Ohio, and the highest number 1775, made for General George Washington. Of the 1190 numbers not taken by O'Bannon, I am unable to state where they were located—a few of those numbers were taken in the district after 1792.

It seems a pity the way General Washington's interests were sacrificed after O'Bannon's surveys. His own agents did not know enough to return his surveys with the Warrant to the General Land Office at Washington D. C. The subsequent locators appropriated his lands, and to add insult to injury, Congress, on March 3, 1899, outlawed his warrant, and thus the Washington estate lost that which at one time would have realized $14,250. The lands which were located under the warrant were doubtless worth at this time, with improvements, not less than $300,000. Washington's estate at the time of his death was worth $500,000, and had it been kept intact, its value now would have been fabulous.

In ascertaining the facts set forth herein as to John O'Bannon, I have pursued every lead to its source and have been baffled seemingly, at every point. The facts that I wished to know have receded into oblivion and cannot be brought to light. There was not a publication, in February, 1813, which had an obituary notice of John O'Bannon. There is no mention of him of any significance in any contemporary history. A man now in full life, has every opportunity to have his record preserved to posterity. If he is of the slightest importance, the Daily Newspapers record his doing from day to day, but of John O'Bannon scarcely anything was preserved, except what the official records disclose.

A ROCK WITH A HISTORY.

BASIL MEEK, FREMONT.

The accompanying cut represents a large granitic boulder, believed to be the largest in Sandusky County, and which possesses local historic associations worthy to be published for preservation with other interesting facts connected with the early history of the Sandusky river region.

It is located in the north and south road on the line dividing Sections 14 and 15 between the farms of W. J. Havens and Hugh Havens in Jackson township, 7 miles south-west from the City of Fremont.

There is a general, and what seems to be an undisputed, tradition, that during his campaigns in the Sandusky and Maumee river valleys, in the War of 1812, Gen. William Henry Harrison, with his military staff, at one time dined upon this boulder as a table.

There was an Indian trail leading from Lower Sandusky (Fremont), through what is now Spiegel Grove, the grounds of the late President R. B. Hayes, passing thence west of the Sandusky river, in a southwesterly direction and intersecting at a point not far east of this rock a similar one from the site of Fort Seneca, and thus becoming united into one trail, which passed near the rock in a northwesterly direction to Fort Meigs, on the Maumee river.

This trail became known as the " Harrison trail," because in his military movements between Lower Sandusky and Fort Seneca on the Sandusky river, and Fort Meigs on the Maumee, Gen. Harrison made use of it as a military road. While passing along the same, according to tradition, he and his military family partook of the repast mentioned upon this substantial table in the then wilderness.

The Messrs. Havens who have owned these farms for fifty years, well remember traces of this trail and pointed out to the writer the ground along which it ran. They remember and speak of it as the " Harrison trail."

In the field notes of the government survey, 1820, of said sections 14 and 15, it is mentioned as the " Road to Fort Meigs," and its location shown to be near the spot where the boulder lies.

In size, the boulder is 12 feet in length, with a slightly convex top surface containing 80 square feet; its circumference at the ground is 37 feet, and near the top 32 fèet; it rises 3 1-2 feet above ground, and as nearly as can be ascertained, lies embedded in the earth about the same number of feet it rises above; which would make it contain 500 cubic feet and weigh 40 tons.

ROCK WITH A HISTORY.

It has been regarded by some as merely an obstruction in the highway, and occasional threats have been made to destroy it, but thus far the better sentiment favoring its preservation, has prevailed.

If this article shall aid in promoting still further this sentiment, and result in the preservation of this historic rock which may appropriately be named " Harrison Rock," and which is suggested as a name for it, the object of the writer will have been accomplished.

TWENTIETH ANNUAL MEETING OF THE OHIO STATE ARCHÆOLOGICAL AND HISTORICAL SOCIETY.

(JUNE 2, 1905.)

The Twentieth Annual Meeting of the Ohio State Archæological and Historical Society was held in the lecture room of the Y. M. C. A. Building, Columbus, Ohio, at 2:30 P. M., June 2d, 1905. The following members were present:

Rev. J. W. Atwood, Columbus; Judge J. H. Anderson, Columbus; Prof. M. R. Andrews, Marietta; Mr. E. H. Archer, Columbus; General R. Brinkerhoff, Mansfield; Mr. George F. Bareis, Canal Winchester; Prof. J. H. Beal, Scio; Hon. M. D. Follett, Marietta; Hon. C. B. Galbreath, Columbus; Hon. M. S. Greenough, Cleveland; Mr. W. H. Hunter, Chillicothe; Prof. Archer B. Hulbert, Marietta; Colonel John W. Harper, Cincinnati; Prof. C. L. Martzolff, New Lexington; Prof. W. C. Mills, Columbus; Prof. John D. H. McKinley, Columbus; Prof. B. F. Prince, Springfield; Prof. E. O. Randall, Columbus; Hon. Rush R. Sloane, Sandusky; Mr. E. F. Wood, Columbus; Prof. G. Frederick Wright, Oberlin. Prof. Frederick Starr, Chicago University, was the guest of the society.

Messages of regret because of inability to attend were received from Trustees Dr. H. A. Thompson, Dayton; Rev. N. B. C. Love, Toledo; General J. Warren Keifer, Springfield; Hon. S. S. Rickly, Columbus; and Hon. D. J. Ryan, Columbus.

The meeting was called to order by the President, Gen. R. Brinkerhoff. The Secretary, Mr. Randall, was called upon for the minutes of the previous annual meeting held June 3, 1904. In order to save time, he referred to the minutes of that meeting as published in Vol. 13, pp. 375 to 391, inclusive. Motion was made and carried to dispense with the reading of the minutes, and the printed report referred to was adopted as the correct minutes of the meeting. The President then delivered the following opening address:

ADDRESS OF PRESIDENT BRINKERHOFF.

The Ohio State Archæological and Historical Society had its beginning about thirty years ago. It was first organized as the Ohio State Archæological Association, and its first annual meeting was held at Mansfield September 1, 1875, and was attended by about fifty of the leading archæologists of the state.

The purpose of that organization was purely to form an archæological society. In 1876 the association was represented at the Centennial at Philadelphia. The Legislature appropriated $2,500 to make an exhibit of this nature. Time was short, but an interesting and creditable showing was made. In the opinion of those competent to judge, Ohio had by far the finest exhibit of pre-historic relics, except that of the Smithsonian Institute.

For ten years the work of the association was given exclusively to archæology, but in 1885, it was reorganized and broadened so as to include events historic as well as pre-historic, and the association has since been known as the Ohio State Archæological and Historical Society.

As stated in its articles of incorporation, "said society is formed for the purpose of promoting a knowledge of archæology and history, especially of Ohio, by establishing and maintaining a library of books, manuscripts, maps, charts, etc., properly pertaining thereto; a museum of pre-historic relics and natural or other curiosities or specimens of art or nature, promotive of the objects of the association, said library and museum to be open to the public upon reasonable terms, and by courses of lectures and publication of books, papers and documents touching the subjects so specified, with power to receive and hold gifts and devises of real and personal estate for the benefit of such society, and generally to exercise all the powers legally pertaining thereto."

How far these requirements have been complied with by the society is fairly indicated by its annual reports and other publications, which are everywhere recognized as of the highest value, and comparing favorably with those of any other state.

In archæology, its prehistoric exhibits at the world expositions at Chicago, Buffalo and St. Louis, as a whole were unequalled by any other state or country and were so officially recognized.

Among its accomplishments, doubtless, the most important has been the acquirement for the state of Fort Ancient and the Serpent Mound, than which, among pre-historic monuments in the United States, there are none more interesting and important. The various mounds and other pre-historic relics of Ohio, located and enumerated by the society, now numbers over ten thousand, and one of its leading and permanent activities has been the examination and excavation of these mounds, more or less every year, by and under the direction of our curator and librarian Prof. W. C. Mills.

Our collection of prehistoric relics now numbers over 50,000 separate objects, and is not surpassed or equalled by any other state in the Union. During the twenty years succeeding its reorganization, the society, as indicated by its publications, has given large attention to matters of history, and its library of books, manuscripts, maps, charts, etc., is now very large and valuable. Of these various acquisitions, both historic and pre-historic, our secretary and curator, in their annual reports to this meeting, will doubtless present a more comprehensive and intelligent review than is possible or proper in a brief opening address.

The greatest need of the society at the present time is, a separate and larger building for our museum and library with largely increased capacity over the quarters now occupied at the Ohio State University, and it ought to be a structure worthy of the first and greatest of our northwestern states.

In response to a recent letter of inquiry to our Curator Prof. Mills, he writes me as follows: — "The facts are we have absolutely outgrown the accommodations provided for us in Page Hall. Every nook and corner is filled, and I have been compelled, within a week, to refuse to receive collections, as we cannot place them on display." I am indeed sorry for this, as we have grown so rapidly within the two years, or since we occupied our more commodious quarters at Page Hall. Not only has the museum grown but the library is well keeping pace with it. Exchanging our publications with like societies over the entire globe has placed our society in touch with those it would be impossible to reach in any other way. However, our society has led in archæological explorations and publications, and these, together with our exhibitions, have created an interest in archæological exploration throughout the middle west. At present many states are following our example."

In view of the approaching bi-centennial session of our state legislature, it would seem proper and advisable that our society, at its present session, should take such action as may seem desirable for the presentation of its great needs to legislators and the public.

The President's address was received and ordered placed on file.

The Secretary then made his annual report, which was as follows:

REPORT OF THE SECRETARY.

(For the year, June 3, 1904, to June 2, 1905.)

Some one has said that that nation is the happiest which has the least history. The theory being that prosperity follows a quiet existence. It is likely that many historians and philosophers would quarrel with the truth of that axiom. Certain it is, however, that the history

·of our society for the past year has been one of unusual uneventfulness, yet one of unusual progress and prosperity.

Since the last annual meeting the society has issued its quarterly regularly as follows: July, 1904 (No. 3, vol. 13), October, 1904 (No. 4, vol. 13) January, 1905 (No. 1, vol. 14) and April, 1905 (No. 2, vol. 14). Volume 13 comprising the quarterlies for January, April, July and October, 1904, was issued in bound volume form in December (1904). It makes one of the most valuable and readable volumes of the series. The reprint of this volume was included in the appropriation ($7,500) by the Sixty-sixth General Assembly for the supplying of each member of the legislature with ten complete sets of the thirteen volumes. The re-publication of these volumes amounting to the printing and binding of some twenty thousand separate books was completed in April (1905) and the books were boxed and shipped at the expense of the appropriation fund to each member of the legislature. Double postals were mailed to each consignee announcing the shipment and requesting acknowledgement of its receipt by return card. In addition to these annuals, five copies of the volume of the centennial proceedings were sent in the shipment above mentioned to each member of the legislature. This was in the nature of a *bonus* to the members. It will be recalled that the appropriation of $10,000 by the Seventy-fifth General Assembly for the expense of the State Centennial held at Chillicothe was not fully expended and there was left after the payment of all bills and the publication of the volume of proceedings a balance of $684.79. It was intended at that time to permit this surplus to lapse into the credit of the general fund of the state. The members of the Seventy-sixth General Assembly made an appropriation of $7,500 to reprint the volume of the Ohio Centennial proceedings for the purpose of supplying each member of that Assembly with one hundred copies. This item of the appropriation bill was vetoed by the Governor. In order that the members thus deprived ·of the results of that appropriation, might receive at least a few copies ·of this book, by approval of the Auditor of State and the Governor, the society expended the $684.79 surplus for the reprinting of this Centennial volume thus permitting the distribution of five copies to each member of the Legislature and in addition giving the society about 750 copies for exchanges, libraries, new members, etc.

The publications of the society are more and more in demand by the libraries and historical and literary societies in all parts of the country as well as in the old world. The editor receives the manuscript of many more articles than he is able to use. The result of his selection for publication speaks for itself. Many admirable articles are received bearing upon historical subjects and events in other states or having no especial significance to Ohio. These articles the editor returns with the statement that the society and its publications are devoted exclusively to Ohio archæology and history.

The policy has been continued of sending the quarterlies as they appear to a list of some 350 leading Ohio papers. This has proven to be of mutual benefit to the society and the recipient papers. Many of them have copied the articles or made copious extracts from the quarterlies, thereby disseminating the literature of the society in quarters where it was of particular value or interest.

MEETINGS OF THE EXECUTIVE COMMITTEE.

Since the annual meeting of the Society on June 3, 1904, the Executive Committee has held meetings as follows:

August 19, 1904, (page 558, vol. 13); September 19, 1904 (page 89, vol. 14); November 28, 1904 (page 91, vol. 14); February 7, 1905. At the last meeting mentioned the Committee took action concerning the charges made against the Secretary of the Society by Professor J. P. MacLean, formerly a trustee of the society, which charges were published in the *Franklin News* of January 7, 1905 and a copy of which was mailed by Mr. MacLean to each member of the society. These charges were made in the form of a letter addressed to President Brinkerhoff. After due consideration the Executive Committee unanimously adopted the following resolution:

Whereas, The communication of J. P. MacLean, of Franklin, Ohio, dated January 23, 1905, and addressed to General R. Brinkerhoff, President of the Ohio State Archæological and Historical Society, has been referred to the Executive Committee by the President; and

Whereas, The Executive Committee after a full and careful consideration of Professor MacLean's letter to the President, and the charges and specifications set forth therein against the Secretary, E. O. Randall, and the Executive Committee representing the Society;

Therefore, Be it resolved that this Committee having the fullest confidence in its Secretary, E. O. Randall, hereby approves and commends his conduct, both officially and personally, during his long and honored career as the Secretary of this Society, and be it further

Resolved, That the Committee has no confidence in, and resents the so-called charges and specifications of Dr. J. P. MacLean and it requests the President, General R. Brinkerhoff, to return the same to its author with a copy of this resolution.

The following members of the Executive Committee were present:

D. J. RYAN,	B. F. PRINCE,
W. H. HUNTER,	S. S. RICKLY,
G. F. BAREIS,	G. FREDERICK WRIGHT,
J. W. HARPER,	E. F. WOOD, AND
C. L. MARTZOLFF,	W. C. MILLS.

Each one of the members present voted in favor of the above resolution. Secretary Randall was present but not voting.

The meetings of the Executive Committee the past year have been less frequent than usual because there was really no necessity for meetings other than those held.

At the meeting on August 19, Mr. E. F. Wood made a verbal report of his visit to Fort Ancient on July 4 and 5 (as per page 558, vol. 13). At this meeting standing committees for the ensuing year were selected as follows: Finance: Messrs Rickly, Ryan and Bareis; Fort Ancient: Messrs. Prince, Harper and Bareis; Serpent Mound: Messrs Martzolff, Hunter and Randall; Museum and Library: Messrs. Wright, Greenough and Brinkerhoff; Publications: Messrs. Wright, Ryan and Randall.

On Monday, August 29, in accordance with the decision of the Executive Committee at its previous meeting (August 19) members of the Executive Committee and certain invited state officials made a visit of inspection to Fort Ancient as described on page 259, vol. 13.

At the meeting of the Executive Committee on September 19, the resignation of Professor J. P. MacLean both as trustee and life member of the society was accepted and at the meeting on November 28, Hon. R. E. Hills of Delaware was selected to fill out Mr. MacLean's unexpired term which would terminate at the next annual (this meeting). At the Executive Committee meeting on February 7, Messrs Ryan, Mills and Randall were appointed a committee to fix the date and the program for the annual meeting of the Society. This committee met at various dates and after a personal consultation with President Brinkerhoff fixed the date of the annual meeting upon Friday, June 2. It was decided to invite Professor Frederick Starr of the Chicago University to deliver an address to the society and invited guests on the evening of June 2d at the auditorium, Ohio State University. It was further decided to arrange for an excursion to Fort Ancient on the following day, (Saturday, June 3d), the Governor having acquiesced in that date as being one convenient for his acceptance of an invitation by the society to accompany the excursion.

ITINERARY OF THE SECRETARY.

In addition to the usual duties of the Secretary in looking after the business affairs of the society and editing its publications, he paid a visit to the St. Louis exposition on June 15 and 16 at which time he inspected the exhibit being made by the society under the direction of Curator Mills in the quarters assigned for that purpose in the Anthropological Building. (See page 55, vol. 13). On September 6 to the 10th inclusive the Secretary accompanied by Assistant Treasurer Wood visited the St. Louis Exposition when further inspection of the exhibit of the society and its value was made. During this visit in company with a party of archæologists including Curator Mills, Professor Starr of Chicago, Messrs.

Wood and Randall, made a trip to the famous Cahokia Mound located in Illinois on the Mississippi River opposite St. Louis. This is the largest mound now remaining constructed by the mound-builders. Prof. Mills in his report will make full statement concernng the exhibit of the society at the St. Louis exposition.

The secretary was invited by the program committee to address the Historical Section of the International Congress of Arts and Sciences, held at the St. Louis Exposition, September 19-25, 1904. The secretary was unable to comply, owing to other engagements at that time, but Prof. Mills, our curator, received a similar invitation and represented the society by an address in the section in Archæology of that congress.

On October 11, the Secretary was invited as representative of the society to be present at the dedication of the Soldiers' and Sailors' Memorial Hall at Columbus. The exercises were held in the open air at the site of the building in the afternoon when the corner-stone was laid. In the evening an open camp fire was held under the auspices of the Wells Post and the McCoy Post, G. A. R. in the auditorium of the Board of Trade (Columbus), at which the Secretary was one of the speakers.

On November 5, the Secretary accompanied by Messrs Harper and Martzolff of the Executive Committee paid a visit to Serpent Mound an account of which is found on page 92, vol. 14.

On Friday, November 18, the famous Liberty Bell, from Independence Hall, Philadelphia, passed through Columbus on its return trip from St. Louis to its home in the Quaker City. Secretary Randall in accordance with the request of Mayor Jeffrey of Columbus represented the society in a committee composed of representatives from other patriotic, educational and historical societies. The purpose of this committee was to give a fitting reception to the Bell upon its stop-over of half an hour in the Union Depot. The Secretary selected a number of the local members of the society to be present at its reception. A full account of this will be found on page 94, vol. 14.

On December 28-30, 1904, Mr. A. J. Baughman, Mansfield, and Secretary E. O. Randall represented the society, as per their selection by the Executive Committee, at the annual meeting of the American Historical Association held in Chicago. There were also present at that meeting Miss Martha J. Maltby, Columbus, Mr. Nelson W. Evans, Portsmouth and Dr. C. E. Slocum, Defiance, all life members of The Ohio State Archæological and Historical Society. A statement of the meeting of the American Historical Association will be found on page 219, vol. 14.

ADDITIONAL LIFE MEMBERS.

Since the last annual meeting (June 3, 1904), there have been received into life membership of the society the following:

Hon. Jeptha Garrard and Judge James B. Swing, Cincinnati; Hon. E. V. Hale, Cleveland; Prof. G. A. Hubbell, Berea, Ky.; Prof. John D. H. McKinley, Mr. Frank S. Brooks and Miss Martha J. Maltby, Columbus; Dr C. E. Slocum, Defiance; Mr. Stephen B. Cone, Hamilton; Hon. Ross J. Alexander, Bridgeport; Mr. George W. Vanhorn, Findlay, Mrs. Mary McArthur Tuttle, Hillsboro; and Prof. Stephen B. Peet, Mrs. Mary McArthur Tuttle, Hillsboro; Prof. Stephen B. Peet, Chicago; Mr. E. F. Wood, Columbus; Prof. J. H. Beal, Scio.

Dr. Newell Dwight Hillis, Pastor of Plymouth Church, Brooklyn, was elected an honorary member of the society in recognition of his being the author of a book entitled "The Quest of John Chapman" founded upon the story of "Johnnie Appleseed," one of the unique and original characters in early Ohio history.

APPOINTMENT OF TRUSTEES.

On February 29, 1905, Governor Myron T. Herrick, re-appointed Professor B. F. Prince, Springfield, and Mr. E. O. Randall, Columbus, as trustees of The Ohio State Archæological and Historical Society for a term of three years ending February, 1908.

The report of the Secretary was unanimously adopted and ordered placed on file.

Prof. Mills being called upon for his annual report submitted the following:

REPORT OF THE CURATOR.

I have the honor as Curator and Librarian, to make my annual report upon the condition of the museum and library and upon the Archæological Exhibit, made by the Society, at the Universal Exposition, St. Louis, 1904.

During the year the Archæological Museum has grown rapidly, advancing far beyond our expectations and adding several collections of value from portions of the state, not heretofore represented in the museum. I also placed on exhibition a portion of the material secured during our explorations in the field.

At the present time every available space that can be used for exhibition purposes has been utilized and occupied, and I hope you will visit the museum in Page Hall and see for yourselves the crowded condition and the many obstacles which materially hinder our progress and that each of you will feel that it is his individual duty to devote every honorable effort to secure a permanent and adequate home for the largest and finest archæological collection in Ohio. If this home is provided, Ohio will have the largest archæological museum, representing one state, in this country, if not in the world.

Situated as we are in the very heart of a country once occupied by a pre-historic people, whose little villages lie buried in almost all

Vol. XIV.— 22.

the river valleys in Ohio, it behooves us as a Society to continue the work of exploration, adding what little we can to archæological science, and keeping abreast with other states engaged in the same work.

A few years ago Ohio was alone in this work but by her explorations, publications and exhibitions she has enlisted the attention of other states which at present are engaging in the care and protection of archæological remains, the exploration of mounds and village sites and the proper publication of the results of such explorations. This means a concerted action along the lines of exploration in the various states. At no time in the history of the science is the outlook for advancement so flattering and widespread and with this combined effort in archæology we will be able to present as perfect a history of early man in this country as it is possible to secure. However to bring this about in our own state, we must not feel that because our explorations have been successful and we have obtained great quantities of valuable specimens our efforts should be diminished, on the contrary, what has been accomplished in our field explorations and publications should be our incentive to still better and greater work, so the society can feel, in later years, no regret over lost opportunities. At present we are practically free from invasions by other institutions outside of our state, for the purpose of carrying away our state treasures, and this will no doubt continue so long as we put forth the effort that is expected of us.

I wish to call your attention to the historical museum and library and ask you to note its rapid growth showing that the quarters are inadequate for our present needs, however, I feel, we, as a Society, are not making the necessary effort incumbent upon us, to secure the state papers and even the libraries of our most prominent men in Ohio, who have figured in making our state and country great.

No other state has such a storehouse of historical material. We need to collect more data during the time before Ohio became a state, for certainly much history must be written concerning Ohio's part in the American Revolution. Although not a state at that time, yet the important events occurring within her borders, between the years 1774 and 1800, makes Ohio the most important western country in the struggle for the independence of the United States. Therefore I feel assured that you are all of one opinion, that the vast resources of our state, both archæologically and historically should be properly collected and placed at the disposal of the public. Our plans have been perfected to do this and what we most need is a building to properly care for and display the many valuable specimens that would come to us merely for the asking. At present we cannot even take care of collections that come to us unsolicited, especially if requested to place collections on exhibition; however we never refuse to receive them and place them in storage in our basement rooms if such arrangements can be made.

I cannot at the present time tell you just how many specimens we have in the museum as we are working on the new card catalog, but it will not fall short of 50,000 and, combined with those belonging to the University we have an archæological museum of more than 75,000 specimens representing Ohio alone. In the Library we have 2,432 volumes recorded in the accession book and have several hundred volumes to add to our accession list as soon as the additions can be made.

During the session of the Ohio Legislature, 1901-2, a bill was introduced and passed authorizing our Society to make an archæological exhibit at the Universal Exposition, St. Louis, 1904, and an appropriation of 2,500 dollars was made to pay the expenses of such an exhibit. The Society directed me to prepare and take charge of this exhibit. Accordingly on the 19th of March I shipped to St. Louis, the exhibit prepared from selections in the museum, together with suitable display cases, purchased for that purpose. The rooms assigned us in the Anthropology Building, Exposition grounds, were not well adapted for a display room, consequently our efforts were taxed to the utmost to make our exhibit attractive and instructive.

We completed the installation some time before the opening day and received congratulations from the Chief of the Department of Anthropology and other officials of the Exposition for presenting the first complete exhibit in the building, ready on the opening day. I remained with the exhibit during the entire period of the Exposition and at the close of the Exposition, packed and returned the exhibit without breakage or the loss of a single specimen, besides the return to the museum of more than one thousand dollars' worth of cases, furniture, casts, drawings, photographs, maps, etc.

The exhibit for the most part consisted of material secured by our surveys during the last four (4) years in the field, consisting principally of artifacts from the Baum Village Site, Gartner Mound and Village Site, Adena Mound and the Harness Mound, occupying in all six cases while the other eight cases were used in displaying typical specimens from various sections of Ohio.

The large plaster cast of Fort Ancient which we had prepared for this exhibit was so large that it was impossible to get it into the exhibit room at St. Louis, consequently this proposed interesting feature of our exhibit we were compelled to leave at home. However in its stead I took the large drawing of the Fort and hung it on the east wall of the room, together with enlarged photographs of all the most important points of the Fort. The large drawing of the Serpent Mound Park was hung upon the west wall together with enlarged photographs of the most important parts of the park. Two large casts, one of the Serpent Mound, which was placed at the west end of the exhibit room, and one of Fort Hill of Highland county, which was placed at the east end of the room, attracted a great deal of attention. Upon the walls of the room were placed enlarged photographs of field explorations.

The entire collection was labelled with neat printed labels for all specimens and a large display label for cases together with maps showing location of all important finds. The photographs and drawings were also labelled, so that it was an easy matter for visitors to examine the collection intelligently without the aid of a guide book.

The personnel of the Jury in the section of Archæology, passing upon our exhibit was as follows:

Prof. M. H. Saville, Columbia Univ. Chairman.

Dr. J. C. Alves de Lima, Brazil, Vice Chairman.

Dr. G. G. MacCurdy, Yale Univ., Secretary.

Madam Zelia Nuttall, Mexico.

This committee was unanimous in awarding to our Society the Grand Prize for the most complete and best arranged archæological exhibit in the Exposition — thus giving us priority over the exhibits of all other states and other countries. The committee further honored our Society by awarding me as the Curator, the Gold Medal, for the successful and valuable explorations made among the Ohio mounds by our Society under my supervision. The Committee especially commended the exhumations in the Gartner and Adena mounds.

During the meeting of the International Congress of Arts and Science, September 19-25, 1904, I was invited to read a paper before the Department of Anthropology, Section of Archæology, and presented a paper upon the results of the explorations of the Harness Mound. I was also elected Secretary of the Section.

During my stay in St. Louis I was invited to speak upon the archæological work in Ohio before the members of the Missouri Historical Society; to teachers of several high schools upon the Cahokia Group of mounds and to several scientific clubs upon the explorations in Ohio.

I also received the following letter from the Department of Anthropology which may be of some interest:

St. Louis, U. S. A., November 15, 1904.

Doctor Wm. C. Mills, *Ohio State Exhibit, Anthropology Building.*

My Dear Sir: — With the approval of the Director of Exhibits under authority vested in him by the President of the Louisiana Purchase Exposition Company, and in recognition of the confidence reposed in your abilities and training, I have the honor to designate you Honorary Superintendent of Archæology in this Department.

This action is inspired largely by the desire to convey to you some token of appreciation not merely of the high value of your special exhibit in the Anthropology Building but of the scientific and scholarly character you have constantly aided in giving to this Department.

In case you find it consistent with your duties toward the institution and state you have so efficiently represented to prepare a general report on the archæologic exhibits of the Department, I should greatly appreciate the favor and should take much pleasure in incorporating the same in the general report of the Department for publication by the Exposition Company.

With assurances of consideration, I remain,

Yours respectfully,

W. J. McGee, *Chief.*

During my work at the exposition the members of the Missouri Historical Society did much to make my stay in St. Louis pleasant and profitable, planning many excursions for our entertainment and in many other ways making our stay most enjoyable.

I wish to thank the officers and members of the Executive Committee who have aided me in the great undertakings of the past year which have been crowned with such splendid success.

Respectfully submitted,

W. C. MILLS.

Following the report of the Curator, the Secretary submitted brief reports from the Chairmen of the Committees on Ft. Ancient and Serpent Mound, as follows:

REPORT OF THE COMMITTEE ON FORT ANCIENT.

The Committee on Fort Ancient have made several visits to the Fort during the past year. They found the grounds well kept under the care and supervision of Mr. Warren Cowan, who has been the custodian for a number of years. The various improvements made from year to year are beginning to show very favorably. The grounds are growing more beautiful continually, and are a delight to all who visit them. The buildings are kept in good order and everything about the Fort shows constant care.

Signed.   B. F. PRINCE, *Chairman.*

REPORT OF THE COMMITTEE ON SERPENT MOUND.

On Saturday, November 5, 1904, the committee on Serpent Mound, consisting of Messrs Harper, Randall and Martzolff, spent the day at Serpent Mound Park. The committee found it in excellent condition. The grounds are covered with a thick growth of grass and everything gave evidence of good care. The mound itself is in a perfect state of preservation, being protected by a heavy sod which prevents erosion.

The custodian, Mr. Daniel Wallace, is careful and painstaking in his duties. He looks after the fences and buildings of the park and maintains them in splendid shape. The Society is certainly fortunate in having such an efficient guardian of its property.

The Serpent Mound Park is becoming more popular each year, being visited by hundreds of people annually. The care and preservation of this pre-historic earthwork by our Society is being appreciated not only by archæologists in all lands but by the officials of our state government and especially by the students of archæology in Ohio.

C. L. MARTZOLFF *Chairman.*

The reports of the committees as submitted were received and ordered placed on file.

The report of Assistant Treasurer E. F. Wood, in behalf of Treasurer S. S. Rickley, was as follows:

REPORT OF THE TREASURER.

[For the year ending February 1, 1905.]

RECEIPTS.

Balance on hand, February 1st, 1904	$1,005 90
Life Membership Dues	250 00
Active Membership Dues	99 00
Books sold	80 50
Subscriptions	21 00
Refunded	8 20
Interest	121 05
From Treasurer of State:	
Appropriation for Current Expenses	2,458 57
Appropriation for Publications	2,228 20
Appropriation for Louisiana Purchase Exposition	2,251 24
Appropriation for Field Work, Ft. Ancient and Serpent Mound	1,773 66
Total	$10,297 32

DISBURSEMENTS.

Express and Drayage	$114 14
Field Work	209 30
Care of Fort Ancient	351 72
Care of Serpent Mound	379 75
Sundry Expenses	33 92
Publications	2,201 55
Job Printing	81 00
Expenses of Trustees and Committees	224 80
Louisiana Purchase Exposition	2,354 13
Salaries (3)	2,000 00
Museum and Library	598 05
Transferred to Permanent Fund	430 00
Postage	96 67
Balance on hand, February 1st, 1905	1,222 29
Total	$10,297 32
Total amount of Permanent Fund	$4,200 00

Respectfully submitted,

S. S. RICKLY, *Treasurer.*

The report of the assistant treasurer was received and ordered placed on file.

Following the reports of the officers was held the election of five trustees for the ensuing year. The secretary announced that those whose terms matured at this time were: Prof. G. Frederick Wright, Oberlin; Col. James Kilbourne, Columbus; Prof. C. L. Martzolff, New Lexington; Judge J. H. Anderson, Columbus; and Mr. R. E. Hills, Delaware (selected at the meeting of the Executive Committee on September 19, 1904, to fill out the unexpired term of Prof. J. P. MacLean, resigned). After some discussion as to the procedure to be followed in the election of these trustees, it was moved by Mr. E. F. Wood and seconded by Mr. W. H. Hunter, that the five trustees whose time expires at this meeting, be nominated and re-elected, and that the rules of the society be suspended and the secretary be authorized to cast the ballot of the society for the five men named. This motion was declared carried. (Ten yeas, six nays, and several not voting). The secretary, in accordance with the action of the meeting thus taken, cast the ballot as instructed, and the five men designated were declared elected as trustees of the society to serve for three years; that is, until the annual meeting in 1908.

The secretary here called attention to the fact that at the meeting of the Executive Committee of the Trustees (September 19, 1903), after the death of Trustee Hon. A. R. McIntire, the committee selected Judge Rush R. Sloane, Sandusky, to fill the vacancy. The election of Judge Sloane, according to the law of the society, could be, however, only until the next annual meeting, which was held June 3, 1904. Judge Sloane was not present at the meeting being absent in Europe, and no action was taken in the matter. Therefore, in accordance with the constitution, which states:

Sec. 1, Art. III. Trustees "shall serve for three years, each, from the time of their election, or until their successors are elected and qualified,"

It is encumbent upon this meeting to take some action in regard to the trusteeship in question. It was moved, seconded and carried that the rules be suspended and that the secretary cast the ballot for Judge Rush R. Sloane as trustee for the next ensuing year, namely, from this annual meeting to the annual meeting of the society in 1906. This the secretary did and Judge Sloane was declared elected.

The Board of Trustees, therefore, as now constituted and for the ensuing year will be as follows:

TERMS EXPIRE IN 1906.

J. Warren Keifer	Springfield.
Bishop B. W. Arnett...........................	Wilberforce.
Hon. S. S. Rickly.............................	Columbus.
Mr. G. F. Bareis..............................	Canal Winchester.
Judge Rush R. Sloane.........................	Sandusky.

TERMS EXPIRE IN 1907.

General R. Brinkerhoff.........................	Mansfield.
Hon. M. D. Follett.............................	Marietta.
Hon. D. J. Ryan..............	Columbus.
Rev. H. A. Thompson..........................	Dayton.
Mr. W. H. Hunter.............................	Chillicothe.

TERMS EXPIRE IN 1908.

Prof. G. Frederick Wright......................	Oberlin.
Col. James Kilbourne..........................	Columbus.
Hon. R. E. Hills..............................	Delaware.
Prof. C. L. Martzolff	New Lexington.
Judge J. H. Anderson..........................	Columbus.

APPOINTED BY THE GOVERNOR.

TERMS EXPIRE AS INDICATED.

Rev. N. B. C. Love, Toledo, 1906.
Col. J. W. Harper, Cincinnati, 1906.
Hon. M. S. Greenough, Cleveland, 1907.
Prof. M. R. Andrews, Marietta, 1907.
Prof. B. F. Prince, Springfield, 1908.
Mr. E. O. Randall, Columbus, 1908.

The routine business of the society having been practically completed, President Brinkerhoff stated that he thought the subject of securing from the legislature an appropriation for a suitable building for the use of the society ought to be considered and some anticipatory action taken at this meeting, although he did not know exactly what form such action should assume. He stated the desirability of a building, alluding to the magnificent buildings of the Wisconsin Historical Society, which cost nearly $600,000 and was furnished by the state, and the New York Historical Society building which is now being erected and which when completed will cost in the neighborhood of $700,000, which amount, however, has been obtained by private subscriptions from the wealthy members of the society. He said there had been a diversity of opinion among the trustees as to where such a building of our society should be located, whether "down town" in the heart of the city, where it would be easily accessible to the public, or whether on the campus of the Ohio State University where it would not be so accessible to the public but would be in closer touch with the university and the educational interests of the state. Personally, at first he had favored the city location, but had become converted to the idea that it would be difficult to get the legislature to provide a separate site for such a building, the state not owning any ground in the city which could be properly assigned for such a purpose; whereas, the State University had plenty of ground which would cost the state nothing, and moreover the trustees of the university would welcome its location on their grounds and supply light, heat and many other necessary expenses for its maintenance.

This subject elicited much discussion, and it was finally decided that the matter be referred to the Executive Committee with the direction that they take the matter up at the earliest possible moment and make such report and at such time to the society as the committee might deem advisable.

Prof. Mills desired to say, while the building matter was being discussed, he thought it only due the university that it be credited with doing all that was possible under existing circumstances for the society. They had given the society the use of a large part of the building known as Page Hall, and in fact, were doing their utmost to care for the present needs of the museum and library. There certainly could be no complaint on the part of the society against the Trustees, President or other officers of the university as they were in hearty sympathy with the work of the society and were prepared to do everything possible and legitimate in the furtherance of its progress.

The President at this point introduced Prof. J. H. Beal, of Scio College, a life member of the society and formerly a member of the legislature. Prof. Beal in a few graceful words acknowledged his interest in the society, complimenting its publications and work, and stated facetiously that he belonged to that section of the society which Mr. Hunter had designated as "the crank section," namely, the archæological branch. He had visited nearly all of the prehistoric works of the Mississippi Valley, and hoped to visit in due time all those he had omitted. He thought one of the chief purposes of this society should be to get the people of Ohio interested in the preservation of the prehistoric earthworks.

Mr. Archer B. Hulbert, a life member of the society and now the distinguished author of "Historic Highways," was present and spoke in a complimentary vein of the work of the society, saying, however, that in his travels about the state he had concluded that the society was more popularly known for its archæological work than for its historical work. He thought the society ought to strengthen its work along the line of the collecting of publications of original historical papers, mentioning as an example the original publications in the British Museum of Boquet's Expedition into Ohio in 1764. He thought there was a great field for activity among the individual members of the society in seeking out valuable original manuscripts and securing them for the society for publication. There were already in the library of the Wisconsin Historical Society and the Carnegie Library at Pittsburg many valuable documents pertaining to the early history of Ohio, copies of which could be secured for the Quarterly of the society.

Prof. John D. H. McKinley, a life member of the society, said a few words complimentary of the work of the society and especially emphasizing the apparent need of the society for a permanent home for the manuscripts and documents which the previous speakers intimated that we ought to collect. It was difficult to secure these valuable documents so long as we have not permanent and secure quarters for their safety and accessibility.

He realized that the next great field for the energies of this society is in harmonious action concerning a building.

Prof. Frederick Starr, the eminent ethnologist of Chicago University, being present as the guest of the society, was called upon for an expression of his views. Prof. Starr proved to be a fluent and most interesting speaker. He stated that he had been greatly interested in the proceedings of the meeting; that his knowledge of the Ohio State Archæological and Historical Society began at the Buffalo Exposition, where, under the direction of Prof. W. C. Mills, our Curator, there was a most commendable exhibit of the archæological department of the society and a gold medal awarded the society as it thoroughly deserved. He was connected with the Louisiana Purchase Exposition at St. Louis as lecturer on the subject of ethnology and instructed a class of students for many weeks during the continuance of the exposition. He saw much of the exhibit of our society and of the work accomplished by Prof. Mills. He particularly commended the efficiency with which Dr. Mills explained to the teachers, school children, visitors and "archæological cranks" the objects of interest which the exhibit of the society presented. Prof. Starr said he was somewhat familiar with the publications of our society and that they were exceedingly high-grade in character and form. He knew of none better. Years ago he made the acquaintance of Prof. F. W. Putnam of the Peabody Museum, and was familiar with the history of the securing of Serpent Mound by Prof. Putnam through the influence of the Boston ladies for Harvard University and its subsequent transfer to our society. That was a much desired achievement both for Prof. Putnam and the Ohio Society, in whose hands it ought to be. The possession now by the Ohio society of Fort Ancient and Serpent Mound, the two greatest and most interesting relics of the mound builders in the United States, places this society permanently in the forefront of archæological institutions in this country; and naturally makes it conspicuous throughout the United States and the world at large. He commended the work of Secretary Randall as active executive of the society, and for his work in the historical department and then emphatically expressed himself to the effect that the society should secure a building that would be exclusively its own and not be combined with any other state interest such, for instance, as the state library.

The remarks of Prof. Starr met with most hearty approval on the part of the meeting, which then adjourned.

ANNUAL MEETING OF THE TRUSTEES.

Immediately following the adjournment of the annual meeting of the society there was held the annual meeting of the Board of Trustees. There were present at this meeting, Judge J. H. Anderson, Prof. M. R. Andrews, Mr. G. F. Bareis, Gen. R. Brinkerhoff, Judge M. D. Follett, Hon. M. S. Greenough, Hon. R. E. Hills, Mr. W. H. Hunter, Col. John W. Harper, Prof. C. L. Martzolff, Prof. B. F. Prince, Mr. E. O. Randall, Judge Rush R. Sloane, Prof. G. Frederick Wright.

Secretary Randall called the meeting to order. Prof. G. Frederick Wright was asked to act as temporary chairman. Secretary Randall read the minutes of the last annual meeting of the trustees, which were approved without alteration except that the name of W. H. Hunter should be inserted in the list of the trustees selected to serve on the Executive Committee. His name occurred in the minutes of the proceedings of the Executive Committee but without indicating his authority to so act.

The trustees immediately proceeded to the election of officers for the ensuing year. The officers elected unanimously were: *President,* Gen. R. Brinkerhoff; *First Vice President,* Mr. G. F. Bareis; *Second Vice President,* Prof. G. Frederick Wright; *Treasurer,* Hon. S. S. Rickly; *Assistant Treasurer,* Mr. E. F. Wood; *Secretary and Editor,* Mr. E. O. Randall; *Curator and Librarian,* Prof. W. C. Mills. The Trustees selected to serve on the Executive Committee in addition to the officers who are ex-officio members, were, Messrs. Greenough, Hunter, Martzolff, Prince and Ryan.

Prof. Martzolff called the attention of the trustees to the fact that Mr. Obadiah Brokaw, of Stockport, Morgan County, had erected a monument on the site of the Big Bottom Massacre. Since erecting such monument Mr. Brokaw is anxious in regard to the future care of the same and the ground immediately sur-

GOVERNOR HERRICK   TRUSTEE GREENOUGH

     GENERAL BRINKERHOFF   SECRETARY RANDALL

[From a photograph taken by Mr. J. W. Newton at the Fort Ancient Station, June 2, 1905.]

rounding it. In an interview between Prof. Martzolff and Mr. Brokaw on this matter, the latter had intimated that he might be willing to accept the services of the society in some scheme of co-operation in regard to the future care of the monument and property. This subject was finally referred to the Executive Committee for discretionary action.

A committee of three, consisting of Trustees Randall, Wright and Ryan was appointed to revise the constitution and by-laws and present that revision to the members of the society at the next annual meeting.

The question of salaries for the officers receiving compensation for services was referred to the Executive Committee with power to act. The Y. M. C. A. was thanked for use of their rooms for the annual meeting.

LECTURE BY PROF. STARR.

The proceedings of the annual meeting on the afternoon of Friday, June 2d, were fittingly followed in the evening by a lecture given by Prof. Frederick Starr, of Chicago University, in the Auditorium of the Ohio State University. Prof. Starr's subject was "The Aztecs of Mexico," a subject with which the professor is not only exceedingly familiar, but upon which he is probably the highest living authority. Prof. Starr has visited Mexico many times during the past years and made lengthy and most careful studies of the remains of the ancient Aztec tribe. His lecture was intensely interesting, bringing as it did the subject at first hand before the audience. It was illustrated by stere-optican views especially prepared by Prof. Starr. The lecturer gave a detailed account of the historic Aztec tribe of Indians, the extent of the territory over which they held dominion, their form of government, civilization and such of their history as has been preserved to the memory of the present generation. It would not be possible to do justice to the lecture by attempting even a synopsis of it in these pages. Prof. Starr overthrew many prevailing ideas concerning the nature of the Aztec people and particularly controverted the universally read descriptions of that people by such distinguished authors as Prescott and Lew Wallace, whose portrayals of the Aztecs, the lecturer stated, belong more to the realm of popular fiction than to that of accurate history. The lecturer gave it as a result of his studies that there was probably no racial relationship between the Aztecs and the so-called Mound Builders of the Mississippi and Ohio Valleys.

EXCURSION TO FORT ANCIENT.

On Saturday, June 3d, the society for the benefit of its members and invited guests, conducted an excursion to Fort Ancient. The party consisted of some sixty in number, among whom were Governor and Mrs. Myron T. Herrick; Col. Webb C. Hayes, Cleveland; Gen. J. Warren Keifer, Springfield; Hon. M. S. Greenough and Miss Greenough, Cleveland; Prof. and Mrs. G. Frederick Wright, Oberlin; Prof. Frederick Starr, University of Chicago; Prof. and Mrs. W. C. Mills; Hon. Tod B. Galloway; Gen. R. Brinkerhoff, Mansfield; Mr. and Mrs. Geo. F. Bareis and Miss Bareis, Canal Winchester; Mr. E. O. Randall; Dr. C. S. Means and Master Russell Means; Prof. M. R. Andrews, Marietta; Col. J. W. Harper, Cincinnati; Miss Kate R. Blair; Prof. W. R. Kersey; Prof. G. H. MacKnight; Prof. and Mrs. Herbert Osborn; Miss Anna Russell; Mr. D. E. Phillips; Mr. J. W. Newton; Miss Alice Brown; Miss Martha J. Maltby; Mr. and Mrs. C. A. Covert'and Miss Florence Covert; Mrs. N. E. Lovejoy; Mr. L. S. Wells; Rev. R. H. Cunningham; Mrs. Francis Sessions; Prof. J. H. Beal, Scio; Prof. Frank Cole; Miss Gertrude Hill, Los Angeles, Cal.; Mr. Sherman Randall; Mr. John L. W. Henney; Mr. E. F Wood; Mr. R. H. Platt and Masters Robert and Rutherford Platt; Mr. P. M. Wetmore; Mr. and Mrs. O. K. Ellis; Mr. Clarence Metters; Hon. Alex. Boxwell, Red Lion; Mr. L. B. Freeman, District Passenger Agent of Pennsylvania Lines, in charge of the party.

The party arrived at the fort about noon and after partaking of a lunch at the station inn proceeded in carriages up the hill to the fort. A halt was made at the Pavillion in the Old Fort, where speeches were made by Governor Herrick, Prof. Wright, Prof. Starr, and Prof. Mills, introduced by Mr. Randall. Prof. Mills made a brief statement of the general plan of the fort and contour of the earthworks. Prof. Wright gave a short history of the explorations which had been made among

the mounds, emphasizing the fact that foreigners — especially
the Englishmen — thought it worth while to take relics from the
American remains to the British and other museums. He said
that in fact to-day to study certain relics of American Mound
Builders it is necessary to go to Salisbury, England, which Prof.
Wright expects to visit this summer. It is only in the last fifteen
years, he continued, that Ohio has been alive to the subject. But
the work of the Ohio State Archæological and Historical Society
represents progress in this line, as the crowded quarters of the
society now reveal. The legislature should appreciate the value of
these things so that we may have a building in Columbus to hold
them. A building which will be the pride of the country. All
scholars of archæology should rejoice in the work of this society
for the past ten years.

Prof. Starr expressed a hope that in the future many other
famous remains of the mound builders might come into the possession of the archæological society and be preserved, as Fort
Ancient and Serpent Mound now are. But he said you must
have the people of the state behind you, you must have a legislature of sense and you must have a governor who will be in sympathy with you and not veto appropriations for such purposes.
You know there is an old saying, "New York for homes, Pennsylvania for barns, but Ohio for schools." It is true. I congratulate
you upon your schools of Ohio. Because of these schools you
have Fort Ancient and Serpent Mound saved.

Governor Herrick, who followed, answered Prof. Starr by
saying that the people might expect even more of the Executive
than merely to refrain from vetoing measures which the legislature might pass in behalf of the society. We should contribute
our part towards the preservation of the works for those who
come after us, he said. "I agree with Prof. Wright that we in
Ohio can afford to look after these, and I trust and hope that our
state exchequer from year to year can spare something to devote
to this purpose. I congratulate the people of Ohio that the evidences are that the race which lived here so long ago were a
virile race even as we are to-day."

Members of the party then strolled to various portions of
the Old and New Forts at their leisure, inspecting the exten-

sive and mysterious embankment and mounds, enjoying the beauty of the natural scenery which was in full splendor of spring verdure; and the delightful weather, for —

> "What is so rare as a day in June?
> Then, if ever, come perfect days;
> Then Heaven tries the earth if it be in tune,
> And over it softly her warm ear lays."

EDITORIALANA.

VOL. XIV. No. 3.   *E. O. Randall*   JULY, 1905

HISTORY OF THE MAUMEE RIVER BASIN.

There has just appeared from the press of Bowen & Slocum, Indianapolis and Toledo, a "History of the Maumee River Basin," from the earliest account to its organization into counties. The author is Dr. Charles Elihu Slocum, a life member of the Ohio State Archæological and Historical Society; he has contributed many interesting and valuable articles to its Quarterly, and for many years has been an indefatigable and enthusiastic student of early Ohio history. The work, as its name indicates, presumably deals with only the northwestern part of the state, one of the richest sections in historic lore, but Dr. Slocum's book, which contains some 650 pages of nearly 500 words to the page, naturally and at times necessarily deals with facts and events pertinent to the history of the entire state. This book is, therefore, to a very great degree, a history of Ohio. Indeed, both from its local limitation and its treatment of certain phases general to the whole state, it becomes not only valuable but is really an indispensable addition to the historical bibliography of Ohio. The interest of this book, therefore, is a general one as well as special.

Dr. Slocum with untiring zeal has gone largely to the initial sources for his information, namely, the original documents, as far as accessible, in the libraries of Canada, England and the United States. This gives a double value to his work. He has begun at the very beginning, his opening chapter being upon the geology of the Maume River basin, a most scholarly summary of the geological and topographical phases of the portion of the state in question. He discusses the earliest evidences of prehistoric man, following it, of course, with the narratives of the first explorers, namely the French and the British.

The long and complicated contests between the French and the British for the possession of this part of the Northwest Territory are entertainingly related. Dr. Slocum has made a comprehensive and devoted study of the character and history of the American Indian, particularly of the races and tribes of the American savages which occupied at various times the Ohio country. He has with much faithfulness and painstaking told of their character, mode of life, warfare, and their various relationships with the French, English and the Americans. Dr. Slocum throughout the entire book insists upon designating the "American Indian" as the

"Aborigine," which may be in itself a proper appellation, but which is so seldom used by other writers that in this instance it often tends to the confusion of the reader as for example when he speaks of "The French and Aborigine War" instead of the "French and Indian War" as it was known. Dr. Slocum has accomplished a great work. We know of no historical monograph on this part of American history which so thoroughly and correctly shows up the continued and persistent treachery of the British Government in its dealings with the Indians, whom they at will cajoled, employed and betrayed as allies in their warfare, first with the French and subsequently with the Americans. The author succinctly recounts the various British and Indian expeditions into Ohio previous to and during the period of the American Revolution. Dr. Slocum clearly portrays in proper color and relief the relation of this western history to the colonial history in the success of the Americans in their war with England and the organization of the American republic, which was the result of that war.

The geographical territory which this history specifically covers embraces many of the most important and picturesque events in the earliest history of our state, such as the Conspiracy of Pontiac, the Confederation of Tecumseh, the Expeditions of Scott, Wilkinson, Harmar, St. Clair, and particularly that of Anthony Wayne; also the chief western incidents of the War of 1812.

The early pioneer history is followed by chapters on the drainage system of the Maumee River Basin and the organization of the counties in the Northwest. His last chapter is devoted to the development of communication, public lands, roads — private and public — schools, libraries and so on. Dr. Slocum writes in a clear, concise, indeed rather compact style, and, although the book is as we have indicated, rather voluminous, there is no waste material and the contents consist of nothing but purely historical matter. The whole scheme is on the plane of high historical character. The value of the book is not marred by any biographical sketches or historical gossip, as the slang phrase is "It is genuine goods all the way through," and the doctor has made a most valuable and interesting addition to the historical literature not only of our own state but to the Northwest. It is copiously illustrated with half-tone cuts, maps, and so on. The mechanical effects of the book might be improved in some respects, but for this the author may not be responsible.

This book deserves to be in every library in the country, and no library in Ohio with any pretense to historical literature of the Buckeye State will be complete without it.

WATER HIGHWAYS AND CARRYING PLACES.

E. L. TAYLOR, COLUMBUS.

The 2d day of May, 1497, was one of the most eventful for great results for good of any in human history. On that day, John Cabot, a Venetian by birth, but who was then living at the old sea-faring town of Bristol, on the west coast of England, with eighteen hardy British sailors weighed anchor on the small, but good ship "Matthew," and passed out upon the broad and turbulent waters of the Atlantic on a voyage of discovery. It is probable, but not certain, that his son, Sebastian, accompanied him on this voyage. The adventure was entirely at the expense of Cabot. He had, however, obtained from King Henry VII., royal permission to carry the British flag, and was commissioned to "seek out, discover and find whatever lands, countries, regions or provinces of the heathens or infidels, in whatever part of the world they may be which before this time have been unknown to all Christians."

Further, he was required, if he should be so fortunate as to return, to report at the port of Bristol and to "take a fifth part of the whole capital, whether in goods or money for our use." The return was made in the following August, but without "goods or money," and with nothing but a vague report that they had discovered land in the north Atlantic, hitherto unknown to the civilized world.

All that could be reported of the voyage was that after leaving the port of Bristol, the vessel held her way to the westward, and late in June they came in sight of land, and after sailing some leagues to the south along the coast, they went ashore and so were the first Europeans to set foot on the continent of North America. They had no thought that they were standing upon the shore of a great and hitherto unknown continent, or that their discovery of land in these far off waters was, or would become of any special importance or significance. They were not looking for a new continent, but were hoping to reach the east coast of Asia, known in Europe since the time of Marco Polo, as "Cathay." Cabot did not live to know that he had discovered a great new continent, which was then and had been for many thousands of years occupied by a race or races of savages, whose energies had been spent in the hunt of wild beasts and in waging war upon each other, which wars between savage tribes and nations were wars of extermination in so far as they could make them.

CABOT.

The place of Cabot's landing has not been definitely determined and probably never can be, but a committee appointed by the Royal Geographical Society of Canada, reported in 1895, that the weight of evidence is that it was on Cape Breton, which is on the extreme north east coast of the Province of Nova Scotia. At the place of their landing they found no human inhabitants, but did find snares and devices for taking fish and game, which were evidently designed by human minds and wrought out by human hands. But wherever it was, they seem to have unfurled and planted the British flag and made some kind of proclamation to the effect that they took possession of the land in the name of the King of Great Britain. Nothing could seem to be more idle or meaningless than this proclamation or outcry to the winds and waves of this unknown, desolate rock-bound coast, and yet it became in time to be the basis of whatever title Great Britain had to the continent of North America.

After Cabot, numerous explorers came to our shores, but they seem to have been satisfied with coasting along the shores with no purpose or effort to penetrate the interior, or learn what lay hidden behind the desolate coast line. It was not until 1534 that the mouth of the St. Lawrence River was discovered by Jacques Cartier, and it was not until the next year (1535) that any successful attempt was made to explore the interior of the northern portion of the continent to which the St. Lawrence was the great highway.

JACQUES CARTIER.

In that year (1535) Jacques Cartier, a French navigator, ascended the St. Lawrence to the point of the present site of Montreal. The great Lachine rapids prevented further progress. This was thirty-eight years after Cabot's discovery of the coast, during which time no special effort seems to have been made by English or other European navigators to penetrate the interior of the northern portion of the continent, or to learn anything of its nature or conditions. This inaction was in strange contrast with the activity of the Spaniards in their enterprises farther to the the south. It was some fifteen years after Cabot's discovery that the Spaniards first saw or set foot on the North American continent, and yet before Cartier's discovery of the St. Lawrence, they had overrun and conquered Mexico, and Peru; and it was but four years later that De Soto penetrated Louisiana, Alabama, Georgia, Mississippi, Missouri and Arkansas, and in 1642 wearied, worn and exhausted from three years of wide and fruitless wanderings in search of gold and treasures, died on the banks of the Mississippi and was buried beneath its turbid waters. But it is stranger still that the matter of interior exploration was allowed to rest with nothing added to the geographical information of the interior, beyond Cartier's exploits for the long period of sixty-eight years.

It was not until 1603 that Champlain appeared upon the scene, filled with the spirit of adventure and discovery, and determined to penetrate the recesses of the vast and gloomy wilderness and bring to light the secrets it had held hidden for so many ages.

CHAMPLAIN.

Samuel Champlain, a French navigator, sailed up the St. Lawrence in 1603 and reached the point (Montreal) where Cartier had stopped sixty-eight years before. He was a most ambitious and self-reliant man, capable of great efforts and of wonderful endurance. He was not then equipped for further explorations, but resolved that he would return at the earliest time possible and explore the depths of the vast and gloomy forest that stretched out before him in every direction as he stood on the top of Mount Real and viewed the wondrous scene as Cartier had done in 1535. It was five years before he could carry out his purpose, but in 1608 he re-appeared on the St. Lawrence equipped not only for explorations, but for the founding of a colony in the new world. On the vessel with him came a "French lad" then about eighteen years of age, Stephen Brulé, destined to become the greatest interior explorer of his time and to lead a most singular and strenuous life and end with a most tragic death.

When Champlain reached the site of the present city of Quebec, he determined that there he would found his colony and so proceeded to clear the space between the river bank and the stupendous cliffs upon which the City of Quebec now stands, and to erect log houses, where he proposed to spend the winter before proceeding with his intended explorations. Brulé assisted in this work and so became one of the founders of the City of Quebec, now the most interesting, historically considered, of any city on the continent.

The winter was exceedingly severe and the colony suffered greatly, but the spring brought relief and Champlain, having made an alliance with the Hurons and Algonquins, set out for the Iroquois country, which was what is now embraced in the State of New York. The Iroquois were the fiercest and most war-like of all the tribes known, and after they had been supplied with fire arms by the Hollanders and English, they carried their war expeditions from the coast of New England to the Mississippi and from the extreme of the northern lakes, and to Virginia and the Carolinas. They swept from Ohio the Eries, one of their own tribe, and all other tribes having before that time had occupancy within the borders of the states of Pennsylvania, Ohio, Indiana and most of Illinois. Those wide and savage excursions and campaigns could only be carried on by means of the "water-ways" which were connected by "carrying places," by the French called "portages."

It is the purpose of this paper to set out as accurately as we can, the main thoroughfares which were traveled by the Aborigines in their savage forays, and by whom they were first

seen and traversed by white men.   Miss Lucy Elliot Keeler has
aptly denominated these highways as "the roads that run."

Champlain had learned from the Indians that there was an
ample water-way from the St. Lawrence to the Atlantic at the
present port of New York and the intention was to ascend the
Richelieu, which is the outlet of the waters of Lakes George and
Champlain, and by carrying their birch canoes from the head of
those waters over the "carrying place" to reach the waters of

PORTAGE OR CARRYING-PLACE.

Hudson River as they flowed down from the Adirondack Mountains, and so surprise and destroy the villages of the Iroquois
in the Mohawk Valley.   But the plan failed, as when near the
head of Lake Champlain they unexpectedly met with a strong
war party of the Iroquois when a battle ensued in which Champlain and his Indian allies were successful and vanquished their
enemies with great slaughter.   This was the first time that fire
arms had been used in Indian warfare among the northern In-

dians, and the Iroquois were so terrified by the noise and deadly execution of fire arms in the hands of the Frenchmen that they fled in every direction and were pursued and slaughtered in great numbers by the savage allies of Champlain. Soon after this decisive battle, Champlain and his Indian allies returned to the St. Lawrence, from whence he sailed for France, and the Indians returned to their own country. He was, however, again on the St. Lawrence the next spring (1610) where he had engaged to meet the Hurons and Algonquins near the mouth of the Richelieu River. Champlain arrived in advance of his Indian allies, and encamped awaiting their coming. While waiting there, word was received by him that the Hurons had surrounded a barricade of one hundred Iroquois, near the mouth of the Richelieu, where a desperate battle was being waged. He and the Indians with him hurried to the assistance of the Hurons. The barricade was stormed and all the warriors within were killed or taken prisoners. Not one escaped. After this battle Champlain arranged to return to France but with the agreement to return the next spring (1611). It was further arranged that the Hurons should take the young man Brulé to their far off Huron country and that Champlain was to take with him to France a young Huron (Savignon), selected by his tribe for that purpose. They were to meet again in June, 1611, and exchange hostages. This was accordingly done.

In this year spent with the Hurons Brulé had acquired their language and habits of life and was able thereafter to act as an interpreter for Champlain in his intercourse with the Hurons and Algonquins both as to war and trade.

Champlain made in all ten visits to the St. Lawrence from 1603 to 1633, during which time he had learned from the Indians much concerning the lakes and rivers of the north-west, but as for himself he discovered or first saw no lakes or rivers of importance except Lake Champlain and the Richelieu River. He wandered far and wide in many directions but it cannot be claimed for him that he was the original first white man to discover or see any of these great natural highways except as before mentioned. In all his wide wanderings, Brulé seemed to have been in advance of him. Nevertheless, Champlain is entitled to the credit, in large part at least, for directing the discoveries made by Brulé.

Champlain has been frequently and generally accredited with being the first "white man" to see the waters of Lake Ontario, but this claim cannot be allowed, as it is surely incorrect. In fact, it can have no support, except upon the assumption that the explorations of Brulé were the explorations of Champlain.

In the month of September, 1615, Champlain had concentrated his few Frenchmen and many Indians of the Huron and Algonquin tribes at Lake Simcoe in the Huron country, with a view of invading the country of the Iroquois, but before the warriors had all assembled, Brulé with twelve Hurons was dispatched to notify the Carantouans, who were allies of the Hurons and other Canadian tribes, and who had promised to assist them in the invasion of the Iroquois country.

Lake Simcoe is directly north from the mouth of the Humber river, near where the city of Toronto now stands. It was but three or at most four days' travel for Brulé and the Indians with him to reach the upper or western end of Lake Ontario and by crossing that end of the lake they would be within the Iroquois country at or near the mouth of the Niagara River; and so if they were fortunate enough to escape the fierce Iroquois, while passing through their country, would reach the Carantouan villages by the shortest and quickest route possible.

The Carantouan Indians were at that time living on the upper waters of the Susquehanna in northern Pennsylvania. Brulé and his Indian escorts reached the Carantouan villages without mishap or delay and urged that tribe, friendly to the Canadian Indians and relentless enemies of the Iroquois, to furnish five hundred warriors, which they had promised, to join with Champlain and his allies in an attack upon Onondaga village.

Brulé set out from Lake Simcoe, directly south, on the 8th of September, 1615, and some days later, Champlain with his Indian allies started for the mouth of the Trent River, which is near where the city of Kingston, Canada, now stands. Brulé's route took him direct to the mouth of the Humber river (Toronto). That they traveled with all speed and haste may be assumed, as their mission was to notify the Carantouans to be present near the village of Onondaga by the time that Champlain should reach this important stronghold which was the objective point of the expedition. Champlain and his allies on the other hand had a much longer and more difficult route. They were required to take with them canoes for the entire party so as to cross the numerous streams and small lakes which intervene between Lake Simcoe and the mouth of the Trent River. They were also required to stop at different times in order to procure a supply of game and fish for their sustenance. Brulé reached the Carantouan villages without hindrance or delay, but the Indians were slow in assembling, and with their feasting and dancing always incident to going to war much delay was had and he was not able to bring them to the point of attack until Champlain and his Canadian Indians had been repulsed at the above named village. Champlain's retreat was by the same line by which he came, and he finally reached the Huron country where he was compelled to spend the winter with them on the shores of Lake Huron (now called Georgian Bay). "The roads that run" had been congealed into ice and the thawing suns of spring had to be awaited.

Brulé reached the mouth of the Humber and stood upon the banks of Lake Ontario many days, if not weeks before Champlain reached the mouth of the Trent River near Kingston, from which point he first viewed the waters of Ontario. The route taken by Brulé with his Indian guides to Lake Ontario was less than half the distance of the route taken by Champlain, and it is certain that Brulé not only saw Lake Ontario but crossed it before Champlain had reached the mouth of the Trent river. Both Champlain and Brulé had long been familiar with the fact that such a lake existed but neither of them had before that time seen its waters. The best and shortest route from the Huron country to Ontario and the St. Lawrence was that which Brulé took to reach Lake Ontario and thence along the north side of that lake to its outlet, and thence along the descending waters of the St. Lawrence to Montreal and Quebec. But in the time of war between the Indians in Canada and the Iroquois this route could not be used except in such force as to be able to contend with such parties of hostile savages as might be met. This is what caused the

Hurons and Algonquins to adopt the long, difficult and circuitous route of the Ottawa, Lake Nipissing and the French River in order to reach their homes along the borders of Lake Huron and Lake Simcoe.

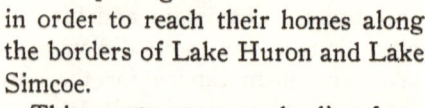

This great water-way leading from the waters of New York Harbor to the St. Lawrence is about four hundred and fifty miles in length, with only seven or eight miles of *portage* or "carrying place." The Hudson river furnishes about one hundred and fifty miles of this water-way, and lakes George and Champlain and the Richelieu about three hundred miles.

It was a singular coincidence that at the same time Champlain was exploring and making war on the waters of the lake which bears his name, Henry Hudson, an English navigator, was exploring the waters of the Hudson river which bears his name, so in the same year this entire water-way was made known to Europeans.

The Hudson river was not, as is generally assumed, discovered by Hudson, but by Giovanni da Verrazzano in 1524, who was sailing under a commission from Francis I. of France. Verrazzano sailed into what is now the port of New York and some little distance up the Hudson. This was eighty-five years before Henry Hudson saw that stream. In the meantime the French fur traders had penetrated that river at least as far as the present city of Albany, but it was not until the year 1609 that the entire water-way from the St. Lawrence to the port of New York became known to Europeans.

For what thousands of years this great route was known and used by the Aborigines can never be known, but certainly from the remote time when human beings came to inhabit that part of the country.   Since the coming of white men with a view of possessing the country, there has been innumerable war expeditions conducted along this great water route between the French and their Canadian allies and the English and their allies, the Iroquois.   Important battles and massacres and conflicts, of every nature, have since that time taken place on these waters and along their shores.   It is not within our purpose to enumerate even important war expeditions, but we will be pardoned for recalling a few of the later and more important engagements which took place, in which "white men" were engaged, as showing the importance of this route as considered by the French and English and the people of our colonies.

On the 16th of April, 1755, a commission was issued to Col. William Johnson of New York, appointing him major general of the forces to be sent by this route to Canada to expel the French from Crown Point, where they had strongly entrenched themselves.   Sir William was to have in his commnad 3,500 colonists and British, and 1,000 Indians.   He commenced his forward movement early in August, 1755, and on the 14th of August arrived at Fort Edward where he was joined by 250 more Indians.   In the meantime Baron Dieskau, in command of the French and their Indian allies, was marshalling his forces to resist the incursion of Sir William and his army.

On the 7th of September the forces met and a desperate battle ensued, which, after varying fortunes, resulted in favor of Sir William and his forces.   Sir William and Baron Dieskau were both wounded and the latter was taken prisoner and sent to New York and thence to England.   He was succeeded in command by Montcalm, who, on July 8, 1758, with 3,600 men successfully defended Ticonderoga against the British General Abercrombie who assaulted that place with 14,000 men, of which he lost 2,000 killed and wounded.

This water-way was also the route taken by Gen. Robert Montgomery in command of the continental troops in the invasion of Canada in 1775. He succeeded in taking all the forts on these waters and along the St. Lawrence until he reached the City of Quebec, which was the great objective point, where, in an assault made upon that stronghold December 31st, 1775, his forces were repulsed with heavy loss, General Montgomery being among the dead.

General Burgoyne was placed in command of the British Canadian forces in America when he arrived early in 1777. He came with a large British (Hessian) force of about 8,000 troops to the St. Lawrence River where he invited the Indians to join him, many of whom did so. He advanced along the line of the Richelieu and Lake Champlain and Lake George, until he reached the headwaters of the last named lake, with a view of taking possession and holding the line of the Hudson River, but his plans were frustrated. He was hindered, delayed and defeated at Stillwater, New York, September 19th, and again at Freeman's Farm, October 7th, and was compelled to surrender with his whole army near Saratoga, October 17, 1777. So it will be seen that this great highway from the waters of the St. Lawrence to the waters of the Atlantic at New York has been, within historic times, a great military highway.

Henry Hudson was most fortunate in having his name stamped upon this important river. Not only the Hudson river received his name, although not discovered by him, but Hudson's Bay and Hudson's Strait will forever bear his name, although he was not the original discoverer or navigator of either.

It is certain from maps and charts of former navigators, particularly that of Sebastian Cabot, that Hudson's Bay had been entered and partially explored nearly a hundred years before Hudson entered those waters. It was on this voyage to Hudson's Bay that he met his sad fate. The ship's crew mutinied and placed him and his son and seven of the seamen in an open boat and set them adrift on the desolate and gloomy waters of Hudson's Bay. No trace of them was ever found, although when the facts became known in England a searching expedition was sent out to look for them. They undoubtedly perished in the waves of that storm-swept and lonely sea.

E'TIENNE (STEPHEN) BRULE'.

As we have before seen Stephen Brulé came to Quebec in 1608 which was the second visit of Champlain to the waters of the St. Lawrence. He was with Champlain at the battle on the lake now known by that name, in 1609. He remained on the St. Lawrence during the winter of 1609-10, when he again joined Champlain in a war expedition, and participated in the battle of June, 1610, near the mouth of the Richelieu River, where a hundred Iroquois who had barricaded themselves, were entirely destroyed by Champlain and his Indian allies. In June, 1610, he went to spend a year with the Hurons in their country on the waters of Lake Huron at the foot of what is now called Georgian Bay. His route was up the Ottawa River to the mouth of the Mattawan, thence up that stream to the "carrying place" leading to Lake Nipissing, thence across that lake to its overflow the French river, thence down that river to the waters of Lake Huron, and thence along the east coast of that great lake to the country of the Hurons. Brulé was certainly the first "white man" or European that ever passed over any part of that long and difficult route or saw any of these lands or waters. In the spring of 1611, he returned by the same way, when the Indians came to barter their furs on the banks of the St. Lawrence and to exchange him for "Savignon" the young Indian whom Champlain had taken to France the year before.

In July (1611) Champlain returned to France and Brulé remained among the Indians of Canada for two years and until Champlain's return in 1613. During this time he roamed far and wide in the wilds of the Indian country.

In 1615 Champlain was again on the St. Lawrence and agreed to go with the Hurons and Algonquins to the Huron country with a view from there of invading the Onondaga country which was in the very center of the Iroquois tribes. Their principal village was in the vicinity of Oneida Lake, New York. The place of assembling was Lake Simcoe in the Huron country and about one hundred miles north of the present city of Toronto.

As we have before seen, Brulé separated from Champlain and his army and left them at Lake Simcoe, and with two birch canoes and twelve Indians for an escort, descended by way of numerous small lakes and other waters to the mouth of the Humber River. This was to the Indians a well known highway by which Lake Huron and Lake Ontario were connected, and, except in times of war, was the best and most desirable route from the Huron country to the St. Lawrence. Brulé crossed the upper end of Lake Ontario to a point at or near the Niagara River and from thence passed entirely through the Iroquois country to the upper waters of the Susquehanna, in Pennsylvania. After the defeat at Onondaga, of Champlain and his allies, Brulé was compelled to retrace his way to the Carantouan villages.

During the winter of 1615-1616, the restless spirit of Brulé impelled him to explore the Susquehanna to its mouth where it empties into the Chesapeake Bay from which he returned again to the Carantouan country, and the next spring the Carantouans gave him an escort of five or six warriors to act as guides to pilot him back to the Huron villages. He was taken prisoner by the Senecas while passing through their country and narrowly escaped death by torture. However, he ingratiated himself with the Senecas, and the next spring (1617) returned to his Huron friends. Here he seems to have rested and occupied himself in the Indian fashion of hunting and trapping until the next spring (1618), when he returned with the Hurons as they went to the St. Lawrence to trade. Here he met Champlain, from whom he had been separated for almost three years, and related to him his various and remarkable adventures. In the last named year Champlain returned to France, but Brulé remained among the Indians. Champlain says of him that he had at that time been "eight years with the Indians" and had acquired their various languages.

When, in 1618, Brulé had arrived from the Indian country and met Champlain at Three Rivers on the St. Lawrence, he was urged by Champlain to continue his exploration to the northward and westward from the mouth of the French river from which country they had received reports of copper mines and had in fact seen specimens of copper which the Indians brought from that country. It is probable that in the summer of 1618 or 1619 he went north along the North Channel to the country of the

Beavers, who then had their homes in the region east of the falls of the St. Mary's. In the summer of 1821 he was again on the St. Lawrence from which he returned to the Huron country where he met his future companion and fellow voyager, Grenolle.

The following diagram will sufficiently indicate the lines which Brulé traveled as the first "white man."

BRULE' AND GRENOLLE.

In 1621 Brulé was again in the Huron country from which place with a companion, a young Frenchman named Grenolle, he started for an extended exploration to the north and west with a view of ascertaining the character not only of the lakes and rivers and Indian tribes but to locate if possible the copper mines of which they long had been informed existed in that country. Leaving the Hurons they urged their canoe past the mouth of the French river and proceeded northward past the Manitoulin islands along the North Channel to the falls of St. Mary's. The entire distance from the mouth of the French river to the falls of St. Marys was unexplored (unless by Brulé in 1618 or 1619) and to Europeans unknown, except by such indefinite and vague reports as they might have received from the Indians. There is but little that is definite about this expedition to Lake Superior, but as they were on an expedition of general discovery with the intention of enlarging the geographical knowledge of the white man, it cannot be supposed that two such venturesome spirits as Brulé and Grenolle would have stopped short at the falls of St. Mary's. They would naturally and necessarily want to know more about the waters beyond from which this vast overflow of clear, cold water came, rushing over one of the most stupendous and beautiful rapids in the world. Standing on the banks of the rapids they necessarily looked out upon the waters of Lake Superior and so were the first white men to see and discover the greatest fresh water body on the globe. They were gone on this expedition for a period of two years, which would give them ample time to have reached the head or western end of Lake Superior where are now the cities of Duluth and Superior. The exact point, however, to which they urged their canoe is not known, but as one of their main objects was to solve the question as to the "North Sea," now known as Lake Superior, it is impossible to suppose that they stopped short of their main purpose. That they went on the waters of Lake Superior to a nation that, to some extent at least, worked the copper mines, of which they had previously heard, there can be no doubt, as they brought back with them a large ingot of copper which could not have been had short of the region of Lake Superior. It is strong evidence of their having reached the extreme head of Lake Superior that the Indians say that the journey from the Huron country was thirty days, while Brulé reported it as four hundred leagues, showing that Brulé's estimate was his own and not what he had learned from the Indians.

The historian Sagard says that Grenolle reported "that a nation living one hundred leagues from the Hurons worked in a copper mine and that he had seen among them several girls who had the ends of their noses cut off having committed offenses against chastity."

Sagard (one of the early priests to visit the Huron waters) who met and traveled with Brulé and Savignon on their return trip down the Ottawa, says of Brulé "that this bold voyager, with a Frenchman named Grenolle, made a long journey and returned with an ingot of red copper and with a description of Lake Superior who defined it as very large, requiring nine days to reach its upper extremity and discharging itself into Lake Huron by a fall."

It is possible and even probable that Brulé was the first white man to see the stupendous falls of Niagara. He was in that immediate vicinity at least on two occasions as early as 1615-16, which was before any other European had visited that region. It may be assumed that Brulé, who was so intensely inclined to see all objects and places of interest, would not have allowed Niagara to escape him.

The last few years of Brulé's life he remained entirely with the Hurons, who in 1632 for some unknown cause barbarously murdered him after a residence among them of more than twenty years. Their savagery did not stop at his death. It is most revolting says Parkman, that "In their wild and horrible ferocity to take vengeance on their victim, they feasted upon his lifeless remains."

The following diagram will sufficiently indicate the lines which Brulé and Grenolle traveled as the first "white men."

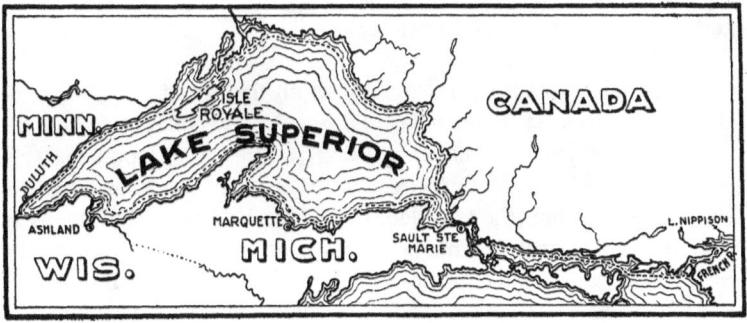

LE CARON.

For more than two hundred and fifty years Friar Joseph Le-Caron received credit generally for having been the first white man to pass up the Ottawa and the first to discover the waters of lakes Nipissing and Huron, and it is only of late years that this error has been corrected. Modern investigation has shown that he was entitled to no such distinction. He in fact discovered nothing whatever which added to the geographical knowledge of the country. He was a devout and zealous priest in the Catholic Church, and ardently anxious to convert savages to his faith, but he was in no sense an explorer and deserves no credit as such. He did not leave France until May, 1615, and in due time arrived at Quebec with three other priests of the Catholic Church. He was assigned to establish a mission among the Hurons, many of whom were then near Montreal where they had come to trade with the French, and he went direct to that place. Champlain had arranged with the Indians there assembled to join them in a campaign against the Iroquois before mentioned. LeCaron had nothing whatever to do with that expedition, but finding the Hurons having finished their bartering with the French traders on the St. Lawrence, were about to return to their own country preparatory to their campaign against the Iroquois, he determined to accompany them. He had no connection with the intended incursion into the country of the Iroquois. That had been arranged for by Champlain and the Indians, and LeCaron simply availed himself of the opportunity to obtain access to the Huron villages with a view only of propagating his religious faith. The Indians with whom LeCaron traveled left the St. Lawrence on the first of July, 1615. It was necessary for Champlain to postpone his departure for a few days, but on the 9th of July, he, with Brulé and another French lad (probably Grenolle) left the St. Lawrence to join in the expedition against the Iroquois. He reached the Huron country a few days after LeCaron and the Indians with whom he traveled, but Brulé had been for five years in that country and had made yearly trips with the Hurons to the St. Lawrence along the route of Lake Nipissing and the Ottawa river, and was as familiar with the route and the country as the Indians themselves.

Years before LeCaron ever saw an Indian, Brulé had lived with them and had acquired the language of different tribes in the regions where he had been; and he went along now with Champlain as his interpreter of the languages of the various tribes. The claim as to LeCaron was based upon nothing more substantial than the fact that the Indians with whom he traveled reached the Huron country a few days in advance of Champlain. Most of the early writers concerning the history of that time mention Brulé as having gone to live with the Indians in the summer of 1610, but they seem to have fallen into the habit of not considering him in their narrations. But when it comes to naming the "first European" or "white man" in connection with these explorations and discoveries Brulé cannot be ignored, but must be given place in history which rightly belongs to him.

LeCaron left the Huron country in the spring of 1616, as soon as the waters were free from ice. He was only a few months in that country during which time he was attending to his religious duties and made no incursions or discoveries. Brulé had left him there when he went on the campaign against the Iroquois and when he returned to the Huron villages, Le Caron had been gone from that country more than a year.

JOHN NICOLET.

John Nicolet, a young Frenchman, arrived at Quebec in the spring of 1618 and was immediately sent by Champlain to the Ottawa country to learn the language in use among the Ottawa tribes. He remained with them two years, during which time he saw not a single white man. Subsequently he made his home for several years with the Nipissings from whence he was recalled by the government to the St. Lawrence and employed as an interpreter and commissary. He went again among the Indians where he remained from 1629 to 1632. This was during the time that Quebec was in the possession of the English, from which place he held himself aloof and remained away during that time in the remote country of Lake Nipissing. He returned to the St. Lawrence in 1633 and the next year (1634) was selected by Champlain to go upon an exploring expedition to the regions further west than had yet been visited by white men. The expedition was in the interest of the "Association of one hundred" who desired to enlarge their knowledge of the Indian tribes and country with a view of extending the fur trade, of which they then had a monopoly. A still further object was to locate, if possible, the copper mines of which they had heard so much from Brulé and Grenolle and the Indians around the upper lakes. Nicolet was selected to make a venture into this, at that time, unknown country except as to such information as they had received from the natives. They had heard of the

Winnebagoes who were at that time located west of Lake Michigan, and Nicolet was especially instructed to visit them and also any other tribes who might be found in that region.

It was in 1634 that Nicolet started on his mission. He pursued the usual route by way of the Ottawa, Nipissing and the French river, and at the mouth of the French river he turned north and west as Brulé and Grenolle had done thirteen years before. He held his way along the north shore of the Huron waters to the falls of St. Marys, as Brulé and Grenolle had done. From the falls he turned south along the St. Mary's river to where it enters the waters of Lake Huron, and from that point commences his original explorations and discoveries. He proceeded along the north shore of Lake Huron, past the Straits of Mackinaw, around the north and west shores of Lake Michigan until he entered the waters of Green Bay. From Green Bay he proceeded up the waters of Fox River to near the carrying place from that stream to the waters of the Wisconsin river and there ended his original or first "white man's" discoveries.

Nicolet returned to the St. Lawrence and was employed in important relations mostly at Three Rivers and Quebec until 1642, when he lost his life by the upsetting of a boat in which he was hurrying on a mission of mercy to save an Iroquois from being tortured by the Algonquins who had captured him.

Nicolet was a devout Catholic but not a Jesuit. His life and character and conduct in his intercourse with the numerous Indian tribes was such that they all reposed the greatest confidence in him in life and entertained the highest respect for his memory of which their natures were capable.

The diagram on page 376 will in a measure show the route of original discovery to which Nicolet is entitled to credit.

JOLIET.

In 1669, Talon, then Intendant of Canada, sent Joliet with a young French companion to explore and locate if possible the copper regions of Lake Superior. He failed in his mission in so far as the copper regions were concerned, but they made a most important excursion over waters that had not before that time been reached or seen by any European. On their return from the northern lakes, they coasted down the west shore of Lake Huron and visited the Pottawattamies then living on that shore. The Pottawattamies had, at that time, never seen a white man. From the Pottawattamie country they coasted on down the west shore of Lake Huron to the point where the waters of that lake flow south through the St. Clair and Detroit rivers. From there these daring explorers held their way with the current

of these rivers until they reached the waters of Lake Erie. Thence they proceeded along the northern coast of Lake Erie to the mouth of the Grand River not far west of Niagara Falls. They turned up Grand River (now the home of the Senecas) and proceeded to a point near the present city of Hamilton, Ontario, where they met LaSalle and the Sulpitian priests. They were the first Europeans to navigate or see the waters along the route which they took from the northern end of Lake Huron to a point near the city of Hamilton. The information which they imparted to LaSalle and the priests as to the waters over which they had just passed, and the condition of the Pottawattamie nation determined the priests to go at once to that country as a field for the exercise of their religious proclivities. It was here that they parted with LaSalle who held firmly to his purpose of exploring the Ohio River country.

Joliet and his companions are entitled to be considered the first white men or Europeans to pass over any portion of these waters over which now passes by far the greatest commerce of any inland waters in the world.

The following diagram will indicate the lines of original travel taken by Joliet and his companion.

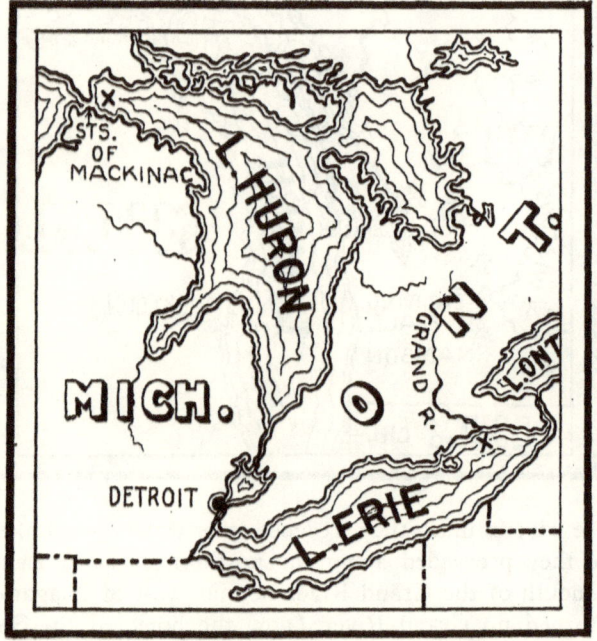

MARQUETTE AND JOLIET.

In 1672, Frontenac, then Governor of Canada, and Talon, the Intendant, determined to send an expedition to the regions further west than had yet been visited by white men and to search out and locate the great Mississippi river and to learn as much as possible of any tribes that they might meet with. Their purpose was largely mercenary, their object being to secure a knowledge of new tribes and new regions so as to enlarge the fur trade on the St. Lawrence. Jolliet was selected by them for this service, for which he was in the highest degree fitted. He had been born at Quebec and brought up in the wilderness of the lake country and was intelligent, hardy and daring, thoroughly versed in the habits of the Indian tribes. He had already made long excursions to the lake country and had made valuable discoveries of new routes of travel by water and of new tribes of Indians. He was to have associated with him Father Marquette who had seen service as a missionary at the falls of the St. Mary's and at LePoint (Apostles Islands) on the south side of Lake Superior. While stationed in these places as a priest of the Catholic Church, Marquette had learned much concerning Lake Michigan and the Mississippi and Illinois rivers. He had come in contact with numerous members of the tribes occupying the vast region to the south and west of Lake Superior and greatly desired to explore it.

Joliet reached Mackinaw on this expedition in the fall of 1672 with instructions to Marquette to join him in the proposed venture which gave great pleasure to the ardent priest, as it was in harmony with his own desires. They spent the winter in preparing for the journey and in informing themselves as fully as possible concerning the regions and tribes they were to visit.

On the 17th of May, 1673, they embarked in two canoes with five men. These two frail canoes were destined to carry them from "the snows of Canada to the more congenial clime of Arkansas" and to tide them over thousands of miles of water which had never before been disturbed by a white man's canoe. From Mackinaw around the north and west shore of Lake Michigan they passed over the same route which had been traveled by Nicolet thirty-nine years before until they reached the waters of Green Bay. From there they ascended the Fox river to the carrying place from the waters of that river to waters of the Wisconsin river. This carrying place was near the point at which Nicolet had turned back. It was but a mile and a half from the waters of one river to the waters of the other, but the way was so intricate through the vast field of wild rice which grows in such abundance in that region as to require the services of Indian guides to pilot the way through them.   When they reached the waters of the Wisconsin they dispensed with their guides and proceeded for six days to descend the Wisconsin to its mouth where it empties into the mighty Mississippi.   When their canoes shot out on the waters of that the greatest of rivers on the continent the adventurers were greatly rejoiced, and well they might have been as they had at last discovered and were upon the waters of the long sought for Mississippi.   The voyagers turned south with the current of the river and proceeded for more than a thousand miles.   They passed the mouth of great rivers emptying into the Mississippi and found many tribes of natives inhabiting the shores, most of whom proved friendly.   They did not change their course until they had reached the mouth of the Arkansas river where DeSoto had crossed the Mississippi 132 years before.   At this point they were able to determine that the Mississippi flowed into the Gulf of Mexico which was an unsettled question up to that time.   From this point on the 17th of July, 1673, they commenced their return up the Mississippi and proceeded with great difficulty and considerable delay on account of the illness of Marquette until they reached the mouth of the Illinois, into which they turned their canoes and urged them up that placid stream to the important Indian village of Kaskaskia.   They found the people of this very important village friendly, and after some stay there, the Indains kindly piloted them up to the mouth of the Des Plaines, up which they proceeded to the carrying place over into the Chicago river.   They then coasted up the west shore of Lake Michigan to Green Bay which they had left four months before. Jolliet proceeded at once to the St. Lawrence while Marquette remained at Green Bay.

Marquette and Joliet are entitled to credit for having been the first white men to pass from the carrying place between the Fox river and the Wisconsin to the mouth of the Arkansas and on their return from the mouth of the Illinois to the mouth of what is now the Chicago river, thence along the western coast to Lake Michigan to Green Bay.

The following diagram will show, in a manner, the routes over which Marquette and Jolliet are entitled to be considered the original navigators and explorers.

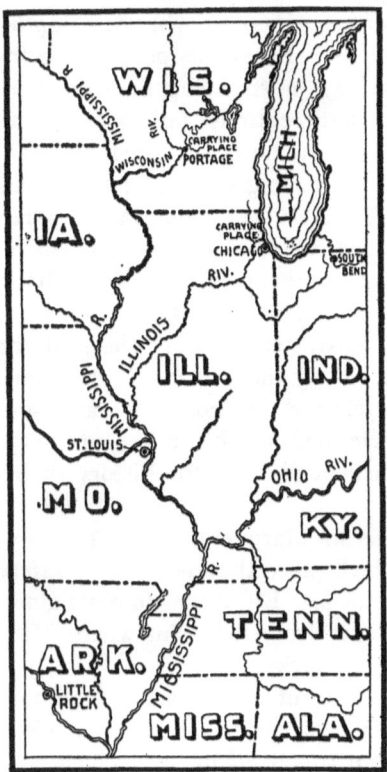

FATHER JAMES MARQUETTE.

When Marquette and Joliet reached Green Bay in the fall of 1673 the former was in infirm health and rested at Green Bay for nearly a year, but his health being in part restored he determined to return to the Illinois river as he had promised the Indians he would do. The course taken by Marquette and associates, two of whom were French, was along the west side of Lake Michigan to the mouth of the Chicago river. He pursued the route from that point to some distance inland where he suffered a relapse and was compelled to spend the winter in a rude hut constructed by his French companions. They suffered greatly during the winter, but in the spring of 1674, Marquette renewed his efforts to reach his Indian friends on the Illinois with a view of establishing a mission among them. He succeeded in this and was most joyfully received by the natives. He administered religious instruction to them for a short time, but his health was such that he was required to make an effort to return to his mission at S. Ignace. A number of Indians accompanied him up the Illinois river to the mouth of the Kankakee; thence up that lonely and crooked stream for several hundreds of miles until they reached a point near where is now the city of South Bend, Indiana, where there was a short carrying place of about four miles from the Kankakee over to the headwaters of the St. Josephs of Lake Michigan, and there it seems the Indians left him. From there he, with his two French companions, floated down that river to its mouth where it empties into the east side of Lake Michigan. From this point his faithful escorts proceeded for several days north along the east shore of Lake Michigan until his strength entirely failing him, and himself realizing that death was upon him, requested his companions to take him on shore that he might die in peace. His every request was complied with. A rude shelter was prepared for him where, after a few days and nights of devotion, he passed peacefully away, and was buried at the place of his death on the desolate and lonely east shore of Lake Michigan.

In reviewing the lives and characters of the priests of the Catholic Church who energized among the Indians of that time, or of any time, Marquette was clearly the most celebrated and most beloved by the Indians. He died in 1674 at the age of 38 years, but his name has a permanent place in the history of his times.

The two French companions of Marquette on his last voyage proceeded to Mackinaw, which place they reached in safety and are entitled to be considered the first Europeans to coast along the eastern shore of Lake Michigan from the point where Marquette was buried to the Straits of Mackinaw.

The diagram on page 382 will sufficiently show the route taken by Marquette on his return from the Illinois river in 1674. This route had never before been traversed by white men.

LA SALLE.

La Salle came to Montreal from France in 1666. His equipment for whatever experiences he might have in his career in the New World was that he was well fitted mentally and physically to meet whatever fortunes or misfortunes might befall him. His ambition and his courage were unbounded and not unmixed with greed of gain. He had visions not only of wealth but of dominion and empire. Before his time extensive explo-

rations had been made, but he soon learned from contact with
the Indians, especially the Senecas, a party of whom had wintered
at his quarters in 1668-69, of still vaster regions that were as yet
unexplored and unseen by white men.   He heard especially of

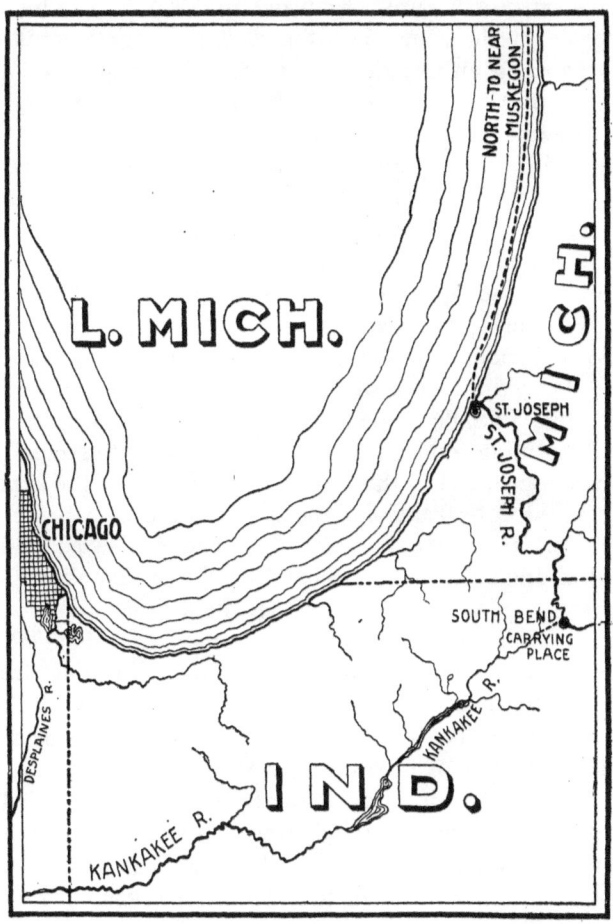

the waters of the Ohio, some of which headed in the Seneca
country and to which his Seneca friends offered to guide him.
He knew that the waters of the Ohio would reach the great Mississippi river and finally flow into the sea, but where and into what

sea was the great mystery. It is probable that his hope in this first exploration to the Ohio country was that he might reach the Mississippi; and in all probability he would have done so had his crew remained loyal to him.

This expedition was organized in 1669 at LaChine, near Montreal. At the same time the Sulpitian priests at LaChine were organizing an expedition for the purpose of searching out and converting to their faith such Indian tribes as they might find in the unknown country of the Ohio. The two expeditions were united in the beginning. LaSalle had procured four canoes and seven men, while the Sulpitians had their own canoes and their own men. The members of this expedition were all Frenchmen and would have to procure guides from the Indians when they reached the upper end of Lake Ontario. On the 6th of July, 1669, they proceeded up the St. Lawrence river to Lake Ontario and along the south shore of that lake to a point not far east from the mouth of Niagara river where the expedition rested while LaSalle visited the village of the Senecas with a view of obtaining guides to the Ohio. He failed to secure guides, as he had hoped, and as the season was getting late the expedition again moved forward along the south shore of Lake Ontario, past the mouth of the Niagara river and proceeded until they reached an Indian town near where the city of Hamilton, Canada, now stands. While at this village he learned of two young Frenchmen being near by, and there for the first time Joliet and LaSalle met. Joliet, as before stated, was returning from the expedition which he had undertaken at the instance of Talon in search of the copper regions of Lake Superior. This meeting caused a separation of La Salle's party from the missionary party. Joliet told them of the Pottawattamies who greatly needed religious instructions, and the missionaries determined to go at once to their spiritual rescue while LaSalle adhered to his original purpose of visiting the valley of the Ohio. The home of the Pottawattamies was at that time in the country west of Lake Huron.

It is conclusive that Joliet in returning from his search for copper mines in 1669 coasted the west shore of Lake Huron for the reason that he visited the Pottawattamies and reported their spiritual condition to the priests who were with LaSalle when they met near the head of Lake Ontario. The Pottawattamies occupied the country west of Lake Huron and in order to visit them Joliet necessarily had his course along the west shore of that lake.

The missionaries failed in their purpose to reach the Pottawattamies, but passed up the eastern side of Lake Huron, and

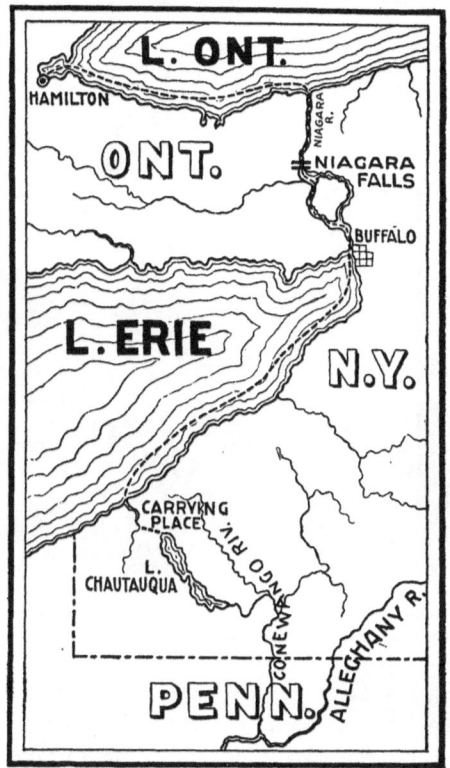

the north channel until they reached the falls of St. Marys, from which place they returned by the way of Lake Nipissing and the Ottawa to the St. Lawrence, having discovered nothing and accomplished nothing. LaSalle succeeded in carrying out, in large part, his original plan. Just what course he took after separating from the missionaries is not known with entire certainty, but it may be assumed that he passed near the head of Niagara river and along the south and east side of Lake Erie to a point opposite Chautauqua Lake. From Lake Erie to Chautauqua Lake there was a well known and much used carrying place of about eight miles. From there the route was over the waters of Chautauqua Lake to its outlet near Jamestown, New York, from where the overflow waters, united with the other streams, flow

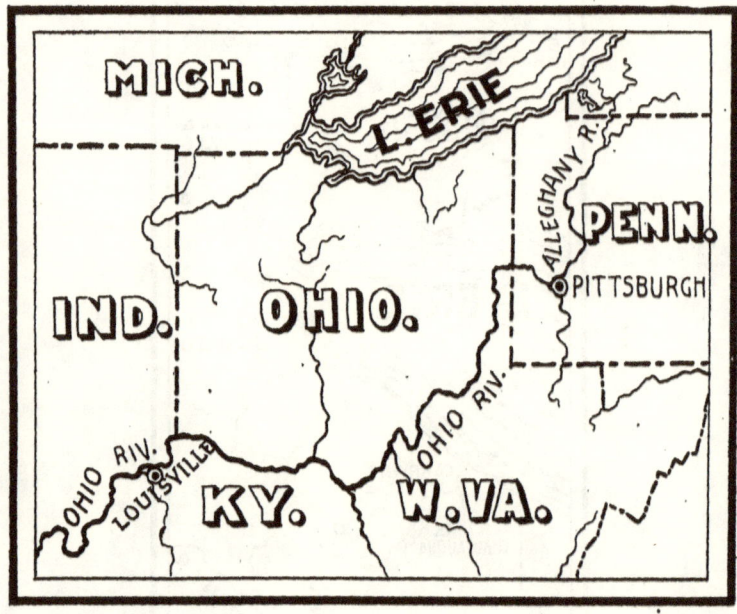

into the Alleghany river near Warren, Pennsylvania, and thence descend to the Ohio. It was by this route that the French subsequently sent a force two hundred strong to take possession of the Ohio.

Not much is recorded of this excursion of LaSalle except that it extended down the Ohio to the falls at Louisville, Kentucky. Here most of his men deserted him and he was compelled to return almost if not entirely unaccompanied. His way of return has not been definitely determined, but it was necessarily by way of the Big Miami and the Maumee (then called Miami of the Lake) or by way of the Scioto and Sandusky rivers. No other routes were at that time opened to him. Whichever of these routes he may have taken he was the first white man to have passed over it. The probabilities are that he went by the Big Miami and the Maumee to Lake Erie, but it is not certain, and not much can be claimed in respect to it.

Between the ending of this expedition and the undertaking of his next important voyage of discovery there elapsed a period of about nine years. In the meantime he was exceedingly engaged with important affairs along the St. Lawrence and in France, to which country he had in the meantime made several voyages.

In 1679 he planned a voyage over Lake Erie, through the Detroit and St. Clair rivers and over Lakes Huron and Michigan with a view of reaching and exploring the Mississippi river, as well as engaging in the fur trade. In furtherance of this plan he built on the Niagara river above the falls a vessel of forty-five or fifty tons with which to navigate the great lakes. They named the vessel the "Griffin." There were three friars of the Sulpitian order in the party that sailed on the "Griffin," among whom was Father Hennepin, a man of considerable learning and a ready and somewhat graceful writer, and had considerable talent for describing places where he had never been and things that he had never seen. He immortalized himself by stories which he related and books which he published when he returned to France which have secured for him, for all time to come, the appellation of "the most impudent liar." Nothing could exceed his audacity in this respect.

The expedition started in the summer of 1679 from the Niagara river and passed safely over Lake Erie, Lake Huron and through the Straits of Machinaw until they reached Green Bay on the waters of Lake Michigan. Here the vessel was loaded with a rich cargo of furs, and LaSalle sent it back to Niagara in charge of his pilot and five men. The vessel was never heard of afterwards. It was lost somewhere between Green Bay and its destination the Niagara river. From this point (Green Bay) LaSalle determined to push forward to the Illinois country, and in pursuance of this purpose passed down the west shore of

Lake Michigan and around the south end to the St. Joseph river.
From Green Bay to the mouth of the Chicago river the route had
been traversed by Marquette and Joliet several years before; but
from the mouth of the Chicago river to the mouth of the St.
Joseph, LaSalle and his party were the first white men to traverse
it. From the mouth of the St. Joseph to the mouth of the Illinois,
and on to the mouth of the Arkansas river the route had all been
explored before this expedition of LaSalle. When LaSalle and
his party reached Illinois country he determined to build a fort

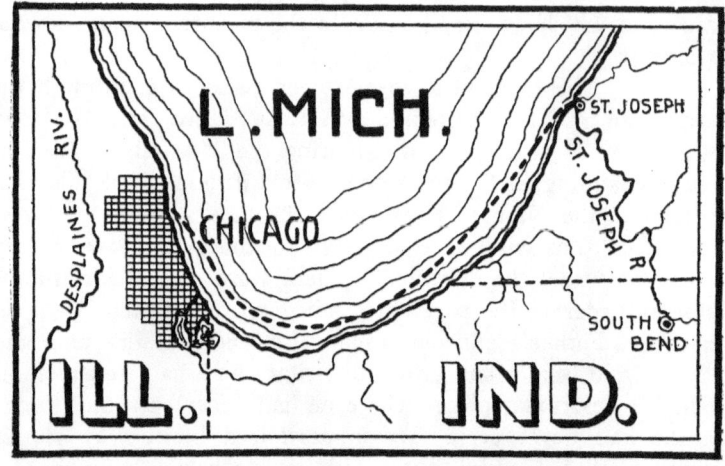

and establish a camp as a basis for further explorations. But
from this place LaSalle was compelled to return to Lakes Erie
and Ontario, leaving the colony on the Illinois in charge of his
faithful Tonty with instructions as to its conduct and management in his absence; and at the same time he instructed Hennepin
to proceed down the Illinois to its junction with the Mississippi
and to make such other and further explorations as opportunity
might afford.

In the meantime, pursuant to the instructions of LaSalle,
Hennepin with two French companions (Michael Accau and a
man known as Picard du Gay), proceeded to the mouth of the
Illinois, thence up the Mississippi to the mouth of the Wisconsin. From their starting point on the Illinois to the mouth of

the Wisconsin they passed over waters that had before that time been explored by Marquette and Joliet. From the mouth of the Wisconsin, however, to the falls of Minnehaha, near the present city of Minneapolis, he and his companions were the first white men to explore that part of the Mississippi river. They were taken prisoners by the Sioux Indians somewhere in that country and were for some time detained by them, but were finally released and Hennepin returned to the St. Lawrence by way of the Wisconsin river, Mackinaw, Nipissing, and the Ottawa. From the St. Lawrence he returned to France where he wrote and published volumes of stupendous lies which made him famous at the time and infamous for all time. He has secured immortal fame in history both as a liar and a plaguerist.

As soon as LaSalle had established his camp and fortified himself in a strong position, which fortification he gave the name of Crevacoeur, he returned to Fort Miami at the mouth of the St. Joseph at the southern end of Lake Michigan, and from there he made a journey on foot with his five French companions across the southern portion of the State of Michigan to Lake Erie and on to Fort Frontenac at the foot of Lake Ontario; but it is not within our purpose to follow him in the strenuous life which befell him until he reappeared at the mouth of the St. Joseph late in the year 1682, where he made final preparations for an expedition intended to reach the mouth of the Mississippi. On December 21st, he dispatched Tonty and Membré from Fort Miami at the mouth of the St. Joseph with a part of his force in six canoes. They crossed from the mouth of the St. Joseph to the mouth of the Chicago where LaSalle joined them a few days later. From the Chicago river over to the Des Plaines there was a carrying place of a few miles, but at this time those streams were frozen and LaSalle and his companions were compelled to construct sheds and put their canoes and baggage on them in order to cross from the Chicago to the Des Plaines which was and is the north branch of the Illinois. They followed the course of the Des Plaines to its junction with the Kankakee and thence down the Illinois to the site of the Illinois village which they found deserted. From there they found the river free from ice and proceeded with their canoes down the Illinois river until on the 6th of February they reached its mouth where it empties into the Mississippi. They tarried here for a few days and then commenced the descent of the great river. They stopped at the various Indian villages with a view of learning as much as possible concerning them and of cultivating friendly relations with them. They in time reached the mouth of the Arkansas where they found a considerable Indian village. This was at the point where DeSoto and his followers first saw and crossed the Mississippi 141 years before and which had been reached by Marquette and Joliet nine years before. The Mississippi had not been explored from that point to its mouth. On the 31st of March they passed the mouth of the Red River where in 1542 DeSoto died and was buried with all his ambition and greed of gold and treasures. The rich cities he hoped to find and plunder as he and other Spaniards had done in Mexico and Peru were never found and his visions of plunder and wealth vanished into nothingness.

On the 6th of April, LaSalle and his companions reached the point where the river divides itself into three channels, through which its mighty waters rush into the Gulf of Mexico. These were all explored until they reached the sea, "then the broad bosom of the great gulf opened on his sight, tossing its restless billows, limitless, voiceless, lonely as when born of chaos, without a sail, without a sign of life." (Parkman.)

In the discovery of the mouth of the Mississippi, LaSalle had reached the consummation of an ambition which he had long and ardently entertained. It would seem that he might well have been satisfied with what he had accomplished in the eighteen years since he left France, and it would have been well for him had he been content to rest upon the laurels which he had gained by his strenuous efforts in exploring and making known the important water highways of the interior of the continent. He and his associates had aided very materially in making known to the world the highways and carrying places by which the Aborigines traveled for thousands of years. The entire distance from the mouth of the St. Lawrence to the mouth of the Mississippi was more than 4,000 miles which had been traversed by means of birch canoes, urged on by energetic adventurous white men. He was not satisfied, however, and immediately returned to France filled with the idea of returning by sea to the mouth of the Mississippi and establishing there a military colony in the furtherance of French interests. Aided by government, he organized an expedition and sailed for the mouth of the Mississippi but miscalculating the latitude and longitude sailed past the mouth of that river and landed some distance west of that point. It is not our province to follow him further. He wandered far and wide over land, hoping to discover the great river, but he failed and on or near the Brazos river in the State of Texas, he was foully murdered by one of his own men.

The original explorations to which LaSalle is entitled as the first "white man" to have traversed are, *first,* from a point near the Niagara river to the waters of the Alleghany and thence

down that stream to the Ohio and on to the falls where the city of Louisville now stands; *second,* the route by water from the mouth of the Chicago river around the south end of Lake Michigan to the mouth of the St. Joseph; *third,* from the mouth of the Arkansas to the mouth of the Mississippi. But these discoveries in no wise represent the explorations and discoveries which his mighty energies prompted.

Champlain in his time and LaSalle in his time were the main springs of most of the discoveries of the waters and countries in the great basin which lies between the western slope of the Alleghanies and the eastern slope of the Rocky Mountains and the Great Lakes on the north and the Gulf of Mexico on the south. It is not at the present day generally appreciated that these two energetic, able and ambitious Frenchmen came near establishing a French empire in the New World embracing this entire territory.

BETWEEN LAKE ERIE AND THE OHIO RIVER.

There were three starting points on Lake Erie by which the Aborigines in their time, and the white men in more modern times passed from the waters of Lake Erie to the waters of the Ohio River. These were all very important and much used as far back as we have either history or tradition. There were practically direct lines of canoe travel with but few carrying places on any of them so that the Aborigines could pass easily from one of these waters to the other.

The first we have to mention commenced at the mouth of the Cuyahoga river where the city of Cleveland now stands, thence up that river to a point near the city of Akron in Summit County, Ohio, where there was a carrying place of about eight miles from the waters of the Cuyahoga to the waters of the Tuscarawas and south with that stream to the Muskingum, and thence along that majestic river to its junction with the Ohio. It is not known who the first European or white man was to pass over this route, but no doubt it was first traveled by French fur traders or *voyagers.* The ubiquious fur trader was everywhere present, in the immediate wake of the original explorers, but they left no records of their travels or excursions. The main lakes and rivers were visited by them soon after their existence was made known.

As early as 1668, Joliet traversed, as has before been seen, Lake Erie and the Detroit and St. Clair rivers; and the next year a few Sulpitian priests traveled over the same route, only going in the other direction, and from that time all the waters were made known to the French traders. On LaSalle's return from his exploration of the Ohio in 1670, all that country was made known and soon invaded by the rapacious and unscrupulous fur traders, so that we may safely assume that all the waters of Lake Erie and the waters leading from Lake Erie to the Ohio were traversed by them, and that they must be considered as the first white men to invade these waters; so that it is almost certain that the Cuyahoga and the Muskingum and the Scioto routes and the Maumee were all known and often used by the French traders prior to the time of which we have any authentic record.

THE SCIOTO AND SANDUSKY RIVERS.

The next important highway between Lake Erie and the Ohio river commenced at the mouth of the Sandusky river and proceeded south against the current of that historic stream to a very noted carrying place about six miles east of the present city of Bucyrus in Crawford County. This carrying place was but four miles long and was the only carrying place between Lake Erie and the Ohio river. When this route was first traveled by white men is not known, but like others it was undoubtedly by the French traders at a period long prior to any written record concerning this route. The first written description that we have was by Col. James Smith, who, in the summer of 1755, was taken prisoner by the Indians. He passed from the mouth of the Sandusky to the carrying place in Crawford County. From there he went with his captors to the south west as far as the Olentangy, now called the Darby. He and his Indian companions spent the winter of 1757 in the neighborhood of what is now Plain City, Madison County, and the next spring they descended the Darby to the point where it empties into the Scioto river near Circleville, Ohio, from which point they ascended the Scioto to the carrying place in Crawford County, and thence by way of the Sandusky and Lake Erie to Detroit. His very interesting

and important narrative furnished the first description that has
been preserved of the country between Pickaway County and the
mouth of the Sandusky river.

From the mouth of the Maumee, the Ohio could be reached
at two widely different points, the one at the mouth of the Big
Miami, and the other at the mouth of the Wabash; but who first
traveled these waterways is like the last two mentioned, unknown.
Lake Erie and the Detroit river, and the surrounding regions,
had been discovered and made known as early at 1669 and '70.
The French trader soon entered into any new field of barter or
commerce with the Indians which was opened to them; and by
the year 1700 the French interests about Lake Erie and the
Detroit river, and other streams in that region had come to be
so important that it was deemed necessary by the French authorities to give it a military protection, and so in 1701, Cadillac, a
French officer, was sent with fifty soldiers from the St. Lawrence
to establish a post at the present city of Detroit. He arrived
at that point July 24th, 1701. At that time there were both
French and English traders around the waters of Lake Erie
and the Detroit and other rivers, so that it is certain that, at that
early date, there was not only French traders in that region, but
that their interests were so considerable that it was thought necessary to protect it by military force. There are facts as well as
traditions which go to show that the Maumee had been traversed
by the French trader as early as 1690, but who the first trader or
voyager was will always remain unknown. The waters of the
Ohio could be reached from the Maumee either by ascending the
Auglaize or by ascending the St. Mary, and thence by carrying
places to the waters of the Big Miami which empties into the
Ohio at the southwest corner of the State of Ohio.

Another very important way to the Ohio was up the Maumee
to a point near Fort Wayne, thence by a carrying place of eight
or nine miles to Little river one of the head-waters of the Wabash.
This led to the Ohio river at the southwest corner of the State
of Indiana. We know that this route was traveled by the French
at a very early day, and French trading posts had been established

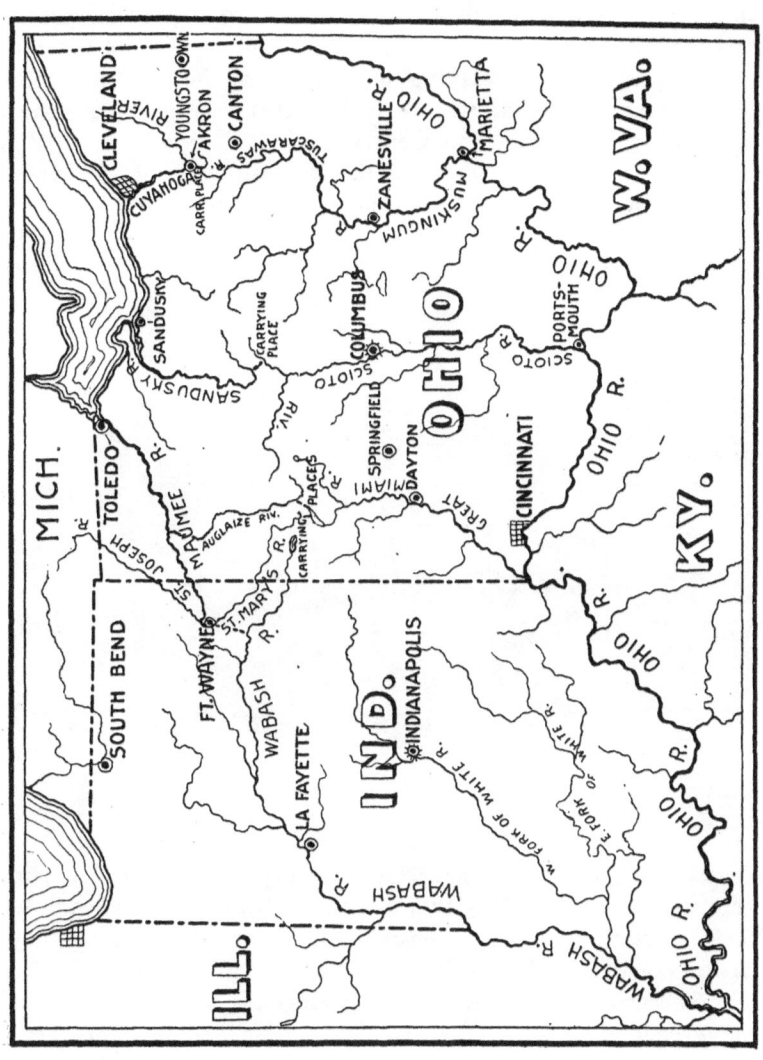

as far south as Vincennes; but it is not easy to fix dates for these events. In 1778 the English general, Hamilton, passed over this route with his army of about three hundred soldiers and Indians, and established himself at the village of Vincennes. He has left a description of the carrying place between the waters of the Maumee and those of the Wabash. This carrying place was about nine miles long, and General Hamilton says of it: "We arrived at one of the sources of the Wabash, called Little river. The stream was so uncommonly low that bateaux could not have

floated but for the fact that, some distance below, a beaver dam kept up the water. This they cut through to give a passage to their boats, and, having taken in the lading at the landing, they passed them all." He further says: "This carrying place is free from obstructions but what the carelessness and ignorance of the French have left and would leave from generation to generation. An intelligent person, at a small expense, might make it as fine a road as any within twenty miles of London. The woods are beautiful; there are oak, ash, beech, nut-wood, very clear and of a great growth." (Butterfield's Conquest of the Illinois, 208.)

Subsequently very important events took place along this water highway, but they are not within the scope of our present purpose.

———

The foregoing paper is mainly based upon the following authorities: Bancroft's History U. S., Weare's Cabot's Discovery of North America; Moore's Northwest Under Three Flags; Cadwallader Colden's History of Five Indian Nations; Brulé's Discoveries, by Butterfield; Nicolet's Discoveries, by Butterfield; Shea's Discovery and Exploration of the Mississippi; Buell's Sir William Johnson; John Fiske's Discovery of America; "Captain Pote's Journal;" Parkman's LaSalle, and The Discovery of the Great West; Parkman's The Pioneers of France in the New World; Butler's Lake George and Lake Champlain; Ketchum's History of Buffalo; Darlington's Col. James Smith; Weise's History of the City of Albany; Butterfield's George Rogers Clark's Conquest of the Northwest; Drake's Book of the Indians; Perkin's Western Annals; Hall's Memoir of William H. Harrison; Simpkin's History of Auglaize County; Knapp's History of the Maumee Valley; Slocum's History of the Maumee River Basin; Prescott's Mexico and Peru; Parkman's Jesuits in North America; Narratives of Marquette, Allonez, Membre and Hennepin.

THE UNDERGROUND RAILROAD.

S. S. KNABENSHUE, TOLEDO.

The Underground Railroad was not under the ground, nor was it a railway; but there was a fitness in the name which caused its general use to express one of the most remarkable phases of the long struggle against slavery and the Slave Power. The term was a popular mode of referring to the various ways in which fugitive slaves from the South were assisted in escaping to the North, and especially to Canada. It was often humorously abbreviated to "U. G. R. R."

The boundary between the slave and the free states began at the mouth of the Delaware river; ran up that stream to Mason & Dixon's line — the boundary between Pennsylvania and Maryland; thence westward to the end of Maryland; then north, between Pennsylvania and what was then Virginia, but is now West Virginia, to the Ohio river; down the Ohio to its mouth; up the Mississippi to the northern boundary of Missouri; along the northern and western sides of that state, and thence westward along the line of 36 degrees 30 minutes north latitude — the noted Missouri Compromise line.

Take a map of the United States, follow this line, and it will be seen that the shortest route to British soil in Canada and, hence to complete freedom, was across Ohio. Only a little more than 200 miles, as the crow flies, lay between the slave and liberty after he crossed the Ohio river. Hence this state was the favorite route. Probably more fugitives found safety by the trails of the Underground Railroad crossing Ohio than by those through any other state. Along the Ohio which fronted slave territory for about 375 miles, there were initial stations at some 22 or 23 river towns; and some of these, such as Cincinnati, had several different routes leading toward the North Star and freedom. This was necessary, for the slave-hunters were often close on the trail of the fugitive, and it was necessary to have more than one route, so that, if one or more were watched, the negro would be sent by another.

It is extremely difficult to get the facts regarding these routes. It is to be remembered that the Underground Railroad was first established in Ohio somewhere about 1815 to 1817; and the work of the road never ceased, but grew increasingly greater, until the extinction of slavery by the Civil War. Thus, for fifty years, it was one of the most traveled of states by the black fugitives. A pro-slavery writer of 1842 declares that at this time there were eighteen or nineteen thoroughly organized routes across Ohio. But the greatest activity of the U. G. R. R. was after the enactment of the fugitive slave law of 1850, and there were doubtless more than twenty general routes, each with side deviations, the paths taken thus forming a veritable network over this state.

The origin of the name "Underground Railroad," is uncertain. R. C. Smedley, in a little work on "The Underground Railroad in Chester and Neighboring Counties of Pennsylvania," says it came into use among the slave-hunters in the neighborhood of Columbia, Pa. They had little difficulty in tracking slaves to Columbia, but at that point all trace was lost, and they are said to have declared there must be an underground road somewhere. As railroads were unknown until after 1830, the term must have originated later than that year. Hon. Rush R. Sloane, of Sandusky, who was actively engaged in underground work, says that in 1831 a negro named Tice Davids ran away from Kentucky. His master pursued him so closely that, when he reached the Ohio river, near Ripley, he was obliged to plunge in and swim across to avoid capture. His master secured a skiff and started after Tice. He kept him in view until he reached the Ohio shore, when the negro disappeared. After a long search his master said he thought "the nigger must have gone off on an underground road." This story created a great deal of amusement along the Underground line. First, the "Underground Road," then naturally the "Underground Railroad."

Gradually railway terminology was applied to different parts of the work — all figurative, of course, like the generic name, "Underground Railroad." Men who were very active in the work, fearless of consequences, were "managers;" "contributing members" furnished money for clothing, food, hiring vehicles, etc., and were generally men who did not wish for social, political, or business reasons, to be known as in sympathy with the work; an "agent" or "conductor" piloted the slaves from one house to another. These houses were called "stations." One man named Levi Coffin, mentioned in the above, was for many years called president of the Underground Railroad, because he personally aided over three thousand slaves on their northward way, in the thirty years he was engaged in the work.

It must be kept in mind that helping slaves to freedom was unlawful. From 1793, there had been a fugitive slave law, which imposed penalties of fine and imprisonment for concealing run-away slaves, or aiding them in any way to evade capture. Hence there was need of the utmost caution. The majority of the people of Ohio, probably, during all the time the underground railroad was in operation, were not in sympathy with its work. For its efficiency and secrecy it depended upon the friendship, sympathy and confidence existing between members of neighboring stations. A fugitive who reached an initial station received food and clothing, if in need, and was hidden in an attic, a hay-mow, a corn-crib, at some places in caves, until arrangements could be made. He was then taken to the next station — usually a farm house. All travel was by night, to lessen the chance of capture of the slave, or of detection of his conductor. As a rule, when a fugitive had been passed to the next station, the person at the initial station never heard of him again — unless he was captured, which very seldom happened. His exact route was not known, because there were always alternate stations, and a negro entering Ohio at Harmar, for instance, at the mouth of the Muskingum, might cross to Canada from Buffalo, Cleveland, Sandusky, Toledo, or from a minor lake port.

The settlers of Ohio along the river, had a good sprinkling of men from Maryland, Virginia and Kentucky, who had strong moral objections to slavery. The Quakers always were opposed to the institution, and they were the most active in underground work. The Scotch-Irish Presbyterians, Scotch Covenanters, and Wesleyan Methodists were also notable in it. Many of these deeply-religious men refused utterly to lift a finger to persuade a slave to escape, or to act as abductors; but the runaway negro who came for aid was never turned away. The majority of slaves who reached freedom ran away of their own accord; but there were, in the many years over which the work extended, a number of people who devoted themselves to abduction. Harriet Tubman, a negro woman, was one of these, and gained the title of "the Moses of her race." She was a Maryland slave, but escaped to Philadelphia in 1849. The next year she went to Baltimore and abducted her sister and two children. From then until the Civil War, she made nineteen trips, and brought over 300 slaves to freedom.

Very few documents relating to the Underground Railroad are in existence. The legal penalties for rendering aid to fugitives were always present in the minds of the operators; therefore, they avoided any written evidence of their work. Records and dairies were kept by some, and letters passing between station-keepers were frequent; but these were all destroyed after the enactment of the fugitive slave law of 1850, which created much consternation by its rigorous provisions and severe penalties.

The total number of fugitives is simply a matter of estimate. Josiah Henson, himself a runaway slave and afterward an abductor, estimated that in 1852 there were 50,000 fugitive negroes living in the north, exclusive of those who had gone to Canada. This is probably overstated. Charges of bad faith against the North in the rendition of fugitive slaves were frequently made by Southern members on the floor of Congress. Representative Moore, of Virginia, in 1822, declared his district lost four or five thousand dollars' worth of negroes every year. In 1850, Senator Atchison, of Kentucky, declared that hundreds of thousands of dollars worth were lost annually by the border slave states. Pratt, of Maryland, said his state lost $80,000 worth each year, and Mason of Virginia, put the loss in that state at over $100,000 per year. Clingman, of North Carolina, said the 30,000 fugitives then estimated to be living in the North were worth, at current prices, about $15,000,000. Claiborne, governor of Louisiana, gave as a defect of the fugitive slave law of 1850, that it failed to provide for the payment to the South of the $30,000,000 of which she had been plundered by the loss of slaves in forty years.

He also declared that the number of slaves in the District of Columbia had been reduced from 4,694 in 1840, to 650 in 1850 by the underground railroad.

Mention has already been made of the number of initial stations along the Ohio river. Many of the fugitives were conducted to Erie and Buffalo; but every lake port in Ohio, from Conneaut to Toledo, was a point of departure for Canada. Sandusky and Cleveland were specially important, because, in the last ten years of underground work, they were the termini of railways running southward to the center of the state. In these later years, fugitives were put on board night trains, in the baggage cars, and thus taken swiftly to those cities, where they were put on steamers bound for Canadian ports, or taken across Lake Erie in sailboats. The steamers out of Toledo were frequently employed also.

The list of Toledo operators of the underground railroad embraces the names of Richard Mott, a Quaker: Hon. James M. Ashley, former congressman; the late Mayor Bringham; James Conlisk, an Irish-American; William H. Merritt, a negro, and several others. As a youth of 17 in Kentucky, Mr. Ashley helped two groupes of fugitives across the Ohio, one of seven persons, the other of five. He was active in the work for years in Toledo and took many risks — not the least of which was taking a party of fugitives in a sleigh, in midwinter, across Lake Erie on the ice from Toledo to Amherstburg.

There was a station in Maumee, operated by A. C. Winslow, who operated a foundry. From there, if there was no close pursuit, fugitives were brought either to Toledo, or taken, via Detroit avenue, to Monroe, Michigan, and thence across to Canada. If the pursuers were close, the negroes were taken to the Sylvania station, kept by Daniel Harroun, jr., and from there Hall Deland, the "night hawk," took them to the French settlers along the Detroit river, who ferried them across that stream to Canada.

At Sandusky still lives, full of years and honors, Hon. Rush R. Sloane, a notable underground operator. In 1854, while he was in the law practice, he was tried for the dismissal without proper authority of seven fugitives from the custody of their captors. Two suits were instituted against him by Louis F.

Weimer, the owner of three of the slaves. The case was tried in the United States District Court at Columbus, and a verdict for $3,000 and costs was returned against him. The costs were $330.30. Some Sandusky friends raised $393, which paid court and marshal's costs, but Mr. Sloane had to pay the $3,000 from his own pocket.

New England had a number of underground railroad routes. The fugitives sometimes came from the South through New York, but many came hidden aboard coasting vessels which traded to Southern ports. From New York a much-used route went up the Hudson to Albany. From here some were sent west through Rochester, the home of Frederick Douglass, thence to the Niagara frontier; some went northward direct to Canada.

There was a network of routes leading from the South to Philadelphia and the Quaker communities in the neighboring counties. From thence some went to New York, and some by routes northward to the Niagara frontier. In western Pennsylvania were a number of routes, the fugitives following the valleys between the mountain ranges of the Alleghanies from the South, and eventually reaching Canada through Buffalo, Erie, Cleveland or Sandusky.

Indiana had many routes, ending at Detroit, Toledo, Michigan City and Chicago. From the Mississippi, along the Missouri boundary, a number of routes crossed Illinois to Chicago, whence the fugitives were taken by lake steamer to Collingwood, Detroit and Amherstburg. In the late '50's, there were routes in eastern Kansas and southern Iowa, all joining the Illinois routes, and with the same terminations.

Thousands of negroes started with no knowledge of what to do other than to have the north star pointed out to them, with directions to go toward it — they traveled at night, and hid during the day — with the information that when they reached Canada they were free, and could not be brought back. Many along in the late '30's and '40's, followed the Wabash canal across Indiana to Toledo; or the Ohio canal from Portsmouth to Cleveland, or the canal from Cincinnati north of Toledo. The desire for freedom was general among the slaves, even when they were well treated. The one thing the slaves in the northern tier of slave states most dreaded was being sold South, to labor in the rice fields of Carolina, the cotton fields of Georgia, Alabama and Mississippi, or the cane fields of Louisiana. And from the time that the desire for freedom inspired slaves to run away, there seems to have been people in the North willing to give them cordial aid. The earliest mention we have of any systematic aid to runaways is in two letters written by George Washington in 1786. On May 24, speaking of the slave of Mr. Dalby, of Alexandria, who had escaped to Philadelphia, he said: "A society of Quakers, formed for such purposes, have attempted to liberate him." On November 20, of the same year, he writes of one of his own slaves, sent under an overseer to Hon. Wm. Drayton, but who escaped in transit. Washington writes: "The gentleman in whose care I sent him has promised every endeavor to apprehend him; but it is not easy to do this, when there are numbers who would rather facilitate the escape of slaves than apprehend them when runaways."

This was before the formation of the national constitution. One of the compromises of that document was the clause which reads: "No person held to service or labor in one state under the laws thereof, escaping into another, shall, in consequence of any law or regulation therein, be discharged from such service or labor, but shall be delivered up on claim of the party to whom such service or labor may be due." This clause, although it studiously avoids the words "slave" and "slavery," meant runaway slaves.

This clause remained inoperative for several years, because Congress enacted no law on the subject. In 1791, a case of kidnapping occurred at Washington, Pa., which directed public attention to the matter, and in 1793 the first fugitive slave law was enacted. From that day until 1863, the aiding of runaway slaves was illegal. But the law was ineffectual to stop it; the underground railroad methods were followed, especially in Pennsylvania. Several states enacted laws to aid in the rendition of fugitive slaves within their borders, but they did not deter underground operators. The national law was amended and strengthened somewhat about 1819; but the work of the underground railroad increased steadily through the next three decades, until in the fierce debates upon the admission of California as a free state, the compromise bill of 1850 was enacted, one of the features of which was the severe fugitive slave law of that year. This stirred up the friends of freedom to renewed activity; and when, in 1854, the Kansas-Nebraska bill repealed the Missouri Compromise, and showed the purposes of the slave power to extend the hated institution into territories, that they might be admitted as slave states, the impetus became greater. For the first time, a great political party was organized to resist the encroachments of slavery. Six years later it obtained control of the national government. Secession followed, and the war for the preservation of the Union destroyed slavery forever.

POWDER MAGAZINE AT FORT HAMILTON.

DR. WILLIAM C. MILLER.

It is generally understood that the Revolutionary War ended with the surrender of Cornwallis, October 19, 1781, and a treaty of peace was signed at Ghent, acknowledging the independence of the colonies, and by this treaty the United States were to have and hold as part of its domain the territory from the Atlantic to the Mississippi River and south of the Great Lakes, except Florida which was ceded to Spain. But did the British adhere to their agreement? No. For twelve years after, they sought in every conceivable manner to reclaim Detroit. They incited the Indians against the white settlers in the Ohio Valley, furnishing them arms and ammunition, so that by 1790 the Indians became so arrogant and the white settlers so dismayed and panic-stricken that they fled from their primitive forest homes to the nearest fort. It was in 1791 when President Washington's attention was called to the condition of affairs in the Ohio country. Then he ordered General Arthur St. Clair, a gallant and brilliant soldier of the Revolutionary War and who had given his fortune to save his country's independence and was then governor of the Northwest Territory, to raise an army and proceed against the Indians for the protection of the pioneers and in order that everlasting peace and tranquility might prevail in the Ohio country. Leaving Fort Washington now Cincinnati on September 8, 1791 by the 17th he arrived at a point 25 miles north of the east side of the Miami River in latitude of 39-26 and longitude of 7-29. Here he built a fort and on the thirteenth of September had finished it and named it in honor of General Alexander Hamilton, then Secretary of the Treasury in Washington's cabinet. A powder magazine was erected at the south end of the fort of square logs laid close together having a hipped roof, a cupola in its center, and a blue ball on top of it. A well was dug in March, 1792, located in the east side of what is now Monument Avenue and for years afterwards was known as the Sohn's Well. Gen-

eral St. Clair, Wayne, Wilkinson and Harrison, and Major Cass,
Col. Buttler and Col. Darke were at this well often one hundred
years ago to quench their thirst. This well and the powder
magazine are to-day the only remaining relics of Old Fort Hamilton. After the treaty of Greenville, the white winged messenger of peace floated over the Miami Valley never again to be disturbed, and General Wayne in the fall of 1796 ordered Fort
Hamilton vacated and the public property sold at auction. Israel Ludlow had purchased the site of Fort Hamilton. Upon its
abandonment as a garrison, many of the old soldiers of St. Clair
and Wayne, such as John Torence, Captain Wingate, John Reily,
Archibald Tolbert, and John Sutherland remained to make it their
permanent abode, thus forming the nucleus for the now prosperous city of Hamilton, a hundred years after. The old well is
still there where thousands of Hamilton inhabitants within these
hundreds of years, now all passed and gone, have quenched their
thirst.

The powder magazine, when the fort was abandoned, was
turned into a jail and remained as such until 1810. The old soldiers of General St. Clair and Wayne, residents of Hamilton,
formed themselves into a militia company and whenever there
was any prisoner, a detachment of ten or twelve would form
a guard to prevent the occupant's escape. In 1803, when the
country was organized the commissioners ordered the magazine
to be reinforced with militia and strengthened, two more companies were organized from the immediate vicinity of the town.
John Winjato, James Blackburn and John Gray were captains
and when any of them were called to duty they were henceforth
paid for their services.

The magazine was strengthened with a door of heavy two-
inch plank driven full of spikes and nails with a hole cut in the
center in the shape of half moon for the admission of light, air
and food for the occupants and fastened with an iron hasp and
paddlock. In 1810, the magazine was abandoned as a jail and
was from that time until 1825 used as a place of worship. Here
the Rev. Lorenzo Dow, the eccentric itinerant preacher of three-
quarters of a century ago, preached. Here Rev. Adam Rankin,
of Kentucky, Rev. David Rush, and Rev. R. H. Bishop, later

President of Miami University, preached to the adherents of their faith, the Associated Reformed and now the United Presbyterians. Here Miss Ellen McMechen, later Mrs. Charles K. Smith, and Miss Jane McMechen, later Mrs. Jessie Corwin, taught school. Here the children of the early settlers were taught their A, B, C's, such as the Blairs', Wilkinson's, Hough's, McBridis', Cameron's, Sutherland's, Wood's, Murray's, Webster's, and Hunter's; a chart owned by Mrs. James McMechen in the early twenties in this building, can be seen at the Magazine building to-day.

Here Mrs. Henry Skinner, daughter of Israel Creeg, once sheriff of Butler County, the venerable mother of Dr. George Skinner, who is still with us, went to school. About the year 1840 the magazine was abandoned as a school. Carl Donges, proprietor of the William Tell Hotel on High Street, whose property extended from High to Court Street upon which the magazine stood, became its owner. He, a man of military attainments and for years captain of the Jackson guards, a military organization, converted this building into a magazine again. Here were kept the two little bull dogs and the ammunition that used to thunder forth the victory of a political campaign at the wee small hours of the night awakening the inhabitants to let them know who was the winner. When two shots were fired in succession it meant a Democratic victory, and one shot fired at a time, indicated a Whig victory.

In 1849, the magazine was purchased by Peter Jacobs, who removed it to a lot on Water Street, purchased of C. K. Smith some years previous and converted it into a dwelling. It was then weatherboarded and the roof changed to a gable fronting on Water Street. It remained in the Jacob's family until 1883 when it fell into the hands of the late Thomas Millikin. Thomas Millikin had an eye on this house knowing its history personally, and the writer has frequently heard from the lips of the leaders in the community in the first half of the last century refer to the last relics of Fort Hamilton, the magazine and Sohn's Well. In 1889, a committee of the Soldiers and Sailors Pioneer Monument Committee called upon Thomas Millikin with a view of acquiring the magazine building and to place it upon the lot at the foot of High Street. Mr. Millikin thought well of the proposition, but somehow nothing came of it. Some time later a committee of the Daughters of the American Revolution called upon Mr. Millikin with a view of getting this building, remodel it, and convert it to its original form as near as possible. Mr. Millikin was most enthusiastic and promised to give them the building; they to remove it. In the meantime Thomas Millikin died and the property fell into the hands of O. M. Blake, who upon being apprised of Mr. Millikin's promise, most graciously and patriotically carried out Mr. Millikin's wishes and thus this historic building became the property of the D. A. R. The officials of Hamilton with a like spirit of patriotism and a desire to perpetuate the memory of Hamilton's early days granted a site for this building on the north side of the east end of the High and Main Street bridge, and furnished every convenience.

NAVIGATION ON THE MUSKINGUM.

IRVEN TRAVIS, MCCONNELSVILLE.

[Mr. Irven Travis, the writer of this article, was born near Roxbury, Windsor Township, Morgan County, August 17, 1849. His father,
John Travis, lived in McConnelsville where he was employed in building flat-boats in the summer and taking them to New Orleans in the
winter. Mr. Irven Travis became a pilot on the river boats at the age
of twenty, serving in that capacity on the steamers "Carrie Brooks,"
"Perry Smith," "Oella," "Gen. H. F. Devol," and "Lizzie Cassell."
In 1887, Mr. Irven Travis became United States Storekeeper at McConnelsville, when the state turned the river improvement over to the
national government, and has had charge of the river affairs at that
place ever since. — EDITOR.]

Our knowledge of the earliest navigation on the Muskingum

IRVEN TRAVIS.

seems confined to rather narrow limits. The needs of the red man were
probably satisfied by the use of the
primitive canoe, its use being no
more than the carrying of himself
and his game when on hunting expeditions. However the time soon
came when the white man encroach-
ed on the hunting grounds of the occupants of this valley and their
progress in the way of civilization
soon made better facilities for navigation necessary.

We find the first attempt, in
the way of improvement, was the
building of crafts, larger than the canoe of the Indians, but still
called a canoe. In its construction often the largest trees of
the then unmolested forest were used, their length being from
75 to 90 feet, their diameters from 30 to 36 inches at the top.
The center of this huge timber was removed, leaving a shell of

from 1½ to 2 inches in thickness, affording a capacity of 10 or 12 tons. We find apples to be one of the first products of this valley to be transported by this craft, the capacity in bushels being as many as 200, after leaving space for the men (generally two, one in either end), who pushed with poles instead of paddling as was the custom with the Indian canoe. Such necessities as could be had at that time were taken in exchange for their cargo, very little money changing hands until the advent of salt making in this valley. The drilling of salt wells having commenced as early as 1817, in the early twenties of the 19th century, salt became the principal article of freight and continued to be until the improvement of the river by a series of locks and dams, which was commenced in 1836.

Larger and better crafts again became necessary and another type of boat called a "Pirogue" came into use, the unique build of which seems to make a description necessary. In its commencement the lines of the canoe, already described, were used and in fact until it was a finished canoe. It was then split through the keelson from stem to stern, with the whip-saw in use in those days. The two halves were then carried apart and cross keelsons of such length as was the desired width of the new craft were placed between. Then by the use of the whip-saw bottom plank were prepared which ran parallel with the gunwale and was pinned with wooden pins instead of spiked as to-day. The seams were then calked with a refuse of flax called tow, no oakum being in use at that time. What was called race-boards were then placed along the top of the gunwales on which the men would walk to and fro propelling the boat. The poles used were from 15 to 20 feet long and about 2¼ inches in diameter in the middle and tapering both ways, the end which came in contact with the shoulder, a trifle smaller than the other which was provided with an iron socket. A silver dollar was considered a proper pattern for the top end of the pole. The Pirogue is now finished and equipped with poles.

We will start her on her maiden trip. The crew, an equal number on either side, facing the stern, set their poles on the bottom of the river and push. The boat now moves under their feet, tread-mill fashion, and when the boat has moved her length,

all walk back to the bow dragging their poles in the water and repeat the operation. Where the current was rapid it was necessary
for a part of the crew to continue pushing while others would
head up and set again so that all would not cease pushing at one
time. In such cases the man at the helm would sing out "Head
two," when the two nearest the bow would return and set anew.
By this time the others would have reached the stern when you
would hear "Up behind," when the remainder of the crew would
go as far forward as could be without interfering with the others
and renew their set. In this way the boat would not lose her
headway as she would have done had all ceased pushing at one
time. With an experienced crew this manner of propelling boats
was rather interesting, for in order to have the boat run steady
the men on one side must set their poles at the same angle as
those on the other. If this was not done the boat would flank
or travel side wise and the pilot swear.

About 120 barrels could be stowed away in a Pirogue in a
single floor tier, 3 barrels wide and about 40 barrels long. There
being few if any roads along the river, such supplies as the valley
then afforded were carried by Pirogue to the different salt works
where we find a number of families collected, many men being
employed in the manufacture of salt. Wood was then used as
fuel and we find that the first places where the timber was entirely
cleared off was in the immediate vicinity of the furnaces. This
furnished employment for wood choppers and teamsters in addition to those who pumped and boiled the salt water. When the
supply of wood was exhausted in the immediate vicinity, shoots
were built from the crest of the river hill where wood was
collected and carried down the shoot to the furnace doors. The
Pirogue continued in use until superceded by the Keelboat which
was of more artistic build, this taking place about 1827.

The Keelboat was managed in the same manner as the Pirogue, but on account of its being much larger, from 60 to 150
tons burden, a larger crew was required, 25 men being necessary
for the larger. Even this apparently larger crew was insufficient in passing up stream through the ripples and chutes of the
Ohio and Muskingum. At such places as Luke Chute, Silver
Heels and Slippery Rock, ox teams were kept in readiness to

help through the chutes, often several attempts were made before the boat could be brought up into the foot of the chute in proper position. Frequently the boat would shear off obliquely across the current. When this happened the cattle must be cut loose in a hurry or the boat would pull the cattle instead of the cattle pulling the boat. Such boats were not common until in the early thirties of the 19th century when regular trips, or as regular as was possible, were made between Zanesville and Pittsburg. Salt continued to be the principal freight on their outward trips, and manufactured iron, dry goods and groceries on their return, cod fish and mackerel always occupying a prominent place on the bills of lading. From three to five weeks was required in making the round trip. However, one case is recorded of an up stream trip between Marietta and Pittsburg being made in 5 days. Sails, which were carried by all such boats being brought into service on this occasion. As Keelboats made no attempt to run at night this shows a run of 168 miles in about 60 hours which was considered a high rate of speed, as often hours were spent in warping up through some of the island chutes. Keel boats generally bore a marked distinction by their color, each owner painting all his boats one color, leaving other colors for other boat owners. So when a Keel boat hove in sight a skipper would know who was the owner and if he wished to ship would generally have plenty of time before the boat would arrive.

Mention should have been made of the flat boats or broad horns as they were usually called before the Keel boats, as flat boats were built as early as 1825. They were built as cheaply as was possible as they were to serve for the one down stream trip only, which was usually to Cincinnati or Louisville, carrying salt 300 or 400 barrels, depending on the size of the barrels. As there was no standard size at that time, from 5 to 8 bushels were packed in one barrel. This was probably a scheme as freight was collected per barrel regardless of size. I speak of this as we know oil barrels of later times were increased in size from 40 to as high as 55 gallons in order to save freight. In 1848 a standard was fixed by law, making 280 pounds net, a barrel. At this time an inspector was appointed and all salt must pass his inspection, the weight being the principal thing to be considered, as green salt decreases in weight by drainage quite rapidly. If the shortage did not exceed 25 pounds the salt was O. K. Jake Marquis was the first salt inspector on the Muskingum. Salt boats were managed with sweeps and gouger instead of poles. The sweeps were large oars and were placed on the sides of the boat while the gouger is simply a steering oar placed on the bow. The inboard end of the steering oar and gouger was so high from the deck that a scaffold called a "lazy board" was erected on which the operators stood.

Steam boats of crude design were now making occasional trips from Pittsburg into the Muskingum. The first to ascend the Muskingum was the Steamer Rufus Putnam, in January, 1824. The first steam boats had but a single slide valve engine which caused the wheel to revolve spasmodically with each stroke of the engine as the energy ceased at the dead points. The feed pumps for furnishing water for the boilers were attached to the main engine. This was no serious objection when the boat was under way, but if lying ashore the wheel must revolve if the pump must run. The boilers were cylinder boilers, no flues being used, so the smoke stack must be at the aft end. This gave no heating surface except the lower half of the shell of the boiler. The engines had no reverse attachment so the wheel revolved in the one direction only. In making landings the engine was stopped at what was supposed to be a proper distance from shore and, if carrying too much headway when near shore, men with poles would bear off. The late Capt. Davis related an experience in this line which was of much interest to his hearers at the time, which I will repeat. On passing down stream out of Symes Creek lock, which is nine miles above Zanesville, with one of the boats which had no reverse apparatus, the boat became unmanageable and ran out above a rocky and dangerous reef, where there seemed to be no help for her. The engineer took in the situation and without bell orders from anyone, threw off the cam hook and reversed the motion of the rock shaft, doing this by hand. The wheel started in the opposite direction and by throwing this rock shaft to and fro at the proper time the engine continued its backward motion until the headway of the boat was checked and a disaster avoided. The captain and his crew now crowded around the engineer, to learn how it was done. The operation was repeated, whereupon the captain on arriving at Zanesville laid his boat up in order to have this new fangled arrangement put in place so the wheel would revolve in either direction, but by a little miscalculation this failed and this improvement in engines was left for another inventor. Later the feed pump was connected to an independent engine which made a self contained machine called doctor and the side pump was done away with. The doctor has now been superceded by an instrument called an injector, so small that it could be carried in one's pocket, while the doctor was a heavy cumbrous affair weighing about a ton.

In this connection we may mention other improvements in steam boats and their rigging. The swinging stage now takes the place of two or three lengths of gang plank which were sub-protected by tressels, clamps, etc., which took much time to place. The stage is operated by steam, is always ready and reaches from 45 to 50 feet from the bulwarks. The balance rudder is another improvement of much importance as boats can now round to in one-third the width of the Muskingum, where by the old style rudder the whole width was required and then many a failure made if there was much wind. Many boats on the Ohio are now steered by steam, but none as yet on the Muskingum. From 1824 until the beginning of the river improvement, steam boats made trips between Pittsburgh and Zanesville whenever there was sufficient water, usually in spring and fall. No inspection of steam boats had yet been required by the government and no license was required of the officers. So any man whom the owner would trust could be his pilot or engineer. No steam whistles were in use, but each boat was provided with a bell which was used in making the necessary signals, when meeting or passing other boats and a mutual understanding being that one tap of the bell indicated that each boat must pass to the right and two taps to pass to the left. Contentions arose and collisions were not uncommon. This brought about legislation concerning the management of steam boats, and as early as 1838 the steam boat inspection service had its beginning, by an act of Congress approved July 7th. On March 3, 1843, an act was approved relating to the equipment of vessels. By the act of July 7, 1838, pilots and engineers were required to take out a license which cost them $10 an issue, their license having to be renewed each year. Engineers to navigate any waters, the pilots on such waters as they were fully acquainted with, their introduction generally had been pushing on Keel boats. We learn from a letter written by Mr. F. R. Hanna, a former citizen of McConnelsville, in reply to an article which appeared in the McConnelsville Herald, Feb. 27th, 18905, that the steamer Defiance was the first boat provided with a steam whistle to reach McConnelsville. I know of no better way to describe the consternation of the people on hearing the whistle than to reproduce the letter of Mr. Hanna:

St. Joseph, Missouri, March 2, 1895.

Editor Herald: — I received a Herald with the list of steamboats since 1840. — There is also a notice in the paper asking for corrections from memory from any source, if corrections can be made; with offer of the paper.

As I glanced over the list and found not the name, my memory ran back to boyhood on the banks of the "beautiful blue" and to one certain quiet, pleasantly warm, fall evening — it must have been during the fall of the later part of the 1840 decade — dark, because there was no moon and 'twas before the days of my noble old friend, Tom Nott's oil lamps or your later day electric lights, when the whole village as though by one sudden impulse driven, rushed down Center street to John Edwards' corner to see a new steamboat. Just as we were well arranged all over the wharf and admiring the brilliant red lights shining through the glass front, with red calico curtains of the cabin and the myriads of sparks flying from the smoke stacks, on her sweeping way from the head of the canal to the "landing," we were greeted — no, overwhelmed, by the most unearthly screech that had ever pierced our ears or penetrated the jungles and rocks of "Red Brush" or "Rocky Glen," till we "little tads" and many of the large, older and wiser, (?) thinking surely the "Old Fellow" had come for his own, ran for the upper street in tumultuous clamor, tumbling over each other in our headlong speed to "git out o' the wilderness." It was the Str. Defiance carrying and using the first whistle up the "Jim Crank."

I know I ran for home and although always considered one of the speediest runners among the boys, "Pierre" Gaylord distanced me on the first quarter in his rapid flight for near the parade ground. And his lung exercise so far exceeded the defiance blown out by the steamer, that she never made another trip up the river.

Yours truly,   F. R. Hanna.

Before mentioning the improvements of the Muskingum by the state, we must remember the prior improvement at McConnelsville, where by an act of the State Legislature, February 22, 1830, Robert McConnell was granted permission to build a dam and lock. This work was completed in 1832 or 1833, the dam being built of brush and rubble stone, the lock of cut stone masonry, the inner wall of the lock chamber answering for the outer foundation of the old McConnell mill. There is still at this writing enough left of this wall to mark the place and to locate the old lock, most of the stone however has been removed, some of them within the last 60 days to be used by the Elk Eye Milling Co., in repairs about the present mill. In a recent conversation with Capt. I. N. Hook, I asked: "Do you remember passing through the old McConnell lock at any time?" His reply was "yes, I have special reason to remember. I was locking up stream on one occasion when the head of my canoe caught under the arm of the upper gate as the lock was filling and the canoe capsized spilling apples, mellons and boy into the water. This was nothing serious as the apples and melons floated and were recovered and I am here to tell the story."

In March, 1836, the improvement of the Muskingum was authorized by an act of the State Legislature and an appropriation of $400,000 was also made for the purpose. In August of the same year proposals were called for to be opened at the Court House in McConnelsville on the 20th of the following October. Nine or ten dams and ten or twelve locks were to be considered. This sale continued from the 20th until the 24th. On the 11th of November of the same year, the names of the successful bidders were published in the Peoples Advocate, of McConnelsville. The editor's card reading thus: "Advocate, printed and published every Friday by John W. White. Office on Center St., two doors west of the Baptist church." Which would be the building now occupied by Mr. Betz, the saddler. How soon active operations began, I am not able to say. But it is to be supposed not until the spring of 1837. From the time of the commencement until its completion navigation on the Muskingum was practically at a standstill. The contractors, many of them as shrewd as those of to-day, considered $400,000 the amount available for this work, inadequate and fearing that the next legislature would fail to make another appropriation, thought to bring pressure to bear by beginning this work in such a manner as would cripple navigation continuously until the completion of the entire system, which they practically succeeded in doing.   However, the energy and persistence of the Keel boat men was shown in an effort to arrange their boats so that at least one would remain in each pool so that freight could be transferred from one to another over the unfinished dams.   Three years was the allotted time in which this river improvement was to have been completed. But on account of the contentions concerning the size of the locks which were to have been 22 x 120 feet and were finally changed to 36 x 160 feet which they still remain.   Another cause for delay was the change of location.   One instance was after excavation had been commenced in the bend of the river below Hooksburg.   This location was changed to the present site of Windsor, the citizens of that vicinity subscribed $3,000, one-half the amount necessary to make this change.   Again, high water interfered so that 5 years elapsed before navigation was opened.   A number of steam boats now made their appearance and most of them plying between Pittsburg and Zanesville.

Soon after the erection of the new flouring mills, which was in the early forties, until as late as 1860, regularly each fall flat-boats or broadhorns were loaded at different mills on the river with barrel flour destined for New Orleans. As many as 5 or 6 of these boats were built on the river front between the foot of Main street and the head of the canal, at McConnelsville, each summer, most of which were loaded here also.   A corresponding number of such boats were built and loaded at other points where mills were located until the number going out of the Muskingum in the fall would reach 20 or 25 boats. — There was great rivalry among the crews of these boats, each striving to be first to reach New Orleans.   It is said that trips of this kind have been made without tying a line, as boatmen would say, that is, without landing after leaving Marietta until reaching the eddy at New Orleans.

In this connection I quote another pioneer boatman, who now resides in our midst, Mr. John Travis, who as pilot on one of these flour-boats, left Marietta in the fall of 1852, making the run to New Orleans in seventeen days and eleven hours, thirteen hours of this time being lost at islands Nos. 101 and 102 on the Mississippi by rough weather. This being the only landing made in this long run of 1,794 miles, gives an average of over five miles per hour. In five weeks and two days the crew had returned to start on a second trip. On this particular trip a light load was taken, being 1,200 barrels. The dimensions of the boat being 18x90 feet, the usual size being 18x100 feet, capacity about 1,400 barrels, depending on the depth of the hold. — Flat-boat pilots received as wages on such trips $1.00 for each foot in length of his boat and acted as "Major Domo," when the owner was not on board. Others of the crew, 6 or 7 in number, received $20 each for the trip, the return expenses of all being paid by the owner of the boat. This class of boats continued making trips of this kind until the Civil War interfered, though in the last few years with less vigor. On many of the later trips the cargo was of general produce which was disposed of on the lower coast among the planters. The last trip of this kind was made in the fall of 1860, when the situation become so alarming on account of national disturbance that a part of the crew returned from Baton Rouge rather than take the chances of being detained at New Orleans.

Having finished a long and probably tedious story concerning flat-boat navigation, we will now return to steam boats of a later date. As we have already stated most of the river traffic prior to 1852 was between Pittsburg and Zanesville. About this time daily packets commenced running between Parkersburg and Zanesville. In 1856 the Str. John Buck and Charlie Bowen were making three trips per week in this trade, which was kept up by different boats until the building of the O. & L. K. R. R. in 1886 and 1887.

Throughout this entire article salt has been mentioned as the principal freight. But this long delayed work of the river improvement effected a material change in this respect. Many of the salt works had gone down and their owners with them, financially ruined. The splendid water power afforded by the now permanent dams caused larger and better flouring mills to be erected, and wheat and flour soon became the principal items of freight. Here I wish to mention another product which to-day would add to the freight list but at that time it was considered of no value and consequently bran was spouted into the river, or in some cases was used as saw-dust for street crossings in the vicinity of the mills.

Although steam boats were now quite common, the Keel boat was by no means discarded. They being built to carry bulk grain, were now used to carry wheat from points on the river where warehouses had been erected by the mill owner for collecting wheat. Roxbury 13 miles below and Gaysport 14 miles above McConnelsville, were the two principal warehouses, both of which furnished wheat for the mill at McConnelsville. One cent per bushel was the freight by Keel boat. This extremely low figure was brought about on account of the facilities of handling the wheat at the ware houses where it was received, as well as at the mill where it was discharged.

At the warehouse the boat come along side and the wheat was spouted into the cargo box. At the mill there was a projecting section of the building directly under which the Keel boats could be moored. An adjustable elevator could be lowered into the boat and the wheat carried up into the mill by water power, where it could be distributed on any one of the floors and at any point desired by a series of conveyors. This elevator was so constructed as to suit any stage of water and by a countre balance followed up as the boat was relieved of her load. The projection of the building remains, but where the boat could lay under drawing 3½ feet, there is now a bank 4 or 5 feet above the normal water level.

I now have occasion to refer to another of Capt. Hook's stories. He having a contract of carrying wheat from Roxbury to the McConnell Mills and Mr. McConnell thinking one cent per bushel "a little high," the latter bought a canal boat, the May Queen, paying $1,600 for her, hired a crew and proceeded to boat his own wheat. Captain Hook being thrown out of employment by this move, made the following suggestion to Mr. McConnell, that he, Hook, would boat the wheat for 90% of what it would cost by the May Queen and asked McConnell to keep an accurate account of the expense. The May Queen carried the wheat for one season, when McConnell accosted Hook in this manner: "Ike, if you will take the May Queen out of my sight so I will never see her again, I will renew the one cent contract." "I accepted."

During the Civil War, the salt industry was revived, and in 1865 as many as 23 salt-works were in operation on the Muskingum between Hooksburg and Zanesville, where there is but one to-day. The price of salt reached $3.00 per barrel, most of which was shipped up stream; much of it by smaller steam boats, called "Propellers," which were of canal size, 14 by 80 feet, and heavy carriers on account of their large cargo box and their depth of hold, about 500 barrels being their capacity. The principal reason for shipping with boats of this class was that the larger boats could not pass up through the canal at Zanesville, which the salt must do, in order to reach the railroad without transfer.

After the close of the Civil War, quite a business was started by one of these propellers, called the "Barnhart," which towed a canal-boat of her own size, called the "Tipton Slasher," making regular trips between Port Harmar, at the mouth of the Muskingum and Cleveland via Ohio Canal and this river, carrying cedar logs on her south-bound trips to the large bucket factories, then operating at Point Harmar. On her return trips, salt was taken to Cleveland. Transient boats made many trips on this route, bringing down iron-ore from Lake Superior region, for points on the Ohio, between Marietta and Cincinnati. Lake ice was also taken to Ohio river towns in this manner, there being no ice plants thought of at that time. I have known boats to pass south twice without going north on the Muskingum.

The Parkersburg packets were now carrying tobacco, wool and live stock to Parkersburg, where it was re-shipped east by the Baltimore & Ohio Railroad. In 1860, an oil excitement struck this locality, which gave an impetus to business on the river. Oil refineries were built — one at McConnelsville, one at Windsor and another at Beverly, and several at Marietta. There was then no net-work of pipe line over the country, so all crude oil must reach the refineries by river, or by teams, from the local fields. Steamboats carried crude oil in barrels for a time, but soon the local oil fields failed to furnish enough for so many refineries, and the flat-boats did service again in carrying bulk oil from the Pennsylvania oil fields, leaving the refined oil for the steamboats for a time only, when "Mr. Flat-boat" took it also, distributing it along the Ohio river, as far south as Cincinnati. I must now relate my exper-ience on trips of this kind, in order to show how much work had to be done to reach Cincinnati. This was in 1864, when two trips, in close succession, were made — one of them with two boats lashed — the other with a single boat, the Ohio being low in both cases. In the pools, as the river is called between islands, there was no current scarcely, so we must pull headway, wishing for an island-chute so we might rest while the current would carry us along; but when the swift places were reached we usually went a-ground, good and hard; then we would wish to be in the pool again! Sometimes we would a-ground so hard that the boat would show out ten inches below the water-line. Then we would unload the oil out of one boat — in case we had two — into the other (there was no trouble about her carrying it, as both had good foundations). In this way, one boat could be freed and dropped down in deep water; then we would build a boom, a frame work, to keep the barrels from separating, and cast the barrels into the river, inside the boom, continuing this until the second boat would float. Frequently the barrels themselves were a-ground when inside the boom, but this did not interfere with their navigation, as the strong current would roll them on their bottom, and when over the bar, we would transfer them to the boats again, unless another shoal place was near when they re-mained in the bottom until it would be passed. Two transfers of this kind were made on one of these trips, and one on the other. As the price of carbon oil, at that time, was so much more than to-day, I must say that it was 85 to 90 cts. per gallon, by the barrel.

During the rebellion many soldiers were transported down the Muskingum and some of the steamboats from this river were pressed into the government service and taken to the Tennessee and Cumberland rivers. Having mentioned several classes of boats we must not omit the gunboat which did service on the

Muskingum. When Gen. John Morgan made his memorable raid through Ohio, the side-wheel Str. Jesse Edington was then our ferry boat between McConnelsville and Malta. In a hurried manner she was transformed into a gun-boat, her principal gun being our old Fourth of July cannon. As Morgan was expected to cross the Muskingum at Eagleport (where he did), the gun-boat with a crew and several gunners started for the scene of action. On their way up the river the several gunners proceeded to load the principal gun to kill and cripple, using some powder and much scrap-iron, and on arriving at Eagleport, they found that Morgan had crossed the river and gone. The gun-boat returned, and on her way down the river, it was decided to discharge their principal gun, which was mounted about midship. After the smoke had cleared away it was found that the gun came as near going overboard at the stern as the scrap-iron did at the bow. This can be explained by the load being nearly as heavy as the gun, consequently the gun shot away from the load instead of the load shooting out of the gun. However this gives us one gun-boat in service on the Muskingum.

In March, 1866, one of the finest steam boats that ever before or since navigated this river, was completed and brought into service between Parkersburg and Zanesville. This boat the Carrie Brooks was built by the Darlingtons of Zanesville. They having sold the Jonas Powell, had neglected their trade while building the new boat and a Portsmouth built boat, the D. M. Sechler, had taken charge. So when the Carrie Brooks was ready to enter the trade, so, also, was the Sechler ready to remain. A most lively opposition ensued. These boats seemed to make no effort to do business. The only desire of each apparently, was to pass up and down the river ahead of the other. I have known these boats to arrive at McConnelsville at 6:00 a. m., which was about the time they should have left Marietta. In 1863, Capt. Monroe Ayres, of Zanesville, who then owned and ran the Str. Emma Graham in the Pittsburg and Zanesville trade, transformed a model barge into a side-wheel steam boat and established a trade between McConnelsville and Zanesville, the Str. Falcon making daily trips, where she continued for about one year, when she was sold and left the river. — The Str. Zanesville, Capt. Wm.

Davis, which had been making three trips per week between McConnelsville and Dresden, now dropped into the place made vacant by the sale of the Falcon. This place has been continually filled up to and including the present, the Str. Valley Gem now filling the place.

Since the beginning of navigation on the Muskingum by steamboats, disasters have been few and the loss of life small, comparatively speaking. The first accident of a serious nature was the disastrous explosion of the Str. Buckeye Belle, which occurred in the head of the Beverly canal on March 12, 1852, when 26 lives were lost. The Buckeye Belle was one of the few side-wheel boats to ply on the Muskingum, as the width of the locks, 36 feet, was not sufficient to allow proper width of hull, after deducting the necessary space occupied by the two wheels. Stern-wheel boats were preferable. At the time of the explosion, the boat was engaged in carrying the U. S. mail between Newport, on the Ohio, sixteen miles above Marietta, and Zanesville. The Str. Dan Converse was also engaged in this trade on alternate days, but just prior to the explosion of the Belle, had been succeeded by the Allegheny Clipper. It is said that these boats made this run in daylight. This seems rather remarkable, as with all the improvements in steam boats, their engines, boilers and other apparatus, boats of to-day could do no better. A singular coincidence was the sinking of the Dan Converse, a short distance below Pittsburg on the day previous to the destruction of the Belle and at about the same hour. The late R. L. Morris, of this place, was a passenger on the Converse at the time of the sinking, and on his return found navigation obstructed at Beverly by the wreck of the Buckeye Belle. Therefore he walked to McConnelsville, arriving in time to officiate as pall bearer at the funeral of Milton Whissen, one of the victims of the explosion.

It is rather remarkable that 27 years elapsed before another serious accident occurred on the Muskingum. Not until February 15, 1879, when the Str. L. C. McCormick exploded her boilers, near the foot of Dana's Island, where she sank. One body, that of the fireman, was never seen or heard of, and this was the only life lost by accident. Several were scalded, but none seriously. — Capt. I. N. Hook took charge of the wreck, raised the hull so far as to recover her machinery, which was placed on the Str. Gen. H. F. Devol, which was immediately built by the owners of the Str. McCormick. The hull was then let go when she sank again and was abandoned.

We will now mention a few minor casualties of later date. On June 11th, 1886, the Str. Lizzie Cassel struck an obstruction in backing out of Taylorsville canal. This was not known at the time, as the timbers of the stern rake were so old and rotten that no shock was felt by any of the crew, consequently she filled with water without warning. The first intimation of anything going wrong was the wheeler revolving slower than usual. The mate then went below to investigate and did not return. The pilot thought best to go ashore and see what the trouble was, but on pulling down toward shore the boat careened and the tale was told. She soon sank, the water coming just high enough to extinguish the fire in the furnace and drown some hogs. This accident was not serious, as the boat was raised in ten days, docked and continued in service. The George Strecker burned at Beverly in 1887. This occurred at night in port when no passengers were aboard. The S. R. VanMetre burned at Lowell in 1889. Both belonged to one man, Capt. Stowe, of Beverly. Each was a total loss. The most singular thing in the estimation of the writer is the fact that in all the years since the river has been improved, no steam boat has ever accidentally gone over a dam, notwithstanding many a close call is remembered.

In conclusion I might mention the steamboating of to-day in comparison with the foregoing. One would imagine that with the river in the hands of the general government whereby it is kept in good repair and nothing to interfere with navigation, except ice in the winter season, and occasionally high water, that boating would be a good business, especially when no tolls are collected, as was the case when the improvement was governed by the state. But with all such advantages, we find but three boats which attempt to run regularly — the Str. Sonoma, daily between Beverly and Marietta, the Str. Valley Gem, daily between McConnelsville and Zanesville, and the Str. Lorena, weekly between Zanesville and Pittsburg. The latter is laid up much of the summer season on account of low water in the Ohio.

Such changes have taken place, that in order to make business, the owners frequently buy the larger part of the cargo in going out of the Muskingum, which consists of produce and live stock and poultry.

In conclusion, I must say that no improvement in boating on the Muskingum can be looked for until the advent of a water way from Lake Erie to the Ohio river via the Muskingum, the initial steps of which were taken as early as 1838. A recent appropriation of $200,000, with a string to it, was made by the state for the purpose of reclaiming the practically abandoned Ohio Canal. If this appropriation should become available and the Ohio Canal made navigable again, together with the improvement of the Ohio, which is now under way, and the "on to Cairo" movement with 9 foot which is sure to come, some of us may live to see the Muskingum a national water way of vast importance.

DARNELL'S LEAP FOR LIFE.

It will be recollected by students of history that in the year 1778, during the Revolution, Daniel Boone, with twenty-seven others was taken prisoner in Kentucky and brought to Old Town, or Old Chillicothe, as the Shawanese called it. Through the influence of Hamilton, the British Governor, Boone with ten of his party was taken to Detroit, while the remaining seventeen prisoners were left with their savage captors. Among the latter number was a man whose name is supposed to have been Darnell. Brave as a lion and cunning as a fox, he resolved to try and effect his escape. One night, how it is not for us to say, he found himself in a wood northwest of Clifton. Beneath the branches of a monarch of the forest, he paused to recruit his strength when daylight suddenly burst upon him. Not seeming to comprehend his dangerous situation, he did not move, but coolly took a piece of pemmican from his pouch and began to devour it. He was not unarmed, for he had stolen his rifle and hunting accoutrements from his captors.

The pemmican had scarcely been devoured when the noise occasioned by the breaking of a twig assailed his ears. His backwoods learning at once told him that a human foot had broken the twig, and in an instant he was on his feet. Turning and looking in the direction of the noise he saw several Indians hid behind the trees. He knew they were Shawanese and therefore his bitterest enemies. What should he do? The redskins were in his very path and to attempt to get beyond them was to court death by their tomahawks or the terrible stake. Flight seemed the only alternative — flight in a direction directly opposite to the course he had marked out. The savages remained behind the trees intensely watching the white man's movements. They could have brought him down with a bullet, but such was not their intention. They wanted him to die by fire in their village. For a minute he surveyed his perilous position and then

(425)

tightened the buckskin belt he wore. I will run he cried, and if they catch me they must stir their stumps well. He was no mean runner and no sooner had he started forward than the Indians sprang from behind the trees and started in swift pursuit. The course of the prisoner lay toward the Miami, and the gorge through which it flows. Suddenly he veered to the left and quickened his rapid pace for the savages were gaining ground. He had miscalculated their speed and endurance and now feared that they would soon overtake him. Presently he heard the roar of the falls and he veered still further to the left. His present course would take him to the falls, and the Shawanese sent their best runners to head him off. But he did not maintain his present path far, but veered again and ran straight forward. An ash tree, which he had marked with his hatchet several years before stood near the edge of the cliff a short distance below the falls, and it now lay directly in his path. Suddenly the hunter looked back at his pursuers. They numbered six in all, and were headed by Shawanese of no mean distinction. "I believe I can camp Little Fox," mutters the hunter as he examined the priming of his gun. The priming was in proper condition and he suddenly paused near a tree which stood on what is now the road leading from Clifton to Yellow Springs. He boldly faced his pursuers and threw his rifle to his shoulder. Little Fox saw that the weapon was directed to his breast and tried to shelter himself behind a tree. But alas; he was too late, for the rifle cracked and the Shawanese had lost a valuable chief. The prisoner smiled at the effect of his shot, but did not reload for with hideous yells the remaining five had darted forward to avenge the death of their leader. Directly before Darnell lay the gorge and from bank to bank it was fully thirty feet. Cedars and bushes grew along the edge of the cliff, while far below it rolled the historic Miami, white with foam from the falls. The hunter was not ignorant of all these facts for he had visited the spot before, and it was photographed on his mind. He knew the foolhardiness of an attempt to leap the gorge, and that almost certain death awaited him on the rocky bed of the Miami, but these thoughts did not arrest his progress. He had determined to make the leap and nothing in the world could have changed his mind. And then the thought of a lingering death at the stake urged him on. Better, he murmured to die on the bed of the Miami, than at the stake in Old Chillicothe. In a moment he had passed the ash tree which stands to this day a witness of the daring deed we are relating, and the next he had actually leaped from the limestone cliff. He had not miscalculated the distance, nor permitted a nerve to remain inactive, every one had been strained for the feat. A moment the brave fellow was in mid-air, and then he grasped a bush on the opposite side of the gorge. With great exertion he drew himself up on terra firma and sprang forward again. But he had no need to exert himself longer for the pursuit was ended. The Shawanese had reached the cliff and were gazing, lost in amazement upon the scene of the white man's daring deed and his form which was disappearing among the trees. "He is more than pale face," said one of the Indians; "he is under the protection of the great spirit, for pale face nor Indian could never jump across the Chekemeameesepe. Let us no longer pursue a spirit. We will never look upon his like again this side of the dark river and the happy hunting grounds. Braves, back to your village." In silence the savages retraced their steps and told to their wondering people the story of the most daring feat ever recorded. The white pioneers could scarcely believe it, but they afterwards heard it from the lips of Darnell himself.

And now, reader, if it is ever your pleasure to visit the mountain gorge referred to in this narrative, do not forget to view the scene of the hunter's leap, which is a few feet to the right of the ash standing near the Clifton and Yellow Springs road, a short distance below the falls.

SONG WRITERS OF OHIO.

TWO SONGS INSPIRED IN OHIO.

BY C. B. GALBREATH.

While much has been said and written of the achievements of Ohio's men, the public has not fully appreciated, perhaps, the extent of the influence of the gifted women of the state. This is due, doubtless, to the fact that this influence is often exerted in ways somewhat obscure and indirect. A gifted woman, of course, is a creature of physical and intellectual beauty, endued with the power to lift man to the heights of fame or drive him to despair and — poetry. The lovers of song owe something to Lorena and that other Ohio maiden with the eyes of "delicious blue."

COATES KINNEY.

Author of "Rain on the Roof."

A few months ago a stranger in Cincinnati might have met on one of the streets of that city a man in civilian dress with the martial bearing and elastic step of an officer temporarily off duty. The only evidence of advanced age was hair and beard of immaculate white.

COATES KINNEY.

Such was Coates Kinney to the world,— a militant spirit with much of the exclusiveness and taciturnity that belong to the professional warrior. Such he was by nature and education. By birth a Puritan and by happy chance a disciple of Horace Mann, he was in walk and conversation something of an aristocrat. But like his famous preceptor, he was not to be judged by the austerity of his manners or the rigidity of his classic standards. At heart he was tenderly affectionate. The inner

(428)

man, as revealed by his writings, was thoroughly democratic and humanitarian.

In his ideal social state, man was dominant by intellectual prowess alone. In the language of Caius Marius his question was ever, "What can make a difference between one man and another but the qualities of the mind?" In the rising power of wealth, he saw the supreme menace to the Republic. He had ambitions in the direction of the public service, but "practical politics" were not to his liking. He had small patience with apologies for modern commercialism. Corruption felt the rapier thrust of his scathing denunciation.

Though born in New York, he reached manhood in Ohio. To the state of his adoption he was passionately devoted, and with it he was identified throughout his literary career.

To be chronologically and biographically specific, Coates Kinney was born at Kinney's Corners, Yates Co., N. Y., November 24, 1826. He came with his parents, Giles and Myra (Cornell) Kinney, to Ohio in 1840, and later taught school in Warren and Logan counties. While in the latter he studied law in the office of Judge Lawrence, at Bellefontaine, and for a time edited the West Liberty *Banner.* In 1849, he wrote his famous lyric, *Rain on the Roof.* Later he was admitted to the bar in Cincinnati. He spent one year in Antioch College, but was not graduated. After resigning a professorship in Judson College, Mt. Palatine, Ill., he returned to Ohio to become associate editor of the *Genius of the West,* a literary magazine founded by Howard Durham. William T. Coggeshall succeeded Durham in the partnership. Elected captain of a local company at the breaking out of the Civil War, Kinney, on the recommendation of Salmon P. Chase, was appointed paymaster with the rank of major. After four years' service, he was retired with the brevet of lieutenant-colonel. Before entering the service he was editor of the Xenia *News.* After the war, he edited the Xenia *Torchlight,* and wrote for the Cincinnati *Times* and the *Ohio State Journal.* In 1884 he became chief owner and editor of the *Globe Republic* of Springfield, Ohio. He served one term in the state senate and was an unsuccessful candidate for nomination to congress. He was twice married. A wife and three daughters survive.

While he wrote much prose, he is best known and will be longest remembered as a poet. He left three books of verse, "Keeuka," "Lyrics of the Ideal and the Real," and "Mists of Fire." One of his earliest compositions, written fifty years before the publication of his last volume, was the well-known and ever popular song, *Rain on the Roof*. Fortunately he has left a record of the circumstances under which it was written. It was composed while he was visiting his old home at Spring Valley, Greene Co., O. In a letter to his friend, Dr. Wm. H. Venable, he says:

"I slept one night next the roof in the little farm cottage which our folks lived in, and which has since been torn away and replaced. In the evening there came up a gentle rain, which pattered on the shingle roof, two or three feet above my head, all the part of the night during which I was awake. Here I lay and conceived the lyric, and then went to sleep. It haunted me the next day, which was bright and green, and glorious; and, on a walk from Spring Valley down to Mt. Holly — three miles — where I went to visit my uncle's folks, I composed most of the poem, finishing it the same afternoon during a sequestration of myself and a ramble in the woods just adjoining the town — woods now long since cleared away. It was the easiest production I ever wrote. It cost me no labor. . . .

"I sent it to the *Great West*, which was then edited by the novelist of Indians, Emerson Bennett. I was personally acquainted with Bennett, and he knew me as a writer, for I had contributed to a little literary paper of his. It was so long before the poem appeared that I had given it up as unaccepted. But finally it did appear, September 22, 1849. . . . I learned later, from E. Penrose Jones, who was publisher of the *Great West*, that the poem escaped oblivion through an accidental discovery of his. He was looking through Bennett's rejected manuscript drawer, and found it. Bennett had thought it not quite up to the standard of Indian-novelist literature, and had tossed it into that drawer."

The song as it appears in the second edition of his poem is as follows:

RAIN ON THE ROOF.

When the humid shadows hover
Over all the starry spheres
And the melancholy darkness
Gently weeps in rainy tears,

What a bliss to press the pillow
  Of a cottage–chamber bed
And lie listening to the patter
  Of the soft rain overhead!

Every tinkle on the shingles
  Has an echo in the heart;
And a thousand dreamy fancies
  Into busy being start,
And a thousand recollections
  Weave their air-threads into woof,
As I listen to the patter
  Of the rain upon the roof.

Now in memory comes my mother,
  As she used in years agone,
To regard the darling dreamers
  Ere she left them till the dawn:
O! I feel her fond look on me
  As I list to this refrain
Which is played upon the shingles
  By the patter of the rain.

Then my little seraph–sister,
  With her wings and waving hair,
And her star-eyed cherub brother —
  A serene angelic pair —
Glide around my wakeful pillow,
  With their praise or mild reproof,
As I listen to the murmur
  Of the soft rain on the roof.

And another comes, to thrill me
  With her eyes' delicious blue;
And I mind not, musing on her,
  That her heart was all untrue:
I remember but to love her
  With a passion kin to pain,
And my heart's quick pulses quiver
  To the patter of the rain.

Art hath naught of tone or cadence
  That can work with such a spell
In the soul's mysterious fountains,
  Whence the tears of rapture well,

As that melody of Nature,
That subdued, subduing strain
Which is played upon the shingles
By the patter of the rain.

The poem as here presented contains a number of verbal variations from the original. The most of them were made by the author in his later years. There is no change in sentiment, however.

Much has been written in praise of this lyric. A production so perfectly rhythmical, so full of tender sentiment and so expressive of the emotions of the universal heart, was, of course, soon set to music. For it a number of appropriate melodies have been composed.

Who was the maid that thrilled him "with her eyes' delicious blue?" Local tradition has no definite answer, and of course the Colonel was too gallant to tell. Many of his earlier poems glow with the Sappho flame and reveal the fact that he felt the tender passion whose power it is the especial mission of the poet to express.

Another song, written, as will be seen, to the tune of *John Brown's Body lies Mouldering in the Grave,* celebrated the liberation of the bondsmen:

FREEDMEN'S BATTLE HYMN.

O, to the Lord be glory! halleluiah to the Lord!
He hath stricken off our shackles and hath given us the sword
To do the righteous judgment of his everlasting Word,
    As we go marching on.
    Glory, glory Halleluiah!

We had waited for his token of deliverance so long
That we feared he had forgotten our two hundred years of wrong;
But at last we hear his signal in the battle-bugle's song,
    As we go marching on.

Ho! fathers, brothers, slaving in the cotton and the corn!
O! wives and daughters wishing that ye never had been born!
We are your armed redeemers, and we lead the hope-forlorn,
    As we go marching on.

For God hath made this people by the light of battle see
That death is on the Nation if the bond do not go free —
That by the sword of Freedmen shall the land regenerate be;
    And we go marching on.

Then watch and pray, dear kindred — when ye hear the battle-cry
Look for Freedom's Dark Crusaders where the Union–banners fly,
And to the Lord give glory! for his kingdom cometh nigh,
    As we go marching on.
    Glory, glory Halleluiah!

No adequate sketch of the life and work of Kinney has yet been written. He breathed his last in Cincinnati, January 25, 1904. Except in the local papers, slight mention was made of his demise. In the obituary notices of the reference year books his name seldom appears. This accident recalls the well-known line of his early poem:

    Our graves are leveled soon, and we on earth forgot.

But as Julian Hawthorne declared, "What Kinney has written will live." Among the "heroes of the pen" he has a place. Without intending to do so, he long ago declared his own title to victor over time:

    Hurra for the true! of old or new,
      Who heroes lived or fell —
    Thermopylae's immortal few!
      Hurra for the Switzer Tell!
    Upvoice to sky the brave Gracchi!
      Hurra for the Pole and the Hun!
    For the men who made the Great July!
      Hurra for Washington!
    Yet old Time Past would triumph at last —
      But hurra, and hurra again,   •
    For the heroes who triumph over Time!
    The Heroes of the Pen.

H. D. L. WEBSTER,
Author of "Lorena."

About sixty years ago a young man came from the state of Connecticut and enrolled in the Collegiate Institute of Columbus,

O., one of the schools of higher learning that in a comparatively brief time rose, flourished and passed away. With fair intellectual capacity, a warm heart and a buoyant, optimistic spirit, he pursued his studies with zeal and entered with zest into the innocent diversions of the little circle of self-dependent students among whom his lot was cast. Like many a youth thus environed, in his more serious moments he had visions of the future and the part that he was to play in life's drama. Air-castles he built, but they did not rise to the regions of the unattainable. His ambition was rational and altogether worthy. He hoped to become a minister in the Universalist church.

For his chosen calling he seemed peculiarly fitted. To the qualities already enumerated were added a fine presence and a pleasing address. His was the gift of eloquence, and the well-rounded periods and glowing metaphors that fell from his lips as he bore the message of salvation to all mankind made him friends even among those who had no sympathy with the distinctive tenets of his faith.

Soon after entering upon the active duties of the ministry, he was called to the little church at Zanesville. The leading spirit of the congregation there was a wealthy manufacturer. His liberal contributions were its main support. He was captivated by the brilliant young minister. He felt that the cause to which he was ardently devoted and to which he had given freely of his means was about to be substantially advanced in the community. Outside of the pulpit the gifted young advocate soon became a favorite with his people. His broad sympathies, love of nature, poetic temperament and conversational powers made him a welcome guest wherever he went. The door of his patron, the wealthy manufacturer, was of course open to him. Young Paul Vane[1] was happy. The people were coming out in large numbers to hear his sermons. The congregation was more than satisfied. The future was crescent with hope.

The church had a choir. The purpose of this desirable accessory is the dispensation of harmony. It is sometimes inti-

---

[1] Rev. H. D. L. Webster. The pseudonym Paul Vane is used in this sketch because it is assumed by Webster himself in one of his songs.

mated that the thing dispensed so freely often does not rule the band of sweet singers. Hence, occasional discords that are matters of serious concern to the good minister and officers of the church. Paul Vane was fortunate in his choir. The members were congenial as well as musical. Among them was a young lady with sweet and cultivated voice, the beautiful Lorena[2], sister to the wife of the chief pillar of the church. By degrees the young minister became conscious of her presence there.

Sometimes in his pulpit when words responsive to this thought flowed freely and held in magic thrall his delighted auditors, he somehow felt the spell of two lustrous eyes from the direction of the choir, which on meeting his own modestly retreated behind long, downcast lashes that but revealed more clearly the secret they sought to hide. In the language of one who knew her then, "She was nineteen, short in stature and petite, with blue eyes, light brown hair, and features that took hold upon 'the poetry of heaven.'" Small wonder that she lingered in his thoughts as he walked to his humble rooms alone.

It followed as a matter of course that his calls were more frequent at the residence of his wealthy parishioner. Church business of the most trivial character took on new importance and was the occasion of numerous visits to the mansion. At such times he was almost certain to meet Lorena. If she learned to recognize his approaching step, in spite of her modest nature she did not flee. The two became good friends. Sometimes they walked with companions to view nature on the beautiful banks of the Muskingum. Sometimes they wandered forth oblivious to all things except the blessed thought that they were alone.

Had the stream of affection moved joyfully on to the ocean of connubial bliss, this chapter of romantic history would never have been written. But smiling fortune gradually took on the sterner form of relentless fate. Lorena, as we have already intimated, had a sister, an elder sister.

The wife of the manufacturer, at least so runs the testimony of the friends of Paul Vane — and the relatives of Lorena are silent on the subject — as she saw the friendship of the two ripen

---

[2] Her real name was Miss Ella Blocksom.

into fonder attachment, became seriously concerned. The young
minister with his attractive personality did not fit into the future
that she had planned for her beautiful and accomplished sister.
The salary that he could command in any denomination must
be meager. Especially would that be true of the Universalist
church whose membership was comparatively small. Judged
by financial and other standards, she herself had made a most
fortunate matrimonial venture. She desired as much for her
sister. Paul Vane did not meet the requirements. The union
must be averted.

The view of the elder sister was gradually unfolded to the
youthful Lorena. One writer tells us that she was not only
poetical and romantic but indecisive and submissive. However
that may be, it seems that after many tears and vain regrets she
saw that she and Paul must part.

The day of separation came. It was a cloudless Sabbath
in May. After church they together slowly ascended the hill[1]
and lingered in the gathering twilight. Of that evening Paul
wrote in after years:

> 'Twas flowery May
> When up the hilly slope we climbed
> To watch the dying of the day
> And hear the distant church bells chimed.

In the gathering darkness he learned his fate. On the following day they parted forever. In a letter of farewell, Lorena,
among other things, wrote: "If we try, we may forget."

The young minister's position was no longer tenable. He
could not look for inspiration to the choir. He could not continue
to be dependent upon his present source of support. He resigned and disappeared from the scene of his triumph and defeat.

For the dear sakes of all lovers of eternal constancy in affairs of the heart, it would be gratifying to relate that the twain

---

[1] Some writers state the reference is to Putnam Hill, but it was
probably Hamline Hill, now thickly covered with houses. On this eminence
the home of the wealthy manufacturer still stands.

pined away under the weight of their affliction, or lived to old age nor found in other lives a comfort for the aching void that followed separation. Such tragedies there have been outside of the realm of fiction, but stern history must here record a different sequel.

About the "Town of Zane," matters resumed their normal sway. The young minister's place was filled in the pulpit. The sun declined as in days gone by. The seasons came and went. In due time a brilliant young lawyer of moderate means but high ambitions and qualities that even then held forth the promise of the ermine that he later wore, led the blushing Lorena to the altar.

The years rolled by. Where was Paul Vane? Through the silence that had closed between him and his former world there came at times a vague rumor that in the far west he was trying "to forget."

In the year 1860, when the voice of discord was loud in the land and opposing hosts were marshalling for the fray, a sentimental song appeared that became quite popular. It was sung throughout the United States and in England. It became a favorite in the camps of the Union and the Confederate armies, The words ran as follows:

LORENA.

The years creep slowly by, Lorena;
    The snow is on the grass again;
The sun's low down the sky, Lorena,
    The frost is where the flowers have been.
But the heart throbs on as warmly now
    As when the summer days were nigh;
Oh! the sun can never dip so low
    Adown affection's cloudless sky.

A hundred months have passed, Lorena,
    Since last I held that hand in mine,
And felt the pulse beat fast, Lorena,
    Though mine beat faster far than thine;
A hundred months —'twas flowery May,
    When up that hilly slope we climbed
To watch the dying of the day
    And hear the distant church bells chimed.

We loved each other then, Lorena,
　　More than we ever cared to tell;
And what we might have been, Lorena,
　　Had but our lovings prospered well.
But then 'tis past, the years are gone,
　　I'll not call up their shadowy forms;
I'll say to them — lost years sleep on —
　　Sleep on, nor heed life's pelting storms.

The story of the past, Lorena,
　　Alas! I care not to repeat;
The hopes that could not last, Lorena,
　　They lived, but only lived to cheat.
I would not cause e'en one regret
　　To rankle in your bosom now;
For "if we try, we may forget,"
　　Were words of thine long years ago.

Yes, these were words of thine, Lorena,
　　They burn within my memory yet;
They touched some tender chord, Lorena,
　　That thrills and trembles with regret.
'Twas not thy woman's heart that spoke —
　　Thy heart was always true to me;
A duty, stern and pressing, broke
　　The tie that linked my soul to thee.

It matters little now, Lorena,
　　The past is in the eternal past;
Our heads will soon lie low, Lorena,
　　Life's tide is ebbing out so fast.
There is a future! Oh, thank God!
　　Of life, this is so small a part!
'Tis dust to dust beneath the sod;
　　But there — up there, 'tis heart to heart.

Paul Vane had broken the long silence. On the frontier among the primeval solitudes, he did not "forget." He sought and found relief in poetry. According to his own testimony, one hundred months after the rending of ties that bound fond hearts the touching ballad was written. Two or three years later the manuscript was given to a musical composer who published it to the world. In the original the name Bertha was used where Lorena now appears. The change was made at the suggestion of the composer.

The song was on the way to fame before Lorena recognized it as a message to her. Three years after its publication appeared another song, Lorena's reply:

PAUL VANE.

The years are creeping slowly by, dear Paul,
   The winters come and go;
The wind sweeps past with mournful cry, dear Paul,
   And pelts my face with snow.
But there's no snow upon the heart, dear Paul,
   'Tis summer always there;
Those early loves throw sunshine over all
   And sweeten memories dear.

I thought it easy to forget, dear Paul,
   Life glowed with youthful hope;
The glorious future gleamed yet, dear Paul
   And bade us clamber up.
They frowning said, "It must not — cannot be;
   Break now the hopeless bands!"
And, Paul, you know how well that bitter day
   I bent to their commands.

I've kept you ever in my heart, dear Paul,
   Through years of good and ill;
Our souls could not be torn apart, dear Paul,
   They're bound together still.
I never knew how dear you were to me,
   'Till I was left alone;
I thought my poor, poor heart would break, the day
   They told me you were gone.

Perhaps we'll never, never meet, dear Paul,
   Upon this earth again;
But there, where happy angels greet, dear Paul,
   You'll meet Lorena there.
Together up the ever shining way
   We'll press with hoping heart —
Together through the bright eternal day,
   And nevermore to part.

Strange to relate, the reply was written by none other than Paul Vane himself. The first song had been a financial success, and as no reply was forthcoming from the fair occasion of the effusion the minister penned these verses.

The whole affair had been discussed pro and con by experts in such matters, but they have arrived at no substantial agreement. One insists that the writer of the song should have assumed the name of Vain, as he verifies the opinion of the satirist that wounded love is largely a matter of personal vanity. Another declares that he chose the correct orthography, as he was blown about pretty freely by the winds of time. In support of this view, the fact is pointed out that he himself, like Lorena, found consolation in matrimony. To the suggestion that regard for the first lady of his choice should have prevented him from pouring forth former woes into the ears of the world, a third expert replies that after the cruel experience through which he passed it was perfectly right for him to cry aloud to all who cared to listen. Paul has also been accused of being a bit insincere — of playing to the galleries. To this a clerical gentleman takes partial exception. "Ministers," he declares, "seldom play to the galleries, because they rarely have them; and when they do, the galleries are not well patronized." The historian must therefore leave this delicate question where he found it.

The song, though in large measure displaced by later favorites, is still sung and enjoyed. Because it was written, many a lady has borne and will yet bear the euphonious name, Lorena. The beautiful air was composed by J. P. Webster, who, by the way, was not related to the author of the words. Pathos and rhythm and music will perpetuate the ballad and the story of its inspiration.

Paul Vane was fairly prosperous and happy in the West. From Racine, Wis., he moved to Neenah in the same state, where in the latter seventies he edited a paper, the Neenah *Gazette*. But in the midst of business cares and other diversions he did not wholly "forget." As late as 1882 he wrote to a friend in Zanesville, and referring to his sad experience there said: "I doubt if all the dark lines are erased from my heart yet." Some years ago he died.[1]   His wife still lives in the city of Chicago.

The young lawyer who won the hand of Lorena rose rapidly in his profession. His home for many years was in Ironton, O. He was finally elected Judge of the Supreme Court of Ohio. He died full of honors, admired and universally respected, March 2, 1887.

In the city of Zanesville, surrounded by the scenes of her girlhood days, still lives Lorena in her widowed age. The hill that she climbed in the flowery May of long ago is now hidden from sight by the intrusive growth of the flourishing city. Of her little family, she alone remains. The sun is slowly declining toward life's quiet twilight.

Still flows as of old the Muskingum, turbid and historic. The changing panorama of its banks has sometimes led the admiring stranger to exclaim, "The Hudson of the middle west." Through these scenes a steamer comes and goes, laden at times with joyous throngs in holiday attire. There is laughter and music and song. And the vessel that wends her way over the rippling waters bears right proudly a name forever linked with the river — Lorena.

---

[1] Rev. H. D. L. Webster was born at Stamford, Conn., August 29, 1824. He was educated in Columbus, O.; preached at Zanesville, O.; left the latter city about 1848; was married February 14, 1850 to Sarah L. Willmot; to them two children were born, both of whom are still living. After the death of his first wife he married Mary M. Skinner at Racine, Wis., December 31, 1867; to them were born two children, one of whom is still living. Rev. Webster commenced preaching at the age of twenty-two years. He was well liked as a minister and thoroughly devoted to his work. He organized the first Universalist society at Tarpon Springs, Fla., and preached there without pay till his health began to fail. He died in Chicago, November 4, 1896.

FAREWELL SONG OF THE WYANDOT INDIANS.

JAMES RANKINS, UPPER SANDUSKY.

[Mr. Emil Schlup, President of the Wyandot County Pioneer Association, is authority for the statement that Rev. James Wheeler, the resident missionary, preached the farewell sermon at the Old Mission Church, Upper Sandusky, in the forepart of July, 1843, to the assembled Wyandot Indians. Squire John Greyeyes, a converted Wyandot Indian, preached the sermon in the Wyandot language, which sermon was interpreted into the English language by John McIntyre Armstrong. Many present were moved to tears when Greyeyes bade adieu to the surrounding scenes amid which his people had long lived. This pathetic event inspired the poet. The Wyandots, about seven hundred souls in number, left Upper Sandusky for the far west, July 11, 1843. — EDITOR.]

> Adieu to the graves where my fathers now rest!
> For I must be going to the far distant west.
> I've sold my possessions; my heart fills with woe
> To think I must leave them, Alas! I must go.
>
> Farewell ye tall oaks in whose pleasant green shade
> In childhood I sported, in innocence played;
> My dog and my hatchet, my arrows and bow,
> Are still in remembrance, Alas! I must go.
>
> Adieu ye loved scenes, which bind me like chains,
> Where on my gay pony I chased o'er the plains.
> The deer and the turkey I tracked in the snow.
> But now I must leave them, Alas! I must go.
>
> Adieu to the trails which for many a year
> I traveled to spy the turkey and deer,
> The hills, trees and flowers that pleased me so
> I must now leave, Alas! I must go.
>
> Sandusky, Tymochtee, and Brokensword streams,
> Nevermore shall I see you except in my dreams,
> Adieu to the marshes where the cranberries grow
> O'er the great Mississippi, Alas! I must go.

Adieu to the roads which for many a year
I traveled each Sabbath the gospel to hear,
The news was so joyful and pleased me so,
From hence where I heard it, it grieves me to go.

Farewell my white friends who first taught me to pray
And worship my Savior and Maker each day.
Pray for the poor native whose eyes overflow,
With tears at our parting, Alas! I must go.

NOTE.— HISTORICAL.

In the excellent article "On the Origin of Ohio Place Names," printed in the July issue of the Quarterly, there were a few slips which should be noted for correction.

On page 277, "Loramie's store was a noted landmark and appeared in all the treaties after 1769." The store was burned in 1782 by General Clark's men, and was never replaced. Subsequent to 1769, three general treaties were made with the Indians; one at Fort McIntosh, in Western Pennsylvania, January 21st, 1785; one at Fort Harmar, near Marietta, January 9th, 1789; one at Greenville, August 3, 1795. Only the last treaty mentions "Loramie's." The following is a part of the boundary named in that treaty: "Thence westerly to a fork of that branch of the Great Miami river running into the Ohio at or near which fork stood Loramie's store." The store "was fifteen miles up Loramie's Creek, a branch of the Big Miami. The stream, the post-office at the mouth, and the Reservoir Shelby County, still bear his name" — so the article continues. There is no post-office within several miles of the mouth of the stream. The post-office "Loramie" is about 15 miles from the mouth of the stream, and is at the village of New Berlin, in the northwest corner of Shelby County. The position of Fort Laramie was fully discussed in this Quarterly about five years ago. It follows that the passage on page 279, wherein it is stated that the line from the Tuscarawas runs "west to Loramie's Store," is wholly wrong.

Again, page 279. The French settlers did not locate at the mouth of the Scioto, but at Gallipolis. See Laws of the U. S., Vol. 2, page 503.

On page 276 it is stated that Mount Logan is on Paint Creek. Mount Logan is on the east side of the Scioto, nearly two miles northeast of the Court House in Chillicothe, and is miles away from Paint Creek, which is west of the Scioto.

Page 286. "College Hill is named from two colleges. College Corner with similar educational advantages has one Indiana and two Ohio counties cornering in it." College Corner has no college at all, and it was given its name because it was located in the corner of the township which was given for the founding of Miami University. No Indiana county has a corner at this village.

R. W. McFarland.

ORIGIN OF THE PHRASE, "KEEP THE BALL ROLLING."

THOMAS J. BROWN, WAYNESVILLE.

[I had the following article in contemplation for a year or more, but it was crowded aside by other matters until midsummer last, some time before the January (1905) number of the Archæological and Historical Quarterly was printed when I wrote it down with a pencil in my note book, and herewith give it with very slight change or correction. Some allusion is made in the latest issue of the Quarterly to the ball fad, but I had no knowledge of the article or inspiration of Mr. C. B. Galbreath until I saw it there.— T. J. B.]

Many words and phrases have come into common use whose origin has been forgotten. In many cases, perhaps the origin never was generally known, or has not been passed on from one generation to another, as others have been.

The phrase, "Keep the ball rolling," was years ago more generally used than it is now, but it is still used; if a man has an enterprise on hand which he wishes to carry to a successful termination and has no intention of dropping or neglecting it, he will probably give expression to his intentions by saying he will keep the ball rolling. If many persons are engaged in it, the phrase is then used for mutual encouragement, although its origin has been to a great extent forgotten. I have learned by pretty general inquiry among aged persons that they have entirely forgotten the origin of the phrase, if indeed they ever knew. It came about in this way:

About the year 1840, it was the custom in some sections when a political campaign was on, to work off a surplus of enthusiasm by constructing a huge ball, say 8 to 12 feet in diameter, and covered, at least in some instances, with stout leather so it would stand a great deal of rough treatment. This ball was filled with most anything that would give bulk, and a proper degree of weight, and yet leave it somewhat pliable so as to save it from too much friction; then several persons would roll it along to a political convention. By the way, all large political meetings were called "conventions" in those days, and every man that went was a self-constituted delegate, or a pole raising, or even from one township or county to another when it would be rolled on to the next county by a relay of fresh enthusiastics.

I remember seeing a picture of one of these balls, more than fifty years ago, being rolled along, while the men were supposed to give utterance to the sentiment, "This ball we roll, with all our soul."

I read many years ago a history of the craze, for so it seemed to be for awhile, which told when and where it originated and when it died away. My recollection of it in its general outlines is vivid enough, but the particulars have been forgotten or are too indistinct upon my memory to venture to go into details. It is my impression, however, that the rolling of the ball was indulged in, in some of the far southern states more zealously than here, but there were several in Ohio, and when the enthusiasm was wrought up to a proper key, it was rolled from place to place. This was certainly what was intended, a ball of such size would be a very inconvenient thing to transport any other way.

Perhaps this will revive old memories in others and we will learn something more definite about it.

THE INDIAN MOUND, MIAMISBURG, OHIO.

This mound is located on the upland about a mile southeast of town, and is the largest of its kind in the world. It was originally about eighty-five feet in height, but was reduced to sixty-five feet by digging of exploring parties. It measures about

three hundred feet in diameter at the base. In 1869 a number of citizens sunk a shaft from the top to two feet below its base. So far as startling revelations are concerned, the exploration was not a success. About eight feet below the summit a human skeleton was discovered in a sitting posture. A cover of clay several feet in thickness and a deposit of ashes and charcoal seemed to be the burial. At a depth of twenty-four feet was found a number of flat stones, set at an angle of forty-five degrees, and overlapping like shingles on a roof, which may have been the top at one time. Several theories have been advanced

(446)

regarding the object of its builders. It is thought to have been a place for sacrifice, or a burial mound. The failure to discover a large number of human bones within it seems to disprove these theories. It was in all probability used as a place of signaling, as it is one of a chain of similar earthen structures through this part of Ohio. Fires on its summit, which rises above the top of the surrounding forests, could be seen at a great distance. The trees which now cover it have grown since the settlement of the country by the whites.

EARLY CINCINNATI.

JOSEPH WILBY, CINCINNATI.

[The following article was written by Mr. Joseph Wilby and read before The Optimist Club, Cincinnati, March 1st, 1902. Mr. Wilby is at present the president of the Historical and Philosophical Society of Ohio. —EDITOR.]

The first council meeting of the *town* of Cincinnati is said to have been held on the 5th of March, 1802. The present occasion lacks a few days of being the one hundredth anniversary of that date, but affords a fitting opportunity for us to recall the beginnings and growth of Cincinnati.

The southwest corner of Ohio was fortunate in the character of the men who chose it out of the wilderness and peopled it, and blessed by the conditions under which these men laid the foundations for a great city.

Where we now stand was, two centuries ago, in the possession of the Indians, hardly known to the white man, except to the adventurous Jesuits from New France. Marquette, descending the Mississippi, had sailed by the mouth of the Ohio, or, as he called it, the Wabash, a name by which it was known for many years.

The French claim to all the vast region north of the Ohio and between the Mississippi and the Alleghenies, was ceded to England in 1763 by the Treaty of Paris. Twenty years afterward, by the War of Independence, we obtained from England the right to all this country south of the Great Lakes. It became known as the Northwest Territory, embracing what is now the States of Ohio, Indiana, Illinois, Michigan, Wisconsin, and part of Minnesota.

Though as colonies of England, Virginia and Connecticut claimed part of what is now Ohio, under grants from the Crown, Virginia, in 1781, gave up to Federal control any rights she had in this territory. Connecticut did the same, reserving, however, a little place in the northeastern corner of Ohio, which has ever since borne the name of the "Connecticut Reserve." The Federal Congress, thereby enabled to make laws for these new possessions, 1787 enacted the famous ordinance of that year. It had many wise provisions; its most benign was that excluding slavery forever throughout the Northwest Territory.

Tribes of Indians still claimed rights of ownership in this land. The Federal Government recognized these rights, and, by treaties made in 1785 and 1786, acquired from the tribes claiming it a large part of southwestern Ohio, including what was known as the Miami country, extending from the Ohio River north between the two Miami Rivers.

Thereupon, in 1787, Col. John Cleves Symmes, of New Jersey, a member of the Colonial Congress, a man of wealth and education, who realized, as did Washington, that this Ohio country, by reason of its climate, soil and exemption from slavery would attract settlers, contracted with the Colonial Government for the famous Symmes or Miami Purchase. He thought he bought 1,000,000 acres, but in fact, got less than 600,000 acres, bounded on the south by the Ohio, on the west by the Great Miami, on the east by the Little Miami, and on the north by a line drawn east and west between these two rivers, somewhere in the vicinity of Lebanon, in Warren County. He paid, or promised to pay, the Federal Government two-thirds of a dollar an acre. He got his patent from the Government in 1794. Some of those who had purchased from him had trouble in making title, and it took an act of the Federal Congress to secure to them lands for which part payment had been made to Symmes. Symmes had his land surveyed into ranges, townships and sections, terms familiar to every property owner in Cincinnati. The next year Mathias Denman, another Jerseyman, bought from Symmes, Section 18 and Fractional Section 17, being part of the fourth township, in the first Fractional Range, on the Ohio River. In the contract of sale the land was simply described as located as nearly as possible opposite the mouth of the Licking River, for the survey had not yet been completed. The tract was subsequently found to contain 740 acres, which may be roughly said to be part of Cincinnati as we know it now, bounded on the north by Liberty street, on the south by the river, on the east by a line drawn from a little east of where is now the former homestead of George H. Pendleton, at the top of Liberty street hill, and on the west by a line drawn from about the corner of Liberty Street and Central Avenue to the river at the old Smith Street Landing. The price paid by Denman is said to have been $500, which was about the price the Government had charged Symmes.

Denman thought his land opposite the Licking River a good site for a town, as it was in the line of the old trail from Kentucky to Detroit. With him he associated Col. Robert Patterson, of Lexington, Ky., who took a share in his purchase, and John Filson, also of Lexington. Filson was needed, because he was a surveyor, to lay off the proposed town into lots. Patterson was a popular man, well known to the frontier, and was to act as promotor in advertising the enterprise. Filson, who had been a school teacher, proposed to call the future town Losantiville, a barbarous compound of Greek, Latin and French, indicating, or supposed to indicate, that it was the "town opposite the mouth;" that is, the mouth of the Licking. That the town was ever called Losantiville has been the subject of much controversy, the weight of evidence being, I believe, against it, and in favor of the theory that it was from the beginning known as Cincinnati. The recent founding of the Society of the Cincinnati had made that name popular and proper.

The owners and promoters of this Denman Subdivision, as it might be called, advertised it in the Kentucky Gazette, at Lexington, in September, 1788. In their advertisement they said it was proposed to have in-lots of a half acre each, and out-lots of four acres; every settler would be given thirty of each of these lots upon paying the cost of making survey and deed for each lot, and provided he took possession before the 1st of April, 1789. The original agreement between the proprietors and the settlers or lot takers is in the library of the Historical Society.

In the same month, September, Denman, Patterson, Filson and their associates, including Israel Ludlow and others not interested with them in this particular purchase, together with Symmes, started out from Lexington to reach this land opposite the mouth of the Licking. Symmes decided to go further down the river before he selected a site for settlement, and he and those who were of his mind decided to start a town at North Bend, at the mouth of the Great Miami.

While engaged in measuring the distance between the two Miami rivers Filson disappeared, and it was supposed that he was killed by the Indians.

Israel Ludlow, who was a surveyor, then took Filson's interest, and began laying out the proposed town site. The survey reached from the river to Seventh Street, between Broadway and Central Avenue.

Meanwhile, Benjamin Stites had bought a tract from Symmes near the mouth of the Little Miami, and began a settlement which he called Columbia.

Patterson and Ludlow and those who had joined in the project of making a settlement opposite the mouth of the Licking, came down from Maysville, Ky., in December, 1788, and, on a date still in some doubt, landed near the foot of Sycamore Street. That may be said to have been the beginning of Cincinnati.

By the terms under which lots were disposed of to settlers, the space south of Front Street to the river, bounded on the east by what we now call Broadway, then laid out as Eastern Row and Main Street, was made common or public ground. We know it now as the Public Landing.

Subsequently, Joel Williams undertook to claim rights of individual ownership within this space, but by decree in the case of Cincinnati v. Williams, he was perpetually enjoined, and it has been a public common or landing ever since.

So there were three settlements on the Ohio River, in this Miami country; that located by Symmes at North Bend, at the mouth of the Great Miami; that begun by Stites at Columbia, near the mouth of the Little Miami; and Denman, Ludlow and Patterson's town of Cincinnati, about half way between.

In those days, and, indeed, down to the Treaty of Greenville, in 1795, the Indians were a constant menace to the settlers through the Miami valleys. It was only the most adventurous of them who dared to take possession of lands at a distance from the river.

The Federal Government, therefore, to encourage the settlement of this new territory by affording protection against the Indians, sent down from Marietta, or Fort Harmar, a detachment of soldiers, with instructions to build a fort at North Bend, where Symmes had laid out a promising town. Emigrants naturally would prefer that point to either Columbia or Cincinnati, on account of protection by the fort.

Major Doughty, the officer commanding the detachment, was susceptible to the charms of women. In looking around for a suitable site for the proposed fort, he became interested in a young woman, who, as bad luck would have it, had a husband. The husband, noticing the flirtation, and fearing the effect of military buttons on his family peace, removed thereupon from North Bend to the new settlement opposite the mouth of the Licking. Major Doughty, discovering that the lady had departed for Cincinnati forthwith realized that Cincinnati would be a more suitable place than North Bend for locating a fort, and accordingly ordered his detachment up the river to the town site laid out by Denman, Patterson and Ludlow. There he located Fort Washington, on a plot of fifteen acres reserved for the Federal Government by the town owners. I wish I knew more about what happened to Doughty, but the fort was demolished and the fifteen acres passed to private ownership in 1808. As you all know, the exact location of the Fort has been recently determined, on Third Street between Broadway and Ludlow Streets.

For fourteen years Cincinnati shared with the rest of the Northwest Territory that government which the Federal Congress provided under the ordinance of 1787. The population within the limits of what is now Ohio grew rapidly, so that in 1802, although the territory had not yet acquired the population of 60,000 required by the ordinance before it could be entitled to Statehood, yet it held between 40,000 and 45,000 people, and upon application to Congress, a law was passed authorizing the inhabitants of the eastern part of the Northwest Territory to frame a constitution and State government. This act prescribed the limits for what was to become the State of Ohio, and its northern boundary, separating it from what afterward became the State of Michigan, was declared to be Lake Erie and a "line drawn east and west through the southerly extremity of Lake Michigan."

This language produced the celebrated controversy which threatened to include Detroit within the State of Ohio, and to put Toledo within the State of Michigan. It was the cause of many interesting lawsuits, and was only settled by an act of Congress almost forty years afterward. It seems that the map of this wilderness available at that time to the convention, made from crude surveys, showed the lower extremity of Lake Michigan as being north of the latitude of Detroit. During the controversy as to where the true line should be drawn, a hunter who was familiar with the southern shores of Lake Michigan brought it to the attention of the convention that their map did not correctly show the location of Lake Michigan, for it extended further south than the latitude of Toledo. And thereupon the settlers at Toledo became disturbed for fear that they should be left out of the new State about to be carved out of the Northwest Territory. A compromise was made by running the line between the latitude of Detroit and Toledo, so as to leave Toledo within the new State, but the line remained in doubt.

The act of 1802, permitting the formation of the State of Ohio, committed the making of a constitution under which the State could come into the Union, to thirty-five delegates from various settlements throughout the territory comprised within the proposed State of Ohio, all selected by the Federal Government. These delegates included men whose names will always be remembered in connection with the history of Ohio—Jeremiah Morrow, William Goforth, Edward Tiffin, Nathaniel Massie, Rufus Putnam and others familiar to you. They met in convention at Chillicothe, in November, 1802, and framed the constitution under which Ohio lived down to 1851, when the new and present constitution was adopted. It is a curious fact that this constitution of 1802 was never submitted to the people of the State. The proposition was made in the convention to let the people approve it, but was rejected by a large majority. It would therefore seem as if in Ohio, for the first fifty years of its existence as a State, there was government without the consent of the governed; that is to say, it was a government under a fundamental code of principles, written by persons selected by the Federal Congress, and in the making of which the people to be governed were not consulted.

Thus, in 1803, Ohio was admitted to the Union, as the fourth State to be added to the original thirteen colonies.

The name is from its Indian name, Youghiogany, which the French, leaving out the gutteral sounds, softened into Ohio. It is the Alleghany, not the Ohio, that by its Indian derivation means Belle Riviere.

But Cincinnati was an incorporated town before Ohio was a State; for the Territorial Legislature made Cincinnati a town by an act passsed January 1, 1802. The town then incorporated was thus bounded: On the north by the township line, about a mile from the river (this was Township 4), on the south by the river, on the east by the east line of Section 12, and on the west by Millcreek.

It was not until 1815 that the town was divided into wards—four of them—by a new act of incorporation, which took the place of the act of 1802. The limit of taxation on real estate was, by the new charter, a half of one per cent, and any increase thereof was to be submitted to the people for popular approval.

The difference between the grade of the lower portion of the town, towards the river, and the upper portion, at Fourth or Fifth Street, was probably even greater then than now. Indeed, there may be said to have been two sudden changes in level, one at the river, and one at about Third Street; but this was slowly, by grading, made a continuous ascent from Front to Fourth Street. There were in those days, according to the account left by Judge Jacob Burnet,, the grandfather of Jacob Staats Burnet, of Oak Street, Walnut Hills, four mounds, possibly made by Indians, within the then city limits; two circular mounds, one intersecting Sycamore, Broadway, Fourth and Fifth Streets, the other intersecting Race, Vine, Fourth and Fifth Streets; and single-peaked mounds, one at the northeast corner of Front and Main Streets, and a larger one at the northwest corner of Fifth and Mound Streets, which gave its name to the latter street.

At the northeast corner of Main and Fifth Streets, opposite the present Government Building, there was, for some years into the last century, a swamp filled with alders, so that persons passing north on Main Street were obliged to go over a wooden causeway.

Lots on the principal streets for the first five years after Cincinnati became a town could be bought for less than $100 each. Thereafter they rose rapidly in value. At the end of ten years from that time the price of real estate on Main Street, between Front and Third Streets, was about $200 a front foot, diminishing in value as one went north. This was then the highest priced property in the city. It kept rapidly increasing in value with the increase in population. It was on Main Street below Fourth that later stood the store of Tyler Davidson, the hardware merchant, whose memory is perpetuated by the fountain in Fifth Street.

At the beginning of the last century, that is, in 1800, there are said to have been but 750 people in Cincinnati. In 1810 the population had increased to 2,500, and in 1820, it was nearly 10,-000. Cincinnati was then growing more rapidly than either of its rivals, Louisville or Pittsburg. Between 1820 and 1850, the population showed a larger increase than it ever has since fifty years ago. It much more than doubled between 1820 and 1830, about doubled between 1830 and 1840, and by 1850 had grown in the then past decade from 46,000 to 115,000. It took more than twenty years to double the population again, for in 1870 it was only a little over 216,000.

Almost all of the Germans, whose descendants now constitute so large and valued a part of our population, came to Cincinnati between 1820 and 1850.

The first census that was ever taken by actual count of the population of Cincinnati, was by Benjamin Drake and E. D. Mansfield, in 1826, at the request of a committee of the City Council, and for which the city paid Drake and Mansfield an agreed price of $75. The enumeration was by wards, and showed a total population in 1826 of 16,230 persons.

The slow growth of the town in its earlier years was due probably in part to losses by the Indian wars and the deterrent effect on immigration of the continued depredations of the Indians.

Some idea of the rise in the value of real estate may be had from considering that the northwest corner of Third and Main Streets was bought, when the town was laid out, for $2.00; forty years afterward it was sold for $15,000. The corner of Main and Front Streets, 100 feet on Front and 200 feet on Main Street, sold in 1789 for $2.00. It was thought to be worth $100 in 1793. Fifty years afterward it rented for about $15,000 a year. In 1802 Ethan Stone paid for a lot 150 feet on Vine Street by 200 feet on Fourth Street, $220; and less than forty years afterward 60 feet of the same property, not on the corner, sold at $150 a front foot on Vine Street. And 60 feet on the next square west of this has quite recently changed hands on a basis of $4,015 a front foot. The most valuable property in the city just before the war was probably on the Public Landing; that is, on Front Street between Broadway and Main Streets, where lots were sold at the rate of $1,000 a front foot.

Hamilton County was one of the four counties established as early as 1796, named of course, for Alexander Hamilton, and included about one-eighth of the whole State. The other counties were Washington, St. Clair and Knox, all also named after distinguished early patriots. Hamilton County was subsequently divided into eleven counties — Clermont, Warren, Butler, Preble, Montgomery, Greene, Clinton, Champaign, Miami, Darke and Hamilton.

Having been a town for less than twenty years, Cincinnati became incorporated as a *city* by an act of the General Assembly, February 5, 1819, while Boston was still the Town of Boston. Our population was then 10,283. Our city charter was amended several times during the next eight years. In 1827, the boundaries of the city were defined by a new charter, as beginning on the Ohio River at the east corner of Fractional Section No. 12, and running west with the township line of Cincinnati to Millcreek, thence down Millcreek with its meanders to the Ohio River, thence eastwardly up said river with the southern boundary of the State of Ohio to the place of beginning.

For the next twenty years the city grew toward the east, the west and northwest, chiefly by gradual accessions of territory through subdivisions and additions made by individuals owning large tracts of land. Thereafter road districts having been established through Millcreek Township and other neighboring townships, and incorporated villages having sprung up in the suburbs of the city, a little more than fifty years ago the process of annexation by ordinance and agreement with the newly acquired territory began to extend the city limits.

The first road district taken in became the Eleventh Ward of the city of Cincinnati, and one of the commissioners for settling the terms of that annexation on behalf of the road district was Michel Goepper.

The city then reached out toward the east for more territory, and in 1854 acquired the incorporated village of Fulton. Then annexation reached to the west, and in 1869 Storrs Township, except the village of Riverside, was made part of the city. Later in the same year Camp Washington and Lick Run were annexed. And, by an ordinance of the same date, part of Walnut Hills, adjoining the village of Columbia, joined the city. More of Walnut Hills and Mt. Auburn came into Cincinnati in 1870, after the question of their annexation had been submitted to popular vote. The village of Columbia united with the city in 1872, also after popular vote on the question. The next year the village of Cumminsville decided to extend the city limits toward the north. Cumminsville got its name in this way; it had been known originally as Ludlow's Station, because one of its earliest settlers, John Ludlow—some relative, I believe, of Israel Ludlow—who laid out the city of Cincinnati — had built a house and established himself in the valley north of Clifton, when the place was considered unsafe on account of the Indians. Later a man by the name of John Cummins had a tannery in the neighborhood of Ludlow's farm, adjoining the land of one Hutchinson. Hutchinson's house, or rather tavern — for he kept a tavern — stood where afterward was built the residence of the late John Hoffner, now a landmark in that part of the city. A stream of water ran from Hutchinson's land, of which Cummins, by his deed, was entitled to use as much as would flow through five three-quarter inch auger holes. The Hutchinsons kept a dairy in connection with their tavern, and needed water. One dry summer they plugged up the holes of the tannery supply pipe to save water for the cows in their dairy. The flow of water to Cummins' tannery diminished. A lawsuit followed. For the purpose of raising money to carry on the suit Cummins mort-

gaged his property; and it, being sold on foreclosure, was bought
in by Ephraim Knowlton, whose stone store on Spring Grove
Avenue, then the old Wayne Road, is another landmark in that
part of the city. The store of Knowlton's has given to its location the name of "Knowlton's Corner"; and Knowlton, having
bought this ground from the Cummins on foreclosure, named the
settlement, which at that time numbered many houses (built
mostly by Knowlton, himself, who was a carpenter and builder)
"Cumminsville," by which name it will probably be known as
long as any of us live. The city next, in the same year as the annexation of Cumminsville, went east for more room, and took in
the incorporated village of Woodburn. Then we were satisfied
with our size until we took a slice off the west side of Avondale,
adjoining the Zoological Gardens, in 1888. Still the city was not
content with its border thus extended, and in 1894, after some
controversy with one or more unwilling suburbs, took within the
protection of its municipal police Avondale, Clifton, Linwood,
Riverside and Westwood. Then three years afterward a piece
of Millcreek Township adjoining Avondale. And in the fall of
last year the city acquired an outlaying tract adjoining Price Hill
on the west. Surely the Cincinnati of to-day shows on the map
a wide-spreading territory. Yet I understand that to this extended area is to be added still more contiguous territory.

One of the first municipal ordinances passed by the city of
Cincinnati was the one dated the 17th day of November, 1824,
declaring it unlawful to play marbles within the city limits on the
Sabbath day; and further imposing a fine of ten dollars upon any
boy who played on any street or alley of the city the game commonly called shinny, on any day.

Apparently the inhabitants of Cincinnati carried the custom
of bathing in the river in front of the city to an intolerable extent
in those days, for in 1826 an ordinance was passed imposing a fine
of five dollars and the costs of prosecution upon any one who
should bathe in the Ohio River within the corporate limits, between sunrise and sunset.

Speaking of water, in the earliest times in Cincinnati springs
in the hillside along the present line of Third Street furnished
drinking water, and the Ohio River water for washing. Later

wells were sunk, and water was carried up in buckets from the river on washing days. Still later an enterprising citizen put a cask on wheels, and filling it at the river, made a business of selling water to the citizens. In 1817 a still more enterprising citizen constructed a tank near the foot of Ludlow Street, into which by horse power, he lifted water from the river, and sold it to men with carts, who in turn sold it again throughout the town. In the same year a corporation, having, for a water company, the rather curious name of the Cincinnati Woolen Manufacturing Company, acquired from the Town Council of Cincinnati the exclusive privilege of supplying the town with water for the term of ninety-nine years, for the sum of $100 a year paid to the city. The Woolen Company was bound by the ordinance to fill, free of expense, all reservoirs the town should build, but no limit was placed upon the price to be charged for water supplied for private consumption. Samuel W. Davies bought this right from the Woolen Company in 1820. He built a plank-sided reservoir on the site of the old reservoir on Third and Martin Streets, into which water was pumped from the river. The pipes were of wood, and the pumps worked by horse power. A few years later the engine and boiler of a steamboat were bought by Davies, and the pumping was thereafter done by steam power. But the pipes were still of wood. A part of one of them, dug up from Fourth Street, may be seen at the rooms of the Historical Society. Davies tried to interest the citizens of Cincinnati in his project of distributing water liberally on modern methods, but failed. He then tried to sell back his plant and privileges to the city at a loss. The city declined to purchase. Then, in 1825, Davies procured the incorporation of the Cincinnati Water Company with a capital of $75,000. The company made improvements; adopted iron pipes; the reservoir was enlarged, and a sufficient water supply was obtained. In 1839 the waterworks, and all its plants and rights, were purchased from the company by the city, and to the city they have ever since belonged. A new reservoir was constructed about fifty years ago on the site of the former one, which may now be seen on East Third Street, just beyond the old Kilgour residence and the U. S. Marine Hospital; and it is of interest, to the writer at least, that this reservoir was built under the supervision, and bears on the stone tablet on its south wall the name of his grandfather, Ebenezer Hinman, then superintendent of the city waterworks. About the time this reservoir was finished, in 1852, saw the completion of St. Peter's Cathedral, corner of Eighth and Plum Streets. In 1874 the first section of the new reservoir was completed in Eden Park.

The paving of the streets in early days was of limestone, easily obtained in the neighborhood. It made a poor surface, and a little more than fifty years ago, at the suggestion of Mr. De Goyler, paving with round boulders was adopted, which at that time was considered, and probably was, a great advance on anything that had been previously used in the making of streets. It is only recently that Cincinnati became dissatisfied with this boulder paving.

The Gas Company was originally the private enterprise of J. F. Conover and J. H. Caldwell, to whom the City Council gave the privilege of supplying the city and its citizens with gas in June, 1841. Subsequently, the Legislature granted to these gentlemen and their associates a charter under the name of The Cincinnati Gas Light and Coke Company, which, as I hope all of you know by exchange of certificates, has only recently ceased to be its corporate name. It is, however, the same old meter, with a different colored bill.

The river of course was, from the beginning, and particularly after the introduction of steam, the great highway of travel and commerce. But in 1825 the Legislature of Ohio, stimulated its Erie Canal, provided by liberal legislation for acquiring rights of way and building of a system of canals throughout the State. The two canals in which Cincinnati was interested were, first, the Miami Canal, finished in 1827, and formally opened at Lockland by Governor DeWitt Clinton, of New York, whose name is so closely connected with the Erie Canal. This Miami Canal, about sixty-seven miles in length, extended at first from Cincinnati north to Dayton, near the mouth of the Mad River. It was afterward built to Piqua and later to Defiance. It no doubt was a great public work to have been accomplished in those early times; was a great convenience to the commerce of the Miami Valley, and, connected as it was with the rest of the canal system of the State of Ohio, deserves much that has been said in its favor in the past. Ever since the writer can remember, however, it has, by many reasonably sensible people, been said to have out-lived its usefulness. I am willing to hazard the opinion that part of it within the city limits has certainly outlived its sweet-ness—yes, I am ready to say that it is an ill-smelling relic. It is doubtful, however, if any of us here present will live to see any honest and rational disposition made of it. The other canal re-lated to the fortunes of Cincinnati is the Cincinnati and White-water Canal, or rather was, for so much of it as came within the neighborhood of Cincinnati has long since been appropriated by railroads, who have better served the original purpose of its con-struction.

The bridges across the Ohio, at Cincinnati, deserve some mention in this connection. Daniel Drake, in his instructive and entertaining account of Cincinnati, published in 1815, says that even at that date some enthusiastic persons already spoke of a bridge across the Ohio at Cincinnati. Indeed, at that time Mr. Drake was bold enough to suggest the necessity of a bridge across Deercreek at its mouth. He also pleaded for the restoration of a bridge that once existed over Millcreek, but had been destroyed by high water. As a matter of fact, it was a long fifty years before Mr. Drake's hopes of a bridge across the Ohio were rea-lized. The writer can well remember, before the war, the short stone tower on the bank of the river which was then the promise of the bridge which subsequently sprang across to Covington with its web of steel. The writer can also remember, during the Civil War, the bridge of boats, called, I believe, a pontoon bridge, stretched across the river. Over it marched General Lew Wal-lace and his troops to intercept Kirby Smith's raiders. From time to time thereafter, making peace with the War Department and the tall stacks of river steamboats, four other bridges have, within the memory of comparative youth, spanned the Ohio in front of Cincinnati.

The first railroad constructed out of Cincinnati was the "Little Miami," completed in 1846, as far as Springfield, O., eighty-four miles. The Cincinnati, Hamilton & Dayton, and the Ohio & Mississippi had been thought of at that time, and indeed, were soon in process of construction. Other railroads followed. But it is impossible to speak of railroads in connection with Cincinnati without giving prominent place to our Southern Railway, planned, possibly, sixty years ago, under the name of the Cincinnati & Charleston Railroad. Ferguson's road, which was to give us communication with the South, but not constructed until, by the indulgence of the Supreme Court of Ohio kindly warping, if it did not break, the Constitution of the State, the city of Cincinnati, after much wrangling, much diversity of opinion and grievous burden of taxation, built, with bonded debt, the road which it is now about, with wisdom and good fortune, to place in the hands of a responsible tenant by a new lease on favorable terms. The history of that railroad, from the act of May 4, 1869, down to the present day, is full of interest to every Cincinnatian; but that story has been so well told by Mr. H. P. Boyden in his recent pamphlet that there is nothing left for me to say about it than to notice a rather odd coincidence, personal to myself. In June, 1869, the people of Cincinnati, under the act of the Legislature, voted to build this road. The preliminary survey was immediately begun. In April, 1870, the writer joined one of the preliminary surveying parties at the mouth of Fishing Creek, on the Cumberland River, below Somerset, and continued work with that surveying party for six or seven months in Kentucky and Tennessee. In the same month, April, 1870, the writer's present law partner, E. W. Kittredge, quite unknown to the writer, brought suit for Bryant Walker, city solicitor and tax-payer, to contest the constitutionality of the Ferguson act which authorized the building of the road. After a short term of use by the Common Carrier Company, Mr. Kittredge, in October, 1881, drew the lease for twenty-five years to its prsent lessee.

Nicholas Longworth, the great-grandfather of the talented Senator from this county, was a Cincinnati lawyer in the early part of the last century and practiced his profession until 1819. He invested his savings in lands and lots in Cincinnati and vicinity. He thought well of the future of Cincinnati, and he was not disappointed. He was a kind and useful ancestor. The story is told of him that a fee he got for defending a man accused of horse stealing consisted of two second-hand copper stills, stored at the tavern of Joel Williams, near the river. Mr. Long-worth presented his order to Williams for stills. Williams was about to build a distillery, and traded with Longworth for the stills, giving him in exchange thirty-three acres of land on Western Row, now Central Avenue, on the west side, from Sixth to Seventh Streets, and extending west for quantity. It has been said that even fifty years ago the advance in value of that real estate had made it worth two million of dollars, not counting improvements. Mr. Longworth probably bought and sold more lots of land in Cincinnati than any other one individual. In 1850 he paid for that year taxes amounting to more than $17,000, which is said to have been at that time the largest amount paid for taxes by any one individual in the United States, except William B. Astor, of New York.

The first bank in Cincinnati was the Miami Exporting Company, which started in 1803. Its charter permitted it to sell farm products to New Orleans and issue bank notes. Oliver Spencer was its president, and it paid from 10 to 15 per cent dividends. Then came the branch of the United States Bank, established here in 1817. In 1826 it was the only bank in operation in Cincinnati, and for years it played an important part in local finance. Afterward there was the Ohio Life Insurance and Trust Company, with its office on the southwest corner of Third and Main Streets. This was long before the war and the era of National Banks. The failure of this company, in 1857, was a catastrophe long remembered, and its trustee in insolvency, the late James P. Kilbreth, left at his death, a few years ago, its affairs still unsettled. For many years Adae's bank, known as the German Banking Institution, occupied this same corner.

Sixty years ago Nicholas Longworth gave a tract of land near his Garden of Eden, now our Eden Park, to furnish a site for an observatory. A suitable building and apparatus were obtained, in part by popular subscription, and John Quincy Adams delivered the address on the occasion of its dedication, November 10, 1843. The hill thereafter took from him its name of Mt. Adams.

A quarter of a century afterward the Observatory was removed to its present site on Mt. Lookout, presented to it by John

Kilgour; and immediately the old Observatory building was acquired by and used as the "Monastery of the Sacred Cross." About a year ago the building was condemned as unsafe and taken down.

Such of us who were born here take an abiding and affectionate interest in the city and its history, which is undisturbed by the Pessimists' statistics of diminishing rank in population, commerce or mannufactures. In the matter of good people — and they beyond all else make life worth living—we need fear no rival. As an Optimist among Optimists, I offer to Cincinnati the sentiment long ago addressed to London :

"Dear, damned, distracted town; with all thy faults, I love thee still."

EDITORIALANA.

VOL. XIV. No. 4.   *E. O. Randall*   OCTOBER, 1905

BIG BOTTOM MASSACRE DEDICATION.

It is one hundred and fifteen years since the little band of pioneers were massacred in their fort at Big Bottom on the Muskingum. This settlement was an off-shoot of the one at Marietta. It was the remotest outpost of the Ohio Company. Scarcely had Marietta been settled when there pushed out from the protecting walls of Fort Harmar small bands of settlers , to build homes and clear the fields in other favorable locations. Belpre on the Ohio and Waterford on the Muskingum were soon begun. In the fall of 1790 thirty-six men departed from Marietta and built a blockhouse on the east side of the Muskingum along the line of the Monongahela trail, about a mile and a half below the present village of Stockport, Morgan county. The winter that followed was a very cold one. Since the Indians were not so apt to go on their predatory raids in winter

OBADIAH BROKAW

as at other times, the usual severity of the season disarmed the vigilance of the inmates of the blockhouse. In fact the fort had hardly been completed. Already cabins had been erected and preparations for the spring planting were being made. In this apparent security the work of clearing and building continued.

On the second of January, 1791, along the high ridge on the opposite side of the river, unnoticed by the inhabitants of the fort, a band of Indians saw the settlement. During the day they continued their watch. They noted the unprotected condition of the blockhouse and the probable number of occupants. Early in the evening they crossed the river on the ice and fell upon the unguarded frontiersmen. The deadly work was soon accomplished. Several pioneers escaped and ran through the woods to the settlement at Wolf's Creek.

No memorial of any kind had heretofore been erected to show the passer-by that the place was historic. But now, thanks to Mr. Obadiah Brokaw, who owns the land upon which the blockhouse stood, there is a suitable and imposing monument that tells the story of that winter day's massacre. The monument consists of a marble shaft whose apex is twelve feet above the ground. The shaft is an octagon, seven and a half feet high. On one of the faces are inscribed these words: "Erected by Obadiah Brokaw, 1905." The shaft stands on a limestone base, which in turn rests on another base of concrete. On the front of the limestone base is carved, "Site of Big Bottom Massacre, Winter of 1790." On the two sides are to be found the names of those killed, as follows: "James Couch, Wm. Jones, Joseph Clark, Isaac Meeks, his wife and two children, John Stacey, Zebulon Troop, Ezra Putnam, John Camp and Jonathan Farewell." On the rear of the base are the names of those who escaped, "Asa Bullard, Eleazer Bullard and Philip Stacey." The monument displays excellent workmanship. It stands in a beautiful meadow near the public road, and only a few rods from the bank of the river. It is plainly visible to the passengers on the passing boats.

Mr. Brokaw, the patriotic possessor of the historic site upon which this monument was erected, desired to make sure that it would be permanently cared for and preserved.

This matter having been brought by Mr. Brokaw to the attention of Trustee C. L. Martzolff, the latter visited Mr. Brokaw at Stockport and broached the subject of the transfer of the monument property to the society. Subsequently, on August 17th, Professor Martzolff and Secretary Randall, accompanied by Mr. C. L. Bozman of McConnelsville, who designed and executed the monument, visited Mr. Brokaw who finally consented to transfer by deed the monument and two acres of surrounding land to the Ohio State Archæological and Historical Society, upon the condition that the society elect Mr. Brokaw a Life member, and further that the society provide for the proper care of the monument and land transferred as an historic park and monument, keeping said property properly enclosed and protected from destruction and injury by the public and maintain the same as a free public park. The negotiations by Messrs. Martzolff and Randall with Mr. Brokaw were approved and accepted by the Executive Committee at its meeting on August 28th, 1905.

On Saturday, September 30th, the Society held dedicatory exercises commemorative of the historic event which the monument marks and celebrated the donation of the property by Mr. Brokaw. The Executive Committee of the Trustees of the Society had appointed a Committee on Arrangements, of which Prof. Martzolff was chairman. This committee arranged for a most interesting program, which was successfully carried out. The day proved to be one of almost perfect weather conditions and an audience of some four thousand people from the surrounding country gathered to participate in the ceremonies. Secretary Randall acted as chairman and addresses were delivered by President Brinkerhoff, Trustees Martzolff, Ryan, Andrews, and Hunter, Hon. William B. Crew of the Ohio Supreme Court, and Hon. Tod B. Galloway, Secretary to the Governor. The program was most properly closed by an original poem written and read by Dr. James Ball Naylor, the poet and historical novelist. The Stockport Brass Band interspersed the program with musical selections.

It was a unique and interesting event in the history of the society as this is the first time that the society has come into the possession of a purely historic site. The proceedings with the speeches in detail will be published in the January Quarterly of the society.

The society will proceed without delay to protect the site with a fitting enclosure, making it an attractive place of resort for all who may care to visit this memorable spot.

Mr. Brokaw has certainly earned the gratitude of all lovers of early pioneer history by the timely erection of this stone. It will stand as a constant memorial to one of the gruesome chapters of the early history of Ohio. It will be a reminder to the coming generations of what it meant to plant settlements in the forests of the west. It will not only be a tribute to those who perished on that January day over a century ago, but it will be an ever present testimonial of the opportune thoughtfulness and the generosity of the man who has erected it.

OHIO IN THE CHINESE UPRISING.

We have been frequently asked the question whether it be true, as often reported in the public press, that the American troops were the first to enter the city of Peking at the time of the invasion by the allied nations, and that Ohio soldiers were the first within the gates of the Tartar City. In response to our inquiry, we received the following from Colonel Webb. C. Hayes, who at the time was upon the staff of General Chaffee:

WASHINGTON, February 1, 1905.

MR. E. O. RANDALL, *Columbus, Ohio.*

> DEAR SIR: — The allied troops who marched to the relief of Peking from Tien Tsin in 1900 consisted approximately of 2,000 Americans, 2,000 British, 4,000 Russians and 8,000 Japanese. There were no German nor Italians in this column. The Japanese headed the column all the way and did more of the fighting than any other one of the allies. Peking consists really of two cities side by side, enclosed by high walls — The Tartar City and the Chinese City.

Under the plan of attack, the Japanese were to take gate No. 1, the Russians gate No. 2, the Americans gate No. 3, and the British gate No. 4.

The Americans reached the walls some time before the British, but through a mistake attacked and captured gate No. 4, and then sent word to the British troops who marched in unopposed and then marched through the sluice-way (5) to the legation, being the first to reach the legation. In the mean-

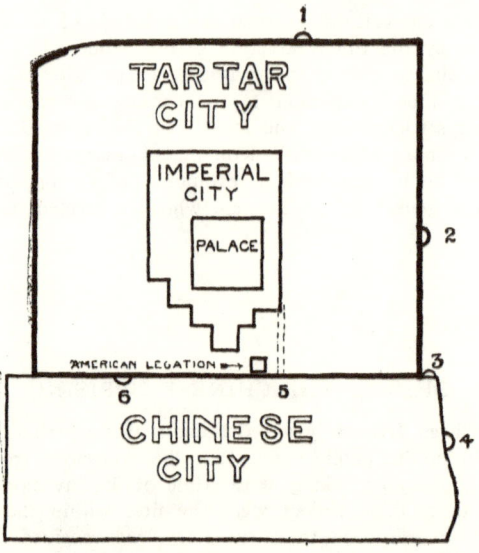

time the Americans, after opening up with artillery the gate No. 4 for the British, then made their attack on gate No. 3. the 14th U. S. Infantry scaled the walls and hoisted their regimental flag on them — the first flag on the wall,— and at the same time the Americans forced their way through gate No. 3, being *the first troops to get inside the walls* of the Chinese City, and then fought their way to the sluice-way (5) through which they followed the British, a close second, to the legation. The Japanese and Russians entered through gates 1 and 2 the next day. The Commander, Major General Chaffee, his Adjutants General Captain Grote Hutcheson and Col. H. O. S. Heistand, his Chief of Staff Capt. J. T. Dickman and myself, all of General Chaffee's staff, besides many other officers are Buckeyes.   Respectfully,

WEBB C. HAYES.

DID THE MOUND BUILDERS HAVE HORSES?

"Did the Mound Builders Have Horses" is the subject of an editorial in the last issue of the American Sportsman, March 2. The discovery of the skeleton of a horse, dug up in the state of Nebraska, started a discussion to which a number of the most eminent archæologists of the country have contributed their opinions. Dr. Phyle treated the subject at length in an essay some time ago. The editorial is as follows:

A horseman is curious to know, after reading Dr. Phyle's essay on the evolution of the horse, whether the "Mound Builders" had horses. We are not expected to answer this question, as all matters in the pre-historic age are exclusively in the domain of speculation. A similar question was asked during a race on the half-mile ring at Newark, Ohio, the location of several notable memorial mounds.

It is supposed that the Mound Builders preceded the North American Indian, but it is not clear that the Indian is the lineal descendant of the Mound Builders. When the white man invaded the Western Continent the Indians had no horses, but it does not follow that the race that built the memorial mounds had no horses. The Mound Builders are an extinct race, and their horses may have perished from off the earth at about the same time.

Scientists and antiquarians who have examined the memorial mounds, especially the famous ones at Newark and in Adams county, Ohio, assert that they have full proof that the builders enjoyed a high degree of civilization. The mound at the Newark Fair Grounds forms a perfect circle, a mile in circumference and some twenty feet high. Upon it stand very large maple, beech and hickory trees, showing, it is believed, that the erection of this mound far ante-dated the arrival of Columbus, over four hundred years ago.

It is thought that the Aztecs, found in Mexico by Cortez, and the ancient Peruvians, whose empire was destroyed by Pizzaro, may have been of the same race as the Mound Builders.

Whether the Mound Builders had horses we can only guess, but that a race preceding the North American Indians had horses we know to a certainty. The evidence of the skeleton horses recently discovered is conclusive.

Prof. Starr, of the Chicago University holds, with many others of the more advanced scientists, that the Mound Builders were Indians and coarse barbarians. Prof. Starr also holds that some of these mounds were built by Indian tribes not yet extinct. The French scientists, Lucien Biart (who has written a very elaborate book on the ancient Aztecs of Mexico), holds that they were a true type of Indians. Prof. John D. Baldwin, author of the "Prehistoric Nations," in his notes on American archæology, holds that the Mound Builders were American aborigines of the Indian type and not immigrants from another continent. Prof.

Baldwin holds that more than two thousand years have elapsed since the Mound Builders lived in the Ohio Valley.

In conclusion we are not in a position to state whether the Mound Builders were the race that exploited the pre-historic horse on this continent or whether they degenerated into Indians. All we know for a certainty is that the pre-historic man had a pre-historic horse, and that he both rode and ate him, and that the horse in improved form still survives, while the Mound Builders are extinct, and the Red Man is where he can see his finish—*Akron Democrat.*

CENTENNIAL CELEBRATION OF CHAMPAIGN COUNTY.

Under the editorship of Mr. Howard D. Manington, a tasty little volume, amply illustrated, has been issued, giving a detailed account of the Centennial Celebration of Champaign County, held at Urbana on the days of July 4th, 5th, and 6th. Under the energetic and patriotic management of the good people of Urbana, the Centennial proved to be an event of great interest, and well worthy the conclusion of one hundred years of the historic county. The inauguarting day of the centennial being also the anniversary day of the nation's natal day, drew an immense crowd of citizens representing all parts of the state to the handsome little county seat. Vice President Fairbanks was the orator of the day and made a patriotic address appropriate to the occasion. One of the features of the day was a grand parade and "a more magnificent spectacle was never witnessed in this state." The procession consisted of platoons of soldiers from the United States Regular Army, State Militia and a great number of novel features as "floats," decorated vehicles, masqueraders in fantastic costume, etc. The day was closed in the evening by a splendid pyrotechnic display in the City Park and followed by a "smoker" under the auspices of the local press committee, in honor of Vice President Fairbanks. This was presided over by Hon. Howard D. Manington, and speeches were made by the Hon. Ralph D. Cole and Messrs. John H. James, Henry C. McCracken, J. A. Howells and L. D. Johnson.

July fifth was celebrated as "Pioneer and Home-coming Day," the exercises being held in the county fair grounds, where several thousand people, bringing their lunch-baskets, gathered from all sections of the county and renewed their early memories of Champaign county life and greeted long absent friends. The formal exercises of the day consisted of an address by Secretary Randall of the Ohio State Archæological and Historical Society, the rendering of musical selections by the Urbana Band and a mixed chorus of some two hundred voices. Judge E. P. Middleton presided.

July sixth was known as "Military Day." A large section of the state militia under the command of Brigadier General William V. Mc-Maken paraded the streets of the city, headed by the Eighth Regiment Band and the Marietta Guards. Governor Herrick and his military staff reviewed the movements of the troops. This was followed by a gathering at tne fair grounds, where speeches were made by Col. W. R. War-nock, Governor Myron T. Herrick and Senator C. W. Dick. In the evening there was held a fitting closing feature which was really the literary event of the week. The exercises were held in Clifford's Theatre, which was filled to its utmost capacity by an interested audience who listened to addresss by Governor Herrick, Senator Dick, Secretary of State Laylin, Lieutenant Governor Harding and Mr. Howard D. Man-ington, who presided.

The volume mentioned at the beginning of this item contains the proceedings of these various days in full, with reports of the speeches and much additional matter pertaining to the history of Urbana and Champaign county. Particularly valuable is the historical matter by Mr. John W. Ogden, Rev. Charles S. Wood, Mr. J. T. Woodward and Mr. I. N. Keyser, Superintendent of the Public Schools of Urbana.

RICHLAND COUNTY HISTORICAL SOCIETY.

The Richland County Historical Society has just issued a neat little pamphlet containing the proceedings of the society, beginning with its first annual meeting, Saturday, June 10, 1899, and closing with the proceedings of its last annual meeting held in the G. A. R. rooms of the Memorial Building, Mansfield, June 7th, 1905. At this latter meeting a most interesting program was carried out. An address was delivered by the Rev. Joshua Crawford on the ill-fated and memorable "Expedition of Col. William Crawford" in the summer of 1782 against the Sandusky Indians. Rev. Crawford is a collateral descendant of the famous subject of his address. We regret that space does not permit of our publishing this address, but the subject has been treated in a scholarly manner by Judge J. H. Anderson in a previous number of the Quarterly. Other addresses were delivered by the Hon. W. G. Geer, representing the Rich-land County delegation; Mrs. James R. Hopley, Bucyrus, by special request delivered the address given by her at the Ohio Centennial Celebration at Chillicothe on "The Part Taken by Women in the History and Development of Ohio;" Prof. Sample, of Perrysville, Mr. Hiram R. Smith and Mr. Peter Bissman, of Mansfield, rendered short talks. Prof. Sample has one of the largest collections of archæological and historical relics in Ohio. Mr. Hiram Smith has reached the honorable age of ninety-three years, and when called for remarks responded by reciting,

"You may scarce expect one of my age,
To speak in public upon the stage."

Mr. Peter Bissman made a most interesting off-hand speech which held the undivided attention of the audience. Prof. C. W. Williamson of Wapakoneta read a very carefully prepared paper on "The Allied Indian Tribes of Western Ohio." Prof. Williamson's address dealt in detail with the early invasion of Ohio by the English traders and the war for extermination which was waged against them by the French from Quebec, who by the aid of the Indians were able to drive back the first of the traders. He also graphically pictured the conspiracy of Pontiac and the plan and efforts of that distinguished Indian chief to regain the Ohio valley from the encroachments of the white men. The Secretary of the Ohio State Archæological and Historical Society delivered an address entilted "Some Phases of Early Ohio History." Humorous recitations were rendered by Miss Lenora R. Shaw of Ashland College and Mr. M. A. Ricksecker of Galion.

This meeting of the Richland County Historical Society, both in interest and attendance, proved to be the most successful of any in its history. The society under the administration of Gen. R. Brinkerhoff, President, and Mr. A. J. Baughman, Secretary, is doing splendid work and gathering much historical material concerning the county and the state which would otherwise be lost to future readers.

*   *   *   *   *

On August 3, 1905, by invitation from Mr. A. J. Baughman, Secretary Randall paid a visit to the far–famed watershed barn, situated near Five Corners, in Springfield township, seven miles west of Mansfield, Richland county, on what is known as the Leesville road. The party from Mansfield consisted of Gen. Brinkerhoff, Mr. A. J. Baughman, Mr. Martin B. Bushnell, Mr. Peter Bissman and Mr. M. D. Frazier, Editor of the Daily Shield and the writer. The party proceeded by trolley from Mansfield to the farm, upon which the barn is located, said farm now being the property of Mr. C. Craig. The barn, a large structure, stands upon the roadside, facing the east and west, and not, as is generally supposed, north and south. The barn rests upon a slight elevation, midway between what are known respectively as the Palmer Spring and Little Lake. Each of these water sources is about a quarter of a mile from the barn. Palmer Spring is the head source of the Sandusky River, which empties into Lake Erie, and the Little Lake is the head source of Clear Creek, which finds its way to the Mohican, thence into the Tuscarawas, the Muskingum, the Ohio and then into the Mississippi. The geographical location at this point is, of course, upon the "divide," having an elevation of 832 feet above Lake Erie, 965 feet above the Ohio River, and 1,265 feet above sea level. Photographs were taken of the barn and the two river sources. The visit proved to be one of special interest, which was greatly heightened by the information gained of the geological and historical features of the section as related by Mr. A. J. Baughman, than whom few in the state are better qualified to speak upon matters pertaining to its geology and history.

INDIAN VS. ABORIGINE.

The following communication is self explanatory. It is from the pen of Prof. R. W. McFarland, Oxford, Ohio, who has contributed many articles of value to the Ohio State Archæological and Historical Society Quarterly.

Mr. E. O. Randall:

In reading your highly commendatory notice of Dr. Slocum's Historical work, I was pleased to see your remark about his use of the word *Aborigine* instead of *Indian.* Allow me to say that the term has never been recognized by Webster, or Worcester, by their co–adjutors, or their successors, as belonging to the English language. It is found in the Century and the Standard, — and we are entitled to suppose that its presence there is because some writer had used it. The plural, *Aborigines,* is applied to the *first* inhabitants of a country; it does not apply to subsequent races. Unless the Dr. can show that the Indians were the first inhabitants of America, the term cannot be applied to them at all.

Further; four hundred years ago when this continent was discovered, it was supposed to be what is now called the East Indies; in discovering the error, the term West Indies was given to the islands between North and South America, and they have borne the name ever since. The inhabitants of these islands were naturally and properly called *Indians,* the name subsequently being applied to all the race, whether on continent or island. And from that day to this, the word has been used alike by writers of fiction as well as of history, — by Cooper, Irving, Bancroft, Prescott, McMaster, Wilson, — indeed, by all standard authors. It has been used by the authorities of the country, both state and national, in regard to civil cases as well as to military; and such has been the practice ever since the English occupied this country. The Spaniard, the Portugese, the French also used the like word. This term has been too long in vogue, and has covered too wide a territory to be called in question at this late day.

It seems to me that the careful and judicious reader of the work in question may be led to suspect that such a lapse may not be an isolated one, but may be accompanied by others no less bad. The tendency would be to detract from the estimate in which the work might be held. The Ohio Archæological and Historical Society cannot, of course, agree to sanction such vagaries.

Respectfully,

R. W. McFARLAND.

ITINERARY OF THE SECRETARY.

On August 18th, Secretary Randall made a trip to Chillicothe and procuring conveyance drove out some seven miles to the location of the "Harness Mounds," where Prof. W. C. Mills, Curator of the Society's Museum, was conducting his explorations. The Secretary spent the day at the mounds, and while there was fortunate to see the discovery of a grave and its opening by the explorers under the direction of Prof. Mills and his assistant, Mr. A. B. Coover. Portions of a human skeleton were exhumed and some fine copper ear-rings and other ornaments were taken from the gave. Prof. Mills was unusually successful in his finds during the summer explorations. He explored completely the largest of the Harness Mounds which had been opened at previous periods, respectively, by Squier and Davis, Prof. F. W. Putnam and Prof. Warren K. Moorehead. Prof. Mills had under his direction an excellent force of eight or ten men. Prof. Mills will prepare and publish in due time in the Quarterly a detailed statement of his explorations for the past summer.

*   *   *

On Friday, August 25th, the Secretary journeyed to Piqua, where he was met by Judge E. L. Hoskins of the Probate Court of Shelby county, Mr. H. R. McVey, Superintendent of the Shelby schools, and Mr. A. J. Hess, President of the Sidney Board of Education. In company with these gentlemen a trolly car was taken to the historic residence of John Johnson, who for many years was the government agent for the Ohio Indians during their residence on the Ohio Reservation. Near this Johnson residence was the old stockade fort known as "Pickawillany," picturesquely located on the banks of the Great Miami River. The party also visited the monument close by, erected by the Daughters of the American Revolution, to commemorate the spot of the last battle of "The French and Indian War." It is a splendid granite rock, upon which is this inscription:

"Erected 1898 by the Piqua Chapter of the Daughters of
the American Revolution in Memory of the Last Battle of the
French and Indian War, Fought near This Spot 1763."

From this point the party took the trolley to Sidney and thence by carriage conveyance drove to the site of old Fort Laramie on the banks or Loramie Creek. This town is now named "Loramie." The site of the old fort is on the farm of Mr. F. C. Arkenberg. While at the site of the old fort the party met Mr. F. J. Uhrich, Superintendent of Schools of Loramie, who imparted to the party much information of historical value.

* * *

Col. John W. Harper of Cincinnati represented the Ohio State Archæological and Historical Society at the "White Water Valley Association" meeting, held September 9th, at White Water, Hamilton county, on which occasion he delivered an address setting forth the history and purposes of the society.

* * *

Mr. W. H. Hunter, Trustee of the Ohio State Archæological and Historical Society, delivered an address to the students of Marietta College and the members of the "Ohio Valley Historical Association" upon the evening of Friday, September 29th, in the college chapel at Marietta, his subject being "General Arthur St. Clair, Territorial Governor of Ohio."

* * *

On Saturday, September 9th, Trustee B. F. Prince made a visit of inspection to Fort Ancient, and on Saturday of the following week, September 16th, Secretary Randall was the guest of Mr. Warren Cowen, Custodian of the Fort. The Secretary remained several days, during which time he made extended examination of the archæological construction of the Fort and noted also the result of the custodianship of Mr. Cowen. The Fort never was in such excellent condition, and in its state of transition from summer to winter — in its all coloring — presented a most attractive and picturesque appearance.

INDEX TO VOLUME XIV.

Vol. XIV.— *31.

www.ingramcontent.com/pod-product-compliance
Lightning Source LLC
Chambersburg PA
CBHW020917020726
47495CB00002B/230